A GRAND OLD TIME

Judy Leigh completed an MA in Professional Writing at Falmouth University in 2015, leaving her career of 20 years as an Advanced Skills teacher of Theatre Studies. She has had several stories published in magazines, including *The Feminist Wire*, *The Purple Breakfast Review* and *You is for University*. She has also trained as a Reiki healer, written a vegan recipe blog and set up a series of Shakespeare Festivals to enable young people to perform the Bard's work on stage.

A GRAND OLD TIME

JUDY LEIGH

avon.

AVON

A division of HarperCollins*Publishers*
1 London Bridge Street,
London SE1 9GF

www.harpercollins.co.uk

A Paperback Original 2018

18 19 20 21 22 LSC 10 9 8 7 6 5 4 3 2 1

First published in Great Britain by
HarperCollins*Publishers* 2018

ISBN-13: 978-0-00-829945-3

Typeset in Sabon LT Std by Palimpsest Book Production Ltd,
Falkirk, Stirlingshire

Printed and bound in the United States of America by LSC Communications

For more information visit: www.harpercollins.co.uk/green

Thanks to Kiran at Keane Kataria and to Rachel Faulkner-Willcocks and her team at Avon, HarperCollins for being incredible and making this novel become real. To the talented MA students and lecturers, Falmouth, class of 2015, and to Sarah and Jim for letting me stay at the villa. To the Totnes writing group – thanks for conversations and creativity. To my early draft readers, Erika, Sarah, Beau, for their warmth and good humour. To Liam and Caitlan for their irrepressible intelligence and energy. To Tony and Kim for wild Sunday lunches. To Big G for all the love and for keeping me grounded. To my Dad, Tosh, and to my own Mammy, my inspiration.

For Irene.

Chapter One

She bounced up and down on the edge of her bed, still in her nightie. When the creaking stopped, the silence closed in around her. Everyone was asleep in Sheldon Lodge. The room was dim and cramped, so she went over to the window and looked outside at the path that led to the road into Dublin. A bird flitted up and away. A single cloud moved across a square of sky. Evie made a puffing noise through her lips and pulled herself away.

She went back to the bed and picked up the thin paperback lying on the duvet. *Season of the Heart*. Recommended reading for the ladies at Sheldon Lodge. Evie had never been much of a reader. There was a picture of a milkmaid in russet petticoats on the front cover, sitting in a cornfield. Her hair was the same bleached yellow as the corn and her face was sad. Evie flipped the novel over and read the blurb. *Dulcie Jones is thrust into the life of a country maid when her gambling father sells her to pay his debts. But Marcus, the mysterious son of her new master Lord Diamant, has other plans for Dulcie . . .*

Evie threw the book away from her onto the duvet. It was six thirty am.

'What a lot of shite,' she muttered to herself, and then she raised her voice: 'It's all complete shite.'

Sheldon Lodge offered its usual deaf ear, although she expected Mrs Lofthouse to run in, all wobbling bosoms and waving hands, to tell her to go back to bed and not disturb the other residents. Evie shuffled into her slippers and dressing gown, and snorted through her nostrils. Most of the other residents were disturbed already, well into their eighties and nineties – even the youngest of them at least ten years older than her.

She wandered into the kitchen, listening for Barry the chef who would make her a cup of tea. She could hear him behind the metal shutters, moving around, organising breakfast. She banged her fist softly to call for his attention and waited. No reply.

Evie sat down at the little table with its plastic cloth printed with yellow roses and realised she was in Maud Delaney's seat. Maud, with her thin hair cropped short, usually spent the day in the chair, humped over the table, her head resting against a cold cup of tea, her eyes covered with her puffy ringed fingers. Maud's place was next to Annie Armstrong, who gulped air like a fish. Every day Evie wondered if Maud was dead until Slawka and Joe, two of the carers, came to move her with the winch. At least it broke the monotony.

Barry would open the breakfast bar shutters in a minute and Evie would have a hot drink and toast. Even better, there would be someone to talk to. Barry would grumble about his daughter Natalie, who had been arrested for taking recreational drugs at a pop festival in the park, and Evie would discuss the problems of poor hen-pecked Brendan, and they would both laugh and chatter. Then there would be scrambled eggs and more toast and it would be halfway through the morning and the *Irish Times*

2

would have been delivered in the Day Room. She'd have two cups of coffee and make her little joke, as she did every day, that it would taste a lot nicer with a nip of cognac. Of course, they let her have a glass of red wine with her meals, but somehow it tasted bitter. Like all the sunshine had gone from the grapes.

Evie picked up a pack of playing cards that had been left on the table and she shuffled them. She didn't know how to play cards, but it was something to do. She sorted through them again and a card poked itself towards her. She took it out. It was the four of hearts.

Evie placed it on the table and smiled.

Four. Her lucky number.

Chapter Two

He stared at his face in the mirror. His hair was still auburn, although faded, the curls flecked here and there with grey, and his blue eyes were crinkled around the corners. He lathered his face with shaving soap and smiled at his white-bearded reflection – a paternal face, like Santa Claus. He imagined how it would be to dress as Father Christmas, surrounded by four children. He'd always thought he'd like two of each: two boys who liked football, a sporty girl, maybe a surfer or a swimmer, and then one for Maura. A chirpy cheeky one with Maura's soft shining eyes.

He lifted the razor and swiped it smoothly across his cheek, then screamed. Thin red blood seeped through his fingers and spattered on the pale tiles of the floor. He swore and dropped his razor in the basin, reaching for toilet roll to plug the small leak in his neck. He looked in the bathroom mirror: sallow face with a foaming beard and eyes round as a fish's. His crisp shirt was going to have to come off. Maura would not be pleased.

He threw the paper in the toilet and applied more, torn into squares, folded urgently. He stiffened and strained his ears. A rustling sound like a cold breeze warned him of Maura's approach; the linen-clad thighs were rubbing together with a soft hiss, a stalking reptile.

He heard her voice before he saw her. It rang ice clear.

'Brendan, for the love of God . . .?' She rounded the corner, looked him up and down and snorted.

Brendan looked her up and down in turn and snorted too, but discreetly. Her cleavage tippled over the top of her V-neck jumper, revealing the tentative lace of a beige bra. The orbs he had first coveted and then caressed now held less fascination for him. The tight slacks and high heels accentuated her curves, and her face, now stern, was topped with little blonde curls pinned high on her head. He mopped his wound and waited for the onslaught to begin.

'Will you look at your shirt? It is completely ruined. I will have to get you another one. The blue one won't go as well with those trousers but never mind, it will have to do.'

Her pause for breath was punctuated by his placatory 'OK, my love' – but even as he said it, he felt a pang of regret that it wasn't OK and there wasn't any love.

She stared at him for a second and he wondered if she was having the same thoughts, then she sighed and started up again. 'Brendan, it's always the same every Saturday afternoon. You know these visits upset me.'

Brendan couldn't help noticing the lines that puckered perfectly around the mouth as she spoke. She has the mouth of an arsehole, he thought to himself. As she stared at Brendan, her eyes were like bullets, small, blue-grey, ready to fire. Any attempt to pass her would be a battle manoeuvre in the making, so he stayed fixed, bloody paper in hand.

Maura rustled away, her heels tapping like nails to the

brain. Brendan flushed the toilet and watched the paper, its perfect whiteness blotched with red spots, as it gurgled, dissolved and disappeared.

Brendan was sitting in the yellow Fiat Panda on his driveway. A wafting fragment of toilet paper was still attached to the dried blood on his neck. The engine thrummed gently.

He listened to the DJ on the radio: 'The birds are singing and summer is blooming here in Dublin, and so let's have the Beach Boys, bringing us "Good Vibrations".'

He banged his head softly against the steering wheel. Harder. Harder still. There were definitely no good vibrations to be had anywhere here. Still no sign of Maura.

He saw a young woman and her child who emerged from their front door. It was Erin from number 27 and little Colm. Erin found her phone and started to chatter. The little boy moved from one foot to another, kicking stones. He only had on a thin jacket. The wind ruffled his hair, shaking the flags of his trouser legs, and he looked cold. He sat down on the kerb, dangling his fingers in the dirt. He scrabbled purposefully in the gravel, found something and picked it up. It was a discarded cigarette. Colm held it in his two fingers, raising his hand in an imitation of an adult pose, pulling a haughty face.

They'd both wanted children, him and Maura. The doctor in the hospital in Dublin said there was nothing wrong with the pair of them, and they should both just relax. That was ten years ago. He was nearly forty. Too late now. It was around that time that Maura's soft eyes hardened. Her sweet smile became pursed lips, puckered and hard. Maura was always the love of his life. Now she was just his wife, who sat across the table at breakfast in a tight suit, her hair pulled back and pinned up and her brow tight with a frown. She used to gaze up into his eyes and promise to love him for ever. Now she slammed his coffee on the table at breakfast and told him not to let it go cold. He sighed. Perhaps that was what love was now; like coffee, it starts hot and strong, only to become tepid and cool.

Outside the car, the child looked up at his mother, who was talking and waving the arm carrying the handbag. Colm put one end of the cigarette in his mouth. He began to smoke as he had seen his mother smoke, as he had seen other adults smoke. He had it off to perfection, inhaling deeply, holding his breath while he smiled like the Bisto kid and then blowing out the imaginary smoke in a steady stream. Brendan laughed, a quiet chuckle. Erin stopped talking, pushed her phone into her bag, turned to the boy and gave him a slap across the head.

Colm dropped the cigarette butt and screamed, his face reddening with furious tears. He looked like a comic book character. Erin grabbed his hand and with a swift pull she yanked him to mobility. His little feet moved in the air, then landed in a run to keep time with his mother. Brendan thought that was no way to treat a kiddie; his hands clutched the steering wheel harder as the Panda shuddered when Maura leapt in. She swung the carrier bags of cakes into the space behind her and looked sharply at Brendan.

'Are we ready to go, Brendan? Do we have everything?'

He nodded. 'I think so, my love.'

Maura stared straight at him, her eyebrows making a deep V in her forehead, her mouth pursed. He knew the expression like he knew his own reflection.

'Brendan, what in the name of God is this stuck on your neck? Toilet paper. Now look at the state of you.'

She reached in her handbag for a tissue. He knew what was coming. Her pink tongue poked through her lips, dampened the paper and scrubbed the hard tissue against his neck. Like a dutiful child, Brendan kept still and closed his eyes and thought that he could feel the love leaking from his life.

She looked at him, breathing out sharply, the moist hanky in her fist. She paused and, for a second, her eyes were soft again. She ruffled his hair, her fingers snagging in his curls. She touched his neck with the tenderness she'd have bestowed on a child. 'There, Brendan, you're all done. Much better. Shall we go?'

The Panda engine was still humming softly. Maura was sandwiched inside a brown checked jacket with a faux-fur collar; she had the red lipstick and crimson nails of a ferocious hunter that had just skinned and swallowed its prey whole. 'What are we waiting for?'

He gulped. 'Maura, I don't think Mammy likes Sheldon Lodge. I mean, she hasn't settled—'

'She is in the best place, Brendan. They can do Tai Chi and cookery classes for the aged. They can give her a good life. Better than she was, by herself.'

'She looks miserable, to tell the truth.'

Maura thought for a second. 'Nonsense. I'm sure she'll be happy as a lark. Come on, let's get moving. Traffic will be terrible in Dublin centre.'

His hands were squeezing the steering wheel. He glanced at the faux-fur collar around Maura's throat. He moved the gears into first. The DJ on the radio was excitedly talking about the heyday of Oasis and the 1990s, then the chords struck out and the song began: 'Wonderwall'. It was a song that was playing all the time, the year they'd met.

The tune epitomised the ecstasy of their young love. Brendan had taken Maura, slender and soft, in his arms, as they kissed and whispered and planned for the future.

They had both been just eighteen and she had gazed at his face as if he was a blessed saint. He had felt that he could achieve anything, for her sake. And the voice sang the words just for them. Words which promised undying love, love beyond measure, love so vast it would last for ever.

As Brendan smoothly turned the Panda towards the edge of the estate, Maura's eyes were half closed in a glaze and she began to sing, in her thin, cheese-grater voice:

'*Wonderwaaaaall . . .*'

She was in her own world, and he had no idea what she was thinking. He wondered if she remembered the happy times; if she recalled their many walks by the River Liffey, how he gave her his anorak once when the rain started, how she squeezed his fingers and smiled into his face. He wondered if she was thinking anything at all. His fingers made deep grooves on the fabric on the wheel, wondering where she had gone, the sweet, soft-skinned girl of his past. He sighed from somewhere, lost fathoms inside him, and looked at the traffic ahead, nose to bumper, grumbling to a halt.

Chapter Three

Four is the luckiest number. Born on fourth of April, 1942. Fourth of five children. Four hundred thousand euros from the sale of the house. Four sausages for lunch today. Four had always been lucky for her. Her da had given her a four-leaf clover, dried between the pages of a book, when she was four years old. She'd had her son on the fourth of March. He'd been her fourth baby, the only one who stuck.

Fifteen is not a good number. Left school at fifteen. Hated school. Married Jim on fifteenth of July. Married life, from then onwards, until he died. Moved to Sheldon Lodge on the fifteenth of December. Room number fifteen. No, fifteen is definitely not a lucky number.

Evie was deep in thought when Mrs Lofthouse spoke to her. Mrs Lofthouse spoke for the second time, and the third, more loudly and with slow emphasis.

'Evelyn. Your son is coming to see you today. Brendan? He is coming to see you.'

Evie blinked. She put on her best confused look and stared directly back.

'I'll just give your hair a bit of a tidy up. Brendan will be here at four.'

'Four.'

'Brendan – and his wife Maura. Lovely couple, Evelyn.'

Evie pulled a face. Maura was always stiff, polite, putting on a pretence of wifely perfection. Evie didn't feel she knew her well at all, even after almost twenty years. Maura was humourless, starchy. She reminded her of the nuns at school, who insisted she must be called Evelyn and not her preferred abbreviation. She'd decided at four years old that 'Evie' was so much nicer, cheekier: it suited her much better than the more formal version. Evie was a chirpy name. Maura could do with being chirpier, she thought. The nuns flitted into her head again and she remembered how they had punished her for using the Lord's name gratuitously. That was the first time she took up swearing as a hobby. The words rolled in her mouth like sweets.

'Bollocks,' said Evie, and looked pleased.

'That's just not nice, is it?' Mrs Lofthouse's sigh showed how much she suffered in her work. She waved the brush in the air. 'There, Evelyn. You look lovely. Shall we put on a bit of lipstick now? Make you look bright and breezy for Brendan?'

Evie took the lipstick from Mrs Lofthouse's fingers and turned it over in her hand. Paradise pink. Mrs Lofthouse had paradise pink lips, which hung like prawns over her huge teeth. Her teeth pushed apart in different directions, one sticking out to the right and one leaning backwards to the left. Evie took the paradise pink lipstick and applied it to her own mouth like a child with a crayon.

Mrs Lofthouse's lips sprang apart. 'If you are going to be silly . . .'

Evie employed the vacuous stare again.

'I'll wipe it off and we can start again. Ah, now. You look a million dollars.'

11

Evie gurned at her, spreading her lips wide. Mrs Lofthouse's prawn pout clamped itself into a thin line. The visitors were due.

Evie watched her waddle away then leaned forward in her chair and gazed around the Day Room. The other residents were in wingback chairs, turned towards the TV where Jeremy Kyle was doing a lie detector test. They were mostly oblivious to the chatter; the flickering screen was reflecting in the glaze of spectacles. Evie looked at the old ladies sitting in the window. Sunlight streamed against their faces, but they hardly seemed to notice the warmth. The flowers were out in the garden; daily, a robin perched on the oak. The old ladies stared straight ahead. One of them, Elizabeth, never spoke a word. Every day, Evie would try: 'Good morning, Lizzie, and how are you today?'

Nothing. Elizabeth continued to stare ahead. The other one, Barbara, could not hear well. Even Alex, the friendly Ukrainian lad who brought the breakfasts, had to raise his voice to startle her from her dreams. At eight in the morning, Alex would be there, his hair stuck up in a little quiff at the front, his face all smiles:

'Barbara, darling, your eggs and sausage – here you are – eggs and sausage – Barbara?'

The aged ladies were dry, thin sticks of women in their nineties, old enough to be her own mother. She saw them in the yoga class each Tuesday, looking around and lifting their twig-like arms. A thought popped into her head: Tweedle Dumb and Tweedle Deaf. She was bored, and being bored made her feel mischievous. What else could she do in this sanatorium of smiles and sandwiches, which smelt the whole day long of perfumed piss?

The clock struck four. They would be here soon. She closed her eyelids and listened to the soothing music that told the residents they were in a caring environment. The armchair had moss-green cushions with silky fringes. Evie sank back into its fat embrace.

Frank Sinatra was singing 'Fly Me to the Moon' in his jolly lilt.

Evie thought about the moon and stars: where were they, exactly? Far up in the heavens? Is that where death was, alongside Frank and Jim and the others? What about after death? Evie decided she would like to come back as a reindeer.

A playful two-dimensional sketch of Rudolph popped into the television of her imagination, its nose a beacon and its legs delicate in snow. Her eyes rolled again beneath their papery lids and suddenly Rudolph exploded and was replaced by a huge reindeer, god-like with antlers and eyes aflame. It spoke in a Hollywood actor's voice:

'I'm Evie Gallagher and I am god-damned pissed off . . .' It glared around the forest, mounted like a sentry on the hilltop of ice, and stamped its regal hoof once, sending soft snow skywards. Evie opened her eyes suddenly to see two looming faces, twins in symmetrical concern.

Evie said, 'I am god-damned pissed off.'

'Mammy,' said Brendan. 'How are you?' and he realised she had already answered. Maura launched herself forward, her dutiful expression on her face.

'Mother, it's good to see you. You're looking well. Can I get you a cup of tea?'

Evie looked at Maura in her suit and tightly pinned curls and decided she would rather eat shit. She closed her eyes. The reindeer was gone. In its place were thin blue veins that throbbed in her lids. She heard Maura whine to the care assistant: 'I think she's getting worse, Mrs Lofthouse.'

'She comes and goes, I think.'

13

Evie wished they would all come and go.

'It's so upsetting for Brendan, seeing his mother like this. It's like she's away with the fairies.'

'We see it all the time,' replied Mrs Lofthouse, hollowly. Evie was not sure what she saw all the time; Mrs Lofthouse was short-sighted and short-witted. In fact just plain short. And fat. Evie felt a hand on her arm; she knew Brendan's touch. Her emotion was visceral and she remembered the little boy who used to clutch at her fingers as a child. She opened her eyes. He was in his late thirties now, but looked older, his hair still thick but greying, his face loosening, hanging from the sharp cheekbones: a worried face. His mouth seldom offered the boyish chuckle he had once used as his trademark, but his eyes were still rounded with hope. Evie was about to smile at him, but Maura's grunts made her turn sharply.

'You're back with us again then, Mother?' Evie twitched her nose; Maura's perfume was attacking her throat and making her choke.

'I am not your mother,' she wheezed.

'Mrs Lofthouse, could Mammy have a glass of water please?' Brendan called out and the care assistant waddled over like a frontline sergeant major holding a cup like a bayonet. Evie expected her to shout, 'Chaaarge.'

Mrs Lofthouse said, 'Come on, Evelyn, drink up.' Evie took a mouthful then sat up, looking at each of them. She thought of the film about the hobbits, sitting around the table for a hobbity talk, each stunted, each poised, each waiting their turn. Evie coughed again and the water in her mouth sprayed in all directions. She spat and choked and laughed at the same time, a cachinnation of triumph. She flopped back in the comfy armchair, put her arms on the supports.

An hour passed. The conversation was slow and stilted.

Evie stared through the window at the place where the path started and wound away towards the road. Brendan shifted in his seat and smiled towards his mother and then at his wife.

'We can't stay too long, Brendan,' Maura said.

He rose up slowly, his eyes on his mother. 'All right, Mammy, I'll see you next week, same time.'

'She probably can't hear you, Brendan. It is so upsetting for him to see her like this.'

'We see it all the time,' mused Mrs Lofthouse.

'Bye Mammy.' Brendan kissed the top of her head. Evie almost reached out to him. Maura shook her head and pursed her lips. Evie scrutinised her daughter-in-law for several seconds.

'Maura?'

'What is it, Mother?'

'Did anyone ever tell you? You have a mouth like an arsehole.'

Brendan's face brightened, a smile flickering on his lips, and he looked at Evie with tenderness and something close to desperation.

'Come on, Brendan.' Maura's mouth was now screwed tightly in anal closure. Brendan saw his mother wink at him before he rushed out after his wife.

Mrs Lofthouse snorted. 'We'd better clean you up, Evelyn.'

'I'm coming back as a stag,' Evie announced.

Evie was sitting at her dressing table in room 15, second floor: her room. On the door was a small notice which read: 'Please respect my dignity. Knock before entering and wait. I may be asleep.' In the mirror, Evie saw the room reflected behind her: the single bed with the red rose duvet cover, her little chest of drawers, the shelf with her photos, the moss-green curtains and magnolia walls and the mouse-grey carpet. This was her home now, thanks to the sale of the house. Maura had said the house was too big for her, but room 15 was far too small. Brendan had thought she would have company in Sheldon Lodge and, when she had first looked round it, the thought of spending her first Christmas alone made the place look like a hotel. The bedrooms were attractive, as was the dining room with the little tables set for four, and Barry, the cheerful chef in his pristine checked pants, had promised her that he would let her have real butter on her toast. The manager, Jenny, had been friendly and welcoming, enthusiastic about the new lifestyle Evie would enjoy – fitness programmes and music nights and watercolour painting. Evie had looked with a child's hopeful eyes at Sheldon Lodge, at the twinkling tree and the decorations, signed the forms and moved in. Christmas had turned out to be turkey, torpor and television.

The triple mirror held her reflection, and her mother's face looked back at her from three angles, hollow-eyed. Her mother had had no teeth when she died. Evie still had all her own teeth, bar one. Her mother had been grey but Evie's hair was soft and brown, although the roots were streaked with silver. Her mother was all done in at forty; Evie was seventy-five, but she was certain she was not done yet.

'Hot chocolate for you, Evie? Rich Tea biscuits or Penguins?' Evie glanced over her shoulder to see Alex, his smiling face peeping around the door. Alex placed the tray down, and lifted off a mug and a plate of biscuits. 'Everything all right for you today, darling?'

'I'd rather have a nice glass of Merlot.' She chewed her lip. 'Alex – do you like it here?'

Alex's cheeks lifted with laughter. 'I am here for three

years, Evie. I have girlfriend here. Work is good and the people are friendly. Dublin better than Kiev for me, that is for sure.' Evie looked miserable and turned away. 'Why you don't like it here, Evie?'

'I am bored, Alex.'

'There is television, darling. Banjo player is coming in later. Maybe now you can play dominoes downstairs with Barbara?'

'I don't give a shite for dominoes.'

'I know what you mean.'

'It's driving me mad.' Evie's eyes were intense. 'I've come here by mistake.'

Alex shook his head. 'Maybe tomorrow things are better?' he suggested, but his face lost its smile as he picked up the empty tray and left Evie alone again. She lifted the cup. The hot chocolate was tepid and the biscuit tasted like grit.

Evie looked around at her room. She could not live like this for the rest of her days. Images came to her of static yoga classes and gurning banjo players and the two old ladies who stared, unblinking, at the television. Her fingers clutched at the neck of her jumper and as the idea came to her she stood paralysed, and could only feel the beating of her heart. In one movement, she was in front of the dressing table.

She tugged open her top drawer, lifting underwear to find her purse, her driving licence, her cheque card. Below were more familiar things: her bus pass, a passport, some jewellery, a small umbrella. She touched the four-leaf clover that her father had given her so many years ago, still dried and pressed in tissue paper, now between the pages of her small photograph album that was crammed with pictures of a younger Brendan in shorts with his father Jim. She found the mobile phone that Brendan had given her for

17

Christmas so they could keep in touch, still in its box. These items were no longer relics of the past – they were tickets to new freedom. Without thinking, she pushed them all into her small handbag. June in Dublin was always pretty, and the Monday morning shops would be full of people. She would spend time breathing fresh air; just a small scent of the real world was already in her nose. Evie knew the door codes and the schedules of Sheldon Lodge. Each day ran like clockwork. It would not be difficult. That night, she slept the sleep of the smug.

Chapter Four

The children swarmed across the pitch, some yelling, some pushing, some straggling behind. Brendan blew the whistle with a *pheep* so loud it hurt his ears. The kids buzzed around him, their voices a cacophony of complaints.

'Get yourself changed now.'

'Mr Gallagher, that last ball was a penalty. Dennis brought the striker down.'

'Did not, you gobshite.'

'And you did so.'

'I'll give you a fat fucking lip.'

'Yeh? Yeh? Come on, then.'

Brendan blew the whistle again. The kids' faces were red with sweat and effort.

'In the changing rooms: showers, *now*. Go on.'

The kids sloped off, shoulders down. One of them muttered, 'Twat.'

Minutes later, Brendan sat in the staff room, clutching a coffee. He looked down at his muddy shorts and saw two pale booted legs dangling. He gazed around the office; piles of paper meant piles of report writing. More evenings at home in front of the laptop. The coffee tasted burnt.

The door swung open and Penny Wray came in, her shorts pristine, her ponytail bouncing. She put a hand on Brendan's shoulder as she passed.

'Was it murder?'

'That group is always murder.' Brendan took another mouthful of coffee as punishment. 'I spend all Sunday night dreading the little beggars.'

Penny sat down and crossed perfect legs. She pulled a bottle of water from her bag and unscrewed the lid effortlessly. 'I just had Year Seven girls doing performance on the trampoline. I have some great little gymnasts in that group.'

Brendan thought that Penny didn't look like she had been on the trampoline. She smelled of something sweet, something fresh, and Brendan sighed. Then he remembered. 'It's the Class From Hell next for English.'

Penny laughed, a sound soft with sympathy and warmth, and she touched Brendan's arm. 'I don't know why they make you teach English, Brendan. You are a sports teacher.'

He shrugged. 'I am thirty-nine, Penny. That is what they do with old PE teachers – farm them out to the classes no-one wants to teach. The losers in front of the losers.'

'I will be a head teacher by the time I am your age.'

Brendan did not doubt it, and that made the prospect of teaching poetry to the worst class in the school almost unbearable. Twenty years to retirement. Years of teaching kids who disputed penalties, who hated Yeats' poetry, who hated him, then home to Maura in the evening to write reports while she grumbled about how they needed a new car and how he didn't have time to take her out in the evenings. Brendan swallowed more coffee.

'I'm running my kick-boxing class tonight.' Penny looked at him and smiled. 'Why don't you come along?'

20

Brendan pictured Penny in her boxing kit, throwing punches and kicks, touching his arm, his waist, as she helped him do the same, their voices loud in one groan of effort. 'Wish I could.'

'You could bring your wife?'

He thought of Maura in her jog bottoms, kick-boxing, and pushed the thought away. She'd never shared his love of sport. The klaxon sounded and Brendan rose up like a trained pigeon and grabbed his battered briefcase, heading for the door. He heard Penny call:

'Good luck with the evil ones, Brendan. I'll get you a baguette for lunch when you're back.'

In the corridor, a sudden gust of wind blasted through the banging door and gripped him by the throat.

An hour later, the klaxon screeched and room E5 was empty again. Brendan put his head in his hands. The silence rang in his ears, more deafening than the shouting and banging on desks that had filled the room minutes before. His head hurt, a dark throbbing behind his eyes. When he opened them, the room looked back at him, a panorama of upturned chairs and screwed-up paper. Brendan picked up the bin and began to fill it with litter. He held a paper ball in his hand, squashed to fist-size. He opened it, with slow care, and read the words:

I have spread my dreams under your feet,
Tread softly because you tread on my dreams.

He bent again and picked up more paper.

'Brendan. Ah. Here you are.'

Nancy Doyle pushed her glasses up from her nose and showed him her practised lipstick smile. He looked around at the mess in the room and noticed Nancy surveying the space: a professional head teacher's assessment of his lesson, based on the amount of discarded detritus.

'Brendan, can we sit down a minute? I need to have a little chat with you.' The smile again; Brendan assumed the worst.

'Of course, Nancy.'

He moved his chair to look at Nancy; the dark suit, silk shirt, hair swept up. She drew a breath. 'Look, Brendan, I'll cut to the chase. I've just had a call from Sheldon Lodge.'

Brendan sat upright. 'My mother?'

'They'd like you to phone them. As soon as you can. It appears your mother left the home first thing this morning, and she hasn't returned.'

Brendan saw an image of his mother in her coat, her shoulders hunched against the cold. It was her back view as she walked along crowded streets. In his mind she was frail, and passers-by bumped her out of their way as they rushed in the opposite direction.

'I'm sure everything is fine. Your mother does seem to have taken quite a few of her belongings, though. I think you should go and ring Sheldon Lodge now. Do you have a phone on you?'

He did not move.

'Go and sort it out about your mother. Give me a call at the end of the day, will you? Let me know she's safe and sound.'

Brendan felt energy rising through his legs; he was up and grabbing at his briefcase, walking frantically to the door, calling over his shoulder:

'Thanks Nancy. Yes, I will. I'll be sure to get back to you later. Thanks.'

He was through the swing doors and moving towards the yellow Fiat Panda, parked between white lines in the car park; his mobile was in his hand, searching for the number of the care home, as he muttered, 'Tread softly, because you tread on my dreams? Oh, Mammy, what in hell have you done now?'

Chapter Five

On the crowded bus to Dublin, Evie sat low in her seat and hugged herself. It was as if eyes were focused on her back, as if she was constantly being watched. She stared through the window, thinking she could be recognised at any moment, identified and apprehended. The idea came to her: she would buy a hat, one which would update her appearance and cover her hair at the same time: a disguise. Her fingers fiddled in the little bag; they were all there, all of her things. Clutching the bag to her chest, she shuffled to the front as the bus slowed.

In a department store, she tried on the whole range, looking at herself in the mirror wearing floppy hats, wedding hats, fur hats, fascinators. Finally, she decided on a red beret. It had panache; it covered her hair completely and she thought she looked like an intelligent outdoor type who might be independent and take walks with a dog. She bought sunglasses, a huge handbag and a jaunty coat in a lightweight fabric and she saw herself in the mirror: a middle-class lady of leisure, or a stylish Parisian tourist. She paid with her card and headed for the chip shop, her old coat and bag in plastic carriers banging against her legs. Fried food was frowned upon in Sheldon Lodge. Evie bought chippers, battered cod and four pickled eggs and settled down on a bench to enjoy them. The chips were hot, mouth-burning, delicious with the forbidden tastes of fat and too much salt and vinegar. The batter crunched perfectly, releasing a stream of grease onto her tongue. It would all go down well with a nice glass of Prosecco, she thought.

A man sat on the bench next to her. He was middle-aged, hunched over, and wore an old overcoat; his face was a dark rash of stubble. Evie offered him a pickled egg.

'And I don't mind if I do,' he told her, pushing the whole egg into his mouth and swallowing it in a gulp.

She offered him another.

'Thank you kindly,' he said and, like an anaconda, opened his mouth into a broad yawn before the egg disappeared.

Evie imagined his neck becoming egg-shaped for a moment before it made the downward plunge. She ate her chips one by one. A pigeon fluttered by her feet, its beak jabbing at scraps, and she almost flicked her foot at it. She thought again; perhaps the pigeon was in need of a chip too. She dropped a couple by her feet and the pigeon pecked, its wings folded behind its back like a dapper little man.

'You're in Dublin on holiday, then?' asked Anaconda Man.

Evie considered her reply. 'Ah, I am a crime writer. Doing research.'

'Oh and what are you researching?'

'Good fortune.'

'Then I am your guy,' said Anaconda Man, licking egg from the corner of his mouth.

'Indeed?' Evie was intrigued. The pigeon fluttered away.

'Yes, I like to take a chance myself. I am on my way right now to place a bet on a certain horse. And why not come along for the fun of it? To find good fortune.'

Evie thought for a moment. Sheldon Lodge seemed a long way away. She smiled.

'I would be delighted,' she said, throwing her warm chip paper in the bin. 'I have never seen inside a betting establishment before.'

They passed two betting shops, both with big double-fronted windows with posters offering luminously coloured deals for bets and odds. She expected him to pause, but Anaconda Man plodded past, his eyes focused ahead. Evie was just behind him; she was about to snatch at his arm, but thought better of it. Both betting shops were names she had seen many times advertised on the television.

'We have missed it . . .' she panted. 'That was a betting shop. Where are we going?'

'Not far now,' he grunted. He'd broken into a sweat, which sat in seamy creases that folded across his forehead. He walked on quickly, Evie trotting behind.

'What was wrong with that betting shop?'

'Nothing.' Anaconda Man was determined and focused. 'Just not the right betting shop, that's all.'

Evie hesitated for a moment. Perhaps he was a deadly and dangerous character like Sweeney Todd or the Ripper, leading her into a dark alley. He might mug her, or worse.

'Come on, nearly there,' he grunted. 'They'll be off soon and there is a particular hot horse I need to back. Are you with me?'

Evie wondered if she was being unwise. They turned the corner into a dim street where the brick buildings had started to crumble. They stopped at a little shop with dark windows and a creaking door that had probably once been green and, before that, painted yellow – Evie could see patches of it showing through the faded green.

The betting shop was fluorescent bright inside and smelled of dust and sweat; it was a furtive gamblers' lair, sheltering little men on stools huddled over newspapers. At the far corner was a counter where two men were whispering and exchanging money. The place was full of people eyeing her suspiciously. She was thinking about walking out again when someone spoke.

'Ah, Memphis. Good day to you,' called the man behind the counter.

Evie watched her smiling companion; so then, Anaconda Man was called Memphis.

'Hello there, brother.'

Memphis looked unlike the man at the counter: she assumed their fraternity was based on the betting.

'I'd like to introduce my fair companion. She is a crime author. Her name is . . .'

'Agatha,' said Evie, holding out her hand and deciding that lies were the safest way forward.

She pulled the red beret down on one side, and glanced over the top of her sunglasses. She would make an excuse in a minute and leave. Memphis raised his arm, holding out money.

'I want to place a bet on the one-thirty. Twenty each way on number fifteen, El Niño.' Memphis shared the newspaper he had just picked up with Evie. 'There you are – El Niño – he's a good hot horse for you, and no mistake, if you want to make some fast money.'

She studied the newspaper. A name in print and the number four caught her attention at once. She looked at the door; she could stay for a few minutes more. Evie bit her lip and thought.

'I want to bet on number four – Lucky Jim,' she announced.

The counter man smiled, his lips a thin U-shape. 'Rank outsider, lady.' Two men behind her guffawed.

'A hundred to one,' agreed Memphis. 'But who are we to stop a lady having a little flutter? After all, you're seeking your fortune.'

'Be quick,' grimaced Counterman. 'Betting closes soon.'

Evie reached into her new bag and pulled out a roll of notes, withdrawn from the bank as contingency earlier. Money just sitting in the bank, doing nothing, which would cover her spending spree with plenty left over. Her hand shook: she remembered selling their home, the place she had lived with Jim and Brendan, then just with Jim, for so many years, and tried to recall her husband's face.

'My bet for number four – Lucky Jim.'

Counterman counted silently, Memphis watching every movement.

'How much do you want to bet, missus?'

Evie nodded her head. She thought of Sheldon Lodge, of Mrs Lofthouse and her pink prawn lips, then she thought of her husband Jim, his flat cap pulled down over serious eyes, a cigarette squeezed between his lips. For a moment, she hesitated, but wasn't four her lucky number? She'd never proven it to herself properly and this was her big chance. She didn't understand odds, but this horse had to win. It had Jim's name and her lucky number. And Jim had been such a good man. Her voice was faint. She crossed the two fingers on each hand. Four fingers. 'All of it.'

'Five hundred euros?' asked Counterman, his eyebrows shooting upwards.

Evie breathed in. 'Number four. To win.'

Counterman winked at Memphis. 'Lucky Jim to win

– a hundred to one. Here, lady, and best of luck to you.'
And he handed her a slip of paper in exchange for her
money.

Evie could see the men's faces staring in disbelief. She
was the centre of their attention, an anomaly, a rank
outsider, just like Lucky Jim. She suddenly wished she had
left the betting shop when she had the chance.

The tinny voice on the radio announced the start of the
race and Evie was aware of the scent of anxious bodies
crowding around her. A short man in a cap smirked at
her through sparse teeth. Evie tried to move back but she
was cornered. A huddle of men gathered around her, all
with the same expression, worry mixed with hopefulness
as they clutched their betting slips.

'And they're off,' announced the lilting voice on the
radio.

Evie breathed in as the mass of bodies came even closer.
El Niño was in the lead, closely followed by Steam Packet
and Argonaut: no mention of Lucky Jim. As the pace
increased, the men around Evie seemed to do an imper-
ceptible jig with their knees. The voice became quicker;
the knee jerk turned into a bounce, their backs bobbing,
quickening with each furlong. Evie smelled the anxiety of
the betting men and she turned her nose as far away as
she could, hoping the race would soon end. The five
hundred euros had not been a good idea at all. Evie almost
wished herself back in Sheldon Lodge. Almost.

'And it's number fifteen, El Niño . . . El Niño followed
by Argonaut and they are turning into the home straight,
El Niño, he is a neck in front but Argonaut, ridden by
Paddy Mills, is giving it everything he has; now it is El
Niño . . .'

Evie thought about dropping her betting slip and
running out of the shop but she was hemmed in by the

fretting throng who started to cheer. Memphis clenched a fist; he began to pound the air; spittle escaped from the side of his mouth. The voice shifted up a gear, the radio rattling with each consonant. The men's eyes were glazed with some kind of religious entreaty and she felt that she was the only sane person in the shop. Her own eyes closed in prayer.

'El Niño has it in the bag but oh, look, now, now on the outside coming up, it's Lucky Jim, number four, his rider is really urging him forward, with less than a furlong to go; he's passed Argonaut but it is El Niño, El Niño, El N— no, Lucky Jim has forced a nose in front, and it's Lucky Jim, Lucky Jim, Lucky Jim. And Lucky Jim wins it by a neck.'

Memphis brought his fist to the counter with a crunch and his fingers splayed, releasing the betting slip. Eyes turned on Evie as if she were an angel. There was no movement, no noise. A strange sensation was seeping into her skin. Lucky Jim had passed the post in first position. She broke the silence. 'Well . . .'

The men responded by clapping their hands; Evie was patted, cheered. The little man with a few teeth grasped her arm. 'Can you tell me a good one for the two-thirty, lady?'

Counterman was calculating her winnings, over fifty thousand euros, as the men watched her, their mouths open. She asked for the cheque to be made out to Mrs E. Gallagher. He handed it to her, shaking his head. She put it carefully in her handbag.

Memphis rubbed moist hands together as he spoke: 'Would you believe it?'

Evie took a deep breath to steady her nerves. She pushed her sunglasses onto the bridge of her nose, held out her hand and took his, her eyes benevolent and gracious.

'Thank you so much for your help today, Mr Memphis,' she cooed. 'You have brought me good luck. Who knows? Perhaps we will meet again. I will certainly mention you in my latest novel.'

She heaved her carrier bags in one hand and swung her handbag in the other. With the men's eyes on her, she swept out of the betting shop, feeling like Marilyn Monroe.

Evie blinked as she came out into the brightness of the Dublin streets. She paused, adjusted her beret and looked about at the shoppers moving up and down on the pavements.

She thought about how Jim never had any luck in his life.

Purposefully, she dumped the plastic carriers containing her old coat and handbag on the top of a brimming bin.

'Holy shite,' she breathed.

Chapter Six

Dublin city blurred outside the windows: clusters of shops, then houses, then roads passed by. Evie was in a taxi, and the driver was turning corners, making her lurch to the sides in her seat. She was rummaging in the bottom of her bag: the new handbag was huge and her few possessions were hiding in undiscovered corners. Her fingers touched the folded envelope in which her winning cheque was hidden. It was empty now that she had deposited the fifty thousand euros at her bank. She could feel the thudding of her heart, pulsing in her throat, beneath the folds of the new coat.

She rummaged again and found the mobile phone that Brendan had given her. It was unblemished and filled her hand. She would phone Brendan and tell him her plans. She would tell him it was only for a few days. She would phone Sheldon Lodge, apologise for any trouble. She squinted at the phone, touching the screen, and pushed the buttons on the side. The screen stayed blank. Evie squeezed the sides again more firmly. Nothing happened. She banged the phone on her handbag twice, and then pressed the square thing on the back above the word

Samsung. The taxi slowed down. The screen remained blank.

'Smart phone, my arse.' She cursed to herself.

As the taxi-driver turned round and asked for the fare, Evie stared up at a modern building with glass windows looming in front of her. She read the words 'Dublin Airport' and felt a shiver clutch at her body.

Brendan was in a queue. Three people were in front of him. He could hear Maura's voice at the reception desk, the familiar tone of chirpy flirtation she used with all her clients, as she called them, and he gave a little cough. He leaned to one side of the queue, waving for her attention. In front was a little man in a mac, bent over, a cap squashed down on his head between pink ears. Over his head Brendan saw a woman's bony back, her pale hair pulled in a knot. As she turned slightly, he could see the huge swell of her belly and the small child she held to her chest. At the front of the queue there was a young man, a skinhead with tattooed arms. He was arguing at the desk. Brendan rocked forwards and backwards on his heels.

'Dr Palmer can't see you today, Mr Lawn. Not even with your bowels being so critical, as you say. Not without an appointment.'

'But I have to see the doctor today, Missus. It has come on bad, and I need something to calm the guts. It's urgent.'

'There are no appointments with Dr Palmer today. He's away on his holidays.'

'But I need—'

'Why don't you pop to the chemist over the road and buy something to sort it out for the time being? Will I make you an appointment with another doctor for tomorrow morning?' She dropped her voice conspiratorially. 'Dr Singh. She'll sort your diarrhoea out for you, sure enough. Nine sharp. Will that do?' Maura smiled prettily, all teeth.

The young man's shoulders slumped. He moved away from the counter and the pregnant girl with the child started to whisper something about painful piles. He saw Maura flash a warm smile and he couldn't remember when she had last turned the same smile on him. Brendan strained up on his toes and wiggled his hand.

'Maura?'

She was writing something down. He shifted from one foot to another and looked behind him. He was the last in the queue. Almost two o'clock. The old man in the mac took his place at the front of the queue. Maura raised an eyebrow at him.

'Yes? How can I help you today?'

Brendan marvelled at how she dealt with the public with such genuine warmth. The man took off his cap and leaned against the reception desk.

'Good afternoon to you, my lovely. I have an appointment with the nurse. Ten to two.'

Maura's tone brightened. 'You're looking a million dollars yourself, but you're still late, Mr O'Malley. The nurse is ready for you. Will you go to the top of the stairs, turn right, and wait?'

Suddenly it was Brendan's turn, and he wanted to tell her his news so that she could sort out the problem. Maura met his eyes and her brows crossed. Her hair was pulled tight to the top of her head; she had combed it smooth and the strands separated into tramlines, the curls pinned and sprayed like a brittle golden crown. Her suit was blue and firmly buttoned across the chest, and the blouse collar stuck over her jacket like twin rasping tongues.

Brendan drew his breath to speak but she was there first.

'Brendan, why in heaven's name are you—?'

'It's my mother, she's gone!'

'God rest her soul.' Maura did not seem unhappy; her face did not move.

'No, Maura, she's not dead, she's run away. Left the home.'

At first, Maura did not speak. Her mouth was open; red lips, the beginnings of wrinkles around the corners. 'Well, she's really lost the plot this time.'

'Jenny Marshall at Sheldon Lodge rang the Guards. They are keeping an eye out for her.'

'And there's a good thing.'

'I've the afternoon off. I'm going to fetch her back. Come on.'

Maura stared at Brendan as if all this was his fault. 'I don't finish till four.'

'The car's outside.'

A loud beeping came from Brendan's pocket and he pulled out his mobile.

Maura frowned. 'The Garda, maybe? Perhaps she's been on the brandy again and they've found her drunk in a ditch.' She smiled at her own joke but Brendan was absorbed with his mobile.

'Hello? Yes, this is Brendan Gallagher . . . Yes, she's my mother. What?'

Brendan listened. His fingers fumbled as he put the phone away in his pocket.

Maura rolled her eyes. 'Well?'

'That was the Guards. They've found Mammy's coat and handbag. In a bin.'

Chapter Seven

Evie was talking to herself. In the airport lounge, sitting with a caramel latte that tasted like creamy pudding. She decided that she was telling herself it was delicious and she liked this modern coffee. As she stared at the froth in the cup an hour later, a clipped voice announced over the speakers that the plane would be delayed for an hour.

She drank two more coffees, visited the toilet twice and, when she sat down again, she noticed her hands were shaking. She watched as other passengers picked up luggage and moved excitedly as if flying was quite normal. Her breathing had become shallow and she wondered if she shouldn't buy herself a small brandy. When they called her flight number, she whispered to herself that people flew on planes every day and what on earth was she so worried about.

In the aeroplane, sitting by the window, lost in thought, she muttered to herself that flying in an aeroplane was quite safe, nothing bad ever happened, well, not often, only in the films. It was a spur-of-the-moment decision, to take her life in her hands and fly in a plane, to do something she'd never done by herself, to be up in the air for over an hour and to go shopping with her winnings. She'd never been on an aeroplane alone before, but she didn't regret it, no, not at all.

Other people were looking at her. She was becoming one of those mad old ladies who talked to themselves because they had nobody else to listen. The flight to John Lennon Airport would only take a short time, it would soon be over and she would touch down in England. The last flight she had made was with Jim to Majorca five years ago and she had squeezed his hand all the way there.

Jim. Evie shook her head; he had been alive last year, but gaunt and coughing in a hospital bed. The sheets were a shroud the day he died and when she returned home the house still smelled of stale cigarettes and the aftershave he wore, once warm and alive. It was a summer day but everywhere was filled with cold.

She fiddled with her safety belt. 'Calm down now, Evie. There's nothing at all to worry about. It'll be grand once you get there.'

'We're sitting here, love – all right?' A red-haired young man indicated the two seats next to her; one held her handbag. He had a Liverpool accent. Evie nodded towards him, wondering if he had heard her talking to herself. He sat down next to her with his friend, who was smaller and dark-haired. Evie huddled towards the window and stared out again. On the tarmac, some people in uniforms were moving luggage on a trolley. The young men slid down in their seats. The red-haired one in the centre next to her tucked his legs under the seat in front of him and withdrew them again, crossing them uncomfortably, and he gave a little laugh.

'We'll get a bevvy when we take off, Paul?' He nudged his friend. Then he turned to Evie.

'I'm Danny; this is Paul.' The dark-haired one, Paul, bobbed his head at her.

'I'm Evie Gallagher. I'm going shopping to Liverpool and I've never been on a plane by myself—' The plane began to rumble and the vibrations rattled in her chest, making her suck in air. 'Oh my . . .' She felt the plane lurch and then the engine juddered. Her fingers twisted around the arms of her seat.

Danny gave his little laugh again, relaxing in his seat, the safety belt riding up towards his chest. The plane accelerated along the runway and she was forced backwards. Evie brought her hands to her mouth. Her eyes were wide.

'This was meant to be a little break,' she said. 'I haven't travelled by myself before. I believe Liverpool's very good for shopping.'

The young men exchanged looks and glanced at Evie, who was pressing bloodless palms together. Danny gave another reassuring giggle. His eyes shone as an idea came to him.

'Eh, Paul, tell Evie the one about that nightclub we were in, and you needed the toilet and you went outside, and that copper stopped you in the road . . .'

'You tell her, Dan.'

Evie pressed her nose against the window. Beneath her the plane shook. The sky was moving towards her; she was hurtling towards clouds. Danny launched into his story.

'Well, Evie, Paul here had had a real skinful, and this copper came over, from Dublin like, and Paul was swaying around like this . . .'

Everything below was small and the plane rocked to one side, its wing drooping. Danny took the opportunity to continue with his tale.

'So, Paul was bursting and looking for some place to – you know. And this copper seen we was Scousers and came over to have a go at us and he says – in this dead deep Irish voice, like – he says, "Well, what do you think you're up to, eh lads . . .?"'

At this point, Paul laughed out loud at Danny's attempt at an Irish accent. Evie saw clouds through the window, hovering fat pillows, and she wondered how it was possible to be so far from the world she knew. Paul and Danny were waiting for her attention, so that Danny could continue.

'So, Paul says to this copper, "Eh, pal, I need a burst," and the copper gets cross and says to me and Paul, he says, "Now, me lads, what's your names?" and Paul looks at me and he starts to stutter and he says, "Eh, eh, don't tell him your name, Danny." And then he falls flat on his face.'

Danny and Paul were squirming in their seats, red-faced. Evie stared at them for a moment, and then she started to laugh too. She breathed out, put her hands in her lap and sat back in her seat. Danny offered his chuckle again. 'So, Evie, you all right?'

Evie looked at Danny's concerned face.

'You were proper pale back there. I was dead worried. I thought you were going to be sick.'

Paul agreed.

'I'm fine now, thank you.'

'So how's about we get something off the drinks trolley, then? Calm your nerves a bit?'

The stewardess was level with them, smart in her blue suit. She glanced at Danny and Paul, and then looked across at Evie. 'Is everything all right, Madam?'

'Fine thanks.' Evie nodded towards the trolley. 'I could do with a drink though.'

Paul chimed in. 'I'm buying – what you having, Evie?'

The hostess looked askance at the two young men, her face conveying something like suspicion. Evie ignored her and offered to buy a bottle of champagne.

Twenty minutes later, Evie and her new friends had drunk a bottle of Veuve de something; she had taught them to say '*Sláinte*', which both Paul and Danny were repeating loudly as they waved glasses. Evie waved over to the stewardess and ordered a second bottle, explaining with a confidential whisper, 'It's a special occasion. You're only young once.'

The stewardess leaned over, which made the boys double over, given the proximity of her uniformed torso. She spoke gently. 'Are you sure everything is all right, Madam?' She was smiling with her mouth but her eyes appeared anxious.

'Thank you, everything is grand now we have another bottle.'

'Of course, Madam.'

She took out the champagne from the ice bucket, uncorked it and turned to Danny and Paul, who cheered when they saw the bubbles froth over. 'Please can you keep the noise down? You're disturbing other passengers.'

The boys burst out laughing again. 'Got a couple of packs of Pringles, love? I'm starving,' said Danny and they began to toast Paul's birthday and the joys of flying.

Evie was oblivious to the changes outside as the plane started its descent. Paul was asleep, his trout mouth puffing out air. Danny, noticing the plane's trajectory, looked furtively at Evie to check she was calm and then began extolling the virtues of Steven Gerrard's free kick and how his slip-up against Chelsea had cost him the Premiership title before he retired. Evie was smiling, but there was a whistling sensation in her ears and a nagging feeling that

40

she might find her route out of Liverpool Airport a little difficult to negotiate.

'I liked him, that John Lennon one,' she mused. 'It was a bloody shame they shot him.'

'Whereabouts you going in Liverpool, Evie?'

Danny raised an eyebrow, pushing Paul upright, before his head flopped onto Danny's shoulder.

'I need to find myself a hotel for a few days. Can you recommend . . .?'

'Yeh, no probs – we'll get you a taxi to the city centre when we get out, won't we, Paul?'

Paul continued to sleep, a snore rattling in his mouth. The wheels on the plane bumped against the runway; the brakes came on and Danny took up the conversation quickly. 'So, you doing anything special in Liverpool, Evie? Besides shopping.'

Evie wasn't sure. So she said, 'Yes. I'm visiting my son.'

'Oh? Does he live in Liverpool?'

She considered for a moment. 'No, he's meeting me there.' She had drunk too much and suddenly mischief popped like a champagne cork in her head. 'He's a rock star.'

Danny looked directly at Evie. 'A rock star? Anyone famous?'

Danny's face loomed drunk and earnest. It was time for another small performance. Evie sat upright, stretched her arms and swept a hand through her hair. 'Oh yes, my son's quite famous. I'm sure you'll have heard of him. He's a singer and he plays with his band all over the world. He's called Bono.'

Danny sat up straight, jerking Paul to a seated position. They stared at each other. Paul blinked and Danny poked him with his elbow and gave a little laugh.

'Bloody hell, Paul,' breathed Danny. 'We just got drunk with Bono's ma.'

Chapter Eight

The clock showed that it was almost nine, and Evie blinked her eyes open, stretching herself in the luxury of the king-sized bed the next morning. She marvelled at how the flight had become so enjoyable after such a nervy beginning. She didn't regret a little bit the fibs she had told the young men about Bono. It had made the boys happy as they'd ushered her into the cab and shook her hand and said: 'It was a pleasure meeting you, Evie. Tell your Bono we loved *Achtung Baby*.'

Evie's stomach groaned; the champagne had furred her tongue; she was ready for breakfast. She had slept in her undies. She'd brought no change of clothes or toothbrush, so she resolved to go shopping. After all, this was Liverpool and she could do as she pleased for the next few days. She would contact Brendan today, and Jenny at Sheldon Lodge. She grabbed the beret she had bought in Dublin and tugged it over her hair. Now she could become someone else, not the Evie she had been, not the wife, the mother, the old lady in the lifestyle home, but someone interesting, someone she had never met. She pulled on her clothes and her new coat, and the smells reminded her suddenly of airports and taxis and betting shops, and she laughed again.

In the hotel foyer, she asked the receptionist for a map of the city, planning her shopping list. She wondered about a good place to have breakfast, one that would have a caramel latte, and the sweet taste was in her mind as she stepped out into the street.

She felt the bump. It knocked her back against the wall and she instinctively clutched at her handbag. She looked up. The beret fell over one eye, and she tugged it off her head. A woman was staring at her.

'Why you don't look where you going?' the woman said.

Evie was stunned. The breath was knocked out of her.

The woman, Italian or Spanish, was annoyed. Her eyes ignited in Evie's direction, raising unimpressed eyebrows. Her face was not young. Her eyes were made up, surrounded with kohl, and her mouth was scarlet; she wore an orange jacket and her hair was piled on top of her head. Evie gaped at her hair, which was magenta red, tied with a pink silk bow.

'You should be careful, old lady,' the woman continued. 'You might hurt yourself.' She turned and swept away down the road.

Evie studied the jacket, the high heels and skinny ankles, and the orange leather handbag that the woman threw across her shoulder as she walked away.

'What does she mean, old lady?' Evie grumbled. 'She was sixty-five if she was a day.'

Evie looked down at two dusty shoes, at her legs in slacks that widened around her ankles and revealed the top of white socks, at the shapeless blue coat she had been so proud of a day ago.

'Hmmm.'

Breakfast would be a priority, a caramel latte and some of those flaky croissants. It would give her time to consider her options.

'I can fit you in now, if you don't mind a bit of a wait, love.'

His name badge said he was called Nathan and his hair was a creative blond quiff, shorn and darker at the sides but rising up from his head in an arc of a bird's wing. He wore a tight purple T-shirt with a slogan that said, 'This Is What a Feminist Looks Like', skinny black jeans and a belt containing scissors and combs. Evie sat down in the reception area, clutching her bags of shopping. She had bought herself some new clothes, including a leather jacket. Evie was still not sure about the jacket – green wasn't a colour she usually wore but it was emerald green and wasn't she Irish, the assistant had asked. It was expensive too, but it fitted well. Of course, it didn't go with the red beret but Evie bought a black cap, not unlike the ones The Beatles wore in the film *Hard Day's Night*, and she paid with her card so it felt almost like the shopping was free.

From behind the reception desk, a young girl brought Evie a coffee while she waited. It tasted like treacle.

'Ready for you now,' called Nathan, ushering Evie to a seat and whisking a matador cape around her shoulders. 'And what can we do for Madam today?'

Evie hesitated. 'I want a change.'

'Hmmm.' Nathan looked at her, stepping back. 'Radical?'

Evie didn't know what he meant but she agreed.

'Leave it with me – some strong colour and a trim and I will have you looking like Madonna.'

Evie didn't want to look like the Catholic icon; on second thoughts she didn't want to look like the woman who cavorted and sang 'Like a Virgin' either. That song had come out in 1984 when Brendan was seven years old. Evie recalled his little legs dancing in the kiddies' disco, singing along to the lyrics with his arms in the air. He had beamed at her and returned to waving his arms and marching with his legs, and she had ached as she watched her child mouthing the lyrics.

Nathan held up her brown locks as if making a decision. Images were forming in her mind: herself as a distorted cartoon with wild hair, and people looking and laughing. Nathan was talking to her but Evie was quiet, watching the whirling maestro at work. He told her about his Mazda MX-5 and had she seen the new Bond film? Evie's hair was painted and piled. The lighting was harsh and illuminated the lines on her face, making her look anxious. The washing took a long time and then she sat before her reflection, a strange elf with a dull cap of hair plastered to her head. Nathan waved the dryer and chatted about his friend's stag do in Goa. Evie twisted around him to peek in the mirror, as he tugged at her hair. The words 'mutton' and 'lamb' slipped into her head. Nathan was an artist, his scissors and the brush in the air, touching up his work, standing back and making a discontented face, then cutting again. He stood back with a flourish, hairbrush aloft.

'I've kept the fringe long and added texture with some layers, not taken too much off – and I think the blonde highlights really frame your face and create a softer look. What do you think?'

Evie looked at the woman staring at her from the mirror and she burst out laughing. 'Ah, will you look at me?'

Her face was beaming and framed with soft golden hair. Her eyes shone. She thought she looked like a fairy-tale queen.

'Don't you like it?' asked Nathan, piqued.

Evie looked up at him as if he was the saint of all hairdressers. 'I love it. It's grand. Now how much do I owe you?'

'That's a hundred and twenty pounds today.'

'Worth every penny,' she told him as she reached into her purse for her card.

Chapter Nine

She returned to the hotel with a travel-case full of clothes; she had a short nap, charged her phone, washed and was back in town in new jeans and the green leather jacket. She was a glamorous blonde now and it showed in her step. This was just what she needed, a little break away from Dublin. Evie grimaced; she must ring Brendan soon or at least text him. As she passed a travel agent's window, a huge blue display caught her eye, and she resolved to come back. She wanted to visit the cathedrals first.

In a side street, she stopped outside a pub and took out her phone, squeezing the sides. She could hear people laughing, and music boomed, and there was a heavy smell of strong hops. She pressed numbers slowly. She would ring Brendan and then Sheldon Lodge. She imagined the conversation. Everyone would be impressed with how she had organised a mini-break for herself. She would come back rejuvenated, blonde, invigorated. Sheldon Lodge still didn't feel like home, but there could be other alternatives – a little bungalow perhaps, not too far from where Brendan lived.

Incredibly, the phone lit up and a bright array of clouds on blue sky showed itself. She pushed an envelope shape and within seconds she was looking at a text box, with the words 'Brendan, Son'. Evie pressed letters and words came to life:

dear brendan I am in liverpool don't worry love mammy

She poked her finger at the icon marked *send* and it was done. She had sent a text. 'Is there no end to my talents?'

Something solid and shapeless clattered into her. She dropped the phone and fell hard onto gravel. A hand shoved her down and grabbed at her handbag but Evie wrapped her arms around the bag and pulled back.

A voice shouted, 'Let go, you fucking old bitch.'

Evie hung on, rolling on top of her bag, as something kicked her arm. There was a crack of pain and she heard her own voice scream from somewhere distant. She curled into a ball and waited for the next blow. There was another bumping sound, shouting and scuffling. Evie raised her eyes; two men were struggling. One was a young lad in a dark jacket with a hoodie, his face twisted like a malignant imp. The other was a man with a huge belly, a red football shirt and heavy arms. One of his elbows was crooked around the kid's neck and the kid was screeching, his eyes livid. The man was swearing; he pushed the kid roughly and he ran around the corner and away. The man turned to Evie and helped her up. She clutched the bag to her body like a shield.

'You all right, love?'

Evie's legs shook and her arm ached. The big man put an arm around her shoulders.

'You want to come inside and have a brandy? You're shaken up.'

Evie's voice was strangled in her throat. The handbag was still pulled tightly to her chest. A brandy seemed like a really good idea. A double.

The man surveyed her again. 'No real damage done there to you, love. You're a plucky one, you are. Jeans are a bit dirty. This your phone?'

He bent down and handed Evie her mobile; the screen was cracked.

'Think you had a lucky escape there, girl.'

Evie was shivering now.

'Where do you live? Let's get you back home.'

Evie told him the name of the hotel and he hailed a taxi and helped her into the seat. She made sure her phone was clutched in her hand and her bag was cradled in her arms. It was only a short ride.

'The police can't find a trace of her. It's been two days and nothing. They've told me to not worry, to carry on as normal.'

Brendan slumped forward across the desk, sending papers in all directions. Penny Wray came to stand behind him; she laid her hands on his shoulders and pressed down on his taut muscles. Brendan tensed his body. 'What if they don't find her? Or what if something has happened to her?'

'It'll all be fine. Wait and see.'

'She's seventy-five, Penny. My head's full of what might happen to her.'

Penny increased the pace of her rhythmic massage to his shoulders. Brendan put back his head and closed his eyes, allowing the warmth of her fingers to seep through the fabric of his shirt. He thought about Penny, who was standing a few inches behind him; how she'd been a friendly presence in the staff room for over a year; how he was grateful for her warmth and kindness. It occurred to him that she had never mentioned a boyfriend. She wore a huge silver ring on her wedding finger: some sort of Celtic design with a big ruby. She wasn't married, she was Miss Wray, and if she'd never mentioned a man in her life, then perhaps there wasn't one. The ruby ring was a deterrent. It was there to keep the wolves away, he decided; she was fiercely single, dedicated to sports, to fitness, health and beauty, to teaching.

Her fingers pressed deeply into the soft tissue of his shoulders and Brendan felt himself give in to the pressure of her knuckles. He knew she had training in sports massage, but she had always been especially friendly to him, supportive and kind. Brendan imagined Penny at weekends, waking early, going for a jog and then a swim. She'd make muesli, for breakfast; a salad, something with lentils for lunch, then off to Pilates or she'd teach a spinning class. He imagined her with friends in the evening. She'd live in a small cottage, have a dog – a Ridgeback – and it would go running with her in all weathers, dog and woman striding as one around a lake at dawn. No, he decided, she wouldn't have time to be married to a man. She pressed her thumbs against the back of his neck and he felt tension seep away like a hiss of gas. His face broke into a wide smile and he wondered if she was enjoying the sensation as much as he was. A sigh shuddered from his throat and he heard the desperation in it. She moved away.

'You're very tense. It must be a heap of worries, Brendan. Is your wife not able to help?'

Brendan's shoulders tightened automatically and he turned round to look at Penny, who was putting on her jacket. She was a practised masseuse. He had seen her pummel the knotty shoulders of other colleagues in times of stress. But she'd spent a long time on his shoulders, longer than she needed. He bit his lip. Her hair was long and glossy: she looked like an advert for shampoo. She made a little mouth at him, to show she was concerned.

He shook his head. 'What can I do, though?'

She pushed one of her sandwiches towards him. It was cheese salad. 'Here. You ate nothing at lunchtime.'

'I've no appetite.'

Penny came over and took his hand in hers and held it. He noticed he was shaking and he had no power over the tremor.

'Brendan, it's nearly five o'clock. Why don't you go home? We're all finished up here. Give the Garda another call; ask them if you can talk to someone who's on the case.'

His head began to feel heavy and a dull ache settled between his eyes. Brendan thought he would rather stay in school than endure an evening with his wife. He wondered if Penny could read his thoughts; perhaps she was impatient for him to go home. Perhaps she had somewhere else to be, somewhere more interesting. Perhaps there was a man after all. He eased himself up from his seat as if stuck to it, slowly, heavy with worry, picked up his case and shoved some papers in it.

'You're right, of course. It will all be better tomorrow. Thanks. You've been amazing.'

She hugged him and Brendan breathed in her warmth. He held his arms away from his body and wondered if he should clasp them tightly around her waist. A sob caught in his throat. He stiffened his shoulders. 'I'll say goodbye then, Penny.'

His mobile bleeped. It was Maura, no doubt, reminding him that he was late for his dinner. He fumbled in his bag and pulled out the phone. He saw the name on the screen, 'Mammy', and his hand clenched around the plastic casing, leaving finger marks of sweat. Penny was at his elbow as he pressed for the message; he read it once, then again. His mother was all right. His eyes blurred as he stared at the text again. She was in Liverpool.

Chapter Ten

Evie sat in the bath and closed her eyes, feeling stiff and sore. The steam rose around her as she cried angry, stubborn tears. She recalled the stifling emotion, the one where you felt not good enough. It was the hollow inadequacy she had felt at St Aloysius School when Sister Benedicta told her she had achieved three per cent in a test on the Scriptures. She'd felt similar pangs of shame on her second day at the bakery when she dropped a whole tray of fresh cream horns. It came back to her, the sense of humiliation and loss which squatted on her shoulders when the doctor had told her about her first miscarriage, and that she might not expect to have a baby of her own. She recalled Jim's sad face, so like Brendan's now, as he observed her from beneath his cap, his eyes misting. Evie clambered out of the bath, wrapped herself in a towel and took another to dry her hair. She looked at the blotching blue bruise and the new heaviness as she tried to lift her arm. Her jaw tightened.

She could go back to the Lodge. At least she'd be safe there. Safe but bored and wasting away. A memory drifted back to Evie like a faint odour, one which made her squirm and feel uncomfortable. She remembered walking in a park in Dublin, almost a year ago. It was early autumn and she'd needed to get out of the house, with memories of Jim whispering at her from each corner and the Hoover sitting squat in the middle of the hallway and the windows smeared and dirty in the sunlight, screaming at her to clean them. She liked the open space of the park, the long pathways, how trees and plants were different shades of greens and reds beneath the wide white sky and how sparse little flowers made dots of vibrant colour. A dog had come from nowhere, rushed at her in a whirl, and then she was on the ground, and its paws were on her chest and she could feel the heat of its breath, smell the stink of its wet pink tongue. A man had grabbed its collar. 'Get down now, will you, Bucket.'

The young man had been ever so polite. He had shouted at the dog and attached a lead to the collar. Her memory became muddled at this point. The young man had a shaved head and a brown jacket, she thought. The dog was big, an Alsatian, perhaps, with huge beads for eyes and slavering chops. Evie had been shaken, deep inside her bones, she had been terrified. The young man's voice was a rattle in her head. He'd helped her stand up, apologised, said something about Bucket being only a pup. She'd muttered that it was all right, she was fine, and she'd turned round, gone home, skulked back to the Hoover and the smeared windows.

Later that week, she had spoken to Brendan and Maura about the dog and the subject of her safety and her loneliness. They had brought up the possibility of her moving to a home. To Sheldon Lodge.

But the feeling of the lurching dog was still with her, the way it rushed at her and bowled her over, its heavy paws poking into her chest. She thought of the young lad who had just attacked her in the dark alley, pulling at her handbag, swearing at her, his voice like a growling animal's. The Lodge was warm, peaceful, safe.

Evie bit her lip and sat up straight, thinking. She had survived. A kind man had helped her, called her plucky. Her handbag was intact and so was she. She was on holiday, she'd been shopping for new clothes and she was newly blonde. She breathed out. 'I'm damned if I'm giving up. I haven't got to seventy-five and learned nothing about fighting back.'

Evie took out the mobile phone. The crack reflected light off the screen but the clouds still came up bright blue. Her green jacket had mud and gravel stuck to a sleeve but it was intact. The jeans would clean up in a wash and the red mark on her face and the bruise on her arm would fade before too long. Evie went to the minibar and poured herself a gin and tonic. The sharpness in her throat gave her a sudden purpose. She would ring reception, organise for the jeans to be laundered. Then she would order a pizza.

When Brendan arrived home, the house was in darkness. He frowned. Maura seldom went to the supermarket without him and it was unusual for her to be visiting friends in the evening. He dropped his bag in the hallway. His copy of the *Irish Times* would be waiting and he would have a quiet read before dinner and then he would mark the poetry homework for a few hours.

A gentle voice came from the dining room. 'In here, Brendan.'

The table was set for dinner, an array of little tea lights, their flames shimmering in the darkness. Brendan recalled his Uncle Patrick's funeral, which he'd attended when he was a teenager, and he felt the draughty air of the church on his skin as he thought of his own father's death last year, the solid coffin containing someone cold he would never touch again.

Maura was sitting at the head of the table and she had a casserole dish in front of her. She removed the lid and steam rose up, the flickering candles casting shadows against the wall, a sorceress standing over a cauldron. A bottle of wine was open and there were two empty glasses. Brendan stared.

Maura slithered from her seat and came towards him. She was wearing a black dress with a low neck, and he could see the pink of her flesh moving beneath the fabric. The straps slipped from their position and she hoisted them back up. Her hair touched her shoulders, sprayed in a shell of loose gold curls. She put her arms around his neck and he breathed in rose petals.

'I've made us chicken chasseur.' He turned to look at the table and she kissed his cheek. Brendan turned back to kiss her but she moved her face away.

'We've a lovely bottle of Pinot Grigio. It's been chilling for hours.'

Brendan shivered without meaning to.

'I thought we could have dinner then maybe we could have an early night.' She batted her eyelids and gave him a flirtatious look.

Brendan took another look at his wife. It wasn't his birthday and he had not forgotten their anniversary, so why . . .?

'Come and sit down, darling. I cooked it specially.'

He had never heard her call him 'darling' before. He sat down like a dutiful child as she stood over him and ladled chicken and sauce onto his plate. She poured the wine into his glass, leaning heavily on his shoulder, and he heard the liquid gurgle and splash. Maura's cleavage was not far from his face and he remembered a time when he used to kiss her there. She had been young and vulnerable in his arms and his chest had filled with the pain of too much love. His mind wandered to a possible bedroom scene after dinner and he tried to recall how long it had been since they had shared any real closeness. In the candle light, her face took on a soft glow and he noticed how perfectly rounded her shoulders were. He shook his head. His eyes flicked back to the tough skin of the chicken.

'Eat up, darling,' said Maura. She moved back to her seat and ladled meat onto her plate.

Brendan tried to cut into the chicken breast, but his knife slipped. He took a forkful of mushrooms and onions and watched the gravy drip between the prongs. Maura's mouth was full.

'How's your food?' she asked him, her eyebrows high in eagerness, and he bobbed his head politely and made a contented sound.

'Lovely, thanks.'

'I thought a nice piece of chicken would be just perfect.'

'It's delicious.'

She looked at him for a moment, their eyes holding, and Brendan wondered whether to compliment her on the dress. He thought the shiny black material and her gold curls gave her the air of a movie star. For a moment, he wanted to tell her that he loved her. He opened his mouth, but no words came, so he filled it with a forkful of chicken.

The clatter of knives and forks on china continued for a few moments then she said, 'And how was your day, then?'

'OK. Busy.'

'I've made us a cheesecake for dessert.'

'Lovely.'

'It's strawberry.'

Maura had almost finished all the food on her plate. Brendan swiped his fork at the meat. He glanced across at her. She smiled back at him as if a stretching grin could sustain the boundaries of a shrivelling marriage.

'Eat up then, darling.'

Brendan took a breath. 'I – I had a text from my mother today.'

'Oh?' Maura's brows came together.

'She's in Liverpool.'

'Indeed?' Her smile had gone.

'But she's fine.'

'When did she say she'd be home?'

'She didn't.'

'That was good of her.'

Brendan couldn't think of a reply.

'Is she having a little holiday, then?' It came out as a sarcastic question and he shrugged.

'I don't really know, my love. Yes, I suppose she is.'

'All right for some, isn't it?'

'What do you mean?'

'Well, Brendan, *we* could do with a holiday. It's been ages since you and I got away.' She paused for a moment, leaned forward and smiled. 'Remember how lovely it was when we were in Corfu?' Her face flushed pink and she was suddenly bright-eyed with recollection.

The chicken flesh was pale against his plate. Maura's straps slipped down again. 'Corfu? That was eight years ago.'

She gave a little giggle and put her hand to her mouth. She looked suddenly excited. He saw the sweet hopefulness of the girl she had been; excitement shone in her face and, for a moment, Brendan wanted to hold her in his arms. 'We never left the hotel room for the whole fortnight. We both came back with skin as pale as when we left. Your father said—'

Brendan didn't want to be reminded that his father said they were just like a honeymoon couple, so he interrupted her. 'Corfu would be too hot this time of year.'

She shrugged and pulled up the straps. 'I thought it would be nice for us to spend time together.'

'Oh . . .'

'Think of it – dinners together, relaxing on the beach, a romantic hotel, a big four-poster bed . . .' She waved her hands to show the size of the bed; it was as wide as her hopes. Brendan nodded. Her eyes sparkled. 'It would be a chance for us to spend some time together. Just me and you. I mean, you work so hard, Brendan. You're always at the schoolwork, evenings, weekends, refereeing the football in the park. I get lonely by myself. Just imagine. Quality time together. A chance for you and me. We could get to know each other all over again. We could see it as a chance to rekindle—'

Brendan was taking a mouthful of chilled wine. He breathed in sharply and it filled his nose. He sniffed. The liquid bubbled and tickled and it snorted like laughter out of his nostrils.

Maura's face clouded. 'What's that supposed to mean?' She stood up, almost knocking over the wine bottle as her body pushed against the table. He snorted again. 'Brendan?' He was doubled over, coughing, a choking, snickering sound. Her face was suddenly sad, her eyes full of round tears. 'I made an effort tonight with all of this, and now you're laughing at me.'

Brendan rubbed his eyes, which were watering. He spluttered. 'I'm not laughing—' and another paroxysm caught his throat and he shook again.

'It's not funny, Brendan.'

He started to cough more loudly, stuffing his hand into his mouth. His face was wet.

Maura put her hand to her cheek and wiped away a stray tear. For a moment, she said nothing, her eyes frantic. Then she breathed out, air coming in a hard gush. 'I hope you're enjoying yourself at my expense.'

The tears were running down his face; he bent over his meal and a second paroxysm caught in his throat and he heaved and spluttered again. Maura's voice was weak, strangled in her throat, as she caught a sob. Her face froze in horror and she stared at Brendan as if he was a stranger, someone she did not recognise. She clenched tight fists and pulled them towards her face, which had broken out in a red flush extending to her cleavage. She bumped against the table, moved away and then turned back to him.

'I've done my best for you tonight. For us. And all you do is throw it back in my face. You can go to hell, Brendan.'

She rushed past him. The door slammed; feet pounded on the stairs and he could hear her crying. He pressed the space between his eyes with two fingers, put his elbows on the table and let his head fall in his hands. He would go up and apologise. In a minute.

Chapter Eleven

She bought two novels at Lime Street station and, by the time the train arrived in Plymouth, Evie knew Emma Bovary quite well. She had never been one for novels, but she had to find something to pass the time between stations and a bubbly woman in her thirties with spiky hair and round glasses had recommended that she read the Flaubert if she was going to France, and a Brontë, if she'd never read it before. Evie laughed; she'd never read anything much before, except turgid stories about saints and sinners at St Aloysius and rubbishy romances at the Lodge.

Evie decided that Emma Bovary shouldn't have bothered with any of the men in the story. Had she won some money while placing a bet on a lucky horse, she would have done much better for herself. Evie started on the Brontë. She would read the rest of *Wuthering Heights* after the crossing to Roscoff. The ticket she bought in Liverpool had a two-berth cabin and, by the time Evie had found her way to number 8215 and let herself in with the cardboard key, it was almost midnight and she wanted to sleep.

She thought the cabin was like the black hole of Calcutta.

She had never been to the black hole of Calcutta, but once the lights were out, the cabin swum with darkness and swayed with the motion of the sea. Evie closed her eyes and felt alone. France was a long way away and she wasn't sure what she'd do when she got there. She'd find a hotel in Roscoff, like she had in Liverpool, do some shopping, eat some French food and drink some nice wine, then come home. She had money and she would be independent – treat herself to a little break. She could do it, an adventure, by herself. She'd use her lucky number again. Yes, she'd stay for four days. Then she'd know what to do.

She shuddered. Home was a puzzle she did not want to solve yet. She needed time to think. But one thing was certain: she was not going back to Sheldon Lodge. That was a certainty. She said out loud, 'Bollocks if I'm going back there. I'll go to my grave first.'

Silence gave no answer from the blackness around her. The cabin was too warm. She rolled over and took the duvet with her. It was like being in a womb, surrounded by water. Or it was like a grave, the grains of darkness like stifling soil. Sleep would not come and Jim's face appeared in her head. Jim as he was when she first saw him, when he came into the baker's shop and asked for a macaroon. He had been shy, looking at her, and she had liked him for his gentleness. He had returned each day; it was weeks before he'd asked her name and months before he'd asked her to accompany him to the pictures.

The starchiness of her wedding gown scratched at Evie's memory; a white lace dress that predicted what was to come: it had been uncomfortable, worn once for tradition, then put away in the cupboard, like hope, like love. The reality had come to her on her wedding night, Jim awkward, taking off his tie and shirt and watching her, his eyes waiting for her to speak. She'd stared at his bare

61

shoulders, noticing a rash of spots against pale skin. What had followed was the beginning of marriage, a tacit compliance, a warm respect for a kind man, each detail on the wallpaper, a routine, a habit. She had lain meekly beside him, stroking his hair. She had encouraged him, soothed him. But it wasn't love, thought Evie. She had never felt what Emma Bovary felt. Nor had Jim been a Heathcliff, a passion to be ridden and never assuaged. He was just a nice man with whom she had spent her married life; he had been the reason she kept the house comfortable and the food hot and filling.

He had given her Brendan, all those years later when they had lost all hope of having children. Those first few brittle months of pregnancy, when her waking thought was for the baby and Jim had been a breath beside her ear, placing cushions and raising her feet. He had marvelled as the baby blossomed into a hard mound of belly, a hidden miracle and finally a wide-mouthed cry in her arms. Jim had stared at them both from a distance, his face twisted in pride. Perhaps that was when they truly bonded, when the mild husband became a playful father and the quiet house was filled with sound. But that was all in the past now, she had laid Jim in the earth and he was gone. She would make her own way in life now, but she would never know what real love was. That opportunity was liquid; it had slipped through her fingers, drained away and dried out.

Evie was in a boat which was bucking and twisting. Water was leaking through a porthole, huge lapping tongues of water, seeping around her ankles. She pulled at a door which would not open and the sea rose high, soaking her white nightgown, making it a dark grey and pulling her down with its weight. She struggled; she looked around but there was no means of escape and no-one to help her. She cried out and held out her arms to no-one. Strange taunting music began to play and a demonic voice sounded in her ears, mocking her. Evie opened her eyes and turned on the light. The lilting music told her it was time to wake up. The French voice heralded the arrival in Roscoff and requested that foot passengers made their way to the foyer. She picked up *Wuthering Heights* and looked at the bleak picture on the cover, the small figure bent against the wind, struggling towards the future, the elements against her. Evie gave a grim laugh and started to collect her things.

She was dragging her case. Her handbag and coat were over her arm and she was heaving along as lorries rumbled by. There was a four-by-four towing a caravan with stacks of bicycles on the back and then a lovely little campervan with floral curtains. There was no taxi rank, bus stop, or anyone to ask the way, nothing but the dawn wind for company. An articulated lorry juddered past and Evie felt the vibrations. 'Roscoff' was the same in French as it was in English, so Evie felt confident of finding a nice hotel. There must be somewhere close to the port, but she'd already walked far enough and her knees were hurting. She pulled the case up onto the kerb and tugged it along the pavement, each movement sending a shock of pain up her bruised arm.

A white lorry with some black writing in French came by very close to her and she raised a shoulder against the shudder, as something twisted beneath her and she felt the clunk like a cracking bone. At first she thought she had broken her ankle, but realised the case was twisted, hump-backed under her grip, and the wheel had come free and rolled away from her. Evie dropped the coat on the case and chased after the wheel, which fell on its side. She picked it up and her hands were immediately grimy. A jutting piece of metal stuck out, but Evie could not make the wheel fit. She turned the case, offered the wheel to the metal, pushed against the fitting and decided another piece must be missing. She hunted around on the pavement.

Evie swore, invoked the Lord and swore again. She looked up for a friendly face but there was no-one around. She considered the French words for 'please help', realising that 'please' was as far as she could go. Someone would understand once they saw the missing wheel, and she imagined a scenario where a nice man put it back together for her and offered breakfast. With determination, she tugged at the handle and tried to drag the case along on its one wheel. It was heavy, reluctant, and the metal made a slow grinding sound as it scored the pavement. She swore again.

A voice came from over her shoulder and she could hear an engine idling.

'Hello. Do you have a problem?'

A young woman in sunglasses was leaning out of the window of an old Renault Espace. Evie exhaled and closed her eyes for a moment. They were British, English probably: they certainly spoke English. Pop music was playing from inside the van. She was about to speak to Evie again, then she turned to her companion who was making a comment in a low monotone. The woman turned back to Evie.

'Have you had an accident?'

Evie nodded. 'The bloody wheel's broken on the case.'

'Can we offer you a lift?'

The woman's companion mumbled something again from the passenger seat. Evie couldn't make out the words but the tone was distinctly hostile.

'Jump in the back.'

64

Evie heaved her case and coat into the van. As she wriggled in her seat, she was assaulted by a loud flurry of barking and a huge yellow Labrador leaped towards her.

'Get down, Iggy!' the passenger shouted and the dog obeyed. Evie's shoulders tensed, although she wasn't sure whether it was the dog's bark or the passenger's that had set her on edge. She wasn't fond of dogs, but the passenger seemed even more difficult to placate.

The driver turned around, took off her sunglasses and smiled. She was a pleasant-faced woman in her twenties or thirties wearing a skimpy vest, her light brown hair in a loose plait. It was hard to tell people's ages these days, Evie thought, when everyone seemed to dress the same, whatever their age.

'Where shall we drop you?'

Evie surveyed the back of the van; behind her, there were cardboard boxes and a sink with taps. She turned back and looked at the woman.

'Where are you going?'

'To the Crozon peninsula, close to Pentrez beach. Is that on your way?'

Evie didn't stop to think. The words 'peninsula' and 'beach' were enough, and the words came into her mouth before she had time to consider her options. 'Oh, the beach, yes. That is where I am going, too. That's grand.' She thought and then added: 'What a coincidence.'

The woman in the front passenger seat did not turn; she had dark hair cut short and spiky, and wore long bright earrings. She offered Evie a cold shoulder, which was visible to one side of her seat. She wore a pale T-shirt, and her lean arms were tanned. Evie thought she made a little grunting noise. She tried to make conversation with the unfriendly girl. 'You have a sink in the back?'

The driver turned over her shoulder to reply. 'It's for the *gîte*. We are renovating it.' She swung the Espace onto the main road. 'I am Maddie.'

'Evie.' She smiled at the friendly girl with the long plait, whose eyes smiled back in the rear-view mirror. Flicking her blonde fringe, her grin broadened. 'Evie Gallagher.'

The other passenger went on looking out of the window. Maddie said, 'This is Katherine.'

'Kat,' said the irritated voice.

'Pleased to meet you,' Evie began.

Kat turned the pop music up louder, a pumping beat and woman's voice repeating the word 'umbrella'. Evie looked through the window at places she could not pronounce as the van pitched through one village after another. She thought about the Crozon peninsula, and wondered if it would be like the pictures in the travel agent's window. Her phone sounded and she fumbled and found a message. It was Brendan. He had written **Come home, Mammy.** The dog was watching her with eager eyes, his tongue hanging from his mouth like a soft pink sock, and she wondered what she would do next.

Chapter Twelve

Evie held the dog by its collar. She was about to knock. The door marked '*Privé*' was ajar and she paused and listened.

'I hate it here. You've ruined everything.'

'Kat, that's not true. We decided—'

'You decided—'

'We agreed—'

'You wanted to live here; it's always about what you want . . .'

'We were going to make it our home.'

'Yes, me and you, Maddie. Now you've invited that bloody woman to stay with us.'

'You don't mind, do you, Kat?'

'You didn't even ask me. She was in the back of the van, saying, "Isn't the beach lovely, do you have any idea where can I stay for a few days?" and you were like, "We have a room here with us." And she was all simpering, "Oh that would be grand," and you didn't ask me what I thought.'

Evie pulled a face at Kat's awful attempt at an Irish accent. Iggy looked up in sympathy, his eyes round.

Maddie's voice was placatory. 'She's sweet. And she can help. She said she'd do a few jobs for us around the place.'

'Look at her, Maddie. She's an old woman. That's typical of you, picking up any old waif and stray, doing just what you want. She'll have to pay rent.'

Old woman? Evie wrinkled her nose, raised a hand to knock and then changed her mind.

'Kat—'

'You didn't even ask me if she could stay. You made the decision. Because I don't bring anything to the table any more, do I?'

'I didn't mean—'

Evie pushed the door and stepped inside. Both women looked horrified. The dog broke away from Evie's grasp and ran over to Maddie, sniffing her outstretched fingers. Evie held up the lead. 'Thought I'd help everyone out by taking Iggy for a little walk on the beach.'

'Thanks, Evie,' said Maddie, her expression uncomfortable, and Kat rushed out of the door, brushing against her. Evie thought she heard a sob.

She had never been sure about dogs. There was something a bit unpredictable about the way they lurched and leaped and barked. The one she was holding on a lead now was tugging her along the beach, pulling forward with relentless enthusiasm. Evie muttered grimly, 'It's a shame the fecking case couldn't do this.'

Evie's brow furrowed as she thought about Kat and Maddie. She would offer to help them to renovate the other two buildings, which had once been a piggery and, to be honest, still looked more like pig sties than *gîtes*. She might enjoy a short working break. She could cook and clean and chop wood for a week or two, but she wouldn't stay long. A couple of weeks would give her time to think. She would be able to arrange something back in Dublin, perhaps.

A damp blanket of warmth hung in the air. She passed the campervans, parked up for the night by the sea wall. The rich smell of cooking onions came from inside a grey camper with a German number plate; a bearded man was on the steps and he greeted Evie by raising his glass as she passed. Iggy tugged at the lead and she hurtled forwards at a fast pace. Her sore arm ached and was still mottled with dark blotches, which were spreading to pale yellow. The sea breeze whipped at her newly blonde hair. It was late now and the wind scattered a few smudges of people to the edges of the beach. The horizon spat out scraps of sunset, red scars across the darkening skies, and the wide stretch of sand merged into the blue of the sea.

'What do you think of Pentrez beach, then, Iggy?' The dog had put its nose into something it found in the sand and was snuffling. The beach was like life should be: open, uncomplicated. There were just a few people with dogs who smiled and said, '*Bonsoir*', and moved on, and Evie had a clear view of where it would eventually end, suddenly and in a flurry of soft mounds. She turned the dog and headed back towards the farmhouse, the little *gîtes* and the bare stones of the renovation project. She was ready to sleep; the day had been a box sprung full with surprises. Above her, a moon was rising, an ancient bronze disc, hard and thin. Iggy strained at his lead and Evie tugged him back, surprised at the strength of her resolve. She looked at the sky. 'I wonder if you ever look back at me, Jim.'

Her voice sounded quiet against the hushing of the waves.

'I wonder about the babbies, the should-have-beens. I

gave them special names in my head. I dreamed them, each one of them, after every time, a little girl with no face, who knocked on our front door and looked at me with no eyes and said, "Don't cry Mammy because I will come back to you again."'

Evie swallowed a lump of unresolved emotion. Brendan had been number four, the lucky one, the one who had stuck. Iggy pulled her forwards, his mouth gaping and eager. Her sob turned into a laugh, brittle and short. Jim was not up in the sky; Evie was not even sure there was a God there, or anywhere. She was not sure about anything at all.

'Is this what it is now for me, Iggy? Am I lurching onwards at a lick, so fast I don't know where I am going? Is that what it'll be until I find it, the meaning or whatever it is?'

Iggy barked and Evie decided she liked the dog. The sea breathed in and out like a sleeping child and Evie wondered how long this peaceful beach could hold her there. As the sun sank low, she thought about time as a smudge of light dimming in the sky. You couldn't hold onto it for long.

Both of the postcards' glossy pictures were the same, divided into three images, all summer yellows, sands and sunshine and bleached prickly gorse. The words 'Pentrez Plage' were blazed red inside a sea-blue ribbon. Evie wrote on the back of the first card: *Thank you all at Sheldon Lodge. I have decided not to come back though. Please can you give my things to my son. I will be in touch soon. With best wishes for the future, Evie Gallagher.* On the other, she wrote Brendan's address and the words, *I'm having a holiday. I am living two minutes from this beach. It is wonderful. Sending love, Mammy.*

She asked the proprietor for two stamps. He frowned at her and she waved the cards. She tried again. '*Deux* . . . stamps.'

'*Anglaise?*' he asked.

'Irish.'

'*Irlandaise*,' he corrected, and handed her two small stamps.

Evie went back into the sunlight and pushed her cards into the box marked '*étranger*' with a swelling sense of having shed all her worries.

The last day of June was intense in the heat and Evie hid in the shade with *Wuthering Heights*. Iggy was at her feet, his tongue dipping in and out of a bowl of water. She could hear the buzzing of a drill and a hammer hitting brick. Kat was in the piggery working on plumbing in the sink and Maddie was plastering walls.

Heathcliff had just plucked Cathy from her grave and Evie marvelled at the power of passion, how it could bind people together and how it could break a man's resolve. Voices shrilled between the vibrations of machinery in the piggery; Kat's dominating, a hard edge to her words. There was a silence and then a single yell. Evie sat up and Iggy pointed his ears. Kat came running from the building, brown and lean in shorts, plaster clinging to clumps of dark hair, a dusting of white on her cheek.

'Come on, Iggy.' Her words were staccato with each breath as she jogged by and the Labrador followed her, down the driveway towards the road.

Evie went back to the chapter and read on; a few minutes later, she was conscious of a shadow over the page, and she looked up. Maddie's hair was over her face; behind the fallen strands her eyes were swollen with tears.

'Evie?'

Evie put her book down and stood, wrapping her arms around the younger woman.

'We just had a massive row.'

Evie waited.

'It's all going wrong . . . Kat's really angry with me. I think – I think she's going to leave.'

Evie blinked. The sunlight was in her eyes. Maddie dropped down beside her and Evie reached over and patted her hand. 'I'm sure it'll be all right.'

Maddie bent forward and snivelled, wiped her hand across her face. 'No, Evie, it won't. It was great when we first came here. We've been working flat out for a year. Then we went back to England last week to see my parents, to buy some things for the *gîtes*. It was our dream, to set up home here together, to run it as a business, but it's all going wrong.'

Evie waited, watching the young woman's shoulders shake, and she put a gentle hand on her back. When Maddie turned to Evie, her face was blotchy and her voice strained. 'My granny left me the money. We both so desperately wanted to make a go of the *gîtes*. I mean, we've been together since the second year at university – nine years, and things have always been good. I did business management, Kat studied foreign languages – it seemed like a no-brainer for us to come out here. There's always been this problem, though, with my parents' interference. We kept it under wraps, hoped it would go away. Then last week, my mother made a stupid comment in front of Kat. Since then, she's been really moody.'

'What did she say?'

Maddie sniffed. 'Something about me providing all the money for the *gîtes* and doing all the brain work and Kat not bringing anything to the table. It really hurt her feelings. She thinks my parents are privileged and I'm spoiled and I think she's lost respect for me. She's very independent; that's one reason why I love her.'

'Shall we take your van and go up to the headland?' Evie said. 'We can have a little walk and you can tell me about it. When we come back, we'll make some supper and open a lovely bottle of wine.'

Maddie felt in her pocket for the keys. She draped her other arm around Evie's shoulders and took a deep breath.

The early evening was still warm and bright. The little kitchen smelled of the warm aroma of herbs and frying potatoes. Kat stood in the doorway, a silent shadow, and Iggy moved towards his water bowl, lapping loudly. Maddie looked up hopefully from the table, which had been covered with a pretty blue-checked cloth and laden with plates full of green salad, sliced tomatoes, olives, cheese, piles of crusty bread. She patted the chair next to her, and Kat slumped down, sullen and tired, running a hand through her hair. Evie placed the Spanish omelette in the centre. It was huge, fluffy and golden, filled with peas and potatoes, peppers and onions.

The chair squeaked as Evie sat down. She poured red wine into glasses. Kat pulled an unimpressed face. 'What's all this for?'

Evie offered her most beatific smile. 'For you, Kat. And for Maddie. To say thanks for putting me up here. For being welcoming. And because you're both so lovely.'

Kat turned away, wrinkled her nose and surveyed the newly whitewashed brick walls. Maddie took a slice of omelette and Evie indicated the rest of the food, then lifted her glass. '*Sláinte.*'

Maddie raised her glass. '*Santé.*'

Kat gulped at her wine, and mumbled to Evie, 'That's "cheers" in French.'

For a moment, there was no sound except for the clank of knives and forks against plates. Then Evie looked up at both girls. 'I've a confession to make.'

Two pairs of eyes darted towards her face, so she winked. 'I'm on the run.'

Kat leaned forward. 'From prison?' Her knife and fork were in the air.

Evie took a mouthful of wine and her laughter bubbled. 'No. From a bloody care home.'

Maddie's brow creased. 'I don't understand.'

Evie chewed thoughtfully. 'My husband died and I just gave up. Felt lonely, so I went into Sheldon Lodge. I was surrounded with lots of lovely old people there and, do you know, it was the coldest, loneliest winter of my life.'

Maddie's fork was in the air. 'I had no idea, Evie.'

'So I ran away. I believe in the power of luck, you know. I've a lucky four-leaf clover in my handbag. Had it since I was four years old. Four's my lucky number.' Kat swallowed the last of her wine, so Evie refilled her glass. 'I took a huge gamble and won some money, and it brought me to Liverpool where I met some grand people, but I was attacked by some poor little lad who was a chancer, and I thought about giving up, but then I came here and met you two.'

Maddie and Kat exchanged looks. Evie passed the bread around the table and took a breath. 'You two, you have it all. This place, youth, a future – each other. Make the most of it all. Before you know it, time's like a whirlwind that has just rushed past and suddenly you're seventy-five and on your own. There's no time to waste on petty squabbles.'

The young women stared at Evie and she beamed. 'So come on, the pair of you. Let's sort out priorities.' She raised her glass. 'Happiness. Someone you love, who loves you back. A good meal shared together. And the biggest priority of all. The present. It's not called the present for nothing. It's a gift.'

Kat looked across at Evie and nodded slowly. 'You're right, Evie.' She turned to Maddie and held out her hand. 'I'm sorry, Maddie. I've been stupid, haven't I?'

Maddie leaned forward, mumbled, 'Not your fault . . . nobody's fault. Come here,' and the two women clasped each other in a hug.

Evie stood up, a grin on her face. 'Will I open up a bottle? Another red one, perhaps?'

Chapter Thirteen

His eyes throbbed. Voices scratched in his head; all around him in the staff room, the low hum of conversation was spattered with the clink of teaspoons stirring coffee cups. He slumped over the table and wished time would stand still. His elbows slipped and pushed some papers onto the floor, reports, assessments: paperwork that would need completing tonight. He gathered them, and they rustled, dry as dead leaves, as he piled them up. He pushed his fingers into his eye sockets and rubbed hard. Penny Wray was standing behind him and she touched his shoulder. 'Last lesson this term. Good luck.' The klaxon sounded.

He nodded and picked up his briefcase.

He put the postcard inside the poetry book, at the right page for the lesson; he opened it and said to the class, 'So, William Butler Yeats. "The Second Coming".'

Someone sniggered. McNally or Fearon, no doubt. Brendan carried on, his reading-to-the-class voice a little louder. He slowed his words, tried to emphasise the most important phrases, to convey the gravitas and beauty of the language.

'*Somewhere in sands of the desert*
A shape with lion body and the head of a man,
A gaze blank and pitiless as the sun,
Is moving its slow thighs . . .'

A laugh vibrated, staccato machine-gun fire. Brendan looked up. 'Kevin Fearon?'

There was a pause, a face twisted in consideration. 'I was just thinking about the slow thighs, Sir.'

'He is always thinking about thighs, Sir.'

Brendan tried to manage the moment with a half-smile. 'All right, Jordan. Back to the poem. Where was I?'

'In the middle of slow thighs, Sir.'

Laughter ricocheted; kids' faces were masks, distorted with hilarity and he felt himself duck a little, pushing his head down into his collar. He started again. '*Somewhere in sands . . .*'

'Yeats is gay, Sir.'

Brendan snapped his head towards the boy. 'No, Gilbert, it's believed not, Yeats married Georgiana H—'

'Are you married, Sir?'

'He is so; I have seen his wife, the blonde one with the big—'

'She works in the doctor's, my mother saw her.'

'Now . . . Yeats is telling us in "The Second Coming" . . .' Brendan's heart drummed in his throat and he lifted the book. The postcard poked out from the page and Brendan pushed it back.

'You and your missus, Sir,' began Jordan Jelfs. 'Do you write poems about her thighs, Sir?'

Laughter crackled again. Brendan felt sweat leak and trickle down the back of his spine.

'Tell us about your second coming, Sir, and her soft thighs.'

'Is she a good ride?'

77

Brendan put the book down on his desk and the post-card fluttered to the floor. He caught the eye of Malandra Shaw, who was applying mascara. She gave Brendan her full gaze.

'Mr Gallagher would rather ride Miss Wray.'

The boys howled, throwing themselves back in their seats. Kevin Fearon waved his fist over his groin. 'I don't blame you, Sir. I could ride her too!'

'So come on, Sir, tell us about the Miss Wray one. Does she have soft thighs?'

Brendan considered each face; the kids were rocking with delight, punching the air and looking at each other, mouths twisted in sarcasm. He brought his palm down hard on a desk. His mouth twisted and held still, a frozen grimace. He spluttered, and then the words came. 'Shut up. Do you hear me? Just shut up, all of you.'

The room went quiet for a moment. The air prickled. Brendan felt damp under his arms, and smelled the stale sweat pooling there.

Softly, Kevin Fearon cooed: 'Ooohh, he's getting angry . . .'

There was a snigger; someone made a farting sound on their arm. Brendan was pale as the page as he walked over to Kevin's desk and leaned over, inches from his face. Something was building inside him, a hard mass of anxiety: the son, the husband, the teacher, the total failure. His mouth was dust-dry. He licked his lips, once, like a snake. Behind his eyes a throbbing pulse was blinding his vision. He brought his hand down on the table. 'All this has to stop. Now. It has to stop.'

His voice was raw and the edges of his words signalled a fury beyond his own control. Kevin leaned back in his seat, a smirk ready to curve on his lips, but something made him hesitate. At the back of the class, someone scraped a chair; someone else exhaled noisily.

Brendan thumped the table again, his fist bloodless. 'Yeats is an important part of our studies,' he began. 'This is all going to change. Over the holidays each and every one of you will write me an essay about Yeats' poetry. You hear me? All of you?'

He banged his fist again, twice, three times, and he was beating at his anxieties, flattening each one. All eyes were fixed on him. Brendan stood up, dizzy, and walked over to the board, pointing at a question projected in print. His voice shook, but his eyes were livid coals. He felt a pain in his hand. A nail was bent backwards and the skin was purpling.

'Right. Right. What literary devices has Yeats used in "The Second Coming"? I want two sides of A4 paper from each of you, handed in to me the first day back after the summer break. Now, write it down in your homework diaries. In silence.'

He stared wildly around the room. Each student bent a head towards the page, writing, and some twisting up to look at the white board, each face a study of perplexed or feigned interest. Brendan bent down and picked up the postcard, his hand a palsy of nerves and triumph, and he read the handwriting again. His mother was on a beach in Brittany.

When the klaxon sounded and the students left, one or two bumping into desks as they went, Brendan collected the papers together and pushed them deep into his briefcase.

'Happy holidays, Brendan,' Penny Wray said when she came into the classroom, cool and confident in her shorts and T-shirt. Brendan's face flushed violet. It occurred to him that he would not see her for several weeks. He breathed deeply and forced out the question that had popped into his mouth and filled it like cement.

79

'Are you away for the summer, Penny?'

She grinned. 'I'm off to Mexico. And you?'

He shrugged. 'No plans. Not really.' He looked at her, all white shorts and glowing skin, and tried again. 'So, will you go to Mexico with a boyfriend?'

She turned away and picked up his copy of W.B. Yeats, examined the cover and put it down again. 'It will be a sporting holiday. Snorkelling, sailing, sunbathing.'

Brendan almost said he wished he could come along. 'Sounds perfect,' he mumbled.

She grinned at him. 'Will I email you some photos then? The scenery's lovely. I've been there five times before.'

He nodded and wondered again if her offer of friendship could have been something more. He was aware that his shirt held the stench of sweat. She sat at his desk, crossing her legs, and he swallowed. She had a newspaper in her hand and was unfolding it. Her ponytail swished and she flicked the pages.

'Look,' she said, pointing at an advertisement. 'I've found us new jobs. Here – this one would suit me perfectly. In charge of sports, just in the north of the city. And this is the job for you. A pastoral post in St Cillian's. The application date is this week. It's just up your street. You'd be great at it.'

Brendan followed her finger and read the print. A new job in a new school. Penny was right, it was what he needed, and he would apply. They would find different schools and have different lives and she would not miss him. But perhaps change was just what he needed.

Chapter Fourteen

'You have been on that laptop all evening. Why don't you come through and watch TV with me?'

Brendan was engrossed in finishing his application to St Cillian's. He pressed his lips together but no sound came out in reply. Maura tried again, her voice saccharine with effort.

'I could open a bottle and we could share some cheesy nibbles?'

Brendan read through his application, adjusted a word or two and pressed *send* with a mixture of disbelief and satisfaction. 'What was that?' he said.

'Wine and nibbles, darling.'

She had been using new endearments throughout the week. Her eyes had taken on a kind of bovine hopefulness and her lashes fluttered, heavy with extra mascara.

'In a minute.' He thought about calling her a new tender name, 'sweetheart' or 'honey' perhaps, instead of the usual placatory 'my love', but it felt awkward. He picked up his mobile and found his mother's number, pressed dial and waited. Nothing, again, except an empty voice requesting a message. He wondered if she had discovered how to pick up voicemail.

'Brendan, will I start the film?'

A sudden thought occurred to him. He started to search for something on the internet, his brows together, his eyes reflecting the moving screen. She was behind him, looking over his shoulder. He pressed the keys and waited. A white page flipped up, a timetable. Maura put her arms around his neck, looking over his shoulder. Brendan made the screen whizz up and down: Cork to Roscoff, Roscoff to Cork.

She leaned against the back of his chair and rested her face against his head. He could hear her breathing, her mind processing the details.

'Is it a little holiday we're having? Are we going to France?' She twirled her fingers in his hair and her voice was light and girlish. 'Oh Brendan, I'd love to go to France. Just you and me. The food and the wine – just think, and the beaches. You'd have a chance to practise your French – you'd like that. And we could enjoy some culture, the churches, the history. You could do a bit of canoeing perhaps and I could sit in the sunshine and get a suntan. I'm so pale at the moment. It would do us both good.'

Brendan put the laptop down and turned around. She was wearing a flimsy dressing gown. It was loose and he could see she had little on underneath, if anything. Her damp hair trailed across her forehead. He became aware he was staring.

'Ah.' He turned back to the laptop. 'Maura. I was thinking of going by myself.'

He swivelled around again and was surprised to see that she was upset. The smile slipped down from her face and her eyes became soft, almost tearful, then colder and hard.

'I thought I would bring my mother home. I'd just be away a couple of days. Not long.'

Frozen disbelief stared back at him.

'She's written to the Lodge and said she doesn't want her place there any more. I need to go and get her, Maura, find out what's happening.'

Maura exhaled. The dressing gown gaped and she pulled it across her chest, tying the belt firmly. 'Why don't you just call her? Tell her to come home?'

Brendan held up his mobile. 'I just tried. She's not picking up.'

'But we don't need to go after her. She's a grown woman. She can come back by herself.'

He frowned. 'But what if she doesn't want to come back?'

'Then let her stay.'

Brendan glanced over her shoulder and back to his hand, which was squeezing the phone. He glanced at the wedding ring on his finger. He had imagined himself going alone to France. It would be an adventure. He would be a sleuth. He wouldn't tell his mother what he was doing; he'd text her, then catch up with her. Eventually, he'd phone, tell her where he was, and they'd meet in a nice restaurant, over some *moules marinières*. She'd be surprised to see him, delighted, and he'd persuade her to come home. She'd say, 'I'm glad you came, Brendan. I'm ready to come back. I missed Dublin too much. But most of all, I missed you.'

'Ring her, Brendan.' Maura nodded towards the phone. 'Then we can see the film.' She raised her eyebrows hopefully. 'And have some nibbles.'

Brendan hung his head. He wondered if his mother was having a great time in Brittany. It occurred to him that she mightn't be missing him at all, that she might not need him. The thought filled like a raincloud and dropped damply across his shoulders. He groaned. 'I'm going to France, Maura.'

83

'Then text her and tell her we're coming.'

He shook his head, looked at his hands for a moment and then glanced around the room. 'I don't like sending Mammy texts. She probably won't read them. Anyway, she might not want to come back. I'll go and surprise her. Tell her we miss her. Tell her she should be back here, in Dublin, with us. Persuade her to come home.'

'Then I'm coming with you.' Her lips made a straight line. 'Book the tickets, Brendan. I'm owed a few weeks off work. You sort out the ferry crossing. I'll go and start packing the cases. There. That's it, all settled.'

Evie walked up the hill, one arm crooked through Maddie's and the other through Kat's. The music was audible, the light playing of pipes lifted on the wind, and the three women were already dancing on skipping feet. Maddie leaned towards Evie. 'You've seen nothing of Pentrez until you've seen some Breton dancers. They come here every Friday evening in the summer, in costume. You'll love it, Evie.'

Kat smiled and Evie grinned back. She had never seen the young woman so happy as during this past week and the three of them had worked hard in the *gîtes* together, chatting all the time. Evie had pretended to be shocked by Kat's raucous renditions of various so-called traditional Irish songs. 'Paddy McGinty's Goat' had been particularly rude. They had been telling tales and drinking brandy. Evie had entertained them with stories of her mischief at St Aloysius' School and the responses of the angry nuns, and she had made them cry when she sang 'Danny Boy' in her high quavering voice.

They caught sight of the little night market. The aroma of crêpes hung on the air and costumed dancers were already in full swing, arm in arm with local people who seemed to know every step. Evie grinned as Kat and Maddie pulled her through the throng. They found themselves in a circle of dancers and they linked arms, following the moves and laughing at their mistakes.

The man who turned to Evie moved lightly on his feet, despite his solidity. He held her waist easily, his other hand slipping into hers in a practised dance move. His face crinkled, his cheeks concertinas of charm. Evie allowed herself to be turned, puzzled by the unfamiliarity of a stranger's hands, and she looked over his shoulder at the musicians in black and white, smart in their tasselled hats. They were singing, playing lusty pipes which blew bubbles of music into the air. Evie turned again on the whisk of a gavotte and Maddie and Kat were dancing together, their eyes glazed with happiness, Maddie's plait swinging in an arc. Evie's partner tightened his grip on her waist. His forearms were muscled and his puffed cheeks reminded her of Popeye the Sailor.

She swirled and the town square passed by in a blur, full of revellers and musicians and vans selling crêpes and couscous. The bars were crowded, drinkers laughed together in doorways with a glass in one hand trying to clap to the rhythms. Evie turned again and her new partner was Kat. They were lifted on the gurgle of the pipes.

Kat raised her voice above the music. 'I can't thank you enough. For everything.'

'Ah, it was a pleasure.' Evie thought of the piggery, now two *gîtes*, neatly painted over the last fortnight and homely with their crisp curtains and yellow walls. Adverts were already in place and bookings were being made for the rest of the holiday season.

'I mean for being so sweet and patient with me. I was a real cow. I was making a mountain out of a silly little thing.'

Evie leaned into the swing and Kat clutched her hands tightly.

'Please say you'll stay with us for the summer, Evie. Maddie would love that and so would I.'

They turned in a spin and changed partners again.

Popeye was back and he claimed Evie in his grasp. He gave her his creased smile again and said '*Charmante*' to her, pulling her into his body. She inhaled the smell of tobacco and thought of Jim, how he had held her lightly when they had danced together to music in the sixties. Jim had shuffled his feet awkwardly but she'd always loved dancing.

Popeye's grip on her waist was determined. It was time to buy herself another glass of Pommeau, and she pulled away from him and walked over to a stall, ordering a small glass. The drink was thick syrup which clung to her tongue. It had a kick like a Saturday night in Dublin. She swallowed in gulps and it prickled her throat. Evie could see the beach down below the road. The day was draining away and a light rain began to nuzzle her face. No traffic passed except for the German in his campervan driving on his way elsewhere. He waved a hand in recognition and Evie waved back. She wondered where he was going, whether he would travel far, whether he would have adventures. His campervan was huge, like a small house, and she thought how nice it must be to point yourself in any direction and go where you choose. The campervan lumbered away and was gone and Evie had the sense of being left behind. She looked at the sea shining, sliced in half by the melting of the setting sun, and her eyes swept towards the arc of the coastline. She wondered what was beyond Brittany. The music and laughter warbled behind her. Evie looked towards the horizon again and felt her pulse quicken.

*

They were driving to Le Faou for a special treat. Kat and Maddie had told her there was a bakery patisserie that sold the best cakes on the presqu'isle, explaining with a grin that they'd sampled most of the cake shops across the peninsular, and, as Evie had worked in a bakery for over twenty years, she must visit, then they would have lunch. Iggy licked his chops and the van was light with laughter.

The cake shop sold macaroons, brightly coloured and crammed with cream. Evie ate three, telling the proprietor that the Dublin bakery wasn't like this in the 1960s. Maddie and Kat held hands and talked of plans for the *gîtes*, themed evenings, parties, music, and Maddie grasped Evie's hand. 'We'd love it if you'd stay and help. As long as you'd like.'

Lunch was delicious, crêpes and salad and bread with a glass of wine, and Evie was in a warm haze as they walked back to the van, arms linked. Maddie chattered about plans for her visiting holidaymakers, barbecues, even Christmas festivities, but Evie's thoughts slipped elsewhere. A sign on a wooden gate caught her eye and she stopped. 'Could we take a look in there for a minute?'

Garage Lasnec sprawled behind open wooden gates, a mass of metal in various stages of repair. Georges Lasnec was languid, lifting the bonnet of a light green Peugeot. He was a tall man with a goatee smudge of oil on his chin. Evie asked him in simple English if he had any campervans for sale. Maddie translated and Evie was led around a path of vehicles in different stages of newness. She stopped.

'Will you look at this lovely old campervan?' she said. It was aqua blue and had a front like a rounded face. She paddled her fingers along the chrome of the little grille. 'Ah, this is ancient and cheeky . . . It's grand. I like it.'

Kat said something to the man and he gave her the keys.

'Jump in, Evie. Do you want to test-drive?'

Evie slid into the driver's seat. It was soft leather, comfortable. She glanced up at the roof, where a few rust spots had formed. It smelled musky, like a river bed, but sweet. Bright curtains hung at the windows, the edges frayed. There were some covers rolled up in the back, a wicker basket which looked like it would hold a picnic. She looked out through the windscreen, which was grimy apart from the lighter arc made by the wiper. It would need a good clean. Her hands slid smoothly around the steering wheel, then her fingers wiggled the gear stick. She smiled. 'This needs some TLC.'

With Kat as her passenger and Maddie and Iggy left behind in the garage, Evie swung the campervan out of the gate and into the road. It jerked and stopped, then lurched forward again to join the traffic. Evie hit the kerb and the campervan ricocheted and bumped onto the road.

'Keep it on the right-hand side. You're not in Ireland now.'

'Oh, right.'

Kat guided her around the town. Evie screwed her eyes and peered over the wheel, thumping the gear stick and jolting up onto the kerb and down again.

'Brake.'

Evie slammed both feet down, just missing the bumper of the vehicle in front.

'Shite.'

She swerved in front of a parked van, passing dangerously close to a cyclist, and she accelerated, remembering it was a while since she had driven the old Micra. It had been Jim who would drive them around Dublin, mostly. After his death, she had taken their car out, usually to the supermarket, several times to the graveyard. She didn't enjoy the Dublin traffic, but here the roads were relatively calm. One driver raised his hand; let her out in front of him. With Kat's guidance, she was able to negotiate a road island, and to overtake a slow car, putting her on the road back to Le Faou. She had driven exactly four kilometres: the campervan was clearly going to be lucky.

They returned to Garage Lasnec, turning sharply in front of a lorry, which sounded its horn. Maddie's face was anxious and Iggy was straining at his lead. Georges Lasnec put his hands on his hips.

Evie slid out of the driver's side and held up the keys. 'I'll buy it.'

'Hang on a minute.' Kat said something to Georges Lasnec who shrugged a laconic reply. Kat launched into fluent French, arguing, her words fast and energetic. Evie passed a hand over her head; the driving and the excitement were exhausting.

The garage owner paused, grumbled and lifted his palms in protest; Kat threw a word at him, a number, a knife in a game of stretch, and he folded his arms across his chest. He grumbled; he forced his hands deep into pockets, turned away and nodded. She had won.

'OK, Evie, he's reduced the price. It needs new tyres too so he'll put those on for you. Three thousand euros all in. How's that?'

Evie found her card in her bag, somewhere at the bottom.

'That's grand. Tell him we have a deal.'

Her case was loaded, with its wheel fixed. She'd packed boxes of provisions, summer clothes, CDs, bedding, water and too many books, including one she had just started reading, a translation of something by Simone de Beauvoir, which Maddie had given her. It was hot and sticky inside the campervan and the beach would have been an ideal place to go with a book, but Evie had a map with a route marked in pencil. She had decided to go south, to see for herself the vineyards and the mountains, and she'd worked out a route based on Maddie and Kat's jaunt to Languedoc two years ago. She leaned forward and stretched out her arms. Iggy leaped up, round-eyed, and Kat and Maddie hugged her, all three gripped in a rugby scrum. When they pulled apart there were tears.

'Please come back and visit us, Evie.'

'Of course.'

'And thank you for everything.'

Kat handed her two pieces of paper. One was an address and mobile number. The other was the cheque she had given them for rent. Evie protested but Maddie began to sniff, so she stopped.

'You're the best of girls. Like daughters. I'll come back and see you both soon.'

They embraced again and Evie clambered into the campervan. As she drove away, the rear-view mirror showed two waving women, their arms linked, and a barking dog.

She leaned over the wheel, blinking, and swung onto the open road via the pavement. The sea was to her right and the highway ahead, shimmering with opportunity. A bend to the left took her up a hill, signposted 'Menez-Hom', which became steeper, a slope furred on either side with scrubby yellow and purple heather. She overtook a cyclist, moving to the far side of the road, and lugged the gears into second, making the campervan lurch forwards as if sprung. She pulled in at the top of the hill, parking between two large caravans, and clambered out. Evie clutched her bag and climbed the path to the top of Menez-Hom, the wind whistling hard in her ear drums.

She could see people rising from the hills into the skies, tied into colourful canopies, looming in front of her then sliding down, out of sight. How free and calm they appeared, these hang-gliders, lifted and held on the wind, then shifting away again. She could see model aeroplanes flying, rising and tumbling, and, to the right, in the distance, there was a clutch of wind turbines and a small town. To the left, she saw a bridge and a river and, as she turned around to look behind, the sea shone back at her, smooth as a mirror. The panorama was vast and generous and she felt surrounded by new choices. She shivered, a delicious feeling composed of cold and opportunity.

She scrambled back into the campervan. The cab was stifling and the air was thick; she started the engine and opened the windows, pushing the curtains apart to flutter in the breeze. The summit was far behind as she hurtled down the hill and saw the road open its arms to the left and the right.

'Today is the lucky fourth of July. The world is my bloody oyster,' she muttered as the gears champed together and she turned towards a sign which said 'Ploeven'. She fiddled with the CD player and a familiar tune took to the air. Evie began to sing along, her voice warbling and light.

An hour away, a yellow Fiat Panda had left the port in Roscoff and was just turning onto the main road. The driver stared straight ahead while a woman gave him directions from the passenger seat, a map under her nose.

Chapter Fifteen

They saw the sea from the road above. It was a shield of silver with a halo of sand shimmering in the sun. The Fiat Panda wound its way down the narrow bends, then the beach appeared to their right, speckled with swimmers. Windsurfers were zipping and unzipping the foam on the horizon. It was hot inside the car, even with the windows wide open. They drove up and down the seafront twice, looking for a hotel.

Brendan's brow furrowed. 'She said she was staying near this beach, so she must be in a hotel. But there isn't one here.'

'There are some little apartments. Maybe she's rented one of those. It would be funny to bump into her in a little café, maybe like that one there.' Maura could smell pizza cooking; a blue and white sign offered '*moules marinières/frites*' as the dish of the day for nine euros. Brendan turned his head from side to side.

'Perhaps we should ask someone? Should I stop at this little shop – maybe she bought her postcards here?'

He pulled up at the kerb and grabbed his jacket, slamming the door as he moved away; his mobile and wallet were in the inside pocket. Maura followed him, too warm even in her sleeveless top and shorts. There were ice-creams for sale, cold drinks, and newspapers. She picked out some postcards with pictures of the sea splashing spray. Brendan asked the proprietor in his best French if he knew of a woman who was staying close by, an Irish woman. The man pushed up his glasses and replied, '*Oui.*'

His lungs emptied in a rush. He asked the man if she was an older woman, in her seventies. The man scratched his head.

'*Oui. Peut-être. Plus jeune . . . On ne sait jamais à ce qui concerne les femmes . . .*'

Brendan put his hands on the counter and leaned forwards. 'Brunette? Petite?'

The proprietor cleaned his glasses on his shirt and replaced them, peering back at Brendan. '*Non. L'Irlandaise elle était une petite blonde.*'

Brendan asked him if he was sure and the man grunted assent. Maura handed over her postcards and bought stamps and two bottles of water. Brendan blew air out through his cheeks, then turned back to the car.

'It can't be the same woman. The one he knows has blonde hair. What should we do?'

'Ring her, Brendan.'

'We've decided. We'll surprise her. She loves surprises.' He imagined his mother being delighted to see him, hugging him, telling him she couldn't speak a word of French and what a good job he was here; he was so good at the language, just in time to help her find a nice lunch, then she'd be on her way back home.

'Text her, then go for lunch?' Maura brightened. Brendan was already busy on his phone.

'Best not to tell her we are here, my love. Not yet.'

Another image came into his head. His mother in a swimsuit, in a deck chair on the sand, a sun hat on her head, her face a picture of surprise and irritation. What if she didn't need him at all? What if no-one needed him again, except for Maura? Guilt descended on him like a sudden downpour and he shivered.

Brendan clutched the phone and typed: Where are you, Mammy? B x

Maura placed a hand on his wrist. She leaned towards him, her lips close to his cheek. 'We should be thinking of finding a hotel for ourselves, Brendan. We could be here for a couple of days, maybe more.'

The mussels were served in a wonderful sauce, the chips were thin and crispy and the afternoon on the beach was lazy and soaked in sunlight; time stretched out in a glorious hammock of haze. Maura waded into the water, laughing, splashing, calling Brendan to follow her in and paddle. His mood lifted, seeing his wife smile with delight, her hair whipping across her cheeks. He checked the mobile repeatedly but there was no reply from Evie.

They found a small, picturesque hotel by the river in nearby Châteaulin, they ate at a little Chinese restaurant and walked arm in arm back to the hotel. The water was smooth, calm as crystal, reflecting the arched bridge and green banks in symmetry. A cyclist passed, then another. Maura knocked back three glasses of wine and she was chattering about going to a French market in the town later in the week. Brendan looked down at his feet and used his spare hand twice to check his phone without her noticing.

They shared a dessert; Maura chose profiteroles, and she giggled with delight as she plucked one from the plate and popped it between Brendan's lips. He tried to push the worry of his mother away and enjoy her company.

She was scintillating, charming the waiter in her meagre French, *merci* and *s'il vous plaît*, and the tall balding man in black was attentive to her, filling her glass and murmuring, '*Vous parlez Français très bien. Vous êtes Allemande, Madame?*' She looked at Brendan quizzically, not understanding.

He muttered, 'He thinks you're German. He says your French is good,' and laughter bubbled from her lips. Brendan frowned at the waiter and wished he would go away.

They walked back arm in arm and Maura disappeared into the bathroom. Brendan checked his phone for messages and then took some maps from his suitcase and selected the Ordnance Survey map of Finistère. In the shower, Maura was lathering herself and singing a song about a new day, her voice echoing against the glass of the cubicle. She was adding the bass line too, punctuating the tune with soft sounds like sucking fruit.

Brendan felt his phone vibrate in his shirt pocket and he checked the text. In Anger. All fine. Don't worry. For a moment he didn't understand; was his mother irritated with him for texting her? He held his breath at the thought of his mother, independent and self-propelled, furious with him for encroaching on her holiday time. He replied quickly. Are you angry with me? Maura took up the chorus again, more booms and grunts, thrusting her hips from side to side to the tune. The phone vibrated again. Staying near Angers. Going south. Nice here. Mammy x and he put it quickly in his pocket as Maura emerged, a towel around her torso.

She tottered into Brendan's arms and fell, covering them both with drops of water. She giggled and the towel slipped down a little from her body. Brendan noticed that the skin on her throat was raspberry-coloured from the hours spent on the beach; below was pure cream. She reached around to clasp his neck too tightly and she smelled of undiluted vanilla. He put his arms around her.

'Tell me you love me, Brendan.'

His lips skimmed the damp forehead. 'You know I do.'

The forehead creased. 'I wish you'd tell me more often.'

'But you know how I feel . . .'

'Sometimes . . . you can be so distant.'

'Maura—'

'So secretive—'

'Maura, don't—'

Tears pooled in her eyes and a fat one splashed over, still for a moment then exploding and running down onto her cheek. Brendan kissed it. He wondered if this would be a good time to explain how she made him feel unhappy sometimes, that she could be critical and he could be uncommunicative and withdrawn, but he still thought she was lovely and to ask if there was a way back to how they used to be together.

Maura's face crumpled, then it was covered in tears and she was sniffling. 'Tell me everything is all right.'

'Everything's all right, Maura.' Brendan looked at her mouth, her jaw trembling and slack, and he wanted to hold her even tighter. Something protective and primal surfaced and he glued his lips to her mouth. She pulled away and blinked, took a handkerchief and blew her nose.

'You know you're still a handsome man, Brendan Gallagher. Come here and let me show you how much I still love you, after all these years.'

She reached up and put her hands on his shoulders and the towel fell away completely. Maura grasped for his head and pulled it down towards her lips, hauling him onto the mattress. He heard her exhale and he rolled across her body and he put his arms around her and closed his

96

eyes. She tugged at his shirt buttons and began to nuzzle his ear. Brendan touched her hair lightly and put his lips on hers. He squeezed his eyes closed and whispered something unintelligible into her hair. She was in his arms and it was like old times. The familiar feeling surfaced in Brendan and he murmured her name over and over. He felt powerful; happiness surged in his chest like a bird in flight. They would make their marriage work. This holiday was just what he needed. They rolled over. The phone slipped from his pocket onto the bed and bumped onto the carpet.

He awoke the next morning and the guilt from his dream sat stiffly between his shoulder blades. He had been swimming in indigo seas with Penny Wray. She was a mermaid with a glistening tail and they'd frolicked and tumbled below the surface of foamy waters. She'd flicked back long hair, sending a shimmer of diamonds into the skies. He'd followed her to a rock where she was suddenly naked, her skin the colour of cappuccino. They'd made love and lain stretched in the heat haze until the salt had dried on her body, crystals glittering in the sun.

He awoke with a start and a pang of shame and rolled over. Maura was asleep, her lips apart, an arm flung across one breast, pale against the red line of sunburn on her shoulder. He pulled on the discarded underpants that were crumpled on the floor, and unzipped his laptop case. He perched himself on the edge of the bed and flipped up the screen. There were two emails: one from St Cillian's acknowledging receipt of his job application and one from Penny Wray, wishing him a great holiday and saying she would apply for the head of sport post before taking off to Mexico to go snorkelling.

Maura woke and was sitting up in bed, watching him;

she was smiling, measuring the curve of his spine as he searched the map of France and typed in 'Angers'. He did not know that she was holding her breath, gazing at him with familiar fondness, a feeling of hope making her heart leap. She was thinking about the hotel breakfast and whether there was time to tempt him back into bed.

Brendan screwed up his eyes at the screen, checking the online maps, trying to work out the arced lines of roads and the dots of towns and cities and convert the distances to kilometres. He made a map in his head, considering where they might stop for lunch and when they would arrive in Angers and when they could text his mother that he was nearby. Perhaps that would be a good time to phone her and tell her he was not far away. He was planning the route to make the most of their time and to miss out any toll roads or busy city centres. They would be heading south today and leaving Brittany, the markets, the mussels in white wine and the beaches far behind them. Maura would be disappointed but finding his mother and bringing her back was as necessary to him now as breathing.

Chapter Sixteen

Evie slept deeply in her campervan duvet. She was cocooned, wrapped in cotton, completely safe. The night before, she had drunk too much wine and thoroughly enjoyed herself. She'd found a *gîte* outside Angers where a sign said '*Les camping-cars sont bienvenus: 8 euros*'. The old lady was a tiny sparrow of a woman with a welcoming smile and a face lined with kindness. Odile had white hair and a bowed body and was eighty-seven years old: she'd explained through writing on a piece of paper and crossing it out that if Evie stayed for dinner for twenty euros with free wine, she could park her campervan overnight for free.

They had dined at the big wooden table, Odile at the head, the perfect hostess, filling the table with dish after delicious dish and carafes of wine, red and white. The guests had been wonderful: there was a Spanish man and his German wife, Miguel and Ursula, and their teenage daughter, Kristina, who spoke in Spanish to her father, German to her mother, French to Odile and English to Evie, translating for everyone. There was a Dutch man in his forties, Adriaan, and an English couple, Tom and Fran from Leighton Buzzard. But the food was unlike any she had ever tasted: a soup of creamy Jerusalem artichokes, then whole globe artichokes, dripping with butter, tomatoes seasoned with fresh herbs, tiny potatoes, and meat and sauce that melted on the tongue. Then wafer-like crêpes, cream, apple pie, brandy. Evie had told the guests about her road trip since Dublin; they'd laughed at her story about betting on the racehorse and the evening had been wrapped in a cloud of warmth and geniality.

Odile had stood and sung a traditional song, her small voice high and hearty, and everyone had embraced and wished each other well before Evie had curled up in her campervan among pillows and soft cushions, taken a last look at the star-spattered sky and fallen into a deep sleep.

The next day the sun was warm even before breakfast. She knew exactly where she was going; in a conversation at the dinner table, Fran had suggested she pay a visit to Limoges and stop for a while in Oradour-sur-Glane on her way south, so she had a map marked in Biro and she was soon on her way.

Evie drove through Limousin in the flickering heat with the windows down. It was almost midday when she arrived in Oradour and the sun was searing. She parked the campervan and walked across the grass. When she reached the marble monument of Oradour-sur-Glane, the air became cooler.

The grey plaque outside the village told the martyrs' story: it had happened on the tenth of June, 1944: number four had not been lucky for the poor villagers who were pulled from their houses and murdered, mistaken for the resistance fighters. The village was preserved, a memorial to the past, and she felt like she was stepping back through time.

Evie had been two years old then, living in a terraced house on the outskirts of Dublin. Her mother had always placed bread and jam at the table and she was a child in a scrubbed frock, reaching out for a slice as her brothers Brendan, Eddie and Patrick stuffed morsels in their mouths with one hand, shoving slices under the table with the other. Kathleen was a baby, sickly and crying a lot, occupying her mother's attention, while her father's cough could be heard rasping in his chest from the next room. He had died months later in his bed. Fragile Kathleen turned out to be the strongest of them all. She was in Australia now and Evie seldom heard from her; Eddie and Pat had died within a year of each other, and her brother Brendan lived alone in Sligo.

Her mammy's eyes had held constant anxiety. Evie remembered the sensation of the hard hand placed tenderly over her hair. Those days were distant now; the world was very different.

In the village, the chill was visceral, the touch of a time and its people which had not yet left. Ghosts lingered on corners, their breath stretching from one house to the next. Birds were silent and the wind hummed low. The signs said '*Souviens-toi*'. *Remember*. Buildings leaned and crumbled, broken and jagged, teeth in a gaping dead mouth. Evie walked slowly along the yellowing dirt road where grass no longer grew. Bricks in tumbled lines suggested where borders and houses had been. An ancient car, rust red, its grille twisted in a leer, squatted on its wheel rims. A plaque on a wall stated '*Un Groupe D'Hommes Fut Massacré et Brûlé*'. She stared at the words until their meaning sank deep. She passed an old bakery, nothing left but rubble, and she could imagine the cries of the families pushed apart, separated by the length of a gun barrel; she could imagine how closely they huddled to the nearest warm human, how their eyes squeezed tight at the crack of a rifle, again and again.

101

She crossed to the burned church. It was hollowed and blackened, its bricks and dust scattered. This was where the women and children were brought. Evie was bone cold; the fire-charred arches of the church held the shrieks of the children tightly inside. No God had saved them. She noticed an empty pushchair, twisted and scorched. Someone had put a bunch of simple flowers on the seat. Evie closed her eyes and let the sounds of their shrieks hammer into her ears. When she opened them again, the ghosts were still there; they hung heavy in the air, watching. She walked back through the brittle buildings, clasping herself inside her jacket.

Outside the village, the warm air lifted, bringing her into the sunlight, and she sat down on a bench and reached in her bag for her phone. Brendan had sent her a message. She couldn't reply yet. She was still among the French men and women in Oradour. It was over seventy years ago but it was happening now. She was wearing a skirt made of thick, itchy stuff, and a dark headscarf. Jim's cap was pulled firmly over his ears. She was carrying four-year-old Brendan, his legs dangling to her waist, wrapping and unwrapping around her, his little shoes kicking and digging into her apron. It was night time, dusk had fallen and it was cold. They were lined up outside the town hall and men in uniforms pointed guns. Evie could feel how tightly she hugged Brendan; she could imagine Jim's worried eyes and the young soldiers who spoke in a tongue she did not understand and held guns, the cold metal of their barrels pointing straight at them.

Evie shivered. The barrels waved them apart, Jim to the group of men and Evie and Brendan to the women's huddle. They were ushered up the hill, to the church and inside. Evie imagined Brendan in her arms; his tiny voice asking her what would happen to them. She could hear the shots

102

going off like fire crackers outside the town hall, knowing that the men were being executed, knowing that Jim would be among them. She saw the eyes of one of the uniformed soldiers, his voice high, as he ordered the women into the church. The wooden door slammed; the silent women held a breath, then there was a smell of smoke. Evie shuddered and opened her eyes.

'*Bist du Deutsche?*' A young man was sitting next to her.

'I don't understand what you're saying. I'm Irish.'

'I am from Stuttgart.' His English was perfect.

She thought about what to say. 'This is the first time I have been here.'

'I come here every year. It is important to remember.'

He was a smooth-faced young man, light-haired, green-eyed. Not more than twenty-five. She thought for a moment. 'I'm Evie Gallagher.'

'Didi Klossner.' They shook hands.

'Didi, have you been round the martyr village? Oh, I expect that you have. I am still a bit shaken by all that. It's all very sad.'

He shrugged. 'The past is still here with us.' He looked away and a breeze blew his hair.

Evie sat upright. 'It was a shocking experience. I need a minute to calm myself down. Do you know where I can get a cup of coffee or a brandy? You could come with me. A bit of company might be nice after—'

'Of course, Evie. It is a good idea. I know a café which sells the best cognac.'

They spent an hour outside a small terraced bar, sitting at a table with iron chairs. The sun warmed their faces and Evie removed the green leather jacket and pulled up her sleeves. Didi ordered drinks in perfect French. As the heat beat down on the pavements, she drank brandy, then a coffee, while Didi told her about his life as a student of languages and philosophy in Berlin and Paris, about his French fiancée, Marie-Claire, and about his views on world peace.

Her companion was a good conversationalist and an excellent listener. She told him about Sheldon Lodge and Mrs Lofthouse; about Anaconda Man and the hundred-to-one racehorse and the betting shop, about buying the campervan and the good friends she had made in Brittany. She told him that she believed in the power of good luck, that she had always been lucky, and four was her number. He'd never heard of the saying about the luck of the Irish. She did not want to talk about Brendan or about Jim and the loneliness that created an aching space. Didi nodded, smiled and seemed to understand without her mentioning it all.

They chatted for an hour and she thought he was lovely company. She could have sat chatting for another hour, but it was probably time to move on and, anyway, one brandy was enough. She wished Didi the best with his studies and his future. She shook his hand, suggested that all governments everywhere didn't give a shite for world peace and returned to her campervan, a happy little song suddenly floating in her head and on her lips.

She drove for a few hours until she was in the open countryside and hills began to rise around her, their green hump-backs suddenly claustrophobic. Tiredness crept across her arms and sank deeply into her shoulders. She parked, locked the door and crawled into the back for a sleep, thinking it would be interesting to see the Pyrénées the next day and maybe even drive to a summit and look down. The newly unwrapped sleeping bag she'd bought in Angers was cold inside but she had socks and a thick duvet. She pulled the curtains together and let her head fall onto the pillow, her mouth still warm with brandy, and sank deep in slumber.

The sky cracked open and the world outside trembled. Evie opened her eyes – it was blanket dark and a storm was blustering. The windows of the little campervan shook in their frames; the curtains shivered. Outside, a reverberating explosion caused Evie to roll up tightly in her duvet. The countryside lit up brightly and as quickly returned to darkness. She thought it was bombs or gunfire from Oradour but the sequence of rumbling thunder and flashing light caused her to breathe out again. Rain rattled on the roof and drizzled down the windows. She reached for her phone and saw Brendan's text again, anxiety in his words. Tenderness for her son flooded through her and she replied, wishing she could send her love to him through the ether.

Chapter Seventeen

She travelled south all the next day through heat that rose in a vapour from the roads in front of her. Finding the right direction out of Bergerac was difficult; she had made a few wrong turnings and been on the receiving end of several blaring horns. Her natural reaction was to gesticulate rudely but she thought the better of it and chose the more sedate wave and a benevolent smile, calling out, 'Have a nice day.'

The air cooled as she drove into a busy town in the foothills of the Pyrénées. There was bunting everywhere, little triangles of bright colour announcing that the town of Marmande, famous for its tomatoes, was *en fête*. As she locked the campervan, she could smell the succulence of meat roasting and hear the sound of pop music played through fizzing speakers. She followed a few people who were making their way to the centre of the town where a market was bustling. A whole pig was roasting on a spit, its mouth gaping in a wide smile through its skewer as it sweated and somersaulted over the coals.

Other foods were being prepared: couscous, onion bhajis and rice, delicious cakes and cheese, the smells warm and intensifying in the air as she passed. The market was a splash of colour and a temptation of textures for Evie's fingers to touch and try: jewellery, fabrics, and pottery. An African man greeted her in English and German, calling on her to buy belts, handbags, clothes, which hung in flashes of vibrant patterns. She bought a bowl of spicy couscous and some red wine in a plastic cup and found a wooden bench near to a stage where some men were connecting wires and testing the volume of their voices through whining microphones. She stretched out her feet and dug her fork into the grains. The first mouthful was an explosion of warm spice. She decided to look at the cakes and the cheese when she had finished her meal. The light faded to dark blues and greys, and little twinkling colours illuminated the stalls. Evie became aware of someone looking down at her.

'Hello. Are all these seats taken?'

The speaker shouted staccato words at her like Morse code. A middle-aged woman in a powder blue jacket and trousers was flanked by a hesitant gentleman in a light grey suit. He was gaunt and a little bent over towards the woman, and his hair was thinning. The woman's suit fitted her tightly and the bottom of her jacket stuck out like a sail as she bent forward to point.

'Can we sit here?' boomed the woman. Evie moved over a little and waved at the space next to her.

'Thank you.' The woman gestured her approval and the man extended her a courteous nod and sat down. The woman heaved a handbag onto her knee. It was blue leather, matching the shade of the linen trouser suit, which wrinkled and folded with her body as she squeezed into the space between them.

'We are English,' she announced. Evie extended her hand towards her.

The woman continued, as loudly as before. 'We are from Winchester, that's in Hampshire, although I was born near London. I adore London, especially the galleries. My husband is from Chepstow originally, that is near Wales, but he's not Welsh. I am Margaret Knowles; all my friends call me Peggy. This is Geoffrey. You can call him Geoff.'

Evie smiled and was about to speak but Peggy beat her to it.

'Are you French? You don't look French. Dutch, maybe. There are lots of Dutch people around here. I think you must be Dutch, with your colouring.'

'No, I'm not Dutch, I'm—'

'Scottish!' Peggy clapped her hands. 'Oh, how charming. A fellow Brit. Lovely to meet you. I didn't catch your name.'

Evie gave Peggy her most winning smile. She couldn't think of a Scottish name quickly enough but she had another ready.

'I am Eartha. Eartha Windass.' She smothered a guffaw by compressing her lips. 'Pleased to meet you, Peggy, Geoff.'

'Oh how nice. Geoff, do go and get, er – Eartha, was it?' Evie nodded. 'Do go and get us all a bottle of wine. A nice Chablis I think, please.'

Geoff scuttled away into the crowds and Peggy beamed at Evie. Her lipstick was perfectly red, turning down with the corners of her mouth above a soft cushion of chins. Evie ran a hand through her blonde hair and thought about Scotland. She'd had a crush on Sean Connery once; it was 1962 in *Dr No*. He was very dashing, Sean Connery, and he was a Scot.

'We're having a little holiday. It's our wedding anniversary next month. Thirty-five years. Geoff is a solicitor. He's just finished work on a big divorce case and he needs a break. I don't work of course, although I do like to keep myself busy. I am very good at flower arranging, you know. I have a garden full of the loveliest flowers and people always come to me for their bouquets and wedding arrangements. Roses are my favourites, and lilies. I am always telling Geoff I should have gone into business.'

'That's grand.'

'Oh, what a lovely word, grand. How Scottish. It's so nice to meet you, Eartha. And what is it you do? I don't suppose you work now, do you?'

Evie's mind was searching for a good story to tell. Her mouth was only seconds behind. 'I am an actress,' she confided. 'Well, we say actor for both men and women now, don't we? I'm very up to date with all the PC. I am here in France making a film just at the minute.'

'Oh I love how you say film, *fill*-um, and such a nice accent. Ah Geoff . . .' The thin man in the suit had returned: he bent long legs and flourished a bottle of wine. There were cool drops of moisture on the neck and label. Geoff poured generously into three glasses.

'Eartha was saying she's in films. How really super.' Peggy took the glass and began to drink in small sips. She stopped between each small mouthful deliberately, as if holding a thought.

Geoff looked anxiously at his wife. 'Do you like the Chablis?'

'Oh yes – it is obviously a good vintage. I can smell peonies and citrus.' She drank again, stopping to reconsider. 'Lemon, I think, maybe a hint of grapefruit.'

Evie looked away and back at Peggy again and thought she was talking complete shite.

Geoff swallowed a mouthful, and looked hopefully at Peggy. 'Apricot notes, perhaps? Geranium? Lychee, yes, I can taste lychee, too?'

Peggy beamed at Evie again. 'What do you think, Eartha?'

She sniffed at the glass. 'Lovely smell of grapes mixed with something close to cat piss. Packs a good solid punch. We Scots like that.'

Peggy turned her attention to her lapels, smoothing them down. 'Eartha is an actor, Geoff. She is here doing a film.'

Geoff gave her a tentative smile and rubbed his chin, as if considering a menu of choices. 'And what sort of film is it that you are making, Eartha?'

'You'd make a good Miss Marple, I think.' Peggy rested her jaw on the soft flesh below. She frowned. 'She wasn't Scottish though, was she? No. So, is it a period saga? Costume drama? Maybe the one about the Scottish policeman? What's he called? Hamish something?'

An idea leapt into Evie's head. She gave her most winning smile. 'Pornography.'

Geoff swallowed breath and Peggy held her glass in the air for a second too long before taking a quick mouthful. 'Oh dear.'

'Oh, it's very tasteful pornography.' Evie waved her wine glass in the air. 'I am the starring role. I play Lady Whiplash. I have a brothel full of girls, all ages and sizes, from all countries, even Scotland, and we beat the men for pleasure.' She lifted her glass again, as if showing how she could beat them with a gesture of her little finger.

Peggy was horrified. 'That's awful!'

'Not at all.' Evie was in full swing; wine was sloshing in her glass. 'It's a great story line. I am a bit of a nympho-maniac and I control my bordello with an iron fist. Then one of the girls becomes romantically involved with a rich man – I think he is a judge or a lawyer, maybe a solicitor, yes, definitely a solicitor – but he's found strangled naked in his bed by his braces and the police enlist my help to find the killer.'

Geoff swallowed more wine and refilled his glass quickly.

'Oh, so it is a little like Miss Marple?' Peggy looked hopeful.

'Sort of.' Evie patted her on the knee as if to reassure her that all was quite above board. 'A kind of modern Miss Marple – with porn.'

'Well,' Peggy began, but her words were drowned in the thrum of a bass guitar tuning up. A drummer banged his sticks hard on every surface, twice, and then faster, in a roll. A guitar twanged and a little riff lifted on the night air.

'Rock music.' Evie was delighted. 'That is grand. I love a bit of punk rock. I hope they do the one about never minding the bollocks.'

Peggy wriggled in her seat. Geoff drank the last dregs from his wine glass, but the bottle in his other hand was a quarter full. The band launched into a frenzy of screaming and leaping, the lead singer cavorting in front of them in leather and ripped denim. Peggy stood up.

'This isn't quite the guitar recital I was hoping for,' she yelled. 'I am afraid I will say good night to you, Eartha. It was so lovely to meet you.' Peggy extended her hand and Evie took it briefly before the woman in the blue suit turned away. She heard her say: 'Perhaps we will bump into you again.'

Geoff took her hand. 'A pleasure to make your acquaintance, Eartha.'

Evie thought she saw him wink at her. He followed his wife; she was a shifting blue shape in front of him as she pushed through the crowds.

'And don't forget to catch my *fill*-um when it's out.' But her words were lost in the yelps of the vocalist who was hurling himself across the stage, his voice a frenzy of gravel and French expletives.

111

Evie drank her wine. She closed her eyes and the lids throbbed in time to the pounding rhythm. Once she would have stayed for the whole party, dancing, allowing the beat to bounce her on her feet for hours. She and Jim had seen some bands in Dublin: The Kinks, or was it Herman's Hermits, and The Bachelors. She'd danced in her mini-skirt, her hair piled high, twirling until her stilettoed feet were sore. But she was tired now; and it felt different: the weariness clung to her bones and settled into an ache in her joints and behind her knees. She swallowed the last mouthful of wine, feeling its bitterness turn to a delicious tingle on her tongue.

'Scottish, indeed. Peggy and Geoff and their complete bollocks.' She pulled her jacket collar up and the darkness enveloped her as she left the group on stage rocking and reverberating, her eyes roving through the dim light for her little campervan.

Chapter Eighteen

While Evie had been exploring the village of Oradour, Brendan and Maura had set off for Angers in search of her. They had not spoken for some time. The sun poured through the windscreen, which intensified the heat like a magnifying glass. Maura stared of the window and he concentrated on driving the car, his brows knit in a taut frown. Every so often, she sighed, folded her arms across her chest or twisted her neck to look at the passing signs on the motorway. One of them read 'Angers, 60 kilometres'. Brendan worried about what sort of accommodation they might find in Angers, whether it would provide anything interesting for Maura. She'd been unhappy to leave Brittany, dumping her case in the back of the Panda with a thud and making sure that the slam of the car door echoed her displeasure.

Brendan waited for her to break the silence. It was two o'clock and they had not eaten. Maura sighed again, more loudly. Brendan took a chance.

'It's very hot. I think there might be a storm later. I hope Mammy will be all right.' She wiped her forehead with her hand and breathed out. 'How are you feeling, my love? Are you hungry?'

Almost immediately, he wished he hadn't spoken.

'No Brendan, I'm certainly not hungry.'

'Are you not feeling so well?'

Maura clenched her jaw. 'I hate every minute of this journey. It was supposed to be a holiday. I was having such a lovely time in Brittany. I thought you were too. I mean, we could've stayed a few more days.' She pouted, made a baby-doll face and then sighed.

Brendan concentrated on the road ahead, at the vapour rising from the tarmac, at the heavy lorry which swished past. Another lorry shuddered next to him and took its place in front. It was hot in the Panda so Brendan opened his window. Maura sighed again. He thought perhaps he'd phone Evie when they stopped for a toilet break, or at least text her; and check if she had sent him a message.

'It is only sixty kilometres to Angers,' he said. His voice sounded futile. He tried again. 'I'm sorry. You know how important it is to find Mammy. We'll have a nice time in Angers. How about I get us a lovely lunch first?' He glanced across at Maura. She tucked in her chin and her cheeks were red. Brendan wondered how he could cheer her up.

He was feeling troubled. He knew now that his idea to follow Evie and to be the knight in armour who would bring her home to safety had been unrealistic. His father would have expected it of him. But his mother's security contradicted Maura's need for a romantic holiday. It was his entire fault and now she was angry. A sigh shuddered from deep inside him. She was right, certainly: they needed a break together, space to remember the good times, opportunity to enjoy more good times together. He thought about his father again, how he had smiled, years ago when they returned from Corfu as if they were a honeymoon couple, and how he'd glowed then, feeling bashful and proud. That holiday had been a great success. Brendan had the uncomfortable feeling that this time he had made a huge mistake.

Cars and lorries swung in from behind, to the left and then back in front of them. Brendan wiped sweat from his eyes and blinked. Steam or something vaporous was curling from the bonnet. He blinked again to make sure. Plumes of steam rose in the air. Maura sat upright.

'Brendan, will you pull over. Something's wrong with the car.'

Brendan looked around him wildly. Her voice became louder. 'For God's sake, stop. There's steam pouring out of the front.'

The fog in front of them was so thick they could hardly see. Brendan swung onto a slip road, drove across a mini-roundabout and into a lay-by. Maura was out of the car before he could pull on the handbrake.

She shrieked at him, 'We're on fire. Oh my God, we'll blow up.'

Brendan picked up her handbag, slid out and slammed the door. He calmly held out the bag which she snatched from him. He shrugged. 'Maybe it's the radiator, love. We will wait until it cools down and just add a bit of water. It will be fine.'

Maura was breathing heavily. 'Can't you call a mechanic out?'

'I'm sure it'll be all right. Perhaps the water levels are a little low.'

'Didn't you check before we left?'

Brendan scraped the toe of his shoe in the gravel. 'I've some bottled water. It will be fine.' He put a hand on her shoulder. She pulled away, and went to stand at a distance from the car and from him.

'Bloody car,' she muttered. 'It's been on its last legs for months. I told you we should have invested in . . .'

Brendan walked down the lay-by until he was a few yards from her. He sat down on a grassy patch and put his head in his hands. Cars rushed by. Maura rummaged in her bag for a tissue. An overwhelming feeling of futility squeezed at his throat and he swallowed.

The radiator was bubbling. Brendan wrapped a handkerchief around his hand to turn the cap. He yelped as it still burned through the cotton to the soft part of his thumb. Steam hissed and he heard a similar sound from Maura who was behind him, watching. He poured mineral water into the radiator from a bottle, replaced the hot cap and stood back, his hands on his hips. He noticed there was oil on his shirt and his hands. He wiped the handkerchief against his shirt and the oil smudged in a wide rasp. Maura snorted. He put the handkerchief in his pocket and looked at the sky. It was cloudless, blue, holiday perfect. Maura moved away, her high heels wobbling below tight leggings and a sleeveless top. Brendan rolled up his sleeves further, wondering if there was a T-shirt packed somewhere in the back of the car within reach. He decided against it; she would make a comment – she had told him this morning that he would be too hot in the shirt. He opened the car door on her side.

'In you get, my love. It will all be grand now. Right as ninepence.'

Maura slithered into the seat and Brendan closed the door, hunkering down in the driver's seat, and starting the engine. The engine roared and he pulled away; soon, he was negotiating the mini-roundabout and was back into the line of traffic on the motorway. Maura exhaled and twisted her body away from him to look through the window. He stared at the road ahead. She sniffed and looked around the car nervously. 'Brendan, will you promise me the car's all right now? I think I can smell something funny.'

He shook his head. 'All will be fine now, Maura. I have it sorted.'

Angers was thirty kilometres away. Brendan thought about finding a hotel, texting his mother. He'd check the car in at a garage just to be sure, find a nice restaurant and relax. Maura would be calmer and her good mood would soon come back. Perhaps they'd cheer up over a pleasant meal. He could suggest that, once they were back in Dublin, there'd be the possibility of finding a late booking in August for the two of them. Corfu, perhaps? Maura would be happy then and Brendan imagined them resuming their happiness of the previous night: good food and wine, lots of laughter from Maura and the shared nights of passion. He began to whistle. Brendan imagined that he would even find his mother, that she'd be pleased to see him, tell him how glad she was she had such a good son who knew what was best. She'd laugh and say she'd no idea what made her take off to France at all.

Steam began to rise from the bonnet; it became stronger until it reminded Brendan of an Icelandic geyser. A laugh seemed inappropriate but it broke through his lips like muffled hysteria.

'Stop the car, Brendan.' Maura's voice was low and thick, like a demon in a film. There was a lay-by to the right and he pulled in and stopped the car with a wrench of the handbrake. Maura was out, slamming the door. She walked away, perched on a stone, and rummaged in her bag, finding a bar of chocolate. She bit into the bar with venom and Brendan reached for his phone.

Four hours later, a van arrived with a trailer. A young

man in his twenties introduced himself as Olivier, shook Brendan's hand and glanced furtively at Maura. She was looking at her watch; it was twenty past seven. Brendan used his best French to explain to Olivier that the water was hot in the car. Olivier looked in the bonnet, swore in French and said something, indicating the trailer. Brendan looked puzzled, so Olivier tried again and Brendan understood: they would take the car to his garage twenty kilometres away and spend the night in the town, where there was a host who would give them bed and breakfast. The next day Olivier would try to mend the car for them. Brendan and Olivier loaded the Panda onto the trailer, and then they squeezed in the cab next to Olivier. The engine shook and rattled violently. Olivier was chattering as they joined the motorway traffic.

Olivier told them cheerfully that the village they would stay in was called Épinard, which Brendan thought meant spinach. They would be able to find temporary accommodation with a woman called Clémence and she was a very good cook. Brendan smiled and moved his head up and down to show that he understood while Maura stared at the passing cars. Olivier said that it was a good thing they had broken down in the Loire region, as they would have time to taste the local wine, which was exceptional, and the delicious produce of the area. Brendan thought that was what he had said and repeated it to Maura.

'Olivier said we could try some of the local wine; the Loire is famous for good wine.'

Maura was livid. 'I can guess what he said.' She turned to look out of the window. 'Some holiday this is turning out to be.' Olivier told Brendan she would be better after a good meal and Clémence's *chambres* were very *confortable.*

It was past ten as they drove into Cantenay-Épinard,

past the river and the town hall, and there were a few lights on in people's homes. Brendan was surprised at how dark it was: absolute darkness, a tight blanket of blackness and no suggestion of the hazy light pollution he was used to at home. Olivier dropped them at a metal gate where a woman was waiting for them; he helped them to unload their suitcases, gave Brendan his business card, asked him to call the next day and drove off with the Fiat Panda rattling on the trailer.

Chapter Nineteen

Clémence was a strong-looking woman in her fifties or sixties, her dark hair short, and wearing a jumper and jeans. The bed and breakfast was situated on some type of small-holding with chickens and goats. Brendan thought it would be a perfect spot to take children for a holiday. The great outdoors, countryside and scenery to explore, cycling, camping. Clémence ushered them inside the house where there was a table set for two. A carafe of wine was laid out on a large farmhouse table, together with crusty bread and a steaming basin of stew. Brendan mumbled, '*Merci*', and sat down, resting his head in his hands. Clémence left them to eat and drink, which they did in silence. Brendan asked Maura twice if she would like more to eat and drink, and she held out her glass and plate without speaking. Clémence brought them a slice of something sweet, a pie made from eggs and fruit, possibly cherries, which tasted comforting. By the time she had put two cups of black coffee in front of them, Brendan's eyes were starting to close.

Their room was at the top of the house. Brendan carried both cases, and Maura followed, shoes in hand. The room was dark, with floral wallpaper and a huge wooden wardrobe with carvings of a traditional peasant man and woman farming the land. The man held a scythe and the woman wore an apron. The floorboards were wooden and creaked beneath their feet and the wind buffeted the rafters, but Brendan could only see the bed with the brass headwork and the embroidered coverlet. They brushed their teeth over a small basin and Brendan changed into his pyjamas. Maura had already slipped beneath the covers and was facing away from him. Her body felt warm and he snuggled close to her, but she jerked away as if she was shocked. He put a tentative hand on her shoulder, which felt cold.

'We'll make the most of this place tomorrow, shall we, Maura? We could have breakfast and go and taste some wine and look at the river while Olivier is fixing the car. What do you think?'

Maura said nothing for a while. Brendan patted her on the shoulder. 'Maura, I know things haven't gone right today. I'm sorry about the car.'

She sighed, keeping her back to him. 'It was all going so well.'

He tried again. 'I know. We'll have a good time though. Wait and see.'

A sigh. 'I hope so, Brendan. I liked Brittany so much . . .'

He stretched out a hand, touching her shoulders, massaging away the tension as he remembered Penny Wray doing to his muscles in the staff room at school. He pressed firmly, with newly acquired skill.

'Ow. You're hurting.'

He was silent for a moment. 'Sorry, Maura.'

'What are you sorry for, Brendan? The car, or ruining the holiday? We were happy last night, weren't we?'

He rolled onto his back, stared into the darkness, thinking for a while. Then his voice came out as a croak, 'Maybe if we'd had children.'

121

There was a long pause and he thought he heard her snuffle. Then her voice came, a whisper. 'It's too late for all of that now.'

He moved his eyes, straining to see something in the blackness which surrounded him, something which might help him figure the problem out. 'We could start again though; try to get on a bit better together, when we get back.'

'It's always later with you, Brendan. Never now. You're not spontaneous.'

He made a sound through his lips. 'You're spontaneous enough for us both.'

'Yes, but sometimes, it'd be a nice thing for you to take the initiative.'

He knitted his brow and stared into the darkness. 'Initiative?'

She huffed, briefly. Then an idea came to him. He rolled back to her, curved his hand into a palm and smoothed it across her hips, held the roundness of a buttock for a moment, then slid his hand to caress the other.

'Maura, we could book a holiday in Corfu? A second honeymoon? What do you think? We could book it when we get back. Spontaneously.'

He tried again, massaging one buttock, then another, and he nuzzled his face into the soft hair at the back of her neck and whispered, 'My love.'

Then the demon voice came again from the darkness: 'Go to hell, Brendan.'

He turned away from her and, as his eyes closed on the day, a small thought wormed its way into his mind. He didn't understand Maura at all. After all these years, he didn't know what made her happy. He doubted that he could do it any more. Those times had gone and he wasn't sure he'd ever get them back.

*

Maura tore a croissant in half and pushed the soft bread into her mouth. She nodded at Clémence as she poured from the coffee jug and Brendan muttered his thanks as his cup was filled up. Clémence smiled and brought in a carafe filled with orange juice. Brendan thanked her again in French and tried to explain that he and his wife might need to stay one more night depending on whether the car could be repaired in time. Clémence nodded, told them she had many English visitors and could speak the language quite well, then she moved back into the kitchen. Maura stuffed the other half of her croissant into her mouth and washed it down with coffee. She pulled a face and added two lumps of sugar. She stared directly at Brendan.

'Well, I hope for your sake the car can be mended today. This holiday has turned into a nightmare.'

Brendan took a breath. 'If you think back, Maura, it was never meant to be a holiday. We came here to get my mother.'

She made a mocking face and put on with it a mocking voice. 'Always your bloody mother.'

'That is not very nice, is it?'

'Oh come on, Brendan, she's never liked me. Not since the day you first took me home.'

'That's not true.'

'It is. The first time I met her she gave me cold tea and then ignored me and spoke just to you. If it hadn't been for your father, no-one would've spoken a word to me all through the dinner, you and your mammy with your heads together all the time. She only tolerated me because she wanted grandchildren. She never has anything to say to me; talks to you as if I'm not there. She's always given me the brush-off.'

'She likes you.'

'Oh, *you* couldn't see it. She can't do anything wrong,

123

your precious mother. And you'd never defend me, Brendan.' Another croissant was ripped in half.

'That's not fair.'

'But you aren't interested in what I think, are you?' Maura shoved the last piece of croissant into her mouth. He could hear the muffled words. 'I hope the bloody woman is dead.'

Brendan stood up and pointed his finger. 'That's enough, now.'

Maura stared at him. 'Well, of course I don't mean that, for sure. I'm sorry for what I said. But I've reason enough to be angry with her.'

'What reason would that be?'

'I've a list as long as your arm. Remember all those years we were trying for a little one, how upset I'd get each month I found out I wasn't pregnant? And she'd be totally insensitive. She'd never ask me how I was feeling. Oh no, it'd be all about her and the miscarriages she had, all the babbies who would've been girls with silly names and how she kept trying and trying till eventually she had you. Well, bully for her.'

'It upset me too. I wanted a baby just as much as you.'

'And she thought we were totally unsuitable for each other.'

'She did not.' He stared into his coffee.

Maura clenched a fist. 'She told me so many times how proud she was you were a sports teacher, and how you loved the cycling and swimming and football. When I told her I wasn't the sporty type, she suggested I buy a bike and try harder. As if I had to change who I was for you. And you know how I hate exercise. I'd rather do anything in the world than climb up on a bicycle.'

'Well, maybe Mammy had a point. It would be good to share things.' He was thinking of Penny Wray, her golden ponytail, her white shorts. 'Maybe we'd be more compatible if we shared a hobby.'

Maura was looking up at him, and the anger in her eyes became wide panic. 'Brendan, why can't you understand—?'

'I don't know, Maura. I've no idea what to say any more. We'll try and get along as best as we can and then we'll collect Mammy and take her back to Dublin.' He sighed, without looking at her.

Maura made her eyes narrow. They resembled mini-missiles, glittering: perhaps she would shoot him dead if she could. He stared harder. She looked away. Brendan took another gulp of coffee and swallowed audibly. Clémence was at Maura's elbow, holding out more croissants. Maura took one and shredded it into pieces.

They walked past the river and through the town, where the roads narrowed and the houses were three storeys tall, in white and brown stone. The card in Brendan's hand gave the address of the garage and Clémence had explained to him how to get there. Maura dawdled just behind him and he knew she was tired; her heels clacked on the pavement and occasionally she would stop and slide a finger into the sling-back fastening, slowing him down. He resolved that today would be different: everything would go well. He'd pick up the car, drive it away; they'd stop somewhere special for lunch. Maura would smile, the skin around her eyes crinkling and happy. He'd make her laugh and they'd hold hands across the table. She'd tell him she was sorry for being angry and he'd promise to be more communicative and affectionate and they'd find a hotel, make love and fall asleep in each other's arms. In the garage, Brendan saw the Panda straight away. There was no-one around, so he walked through the lines of vehicles and into the office, leaving Maura slouching, sullen, leaning on the car.

There was no-one in the office; papers were strewn on the table and on the wall there was a calendar with pictures of the town, Cantenay-Épinard, showing, for this month, a colour photo of the river and surrounding greenery. A clock shaped like a wine bottle ticked on the wall. It had a slogan which read 'Pays de la Loire'. The time was ten forty. Brendan walked out of the office hoping someone would be outside working but there was no-one.

He went back to Maura, who had opened the Panda's door and was sitting down with one shoe off, rubbing her heel. She looked up at Brendan. 'Well?'

'There's no-one here.'

'OK, that settles it. Let's get in the car and drive off.'

'Maura, we—'

'The keys are in it. If no-one can be bothered to turn up to ask us to pay then that is their fault.'

'But—'

'There are no buts about it, Brendan. I am not staying here any longer.'

A cheery voice called, '*Bonjour*', and Olivier appeared around the corner, wearing extremely clean-looking red overalls. He shook Brendan's hand and started to talk about the car. Brendan asked him to slow down please and to repeat. Olivier put his hands out and showed the size of the problem. It was a big one. The radiator was finished, terminated, kaput. He could fit a new one but the car was a Fiat and they did not have one in stock. Someone in Angers could bring one out tomorrow or, at worst, in two or three days' time. Maura seemed to have understood because her arms were folded tightly across her chest and her face was thunderous. Olivier was sorry, but Clémence had a lovely kitchen, he knew this because she was his aunt and why did they not enjoy a little holiday while he fixed the car for them with a brand new radiator which would be very reliable? Brendan thanked him and said yes, a new one would be a good idea and they would be happy to wait. He turned to see Maura walking out of the garage, standing by the edge of the road, looking uncomfortable in her heels. Brendan thanked Olivier, who leaned forward and tried out his English, indicating Maura with a flick of his head and using a low tone. 'The women. They kill us every day, *hein*?'

Brendan agreed and he glanced at Maura first to see if she was listening. Then he went over to join her by the side of the road.

'How many days did he say it would take?'

Brendan waved his hands as Olivier had done to show the extent of the problem. 'Tomorrow. Maybe the next day. Never mind. We can spend time here. We could even take a bus into Angers—'

Maura heaved herself to full height, wincing in the heels. 'I am not taking a bus. Anywhere.'

She walked away to the other side of the road. There was an *immobilier,* a local estate agent, with photos of houses for sale, and she was gazing at the window. Brendan pulled out his phone and turned away. He found his mother's number and typed in a message: Where are you staying in Angers, Mammy?

Maura did not move except to shift her weight from one foot to the other, her shoulders slumped, her face unhappy.

Brendan's phone vibrated in his pocket and he pulled it out, pressed the button and read his mother's reply: Very stormy weather yesterday. Gone south to the sun. Brendan heaved a deep sigh before he could stop it and wondered what to do.

Chapter Twenty

Evie was feeling very pleased with herself. She'd left the campervan in a little car park just a short walk away and found a lovely restaurant, Le Petit Ours. The sign showed a picture of a small bear smiling and dancing, and Evie repeated the French words softly to herself. She watched a middle-aged couple eating seafood at the table opposite and she was intrigued by what they were doing, as they lifted the shell-shaped cups to their mouths and seemed to sip the contents, one by one, before placing the shells in a bowl.

The waiter was a friendly young man in his late teens, his hair swept back from his forehead by an elastic head-band, and he asked her what she would like. She pointed in the wine list to a bottle of Chablis and said: '*Un, s'il vous plaît, Monsieur.*' He returned with a bottle, not a glass, but she did not mind as the wine was cool and went down so easily. He brought her crusty bread and asked what she would like to eat and she pointed at the couple sipping at their shells at the opposite table and smiled at him and said: '*Un, s'il vous plaît, Monsieur,*' and he came back with a metal bowl full of *moules marinières*.

She began tentatively, tipping the juice into her mouth,

tasting the flavours of garlic and wine and herbs, then eating the little bit of flesh. She wondered what Jim would have made of it all. Jim liked his food plain with plenty of potatoes and gravy; for him a treat was a pastry filled with cream or a sweet biscuit with chocolate. No, Jim wouldn't have understood this *moules* lark at all; he would have shaken his head and grinned shyly and asked if they had chips and bread and butter instead.

Evie ate her bread and *moules* and garlic and topped up her own wine glass, her green leather jacket on the seat next to her, covering her handbag. She was a woman of independent means, a traveller, a character who knew her own mind, like Simone de Beauvoir, whose book she had just finished reading. Simone had some strong views on a woman's place and what to expect from the world; she believed that women should demand more of life and of themselves. Evie agreed. Simone was her new favourite role model. Evie had started a new book today; it mystified her, but she guessed that these French writers were very different to the authors of the simple romance books in Sheldon Lodge about troubled girls who needed rescuing. Certainly this English translation of a book by Albert Camus, about an odd man who didn't mind when his mother died and went swimming with a new girlfriend instead of mourning, shocked her a little. But she was enjoying reading it and something exciting was bound to happen soon. Evie admired the French, the way they slowed down the pace: their books, their food, their way of life. And anyway, she had not understood *Dubliners* when she read that at school, but perhaps she might come back to Joyce later. After all, wasn't he an Irish treasure?

She ate the last of the *moules* and finished off the bottle of wine. She wondered whether to ask for another bottle. She'd always liked wine, a glass here and there with a meal, but somehow the French wine was so much nicer than the stuff she'd bought in the supermarket in Dublin. Perhaps it was because she was in France, on holiday, now an independent thinking woman like Simone de Beauvoir. She waved an arm, and the waiter was beside her, offering a dessert. Evie had never tried tiramisu before, so she ordered one with no idea what it was. The waiter praised her choice, cleared the table and was gone.

The couple opposite had finished their food and were talking. They were holding hands across the table and the woman threw her head back and laughed. The man lifted her hands to his lips, never taking his eyes from her. Evie brushed back her hair with her fingers and wondered if she missed the company of a man, if she would like a romance in her life. The tiramisu arrived and she decided she didn't, as she dipped the spoon deep into chocolate and closed her eyes to better taste the coffee and whipped cream. She finished the dessert in moments and then she ordered a cognac. She'd had plenty of cognac before, but never as smooth and unctuous as this one.

She waved at the waiter and giggled as he moved to her side. '*Un* more, *s'il vous plaît, Monsieur.*' He frowned for a moment and then whisked away, whirling back with another.

Evie leaned on her elbow and swayed a little. The couple opposite were kissing across the empty plates and she turned to them and laughed. 'You're never too old for a little bit of romance, now, are you?' They stared at her and the woman looked offended.

Evie drank the last of her cognac, slurping the remains from the bottom of her glass. She poked a finger in the last of the tiramisu and pushed a smear of cream into her mouth. The waiter was by her side. She blinked up at him, pointed at the empty glass and said, '*Un* more?'

The waiter pretended not to understand and handed her

a piece of paper in a little dish. It was a bill, written in strange scrawl, the numbers leaping across the page. She dug deep into her bag, found her purse and attempted to count thirty euros. The notes stuck together in her fingers, so she flung a handful onto the dish and eased herself up, pushing the table back as she moved. Her legs felt soft beneath her. She thought of the slithery *moules* in their garlicky sauce.

'I'm sauced too,' she giggled and moved away.

She struggled into the green leather jacket. The young waiter was by her side. His forehead was furrowed, eyebrows up near his headband. 'Madame?' He steadied her elbow. 'You give me – too many.' He pushed several notes into her hand and they fell to the floor, He stooped down and picked up the money, wrapping it in her fist, curling her fingers around carefully. With a studied insistence, she unfolded a single note and gave it to him with a flourish.

'For you, Monsieur.'

He stared. '*Vingt euros?*'

'It's a tip. You've been lovely. I'd love to have had a grandson, just like you.'

She sailed past the canoodling couple and found the door. 'If that's what eating the saucy *moules* does for you, I'm having them again,' she told them, her face earnest.

The cold night air hit her in a blast and, for a moment, she couldn't remember whether to turn right or left. She wrapped her arms around the handbag and began to snigger. 'If there are any muggers in France, I'll bash them with the bag, so I will.'

She turned herself towards the car park, a deliberate repositioning, and set off at a pace as if she'd been pushed, leaning forward and taking little steps. She stared up at the stars which swirled like milk stirred in coffee above her head and she staggered.

'I haven't been this pissed since that Christmas, years

ago, when we went to Brendan's for lunch and drank gin and tonic. Maura cooked us that dry chicken. Or was it a duck? Goose! Of course it was a goose.' She spluttered. 'You had to heave me home that night, Jim. Where are you now, now a lady needs an arm to lean on?' She lurched forward, her steps meandering. 'Who knows where you are now, Jim? I don't have a clue. You could be anywhere. Or nowhere at all. Who knows? Not me, that's for sure. But I know where I'm going.' She stopped by the little campervan and fumbled in her bag. Her fingers touched metal and she flourished the keys, tried to ease them towards the lock, missing the key hole. 'I'm going to bed, for sure, if I can ever get this fecking door open.'

She awoke as the skies were spattered with pink, rolling over in her sleeping bag and curling her legs to her chest. Her stomach was twisting, her head was throbbing and her throat thickened with the threat of nausea. She tried to make her mind control the rising sensation in her stomach. Her body rebelled; her face and hair were drenched in sweat, and dizziness pulled at her eyes. She was still for a moment, breathing deeply, then she slipped out of the sleeping bag and tugged at the door.

The car park was quiet and the cold air slapped her face. She swayed a little. Then her stomach could contain its burden no longer; there was a heaving from her belly which she couldn't control and a violent upsurge, followed by another. Evie leaned out of the doorway, watching the vomit hit the gravel, wiping the spittle which swung like elastic from her mouth. She sat back and, although no-one could see her, she felt embarrassed. She waited a moment, willing the nausea to calm. Her body heaved with another wave, and her mouth was suddenly full. Her stomach had a muscle of its own, and she leaned out of the doorway

132

and was sick again. She could taste the soured warmth of *moules* and wine. Her head was knocking, and she slumped back on the sleeping bag. For a moment, she lay still, wondering what to do, not able to think of a solution. Then her fingers found a bottle of mineral water. She unscrewed the cap, took a swig and spat onto the heap of vomit, rinsing her mouth. There was half a litre left and she poured it all outside the van onto the gravel, hoping her embarrassment and nausea would disperse with the dissipated contents of her stomach.

She was weak and dizzy, so she slumped back onto the sleeping bag and closed her eyes. When she awoke, it was hot inside the van under the powerful glaze of the closed windows. Her hands were ice-cold and she covered herself with the duvet. Evie rolled over and wondered if she would be sick again. Her mouth was dry and her bones ached. Sleep enfolded her again and when she opened her eyes she could not remember where she was. She looked at familiar things – her jacket, her clothes, her books – but she felt confused. She sat up and wiggled the door handle; she had left it unlocked. Her bag was still safe: her money, passport, cards and phone were still there. The time on the phone was ten past four. It took a while for her to understand that it was afternoon. She needed water; she remembered that she had tipped the last of her bottle away, so she would need to buy more. The keys were in the bottom of her bag, but she didn't think she could drive. Evie decided it could not be far to a supermarket or a baker's. She'd buy water and maybe some fruit, although she did not want to eat a thing.

Evie struggled out of her clothes, changing damp pyjamas for T-shirt and jeans. Her skin was a grey colour, her arms cold and mounded with goose pimples, so she tugged on the green jacket and some shoes and wriggled out of the van, hugging her bag to her against the puff of fresh air. She locked up, and stepped over the pile of vomit which had set like jelly in a cluster at the edge of the campervan. Each movement, each decision was difficult. She pulled on her sunglasses: her head was a boom-box, and her eyes hurt.

She crossed the car park, her legs only just holding her up. When she reached a low wall, she stopped and leaned on it for a moment to catch her breath. The buildings about her seemed to be shifting, as did the cars, the little shops, the restaurant where she'd eaten. Evie hoped she could find a pharmacy and buy something to calm her stomach and give her some energy. She checked the road for traffic like a child, looking right and then left, making sure she could cross. She would laugh about this tomorrow; indeed, she would never drink alcohol again. Perhaps it was the *moules marinières* that had disagreed with her, or simply that she'd enjoyed too much of a good thing. Her stomach heaved; bitter bile lurched into her mouth and she swallowed it, regretting it instantly as her tongue tasted acid and a fist of pain grasped at her stomach again.

There was a little shop and she made her way towards it. Pushing open the door was an effort, then she realised she needed to pull the door towards her. The action of tugging made her tired. Inside the shop were pungent cheeses, and some ham hanging from a hook. Evie saw sausages curled in the chilled counter; they looked like intestines and she had to hold her hand to her mouth just in case. A woman was being served and the man behind the counter was hacking at a joint of beef. The acrid smell filled Evie's nostrils and she retched, but nothing came up except the taste of bile. She shivered inside her jacket and felt her body jerk forwards. She steadied herself by putting out her hand, almost knocking down a display.

Evie raised the sunglasses a little; the shop lights were

an intense white, so she lowered the shades again. Her body sent her mind an immediate warning: standing up was not easy and she should not do it. She looked for somewhere to sit, hoping that she could hold on a few seconds, then dizziness enveloped her and she crashed forward. The last thing she felt was the bouncing of tins around her and the hardness of the flagstone floor as she fell.

Evie was conscious of blankness, then whiteness; walls, a small window, a tight cover folded over, holding her down. She was lying on a bed in a hospital. She gazed around herself slowly; there was a drip in her hand and her head hurt. She raised a hand to her face and felt the folds of a bandage over her forehead. She leaned back on pillows, groaned softly and closed her eyes.

They flickered open again and a nurse was standing over her, calling her name. The nurse wore a crisp uniform and was bending forward, touching her hand. Evie moved to sit up. The nurse told her to be careful, to be slow, and someone would come and talk to her in English. She helped Evie to sit up, propped by pillows. Evie took in the room: small, the walls white but grubby, a window: she was looking over a courtyard; a town was behind and into the distance. The light hurt her eyes.

Another woman came in, this one thin, tall, with greying hair which had once been black. She wore tiny pearl earrings and she looked severe. Evie managed a laugh; the woman did not smile back, but introduced herself as Dr Masson.

Evie looked at her directly. 'Am I better now? How did I get here?'

'You were in a shop. You fainted, Madame Gallagher.'

'Am I all right now? I think I ate some dodgy seafood . . .'

'Evelyn, you were dehydrated. You hit your head when

135

you fell. We have put you on a drip to put fluids back into your body. You are not badly hurt but you must rest.'

Evie held the doctor's frown in her gaze, for a moment, taking it all in. The doctor tried to help her by explaining again.

'In your bag you have a passport and so we found out your name, and your details. Your handbag is safe in your locker with your purse and other belongings. Someone in the shop called for an ambulance. I hope you have the insurance for travel abroad in Europe. Are you on holiday here?'

Evie nodded and thanked the Lord she'd sorted out her insurance when she booked the ticket in Liverpool. All would be fine. 'Can I go now? I have a campervan in a car park.'

'Who is travelling with you?'

'Oh, I am on my own. It is a sort of road trip, you see. I have a campervan and—'

The doctor exclaimed, a light sound falling from her lips. 'Alone? Surely not, Evelyn. You have a relative we can contact? Husband? Children?'

Evie shook her head and it hurt a bit. 'No-one. I have nobody to contact.'

'But you are seventy-five years old.' The doctor was indignant.

Evie was puzzled. She knew how old she was. She gave a little snort. The doctor continued.

'You are not young. You should not travel alone. You should respect your body. It is no longer the body of a young woman and you should not travel without assistance.'

Evie's teeth came together. 'I'm not demented,' she replied. Then she found another word. 'I'm not decrepit.'

'But, really . . .'

'There are no buts about it.' Evie was insistent. 'I have a campervan. I'm having a little holiday. By myself.'

The doctor looked horrified. 'You have no-one with you? No friend? No helper?'

Evie shook her head again, more with disbelief than as acknowledgement of the doctor's words. Dr Masson wrote something on a clipboard and put it at the bottom of the bed. 'Are you hungry, Evelyn?'

Evie was, surprisingly, and said so.

The doctor still did not smile. 'We'll keep you in overnight and then, tomorrow, we will consider letting you leave the hospital. But I strongly advise you go home to Ireland where you can be looked after properly. You need to slow down, at your age.'

As the doctor turned to leave, Evie called out to her. 'You wouldn't say that if I was a man. It's all just plain wrong if you ask me.' The doctor had gone.

Steadily, she eased her aching body to the side of the bed and sat up. She felt fine. She opened the locker beside her and took out her things: passport, purse, phone, debit card, car keys; all looked fine. She smiled.

'Bloody doctor.' She gave a grim little laugh. 'Complete bollocks. I'll show her.'

Evie pulled out a map and spread it across the sheet on the top of the bed. She looked at the pencil lines she'd drawn and put her finger on the place where she thought she was. She moved her finger right, and further to the right, mouthing the place names to herself. Finally she settled on a dot.

'Now where was I going? Here we are now. Carcassonne,' she read. 'Walled city. Lots of history. Nearby Limoux. That will do me fine. That's where I'm going. No more of this sexist, ageist nonsense. Simone de Beauvoir wouldn't let them get away with it, I'm sure of it. I'll show them.'

Chapter Twenty-One

'You can phone me to tell me the Panda is ready, Brendan.
Clémence and I will be back sometime later. We are going
to treat ourselves this afternoon.'

Maura was chirpy as she spoke through the window
of Clémence's car; they had dropped Brendan off outside
the garage and were off to Angers to do some shopping.
Clémence had become Maura's new best friend over the
last two days; they watched television together in the
evening in Clémence's lounge, while her husband checked
on the animals for the night. They had shared a bottle of
white wine late into the early hours and Brendan heard
them chortling together when he was in bed, their voices
whispering and scratching in his head as his mind drifted
into sluggish sleep. Bad dreams came, which seemed to
last the whole night, and he woke at dawn to hear the
birds chirruping, feeling the coldness of Maura's shoulder
turned against him as she lay across most of the bed, a
snore purring in her nose.

And now the women were off to explore the shops and
have lunch in Angers. Brendan's job was to make sure the
car was fixed and that they were ready to leave tomorrow

morning first thing. He watched the car turn the corner. Maura was gone for the day.

He walked into the garage yard, his hands in his pockets. The yellow Panda was where it was when he left it. Olivier came from the office; when he saw Brendan, he smiled and held out his hand. Brendan asked about the car and, in particular, the new radiator. Olivier's face was bright with optimism, as he explained that the radiator had arrived the previous afternoon, but when he'd tried to fit it, it was the wrong one and he had sent it back again.

'Maybe tomorrow or the day after, then you will be on your journey. You are comfortable at Aunt Clémence?'

Brendan replied that Clémence was the perfect hostess, and yes, he would be happy to stay another day or two. He took out his phone to ring Maura. He thought for a moment, and put the phone in his pocket. It would keep.

Brendan walked down to the river and leaned against the brickwork of a bridge. The water was green-tinged and still. He wondered if Maura would enjoy hiring a canoe and spending a few hours on the river. Perhaps there was somewhere locally where they could rent a raft or just have a swim. Brendan enjoyed the water, although his memory was a little soured by supervising swimming lessons at school. He'd stood helplessly by the pool and listened to countless stories of why one of his students couldn't go in the water but had no note from home; at the other end of the spectrum, there was the splashing and pushing and tomfoolery of the bigger boys, roaring and swearing and bullying, which he punished with detentions.

Brendan wondered if Maura might bring him a new pair of swimming-trunks back from Angers. He had left his on the bed in the hotel in Brittany. He took out his phone; there were no messages so he put it back in his pocket again. He imagined his body lifted and supported by water, the pushing strength of his arms as he moved forwards, the sense of propelling himself forward against pressure. He thought of water lapping around his ears, the coldness tingling against his chest, the droplets filling his eyes. He wondered for a moment if Maura would agree to go swimming with him in a lake. She wasn't a strong swimmer, but he could teach her. He imagined them both together in a *lac*, clear cool water lifting them. In the image Maura's hair was damp, little strands across her face, and her head was back, laughing. His arms were around her and he imagined her leaning back into his grasp, trusting him, closing her eyes as he and the water carried her along. He wondered if they would kiss, and he'd gaze at her wet face, slide his hands over the smooth texture of her swimsuit and her strong body beneath. He breathed out and wondered if Penny Wray was snorkelling in Mexico. His daydream shifted to himself in mask and flippers beside a young woman, her blonde hair streaming behind her; they were both surrounded by gleaming light and shoals of vivid fishes. Brendan opened his eyes.

He found somewhere to sit where the grass was dry and straw-like, and he stretched out his legs. The river was glass-smooth, reflecting trees and bushes and a small house upside down. Brendan felt his heartbeat begin to slow down.

Two children and a man were approaching from the road. They were on bicycles; the girl was a teenager and the boy a few years younger, maybe nine or ten. The man had a dark beard and wore cycle shorts and a top advertising soya yogurt. They stopped on the bridge and wheeled their bikes down to the riverside. They were talking together in French. They laid their bicycles down and the man began to point something out in the river to the children. The girl made a quiet reply and sat down. The boy pulled a ball from a backpack; it was a small football and he and his father started to pass the ball. The girl joined in and the three were running and giggling. The man called his son's name. Alexandre certainly had a good kick on him. Brendan watched them as a sports teacher scouting for potential talent; both children were skilful and competitive and the girl could head the ball well.

Their dad's encouragement was gentle and humorous; there was no sense of disappointment if a kick was missed or went in the wrong direction. Brendan thought how nice it would be to have a kick-about on a day like this, next to the river with such a breathtaking backdrop; how good it would be to share ice-creams afterwards and then get back on the bikes and have a ride home, the children chattering and laughing. He wondered where the mother was. Perhaps she was working, perhaps the parents were divorced, but the man had two fine children who clearly enjoyed their time with him. Perhaps the mother was like Maura and didn't enjoy cycling, but was waiting at home with a smile, maybe with cinema tickets, ice-cream. Perhaps he was a widower, and something tragic had happened. The children wore clean clothes and their game was care-free.

Alexandre booted the ball high. It came down with a thud, bobbled over towards Brendan and came to a stop near where he was sitting. He leapt up and returned it on his right foot. His kick was confident but not too hard. The boy was appreciative with his '*Merci, Monsieur*' and there was admiration in the child's tone. The father looked over and smiled his gratitude. Brendan waved back, half hopeful that they might invite him to join in or at least ask him to go in goal.

But the family finished their game and packed up their belongings; the father pulled on the backpack and they pushed their bikes back to the road where they mounted, and were off, the girl first, then Alexandre, who turned and waved before the father ushered them safely on their way. Brendan was sad to see them go. His hand was still in the air when they were out of sight. He lowered his arm and wondered where everything had all gone wrong.

An hour later, he was sitting inside a little café where betting was being shown on a large monitor. The racehorses were out and they were being led up and down, their names flashing on the screen. Brendan drank the dregs of his *bière blonde*, then he ordered a second beer and a plate of *côte d'agneau*. He was served by a pretty woman in a blue dress, her hair cut in a dark bob, her lips a vivid red. She told him he spoke French well and asked him if he was Belgian. He told her no, he was Irish, and she put a hand to her mouth and said how she loved Ireland and had visited County Kerry once many years ago and did he live near there. Two men in the café were looking at him. One of them was sitting on a stool at the bar, his back turned, reading a paper and occasionally looking over and frowning. He wondered if that was her husband but the man looked considerably older.

The side of lamb was pleasant and the gravy was plentiful, so Brendan decided to stay a little longer. He had nowhere else to go. He ordered a third beer and a *crème brûlée lavande*, which the woman told him was a speciality of the house. It was displayed in a lilac glass bowl, looking professional with its moat of sweet sauce, a crunchy sugar topping giving way to a delicate lavender cream. He wished the portion had been larger.

He ordered a coffee, and the waitress asked him where he was staying and for how long. He told her and she

142

replied enthusiastically that Clémence was a friend of her cousin, Jeanne, and that it was a nice place to stay. She glanced at his wedding ring as he paid the bill and she made him promise to come back for lunch again, perhaps with his wife. Brendan made an unequivocal humming sound between his lips, thanked her for the lovely meal and walked into the sunshine. The beers made his head feel fuzzy and blurred his vision; his mood lightened. He took out his phone. There were no messages and he did not intend to ring Maura. Stubbornness was stiffening his jaw. He found his mother's number and texted her. Where are you going in the South? Send an address, Mammy.

He put the phone back in his pocket with a smile. Action was what was required and, as he sauntered back to Clémence's for an afternoon snooze, he was a man of action, decisive and capable. Tomorrow he would buy himself some brightly coloured swim shorts. He began to whistle a little tune.

Chapter Twenty-Two

The doctor's comments were still buzzing in Evie's head the next day. She picked up her handbag as the doctor dismissed her with the stern words: 'Remember my advice, Madame. You are no longer a young woman.'

Evie muttered 'Shite' to herself inside the hospital, and several times as she walked the kilometre to the car park, the word banishing her bad mood for a few seconds before she felt cross again and said it once more, a mantra against capitulation. This morning the bandage had been removed from her head but the swelling was still visible, although it did not hurt as much as her knees, which ached constantly. They must have been jarred by the fall.

By the time she reached the campervan, she was exhausted. Evie checked that everything was still in its place. She opened all the windows and smoothed the pages of the map, then she was ready to start on the drive, which would take the rest of the day. She would drive to a *supermarché* – she was glad it was nearly the same word as in English – and buy herself some treats for the journey. She was about to start the engine when her mobile sounded from her bag. She read Brendan's message: he wanted to know where she was going. She smiled. He was a good son and was clearly interested in the trip she was making. She imagined him at home, a map of France on the coffee table or on his laptop, tracing her journey proudly. Brendan would be impressed with her choice of a historic city. She typed in Carcassonne quickly with her thumb and pressed *send*, putting the phone back in her bag without checking the screen. Her knees hurt as she pushed the pedals down, in particular the one she was using for the clutch. She pulled out of the car park and into the town traffic, peering over the dashboard to find a signpost.

She yawned: she had been driving for a few hours. The sunshine streamed through the windscreen as through a magnifying glass and her head began to hurt over one eye, pulsating steadily where the bump was. There was little traffic in the town, so her attention was on signposts and she glanced from her map on the passenger seat to the signs, searching for Carcassonne, negotiating a roundabout and several sets of traffic lights, then she turned onto a main road, a straight avenue flanked with trees. Her mouth was dry and her tongue thick, so she resolved to stop at the next lay-by and have some orange juice and maybe some fruit. A thought was rattling in her head: she might even take a nap and rest her knees. A car passed her closely, obviously in a hurry, and Evie wondered if the driver was annoyed that she was only travelling at forty kilometres an hour. She clutched the wheel tightly and peered over the dashboard at the road. There was a low shimmering of heat haze on the tarmac and hills were rising to the left.

A police car passed her with its blue light flashing and a *gendarme* waved Evie to pull over. She saw his little cap and smiled and waved back. He overtook her and an arm came from the window, a strong finger indicating a lay-by to the right. Evie exhaled and followed him, braking steadily so that she did not stop too close to his bumper.

The little man in the blue shirt was marching towards her, a frown on his face, and Evie glanced at his smart uniform. She was about to grin at him but she wound down the window and proffered a solemn expression. He spoke to her and she had no clue what he was saying but his face looked serious. Perhaps there was a killer on the loose. She shrugged and he spoke again but it was still no clearer. She leaned out of the window and raised her voice so that he could hear her over the noise of the passing traffic.

'Hello to you. I don't know what you're talking about though, Officer. I don't speak French very well. I am here on holiday.'

The policeman gesticulated over his shoulder; the other policeman came to join him, and they spoke together in hurried voices. The other officer couldn't have been more than twenty-two. He was obviously the junior partner.

'How can I help you?' she asked, smiling as widely as she could.

'English?' the young officer asked, his face sombre.

'Irish,' she replied. 'I am here on holiday.'

'Where are you going?'

'Carcassonne.'

'May I see your driver's licence? Passport?'

Evie took them from her bag and handed them over. The police officer studied them for a moment, then made a curious expression, wrinkling his nose, and handed the documents back.

'You are Evelyn Gall-agg-her?'

'Evie,' she smiled. 'Officer,' she added as an afterthought.

'This vehicle is French.'

146

'Well done,' she said, congratulating the young man on his skills of deduction. 'I bought it in France.'

'The vehicle belongs to you?'

'Oh yes,' said Evie. 'I certainly haven't stolen it. I paid with my winnings. I put a bet on a horse and it came in at a hundred to one. I had a streak of good luck. Four's my lucky number.'

The young *gendarme* did not understand. He spoke to his surly companion, who replied in a low voice, and then the younger one spoke again.

'Back there in the town you drove through a red light.'

Evie didn't remember doing it.

'Are you alone? No-one else is with you?'

'Oh for God's sake, can't a lady travel by herself?' Evie decided her tone was a bit rude and then gave the young officer a winning smile. 'Yes, I am on my own, Officer.' She thought for a few seconds. 'But when I reach Carcassonne there will be a whole bunch of us. Twenty old people, all from Ireland. An old folks' bucket list club – we're all on holiday together. It's our last holiday. Ever. You see, we're all very ill with a terrible disease and we only have about six weeks to live, Officer. That is why this holiday is so important. It's our last holiday. Before we die a very painful and terrible death.' She gave a little sniff to prove that she was telling the truth and wiped at her eye with the crook of her finger.

The *gendarmes* had a conversation. Evie listened closely but could make nothing of their words. The young man put his hand out and laid it on Evie's arm, which was resting on the open window frame. He patted her twice and nodded his head up and down before he spoke.

'I see you have an injury on your head. I understand now. You are a brave woman and we wish you a good holiday with your friends.'

147

Evie was about to ask what friends, but then she remembered and said, '*Oui, Monsieur*,' twice. She put a hand to her head as if she had a serious and painful wound and then she gave the officer a heroic smile as she imagined Joan of Arc might have smiled before she was taken to the stake. She put on her humble face. '*Merci*, Officer.'

'Drive safely, Madame. Look out for the red lights next time.'

'Oh I will, Officer. You can be sure of that. If there is a next time, of course. Time being so short and all. Yes, indeed I will. Thank you.'

The young policeman was grave. 'I wish you good luck.'

The other *gendarme*, the older miserable one, reached out and took her hand and said something in French, as if bestowing a blessing. Evie thought they were both charming.

'You take care now, Officer. You're doing a grand job.' She thought for a moment and then waved to them through the window. 'Have a nice day.'

The two *gendarmes* saluted her politely as they made their way back to the police car and drove away. Evie breathed out. 'Bollocks.'

She rummaged in her bag for the orange juice. It was warm and the top was sticky but she took a swig, then another. She looked over her shoulder to the back of the campervan and decided a snooze was in order.

Chapter Twenty-Three

She slept until late afternoon. The sun's heat pooling through the windows against her back made her roll over and hug the pillow. Her stomach growled and the muscles in her legs and back felt tight. Evie craved a hot shower and a soft bed and time to recover from the fall. A good wash-down in a public toilet, spitting toothpaste into a cracked sink, was an adventure for a while but she could afford the luxury of a hotel and her body deserved some rest and comfort. She'd drive to a small village, clean herself up and find a nice little café: the bitterness of a coffee and something warm and stodgy would go well in her stomach. Then she'd find somewhere to stay near Carcassonne.

She drove for hours and it was well into the evening when she saw it. She blinked her eyes and wondered if she'd misread the sign but it was there clearly, with an arrow pointing the way. 'O'Driscoll's Irish Bar: 1 kilo-metre'. Evie followed the arrow, leaning heavily over the steering wheel to look for the next sign. A car behind her blasted a horn and she wondered whether she was going too slowly or whether they were upset that she just changed lanes without indicating. The pub was to the right. 'À *droit*', an arrow pointing the way.

She found it, a dingy-looking building with a dark door. The paint was peeling in rough strips, showing a bruised pink colour beneath. A sign above in black and red said 'O'Driscoll's Irish Bar'. By the door was a green and gold logo declaring that a range of Irish beers was available. There were several parking spaces opposite, so Evie reversed into one of them twice, carefully, stopping close to a battered red sports car, and then she grabbed her handbag and made for the door.

At first she thought the pub was closed. The door knob twisted in her hand: she pushed her weight against the wood to heave the door open, but it would not budge. It was almost seven o'clock, but perhaps the pub was not yet open. She turned away, then the door yawned open and a young man with a huge moustache and sideburns crashed into her, slurring in French. He blinked at Evie, then took her hand, patted it twice and muttered, '*Pardon, Madame,*' before lurching into the street. Evie caught the door before it closed and went inside.

O'Driscoll's Bar was lit with foggy yellow lamps; it was a long thin room with huge wooden pillars supporting ceilings that were crusted and cracked, low-hanging and dull grey. The room smelled of stale bodies, beer and damp, each smell distinct from the other. Wooden tables were scattered to the right, mostly empty, beneath a video screen where a football match was being played out soundlessly. A man and woman were sitting at one table, half-pints of beer in front of them, their heads close. The bar was in the corner, on the left, arrayed with glasses hanging from the ceiling and beer pumps sticking up around the red surface of the bar.

Three men were at the bar, their backs to Evie. Two

were little men, their bodies leaning forward, drinking together. One wore a sort of beret perched on the side of his head. Evie remembered her red beret, which was abandoned now beneath the rest of her luggage, along with the new coat she'd bought in Dublin. Dublin and Sheldon Lodge, and even Jim, seemed a great distance away. The two little men chortled softly and emptied their glasses, raising them towards the barman to order a refill. They turned to Evie; one raised his hand to her and she replied, '*Bonjour*', feeling ridiculously pleased with herself.

The last man was probably in his seventies, standing separate from everyone else; he wore a black leather jacket and, as he turned slightly to observe the newcomer, she noticed he wore a Bob Dylan T-shirt. He was very tall. He twisted back to the bar. His hunched shoulders seemed to warn the world that he did not wish to be disturbed. Beneath a cap his hair curled and was held in a small ponytail, which was iron grey in colour. Evie approached the bar and saw the barman refilling glasses for the two friends. He spoke to her in French and she nodded, assuming that he'd said he would be with her in a minute.

Around the bar were fading pictures of Ireland in its pastoral glory hanging from nails hammered into the walls, and one or two photos were arranged closely together. They had dark wooden frames and showed two men in caps working with spades in the fields; a woman in a bonnet serving food to a family in a dingy house. There was a larger picture of two men with raised fists, their knuckles shiny and pale and their faces contorted in pugilistic parody. The bar was lit with little white bulbs; on the wall was a sepia picture of an ocean liner and some people boarding it, wearing old-fashioned clothes. Evie eased herself onto a high stool to rest her knees. A fairground display of drinks was available and she was about to order an orange juice, as she was driving, when she saw a pump offering Guinness, which she'd drunk in a Dublin bar with Jim, years before. A half wouldn't hurt. After all, wasn't it full of vitamins and iron?

The barman had dark hair and thick eyebrows, a stubble-rough face, lively blue eyes and muscled arms. He wore a T-shirt with a cartoon picture of a Dublin bar on it. The slogan said: 'My idea of a balanced diet is a beer in each hand'. Evie smiled. 'I'll have half of your Guinness, please.'

The barman laughed out loud. When he spoke, his accent was Northern English, all elongated vowels and brimming enthusiasm. 'You're an Irish lady. Well, I'll be jiggered. Eh, you're a long way from home, love.'

'On holiday.' Evie extended her hand. 'Evie Gallagher. From Dublin.'

'Ray Deakin. From Salford, Manchester. My parents were from Ennis, County Clare.' He indicated the pictures. 'All this stuff was theirs, God bless them. When they went, I sold up and came over here, fancied a bit more sunshine really, and I started O'Driscoll's. My mother was Doreen O'Driscoll.'

'Pleased to meet you, Ray. This is a grand bar you have here.'

'I try not to drink away most of the profits.' Ray passed Evie her half-pint of dark liquid with a creamy topping. 'On the house, since you are my first Irish customer for a long time.'

She took a mouthful, supping from the top and allowing the froth to stick to her upper lip like a soft moustache. She let it stay for a moment and then licked it clean. 'Mmm. That's good.'

'Well, it's nice to meet you, Evie.' Ray beamed across at the men on the bar, indicated Evie and said something in French. She recognised the word '*Irlandaise*' from her encounter in the post office back in Pentrez. She raised her glass to the two men talking together and again to the tall man. The drinking pair raised their glasses warmly; the other man, aloof and unfriendly, leaned away from Evie. He downed the last of the brandy in his glass and slammed it on the counter with a single word. The barman went to fill it up again and the tall man scratched his head underneath his cap and looked directly at Evie. His eyes were chestnut brown and intense. Evie thought he was rude, so she swallowed another mouthful of her beer, ignored him and started to chatter to Ray. 'So, how long have you been here?'

'Twelve years. Married a nice girl from Foix, Paulette: she's upstairs with the kiddies. She helps out down here when it's busy, which it is usually this time of year. I get all the British football and the big fights in here on the screen. The French love the boxing. And on St Pat's Day we have a party. It goes on until the early hours. Even the mayor comes in. There's sometimes a fight or two, plenty of singing and dancing. It's a riot.'

Evie ordered another half of stout and decided she would probably sleep in the campervan in the car park. She'd ask first, but Ray seemed very laid-back and kind. She'd find a hotel in the morning, and review her plans after Carcassonne. She imagined postcards of the walled town and thought how nice it would be to send postcards to Brendan and to Sheldon Lodge and a nice message to Maddie and Kat and maybe to Odile in Angers, where she had enjoyed such a lovely meal. She'd call in and see them all on the way back.

'Ray, do you have food here?'

'I could rustle you up something, love . . . a plate of stew perhaps and a piece of apple pie.'

Evie beamed. 'That would be grand.'

Chapter Twenty-Four

Four hours later, Evie was feeling relaxed and happy. She had eaten a plate of rich stew, some melt-in-the-mouth apple pie and had drunk four more halves of stout and two cognacs. She struck up a conversation with the two little men, although none of them really understood each other, but the men pointed at the array of bottles and Evie said, '*Non . . . Non . . . Non . . .*' until they reached the huge decanter of cognac. She then said, '*Oui, s'il vous plaît,*' and the men each bought her a brandy. Her knees had stopped aching. She noticed the tall man, the septuagenarian with the dark eyes and little ponytail, glowering at her from behind his glass. Evie wondered what he was staring at, stuck out her tongue at him and looked away. His gaze was unflinching: when she looked back, he was still watching her. She offered to buy the two men a drink, pointing at the optics, and they laughed and asked Ray for a beer each. Evie glanced again at the disgruntled man, on his own at the bar, emptying the dregs in one gulp.

'Can I buy you a drink, Mr Grumpy?' she offered, and laughed. She saw a look of disapproval on Ray's face. The

154

bad-tempered drinker shook his head and said something in French to Ray, who refilled his glass.

Ray came over to her. 'Jean-Luc prefers his own company. Don't pay any attention to him, let him be.'

Evie shrugged and started to ask Ray about his family and if he missed Manchester. She was holding forth about Dublin and how lovely it was this time of year. 'It is grand when the flowers are all out and the birds singing. And the people are so friendly, Ray.'

Ray was agreeing with her when an echoing bang came from the bar to her left. Mr Grumpy had slammed down his glass. Ray asked him if he wanted another and brought over the bottle for him. The tall man with the little pony-tail was in a bad mood, and he swallowed his refill in one gulp. Evie noticed the two drinkers moved away from him a little and then the couple at the table picked up their bags and left.

Evie wrinkled her nose and looked at him again through the corners of her eyes. 'He's a bad-tempered one, isn't he?'

Ray gave her his warning look once more but Evie didn't care. She was bathed in the glow of beer and cognac, good food and a friendly Irish bar. 'I mean, you come out for a drink to relax and to have fun, don't you, and not to bring a miserable face to show to everyone.'

The irritable man emptied the bottle into his glass and put it down firmly. He delved into his pockets and found several euro notes, unfolding them and laying them flat on the polished wooden surface. He turned his gaze on Evie and the dark eyes were flecked with fury. He spoke in English, perfectly clear, his French accent tinged with American, his voice gravelly and heavy with contempt.

'Some of us come here to be alone with our bad temper, Madame. If I have offended you, quite honestly, I could

155

not care less.' He turned his head away and spoke to no-one in particular. 'I will say good night.' He said something in French again to Ray, turned and walked out of the bar without a glance back. It was silent for a moment, and then the two little men ordered more drinks for themselves and one for Evie.

Evie refused; she'd drunk enough, *merci*, and she turned to Ray and apologised for offending his customer. 'I hope I haven't spoilt your night, Ray. I've had such a lovely time.'

One of the two little men drinking, the one with the beret, turned to Evie and said something, called her 'Madame', and waved his hands earnestly.

'Maurice is right,' Ray told her. 'We are delighted to share your company. Don't pay any attention to Jean-Luc; he is miserable most of the time. He spends what he has in here on drink and he seems happy enough as long as no-one speaks to him. He has his own troubles, but he never shares them.'

Evie tried to forget about the man Jean-Luc and his bad temper, but the image of him stooped over the bar, his shoulders tight, a glass in his fist, stayed with her. She thought about his dark brooding eyes. He could have been a character in *Wuthering Heights*.

'I'll have that drink after all,' she said. 'Oh and Ray, I'd like to stay around here for a day or two before I go on to Carcassonne. Can you recommend somewhere?'

Ray chortled. 'I can do you a good bed and breakfast here; full Irish, with soda bread thrown in and the best coffee in town. Evening meal too, if you want it, love.'

'It's a deal,' Evie told him, her eyes shining. 'And I would like one of the best coffees in town now, with my cognac, if I may, please, barman.'

'Coming up.' Ray busied himself with the coffee

machine, and a cup and saucer. 'Are you parked nearby? I'll give you a hand in with your things and then you can meet my wife, Paulette.'

The next day, Evie found herself in the market at the nearby town, Saint-Girons. It was a forty-minute drive; she took another half an hour to find somewhere to park and it was a ten-minute walk downhill to the market. Ray told her over breakfast that Carcassonne was under an hour away, so she decided to stay where she was for a few days, until the lump on her head was flat again and her knees and muscles less painful.

Saint-Girons was lovely, a town full of hippies and interesting-looking people, and the market was colourful and lively. Music throbbed on the air – African drumming and a man in a long kaftan who had a type of harp that he played with the neck sticking out in front of him, and a little band of three French men in berets who had an accordion and a guitar and put their hearts into singing traditional songs.

Rich smells of cooking followed Evie around: scented couscous, roasting chicken, spicy bhajis, and tangy cheeses. People smiled and chatted to her, many in English. There were stalls of clothes hanging, brightly coloured as flags. An English lady, tall and slender, probably in her fifties with wavy auburn hair and a long fringe, was selling pots of jam and chutney and Evie bought some yellow bean chutney and stopped for a chat with her about her life in France. She was called Caroline. She wore a long print dress and leather sandals. She lived with her partner, Nigel, out of town, halfway up a hill. They'd done up a guest house and the jams were just a sideline. Caroline told her it was a great place to live; summers were glorious and winters often snow-bound, which made the area exciting

157

and cosy. Caroline gave Evie her business card with her mobile number on it, and invited her for coffee whenever she liked. Evie promised to give her a call. She drew some money out of an ATM and bought some crazy jewellery: two leather-and-bead bracelets, a brooch shaped like an owl, a chakra necklace, and two toe-rings. Evie felt her mood soar as she moved past stalls of home-made honey and leather belts, piles of fresh strawberries, sandals and shoes and hats. She bought herself some blue leather sandals to show off the toe-rings, as well as an African print dress and a bright scarf, and some curried okra and organic rice to eat for lunch.

There was a stall selling bright rolls of plastic fabric. Evie ran her fingers over the soft squishiness and stood back. There was a pattern of a Paris café, an Eiffel tower and an elegant woman with a little dog on a lead. There were brightly coloured balloons, a sunshine-yellow fabric with blue cornflowers. She smoothed her fingers over a design with repeated lemons in green leafy squares; another fabric displayed bunches of grapes but the most attractive was a repeated pattern of colourful macaroon cakes like the ones in the shop in Brittany. Evie asked the woman at the stall about the fabric and she worked out that these were tablecloths which were sold by the metre. The designs were cheerful and she thought she would buy some to take home. She stopped for a moment. Home was not Sheldon Lodge, not any more. It could be somewhere else. Dublin? Her home could be wherever she liked. The thought felt good, and she breathed in the atmosphere of the bustling market and smiled.

She arrived at a stall that sold wine: bottles of white caught the sunlight and shook out a golden shard of brightness; deep burgundy reds in dark glass; unusual spirits in ornate bottles; all bearing the label 'Cave

Bonheur' and the logo of a smiling farmer holding up a clutch of purple grapes. Evie spoke to a young man, about eighteen or twenty years old she guessed, his face fixed in a wide grin. He had an exclamation mark of wheat-coloured hair and his thin arms and legs were sticking out from a T-shirt and baggy shorts. Evie greeted him in plodding French, asking if he spoke English.

He nodded, looked nervously over her shoulder and rubbed a flat hand across his brow. 'A little, Madame. I can try. How can I help you?'

'I want a nice bottle of red wine, something really special. It's a present for the lady where I am staying. Paulette. To drink with dinner. What can you recommend?'

The yellow-haired boy looked around him, choosing. He spoke to himself in French, presumably saying the names of the wines aloud. Then he offered a bottle to her. 'You like the nice Bordeaux?'

Evie pointed to another bottle. It was litre-sized, and had a plain label. 'What is this one?'

He looked anxious, put the Bordeaux back and offered her the larger bottle. His brow was soft with sweat. 'Languedoc-Roussillon. Product of the *pays*.'

Evie frowned. 'Product of the peace?'

The boy shook his head. '*Pays*, *Madame*. *Pays*. *Pays*.'

Evie didn't understand. 'Pee? Did you say it was pee?' She started to laugh.

The boy's face was serious; his brow was knotted with worry and he began to wave a hand in front of his face and rubbed the back of his neck with his fingers. 'Produced in the *pays*. In the *région*. Here, in our vines, at Cave Bonheur.'

She gave him her best smile. 'Oh. Is it good wine, then, this one?'

He nodded, his chin bobbing up and down. 'Very special.

Six euros, Madame. If you buy ten bottles, I can sell you four euros fifty each bottle.'

Evie delved into her bag. 'I'll have two bottles of the Long Dog, please. If I like it I can come back and buy more. It's difficult to carry lots of bottles away by myself and it's uphill all the way back to the bloody van.'

The boy grinned and he seemed to relax. His smile pushed out his cheeks. 'No problem, Madame. Here is the card of our business. You can visit and we do the free *dégustation*.'

Evie pulled an alarmed face. She was not sure what he meant – it sounded like free disgusting, which couldn't be right, could it? – but it didn't sound good. She wondered if it was drinking the last of the wine dregs and paying nothing for the privilege.

The boy rubbed his neck with his fist and tried again. 'You taste the wine before you buy. Free to taste, so if you like, you can buy.'

'Free wine?' Evie chortled at the thought. 'Sounds grand. Is your place far from here?'

'Two kilometres outside Saint-Girons on the road to Foix. The direction and telephone are on the card. You can come and visit.'

'I would love to.' Evie paid for her wine, shoving the large bottles into her handbag so only the necks stuck out. 'Nice to meet you.'

The boy shouted after her as she walked away, waving his arms and leaping in the air. He was clearly excited. 'My name is Benji. Remember me. I have the wine ready when you come.'

Evie hauled her handbag onto her shoulder, gripped her other purchases in her hand and headed for the winding street which would take her back to the campervan. She'd enjoyed Saint-Girons market and was looking forward to a nap and then another evening in O'Driscoll's.

Chapter Twenty-Five

'Caucasians, Brendan? What on earth do you mean?'

Brendan came out of the en suite, a towel round his waist. He'd been by himself for most of the day and he sat tiredly on the edge of the bed, where Maura had placed her bags of shopping from Angers. 'That's what she texted me. I asked her where she was staying in the south and she replied Caucasians. But it's not on the map anywhere.'

'It has to be.'

Brendan looked at Maura, at her serious face, and wondered when they had last exchanged smiles. They had been in France for well over two weeks. He recalled the night in the hotel in Brittany when they had been happy, at least for a while, and shrugged. 'I can ask her again. But she said she was off to the south and was staying in Caucasians. Perhaps it's a mountain pass. The Caucasians?'

Maura raised her eyebrows. 'And the Panda?'

'Should be ready for collection tomorrow afternoon. About two.'

'So what will we do with ourselves tonight, Brendan?' She looked at him hopefully and he thought for a moment.

'I know a nice little café where they serve good food.'

Maura wriggled from the edge of the bed. It was late afternoon and the window was wide open, the sun spilling into the room, a deep yellow strip of heat. Dust danced on the air, little twirling specks hovering. Maura walked through the slice of light and over to the wardrobe, her back towards Brendan. 'Right. If we're going out, I'd better put on my glad rags.'

She seemed not to notice him as she pulled clothes from the wardrobe, her mouth twisted in indecision, and put them back. 'I hope it's not too far to walk. These country lanes are playing havoc with my feet.'

Brendan watched her struggle out of her jeans and T-shirt. She glanced at him, then turned her back to him. He watched her hoist a pretty emerald-green dress over her head and pull it down over her hips. He noticed the furtive way she dressed, quickly, her arm a shield across her body. Brendan turned away, looking at his fingernails. He glanced at her again, trying not to stare. Maura smoothed the material of her dress and scrutinised herself in the mirror. She combed her hair, leaned forward to put lipstick on her mouth and caught his eye. She smiled and Brendan saw the sweet, bubbly girl he knew years ago. He moved over to stand behind her and placed a hand on her shoulder. In the mirror, he noticed her eyes twitch towards him and she reached an arm round behind her, took his hand and pulled it around her waist. Brendan examined his reflection: an unhappy man whose cheeks had begun to sag, who had started to look like a hapless bloodhound, and a feeling of futility and guilt grasped at his throat. Their reflection looked back at them, a hopeful couple who were once happy, who could be happy again perhaps, but he had no idea how to achieve it.

The meal passed quietly. The woman in the blue dress was not there. The waiter was dark, his hair lank, and he

162

wore heavy spectacles and a sombre face. They ordered the beef and shared a bottle of red wine. Afterwards, Brendan suggested they went for a walk by the river. Maura asked him jokingly if he was going to push her in, and he didn't reply. They walked down to the bridge where he had seen the father and his children playing football. Brendan leaned against the same brickwork and Maura rested against the bridge and they stared into the river beneath. The air was cold and Maura shivered. Her arms were covered in pinpricks of goose-flesh and she hugged the thin fabric of her green dress close to her body. Brendan took off his jacket and put it around her shoulders. She continued to gaze at the river, into the depths. Brendan took her hand, which lay limp in his fingers, and turned towards the road winding away towards Angers. He would need to contact Evie again and find out where she was staying.

A line of cyclists went by in colourful tops and shorts and Brendan thought about a cycling holiday. It would do wonders for his muscle tone and he imagined his legs brown and strong in Lycra shorts, his bike loaded with a tent and cooking equipment. The hedgerows would be bursting with wild flowers and honeysuckle smells, the burr of bees, and the road would be wide and edged by fields of sunflowers raising tall yellow heads to the sky. He imagined his companion riding up to come alongside him, wearing her safety helmet, a smile on her face and a long ponytail twisting in the breeze behind her. It was Penny Wray.

Brendan pulled himself out of his daydream, back to Maura. He let go of her hand. 'Shall we have a seat down there, on the riverbank? The grass is quite dry. We could watch the sun set.'

'Don't you think it's a bit late for romantic gestures, Brendan?'

'I thought it might be nice if we—'

'Nice? Nothing's nice at all.' Her eyes glittered. 'We've just eaten a meal together, a lovely meal, and you hardly said a word. I thought spending time together would make us feel happy again.' Tears filled her eyes. 'But it hasn't worked, has it?'

'I'm trying my best.'

'But you won't tell me what's wrong.'

'I just don't know how I feel any more.' They were silent, then he mumbled, 'How do you feel, Maura?'

She shook her head. 'Sometimes I'm afraid I'm going to lose you. Sometimes I just want to cry. It's as if all the love we had has leaked away and we're just going through the moves. The thing is, I still feel something for you, Brendan. But I'm not sure who you are any more. Or what you want. Then I think you must want something, but perhaps it isn't me. So I feel angry and then I don't know what I want either. It's just not quite right between us, is it?'

Brendan shrugged. 'What can we do?'

Maura slumped forwards. He thought about putting an arm around her shoulders but somehow his limbs wouldn't move. The silence hung between them, a thick brick wall. The silence became brittle. Minutes passed.

'Maura,' he began. He saw her face was streaked with tears. He forgot what he was about to say.

'Do you still love me?'

'Yes,' he began but the word filled in his mouth and he could say no more. She looked away and her shoulders were shaking. Brendan put a hand on her arm and he was aware that it was a hand of pity. He waited for the other feelings to follow: love, affection, a familiar caring that might still be there, the glue of their past. Brendan felt the cold wind blow through his shirt.

164

Maura stood up, wiping her tears from her cheeks and pulled his jacket tightly around her. Her face twisted, holding back another sob. She jolted her chin up but there was regret carved in the sadness of her face. 'I'm going back to Clémence's. I think I'll have an early night, Brendan. We both have some thinking to do.'

'I'll stay here a little bit.'

'Good idea.' She turned to go. 'I think we both know that things are not good at the moment. We need to decide if this marriage is important to us. Or if it isn't.'

Brendan bit his lip.

She waited for him to speak, and when he said nothing, she whispered, 'Shall I see you back at the bed and breakfast?'

He nodded. She hesitated then bent over and brushed her lips against his cheek. He shivered again. Her eyes lingered on his face and she was lost in her own thoughts.

'I do care, Brendan. I know I don't show it enough but I care more than you think.'

She walked away in her thin dress and his jacket and her silly sling-back heels, and he watched her with sadness. She became smaller in the distance, more fragile, and he thought about running after her, grabbing her in his arms, telling her that he'd try again to make her happy, even harder. He clutched his knees and leaned forward. A sob heaved in his chest, another, and he let out a cry and wept like a child.

The sun had almost gone; there were smudges of red on the horizon but the sky was dark blues and purples, streaked with scratches of orange. Brendan's hands and fingers were becoming numb. The bells of a clock crashed in the distance. He remembered a time when he was younger, when he had been afraid to go home because he had broken a window. In one of his rare teenage moods

165

he'd slammed a door and one of the panes had fallen out and shattered. Evie had swept it up with a broom and told him that it was his responsibility to sort it out with Jim when he came back from work. She had said, 'Your da will be furious,' and Brendan had run off with his football to the park and stayed there, brooding, until the bite of the cold was worse than any rocket he would get from his father. He'd dawdled home and Jim was mild and good-natured about it. They'd put in the new pane of glass together, Jim showing his son how to smooth the putty around the pane.

Brendan's childhood had been a good one. His parents had loved him and encouraged him. Jim had watched him play football each week and Evie had clapped and smiled when he won the poetry prize at school. They were both pleased that he'd become a sports teacher and their wedding present had been sensible: money for a deposit on the house. They had been practical parents but Brendan needed some softness now. He wished he could ring Evie and tell her about Maura, but he would feel awkward asking for help. He envied his mother her capacity for fun; he and his father had been the quiet ones while she was the one for a song, a dance, a laugh. They both used to watch her in action as she chattered away, the same fondness in their eyes.

He and his father were made of similar stuff: words were more often thought than spoken. And now his father was gone, his mammy was far away and his marriage might be dissolving to dust. He had no-one to talk to. He took out the phone and found Evie's number. He could text her and ask where she was. He could ring, but she'd know right away in his voice that something was wrong. He put his fingers through his hair. What was love? Was it just physical passion or romantic sentiment, or was it just a habit to keep the loneliness away? He would walk back to the bed and breakfast, slide his cold bones next to a slumbering Maura. Tomorrow they would have to sort it all out, the Panda, Evie, their marriage. Brendan pulled himself to his feet, put his hands in his pockets and turned in the direction of the shadows.

He woke up the next morning, warm and soft in the bed, and suddenly the remembrance of the troubles of the night before hit him. The bed was empty. When he went downstairs, Maura was sitting at the wooden farmhouse table eating croissants and drinking coffee. Her hair was piled up and fastened with a clip and she wore a bright yellow top and red earrings. Her face was flushed pink, a healthy glow. She smiled at Brendan and he noticed she was wearing pink lip gloss. 'I didn't wake you. You were fast asleep.'

He sat down and interlocked his fingers and she poured coffee from the metal jug and passed him a *pain au chocolat*. She stirred his coffee. 'I have decided we need to get organised today. What time are we picking the Panda up?'

Brendan found his voice. 'Two.'

'OK, we'll pack, then I'll go and buy us some provisions for our journey and a little something for Clémence to say thank you. Then we can have lunch in that nice café again and be on the road for half two.'

'What shall I do?' Brendan was annoyed with himself, allowing her to make decisions. That would need to change if he had to make his way alone in life.

'Find a map and work out our route,' she told him. 'Saying we're going south just won't cut it – who knows where the Caucasians are. Speak to your mother and ask her straight out where she is.'

'OK.' He pushed the plate and the bread away from him. 'I don't feel like food.'

Maura was surprised. She reached out and patted his hand. 'We've a long day ahead of us. You'll need a proper breakfast if we're going to drive halfway across France.'

Brendan stood up. 'I'm not a child,' he said and walked towards the staircase, aware of her hurt expression. Once in the bedroom, he felt his head clear. He would ring his mother, find out where she was and arrange to meet her the following day. He took out his phone and pressed the button for Evie's number. The phone rang a moment, then he heard her voice and he felt his heart lurch.

'Mammy, it's—'

'Brendan. Oh it's good to hear you. How are you? I'm having such a good time.'

'That's nice. Where . . .?'

'I have a little campervan now but I am staying in an Irish bar at the minute in a lovely little town. Oh, it's so nice here in France, the people are so friendly.'

Brendan's mouth filled with cunning. 'Irish bar? Sounds lovely, Mammy. Where is it?'

'Between two towns, Saint-Girons and Foix.' She pronounced it 'Foykse' and Brendan reached for a pen and wrote it down. 'You'd love it. And the market, oh, it's wonderful, Brendan, and the food is delicious, and do you know, they have free wine-tastings and . . .'

'Sounds grand.'

'Oh it is, it is. I'll send you a postcard in a day or two. I might even be able to take a picture on my smartphone and mail it to you.'

'That would be good.'

'Brendan, I have to go now. Paulette is doing breakfast and I'm showing her how to do potato farls so I'll have to get off and away. Is everything grand with you?'

Brendan hesitated. He thought about telling her where he was. His plan had been to meet tomorrow. He thought about Maura downstairs at the table, her cheerful face and smiling pink mouth, and about his mother, who was having such a good time on holiday that she didn't need him at all to help her. His resolve weakened and he shrugged. He would tell her next time he rang, and suggest they meet. There was plenty of time. Perhaps he'd try to sort things out with Maura today, then everything would be back to normal when he reached his mother. He smiled at his plan.

'Fine, Mammy – you enjoy your holiday.'

'Oh I will, Brendan. I'm having such a good time. Now you take care.'

'Bye, Mammy.'

'Give my best to Maura and you take care of yourself.'

'Yes, I will. Lots of love . . .'

She was gone and Brendan felt a pang of shame for his lies and lack of determination. He sat down on the bed and put his head in his hands. He didn't know what to do about Maura; whether they had a future to rescue or whether they had grown apart. He didn't know what to do about his mother, who had sounded so carefree and so distant from him that he was afraid to tell her he was coming to bring her home. Brendan looked around the room and scratched his head, feeling foolish. He delved within himself and decided he would take action. He stood up, breathed in and picked up the note he'd scribbled. He checked the two place names and opened the map, pen in his hand, and started to draw a line from Angers to Foix, his lips clamped together in concentration.

Chapter Twenty-Six

Evie put the phone in her pocket and smiled. 'That was my son, Brendan. He's a sports teacher, you know.' She pushed her hands back into the flour, raising powdery clouds around her as she lifted and patted the potato farls into shape and dropped them into the skillet. Paulette watched with round brown eyes, her chin resting in her palms.

'Ray tells me you come all by yourself here, alone in the camping car?'

Evie nodded, flour on her hands. The skillet sizzled.

Paulette shook her dark curls, tied them back and set the table while young Alice and Sophie sat in front of empty plates, their forks lifted in the air, waiting for a real Irish breakfast. 'I think you are very brave, Evie, to do this journey by yourself.'

Evie looked at the slight woman in the cotton frock, her feet bare and her hair tied in a blue ribbon. 'Sometimes, Paulette, you just have to get up and do things.'

Paulette rolled her eyes. 'It is difficult for me. The girls are still young. Five and seven years. Maybe later when they are grown up, I will do something brave for myself.'

The farls sizzled and were flipped. Evie piled them onto plates and added more potato dough to the skillet. 'When you've young ones, you give all of your time to them. All of your life and soul and energy. But they grow and find their own way. Now I've time for myself, and I don't want to waste it any more.'

Paulette handed plates of steaming food to her children and their eyes widened.

'They're nice with butter. *Beurre*,' Evie explained and the children nodded and poked their knives into a slab of golden butter. There were soon greasy smudges on their faces; their chestnut hair tied back away from damp fingers.

Paulette made a soft humming sound. 'What was it like to be in the home for the old people?'

Evie placed more farls on a plate. 'To be honest, it was sucking the life from me, Paulette. I was getting old. Here I'm just a person, no age. Age is just a number. We have to be alive and have adventures if we're to be who we are. Does that make sense?'

Paulette pressed her lips together and held a farl in delicate fingers, nibbled the end thoughtfully. 'I am thirty-four years old. For me, I have much to do with my life. But for now I am just *Maman*, or I am just the wife of Ray or I am the barmaid. Or sometimes I am the cook. I want so much to be more than that.'

Evie sat to table and reached for the butter. 'What do you want to do with your future, though? For yourself?'

The young woman shrugged. 'I don't know. Good wife. Good mother. They are enough, *non*?'

'For a while.' Evie chewed and thought. 'Yes, all that is grand, and it's important to do it well. But what else would you like to do, Paulette? Later on, for yourself?'

Paulette shook her curls free of the ribbon and then

171

tied them again. 'I don't know. I have no talents. Maybe I could be like you, Evie? Be strong, independent, brave?'

Evie laughed. 'You'd be surprised about your own talents, Paulette. Sometimes they wait their turn and show themselves when you're ready for them. For now, maybe you just concentrate on the babbies, you've plenty of time afterwards. But I could lend you a good book for the time being, to give you something to think about. Have you read much by Simone de Beauvoir?'

Later, as the children wiped the butter from their mouths, Paulette explained that there would be a party in the bar that evening as it was Ray's birthday and asked would Evie like to help with ideas for Irish food. She had intended to go to Benji's free wine-tasting, but that would keep until tomorrow in favour of making soda bread and Dublin coddle, colcannon, stew and dumplings, sausages and finally caramel rice pudding. She was writing a list: they would have to buy cheeses, cream, fresh vegetables, fruit. Evie was keen to make a banquet for her new friends and there would be live music in the bar from Billy the Banjo, and new people to meet. Paulette put a sign up outside in French and English advertising the birthday bash and she tied back her hair in a fresh ribbon and put the kids in little aprons so all four of them could cook up a feast. Alice and Sophie stood on chairs and delved little fingers into flour as Evie showed them how to make soda bread. Paulette flitted between chattering in French to her children, interspersed with giggles and warnings, and English to Evie, asking for help and instruction, and Evie washed her hands and set out ingredients. It was going to be a busy day.

The Irish bar was decked out with little candles in jam jars and they made a space for a stage at the other side of the room, opposite the bar. Tables were pushed closer together to accommodate the food, and people could help themselves. Paulette's dark eyes flashed as she pointed out that the cost of the food would easily be offset by the amount people would drink. Evie and the children helped her get the pub ready while food was in the oven. Ray was out for the day, playing golf with friends, and although he knew they were planning a party, he was banned from seeing their work until opening time. There were 'Happy 40th Birthday, Ray' signs, which Paulette made on poster-sized paper with a realistic-looking cartoon of Ray's smiling face and his body in golf kit, and Sophie and Alice quietly coloured them in. They stuck photos around the bar, Ray as a teenager, gawky in skinny jeans and floppy hair; photos of him on his wedding day and more recent ones of him in the bar, pulling pints and grinning into the lens.

The kitchen smelled of cooking at its various stages: the hot fat of meat roasting, vegetables frying and steaming, and a delicious smell of caramelised sugar. Billy arrived with his banjo and his wife, Marion. He was an Irishman from Waterford who had lived near Foix for twenty-five years and was now in his sixties. Marion was tall, dark, with red-framed spectacles. She spoke little English but she hugged Evie and said hello to Paulette and the kids and rolled up her sleeves to help put out the food while Billy enjoyed a pint of the strong stuff.

Evie wrinkled her nose and turned to Paulette. 'Simone de Beauvoir wouldn't be too pleased. Here we are again, the women presenting the food while the men sit on their arses and drink.'

Paulette smiled politely and agreed but Evie thought that she didn't have a clue about Simone or her ideas on misogyny – and Paulette was French! Evie resolved to definitely lend her the book.

Evie thought about her life in Dublin, with Brendan

and Jim, then at the Lodge, and she decided she too had so much to learn and so much to think about – what was the word? – sisterhood? The women getting together, sometimes cooking, but mostly talking, sharing support and ideas. Maybe that was what was happening. She had never had any real female friends. She and Jim had been out with other couples but they'd never really talked or shared more than a drink and a laugh. And Maura had never been friend material.

Evie pulled a face. Maura wasn't even daughter-in-law material. She'd been a bubbly one at first, but Evie could see that she'd been determined to get her claws into Brendan and Evie had noticed sadly how her sweet-natured son was always so attentive and thoughtful. Maura would giggle and pout and Brendan would be at her side with a soft word, holding out his coat to keep her warm and dry. If they'd had children, perhaps they'd have had a common interest. But, Evie thought as she pressed her lips together, Maura's only interest was to keep Brendan under her thumb. She smiled. Brendan was like Jim, good-natured, indecisive and affable. But he was also her son, and he had her stubbornness. The worm would turn. She had sensed it when they last visited her in Sheldon Lodge. He was made of strong stuff; she was sure of it.

Evie surveyed the bar. Guests had started to arrive in groups. Billy the Banjo was already on his second pint and eating pork scratchings. She popped out into the backyard to ring Caroline, the friendly English woman she'd met selling her preserves in the market, and asked her if she and her partner would like to come to a proper Irish party at the pub in an hour or two. Caroline's voice was full of enthusiasm. She and Nige would be there later and she said how kind Evie was to think of her.

174

Evie leaned against the wall and her life in Sheldon Lodge popped up as a picture in her head. Bereaved, bored and going barmy, she thought, as she remembered the yoga classes with the old ladies and the ill-tempered Mrs Lofthouse and Barry the chef and lovely Ukrainian Alex. But now she was in France, organising a birthday bash and inviting friends. This was the life for her.

Noisy voices brought her out from deep thought; Paulette and the children shepherded Ray up the stairs to shower and change so that he wouldn't see what was going on in the bar. Ray protested good-naturedly in French and the children laughed as Paulette waved him on with a tirade of language Evie didn't understand.

The grin on Ray's face as he walked into the bar later stayed with him all night. As he took his usual position behind the pumps, everyone clapped and sang 'Happy Birthday', led by Billy. Ray beamed as he pulled the first pints. He sniffed the food and his nose turned up like the Bisto kid. Billy the Banjo took to the stage and launched into 'The Irish Rover' and Ray was still smiling at eight thirty, when Paulette joined him behind the bar in her party dress, the kids now fast asleep, to give him a huge kiss on the lips.

Caroline turned up in a long flowery dress with Nige, who had grey hair cropped closely to his head and round glasses. She and Evie discussed Simone de Beauvoir while Nige chatted fluently to a man in a cap who apparently lived near them and brought logs twice a year. Evie recognised the two little men she had been drinking with the night before. One of them was called Maurice; he remembered her and waved a greeting. She couldn't see the tall irritable man with the little ponytail and she was glad he was not there, brooding in the corner with his gloomy eyes.

175

The food was a great success and Evie felt the centre of attention. She drank two glasses of red wine and was talking to people she'd never met. A woman asked her for the Irish stew recipe and she promised that she would write it down with Paulette to help with the French. Caroline ate two helpings of the caramel rice pudding and said it was the best she'd ever tasted. The bar was busy. Paulette was right; people were standing in huge clusters, their arms straight out holding glasses for a refill, and Ray and Paulette were constantly darting about, fetching bottles and replenishing glasses and taking money.

Nige handed Caroline and Evie another glass of wine each, although neither had asked for one. Nige was chewing colcannon and bread and sipping his orange juice. Billy the Banjo was playing 'Whisky in the Jar' and a thought popped into Evie's head.

'Caroline, do you think you and Nige would ever go back to England?'

Caroline shook her auburn hair and answered without hesitation. 'Definitely not.' She explained that they had been living in the converted guest house for almost twenty years and as they had no children or ties, there was no reason to go back to England.

'But what about the people you left behind? Don't you miss friends and family?'

Caroline laughed. 'We have all we need here. Oh, I'd never go back, Evie. We did go to England for a few weeks when Nige's mum was ill. We stayed for the funeral, but we don't go back there much now. I have a brother but he lives in South Africa, and Nige's sister comes over for Christmas with her three kids and the dogs, but our friends are here. And we make new friends all the time.' She clutched Evie's arm and hugged her. 'Why'd you ask?'

'Not sure, really. I was just wondering what it is like to be here long-term. I'm just having such a good time here on holiday, but I don't know how long I will stay. I've a campervan so I can go wherever I like.'

'You travel by yourself? In a campervan?'

'Don't you start.' Evie laughed. 'I was cross with a doctor in the hospital. She told me I was too old to be travelling alone—'

'I think you're bloody marvellous,' Caroline interrupted.

Evie had never thought of herself as a role model. Suddenly, a hand touched her shoulder and a face came close to hers; she recognised the strong breath and the Waterford accent. It was Billy the Banjo.

'Evie, do you know "Danny Boy"?'

She nodded. 'Everybody knows "Danny Boy".'

Billy began to propel her towards the stage area. 'Duet with me. "Danny Boy".'

Evie took a gulp of wine. 'Ah, but I am not really a singer.'

Billy the Banjo indicated the room with a toss of his head. 'Sure, they're all pissed. Nobody will notice.'

Then they were on stage and he pushed the microphone towards Evie. He put on his warm voice for the crowd. '*Mesdames et Messieurs*, Ladies and Gentlemen. *Voici la chanteuse la plus célèbre Irlandaise, Evie, et la chanson la plus célèbre de mon pays, Irlande.* "Danny Boy".'

'What did you say to them?' Evie asked in a whisper.

'Oh I just told them it was your first time on stage and to give you a big round of applause.'

Certainly, everyone was cheering and, as Billy the Banjo played the first notes, Evie took a gulp of wine, closed her eyes and started to sing. She and Billy the Banjo got through the first verse about the pipes calling and she found her voice on '*But come ye back when summer's in*

177

the meadow', and by the final '*I'll simply sleep in peace until you come to me*', she and Billy were competing with each other for the mic. Evie's voice wobbled on the high notes but she was enjoying herself. A cheer went up for an encore and she decided to sing an octave lower as they began the last verse again. She opened her eyes and was thrilled to see the crowd smiling and clapping. The man in the beret, Maurice, was wiping tears from his face and Caroline and Nige were clenching their fists and encouraging her on. She glanced across at Ray who blew her a kiss and Paulette waved.

The song ended, Billy the Banjo offered up a flurry of final notes and the applause echoed around O'Driscoll's Bar. Evie was mouthing her thank-yous when she saw him. He was leaning on the bar, a glass in his hand, not clapping. His little ponytail stuck out from beneath the cap and his eyes were shining. She felt mischief rising through her lungs and she blew him a kiss. He continued to stare without looking away.

Evie grabbed the mic and brushed the blonde fringe from her eyes. 'I am so glad you are all having a good time tonight, on this special celebration, Ray's birthday,' she cooed sweetly, batted her lashes and looked directly at the grumpy man. 'I want to say how nice it is to meet such lovely people in France, so kind and so welcoming and so friendly.' The applause became louder and she curtseyed.

At this point she was Edith Piaf in her little black dress; she was on the verge of asking Billy the Banjo if he knew '*Non, Je Ne Regrette Rien*' when she realised she didn't actually know the words. She smiled beatifically at the audience and suddenly wanted to speak to them in French. She raised her hands in appreciation, then took a bow. '*Merci.*' She thought again. '*Je t'aime.*' The applause was even louder. She racked her brain for another phrase but decided that '*Voulez-vous coucher avec moi ce soir*' wasn't really going to fit the bill.

She bowed again and Billy helped her down from the stage area and began playing another tune. She joined Caroline and Nige who both said she was wonderful. She made her excuses, saying that she was going to visit the ladies' room, and edged towards the bar, deliberately squeezing through the drinkers until she was behind the ill-tempered man who was leaning over a drink at the bar, his back hunched and square. She was not about to let a grumpy man ignore her performance. She muttered to herself, 'So he won't clap, then? I'll show him.'

She wriggled between him and a man holding out a glass and she called out to Ray, who was pulling a pint from a long-handled pump. 'What did you think of my song, Ray? It was for you, on your birthday.'

Ray winked. 'Wonderful, Evie, love. Top class.'

She heard the cantankerous tall man make a sound through his nose. She looked at him, directly meeting the chestnut eyes. 'And just what is your problem?' She batted her eyelashes. 'You have a problem with emancipated women who enjoy themselves, do you?'

The man was a little taken aback at first, but he soon found his composure. 'I have no problem, Madame. But it appears that you do. You sing like a frog.'

Her heart pounded. She met his eyes. They were dark and brooding, tormented eyes as she'd imagined Heathcliff's to be, but she wouldn't look away. He had just insulted her singing.

'And you look like a bloody toad.' Evie made herself as tall as she could, but she barely came to his shoulder. 'A big, ridiculous, rude toad. No wonder you are by yourself and have no friends. You are just fecking miserable.

179

You need to get a life and stop being such a miserable bollix.'

She narrowed her eyes and watched what he would do next. He gave an exaggerated shrug with his big shoulders, and pulled a creased face. 'Who knows? Maybe you are right.'

He looked sad for a moment, and she felt the instinct to put out her hand and pat his shoulder, to comfort him. She looked at her hand and mentally willed it to be still. She had drunk too much wine again. She supposed it was part and parcel of being in France. She met his eyes again and found she couldn't look away. The big man breathed out deeply, a sigh like a volcano, then he turned his face back to Evie.

'But it was a miserable song, all about death. I dislike all this morbid remembrance of death of which you people sing. And you, Madame, you still have the voice of a frog.'

He took another swig from his glass. Evie put her hands on her hips and stared at him.

'And just why are you so rude? What is it you have a bee in your bonnet about, for goodness sake?'

He shook his head. She noticed his broad shoulders, his deep-set eyes, and she felt her pulse pound in her throat. He would have been good-looking once, but his face was sad, ravaged by lines around his mouth, presumably from being so miserable.

His voice rumbled from somewhere deep in his chest. 'You English people with your sayings, bees and bonnets. I suggest you go back where you came from, Madame, and take your terrible songs with you, and leave me in peace.'

'I'm not English, I'm Irish,' she breathed, and stared at him for a few moments, taking in the leather skin and iron grey hair, the tattered jacket and the Bob Dylan T-shirt.

180

'I'd wish you a nice night, but I don't think you'll have one, you being so grumpy and all.' She marched away, her heart beating hard and her fists clenched.

Ten minutes later, she was talking pointedly about 'Danny Boy' to Caroline and Nige, trying to push Mr Grumpy away from her thoughts. Nige thought it was a Scottish song. He was offering cashew nuts from a bowl to everyone who came past.

'Why does everything have to be Scottish?' Evie asked, remembering the couple she had met at the night market in Marmande. 'Or English.' She glanced across towards Mr Grumpy, who was still leaning against the bar and had his back to her. She noticed the stretch of muscle across his shoulders encased in the leather of his jacket.

'It mentions pipes and glens – aren't they Scottish?' Nige had drunk three orange juices but he appeared merrier than anyone, swinging his hands up and down to show what glens were.

Caroline took his arm affectionately. 'It was written by an English lawyer. Based on a tune called the "Londonderry Air".'

'Irish, then,' Evie insisted.

Nige was round-eyed with admiration. 'How did you know that, Caroline?'

'Pub quiz champion, 1985.'

They laughed and Nige began to talk to them about his plans for the cellar and how he could use it for wine storage. Caroline was explaining that they could create a gym or a sauna, even a hot tub, and she invited Evie to visit them and stay for dinner in a few days' time. Evie peeped between them and noticed Mr Grumpy was still at the bar. She resumed listening intently to them both talking across each other; her mouth was full of nuts and she tried to think about dinner with Caroline and a visit to the free tasting she had promised herself, when there was a crash of glasses from the bar.

Over her shoulder, she saw two men were fighting, fists raised and legs kicking, and Ray's worried face as he steered Paulette to the back of the bar area. There was another loud shout, which sounded like swearing, and one man had a beer glass which he broke and pushed towards the other's face. An arc of beer flew from a glass and there were punches and a wooden stool was shattered as someone fell back onto the floor, knocking into an old man. There was more screaming and the flurry of knuckles. Ray was trying to position himself between the two men but they were locked like battling bulls and he couldn't separate them. A space widened around them, and they lurched backwards into the crowd; one of them knocked Evie forward and Caroline caught her and kept her upright. The men were on the floor and the sound of their voices snarling was like slavering dogs. They rolled and spat and fists rose and descended.

They were pulled apart and noise became silence as the two men snarled at each other. The tall irritable man held them up, one in each hand, where they drooped like coats from a hanger. He said something to them in a soft, slow voice and put them down gently, at a distance from each other. One of the men had spattered blood on his shirt and Ray was there with a first-aid kit. The injured man was still angry and he pulled his hands away from his stomach and cried out.

There was blood on the other man's forehead, a handkerchief stopping the cut. Ray and Paulette were tending to the groaning man who was bent double, clutching his belly, a woman next to him, holding his hand. Ray joked that it was nothing more than a little flesh wound, a plaster would probably do it and he'd be right as rain in the morning. The other man moved away.

182

Evie's eyes sought out the bad-tempered man. He was leaning over, catching his breath at the bar, as he swallowed the last of his drink. He met her eyes, and he nodded briefly at her before walking away, his wide shoulders and his black cap sliding swiftly through the crowd before he disappeared behind groups of drinkers. She watched him go, and wondered what made him so grumpy, whether he had a difficult life, whether he had a nice wife at home to cheer him up. Obviously not. He was too miserable – who'd want to live with a man like him? Billy the Banjo struck up his chords and he began to sing 'Dirty Old Town'.

'What was that all about?' she asked Caroline.

'It happened so quickly.'

Nige shrugged. 'A party isn't a party without a good fight.' He finished his orange juice in a swig. 'They'll be best friends again tomorrow.'

It was almost midnight. She went over to the food and helped herself to a sausage and some cold colcannon. The last of the Dublin coddle bubbled in a slow cooker, still warm, so she spooned it on top of the potatoes and cabbage. She lifted the fork to her mouth, watching Ray move chairs and Paulette clean glasses. Billy the Banjo packed away and put his arm around Marion, who looked at him with adoring eyes. Caroline and Nige helped each other into their coats and the man with the winded belly was happy enough, his arm around his opponent, who now had a plaster over one eye. Evie finished her food and watched the couples going about their business and she yawned: it had been a long day and she was ready for bed.

She turned to go upstairs to her room, but stood still again and recalled her conversation with the irritable man. He spoke good English, with a little American twang, and she wondered where he had lived to become so fluent. She frowned and remembered Ray's words; the reverential way he spoke about him . . . she recalled his name, Jean-Luc. She thought of how readily and skilfully he had stopped the fight, how others seemed to respect him. She thought again about the glow of his eyes, the rumble of his voice, and how sad he seemed. He had leaned against the bar, alone, his broad shoulders set, as if the troubles of the world rested on them. He had criticised her voice, been quick to insult her. She had set him straight though, she thought, and she felt pleased with herself. She took the thought upstairs with her and was still thinking about the irritable man as she slid between the covers and closed her eyes.

Chapter Twenty-Seven

The Panda, with a full tank and its new radiator, idled outside Clémence's bed and breakfast and the sun was seething. Brendan was at the wheel and they were saying their goodbyes. Maura stood with her new friends and she was effusive, kissing Clémence and her husband and Olivier on both cheeks and handing Clémence flowers and saying what a good time she had shared with them. Brendan was conscious of the nagging ache in his chest. He glanced out of the window at the road in front of him. He stared at his hands on the steering wheel, at his wedding ring and up at Maura who still had her back to him.

'We should be leaving, Maura. It's past three.'

'We have a map, Brendan.' She spoke without turning, as if a map solved all their problems. He made a mental note of distances: it was seven hours to Foix and so he could do it in two days if they made an overnight stop. Bordeaux was halfway there, somewhere in the middle of the route, and there might be a nice hotel, although he dreaded the hours he would spend in the car with Maura, or the minutes they would spend sitting across a table. He waited quietly until she was in the passenger seat and he drove the car away, Maura trailing her waving hand through the window. The face she turned back to him lost its smile almost immediately.

'Where are we staying tonight?'

His mouth searched for placatory words but those days were over and he needed to be clearer, tougher. 'Bordeaux,' he replied, thinking that a laconic answer would be safest.

'How many hours to Bordeaux?'

'Three, four. We can be in Foix tomorrow.'

'Thank God for that.' She delved into her bag, took out sunglasses and put them on, then found a CD of her choice and leaned back in her seat. Brendan swung the Panda onto a busy road and took his place in a line of traffic.

It was half past eight when they arrived on the outskirts of Bordeaux. Maura demanded a hotel with a restaurant and Brendan was happy to oblige her; it was her only conversation with him for the whole journey. They put their cases in the room, changed and shared a silent meal. Brendan yawned and made a move to go upstairs. Maura put a hand on his arm and her sudden touch made him jump.

'Should we have a little walk outside and get some air before we go to sleep, Brendan? Just to take the air and have a look at Bordeaux at night? I expect we shall be off to Foix tomorrow straight after breakfast, to find your mother.'

She was trying her best. Brendan's stomach lurched in anticipation and he left her in the foyer looking at the décor while he popped upstairs for a jacket for them both.

As they stepped out, she took his arm and he wondered if she was holding onto him for her own protection. He inhaled the strong cloud of perfume that surrounded her. They walked without speaking for a while, looking pointlessly in shop windows. A clock from a church chimed eleven; Brendan hoped the hotel doors would not be shut, and he suggested that they turn back soon. Maura was thinking; she was working out how to say something to him. He did not help her out – the silence was a better companion than anything she might say. He heard her breathe in.

'Brendan . . .'

He waited.

'Do you think . . . you know, when we find your mother and we go back to Dublin . . . Do you think . . .?'

He could hear her struggling to find the words.

'Is there any chance that we might . . .?'

Brendan was quiet for a moment. He could feel her thoughts, but the memories of her, tender and twenty and clinging to his arm, resting her head against his shoulder, left him hollow. 'A fresh start? I hope so. I don't know, Maura.'

They walked on. She took another breath. 'I'd like it if we could both try.' He felt the tension in her body as her arm, looped through his, became stiffer. 'Can I ask you something?'

'Anything.' He wondered if she would ask him if he had feelings for another woman, if he had feelings for anyone else. Or if he had any feelings left at all.

She was swallowing something painful. Perhaps it was pride, perhaps it was the softness of memories, but they clogged her throat. 'In a perfect world . . . you know, Brendan, if everything was ideal . . . what sort of wife would you like me to be?'

Brendan didn't reply. She went on. 'I mean, what might make things better between us? How could I win you back?'

He winced. The word 'win' implied that Maura was prepared to make some kind of effort to make their

187

marriage work again. He lurched for an answer and one didn't come, then out of desperation, a sentence came out of his mouth.

'We would share more things together.'

'What sort of things?'

'Activities.'

'Oh, you mean sex?'

The muscles in his stomach contracted as he thought of her cold back, turned against him for the last few nights. Her fingernails gripped the flesh of his arm. He forced a smile. 'Not necessarily, I mean other things too.'

'What other things?'

He thought for a moment and it came to him. 'White-water rafting.' He tried again. 'Cycling, maybe.'

Her placatory mood suddenly shifted and her eyes narrowed. 'You want me to go white-water rafting, Brendan? Are you mad?'

He pulled his arm away. It was better to say nothing. She spoke again, more insistent.

'You want me to ride a bike?' Her nose wrinkled with the memory of Evie's words about how she should share her husband's hobbies, and she puffed air from her lungs, annoyed. 'Me? On a bike?'

Brendan tried to keep his voice level. 'No, Maura, I don't want you to ride a bike. I don't want you to go white-water rafting. You are right. It wouldn't work. We don't seem to be able to share anything.' He put his head down, turned them around and they began the walk back to the hotel. When they arrived in the foyer, he wanted to go up to bed and Maura hesitated. She was quiet, thoughtful; she had something on her mind. Turning away from Brendan, she said she'd stay in the bar. She needed a coffee and some time to think.

He climbed the stairs feeling miserable. In the bedroom,

he pulled on pyjamas and rolled onto the cold bed. His mind was crowded with images, he recalled some photographs of himself and Maura as they were five years ago, their arms around each other, smiling. He'd suggested a walking holiday in England and they'd visited the Lake District together. He'd bought her walking boots and they'd taken packed lunches and backpacks and set off to climb Great Gable. He'd found a steady rhythm in his legs and a repetitive pop song in his head, which had given his stride speed and purpose. Before long, Maura was lagging behind, and he'd turned to see her, red-faced and tired, holding out her hand to him. He'd pulled her along, helping her climb the scree section, which she managed on hands and knees. He'd been impressed by her humour then, and her gritty perseverance.

At the top, they'd stood, the wind in their faces, gaping at the greys and greens of the hills. Brendan had been exhilarated and Maura thrilled that she had made it to the summit. She'd hugged him and told him she felt on top of the world. He'd promised he'd get her the Death by Chocolate pudding in the hotel that night, with extra cream; she'd been so determined and they'd asked a passing hiker to take a photo of them, the lakes in the background. He remembered, he'd felt like his heart was singing and he could never be happier than he was with this spontaneous, lovely and affectionate woman, his own wife.

Brendan blamed himself, and he felt the blame crash down on him like a tall pile of toppling books. One after the other, he saw each reason why it was all his fault. He did not communicate well. He could not make a decision. He'd become critical, negative, inattentive. His mother had never liked Maura; she'd never thought her an equal partner for her golden boy, and Brendan worried that he had been influenced, made arrogant by his mother's doting

189

fondness. He had become detached, selfish, and he was entirely to blame.

He turned over in the bed and became aware of the emptiness of his arms. He picked up the pillow on Maura's side, folded it, hugged it close. He put his lips against the cotton of the pillow case, breathed in the scent of her musky perfume and wondered how it would sound if he murmured her name, practised how it would feel to kiss her lips, a long lingering kiss. Brendan realised that he missed those days when everything was easy between him and his wife. The days they dreamed of the same things, hoped for the same future. It could have been so different. Conversation, laughter, love, children. He frowned and put a hand to his face. His cheek was damp.

He rolled over again and stared into the darkness. What would happen when he went back to Dublin? Would they still have a marriage? How could they repair the tattered shreds of what was once whole, warm and good? Brendan thought about his mother. She wasn't far away. He could ring her, tell her where he was, ask her to help him. His brow creased. She was an old lady now. He was nearly forty himself and wasn't he man enough to sort out his own marriage, to find his own mother and to take her home? He scratched his head. He wasn't even sure now that his own mother would be pleased to see him. He wondered again what he was doing in France, intruding on her holiday, and he suddenly had no idea what he should do next. He felt alone, precariously dangling from a rope and he could not see what was above him or below. He squeezed his eyes closed and fell into erratic sleep.

Breakfast the next day was at eight thirty and Maura was humming a cheerful little tune. She was wearing jogging pants and one of Brendan's T-shirts and pink trainers and was obviously hungry. Her crimson nails snatched at the fibrous softness of a baguette and Brendan thought of a dinosaur eating its prey as she ripped the bread apart and the jam stuck to her lips. He sipped coffee and looked worriedly out of the window. She continued to hum happily to herself, dabbed her mouth and then remarked about the weather.

Brendan noticed the flirtatious way she looked at him and away again, the smile which kept playing around her lips until she hid it coyly with the back of her hand. He felt nervous and refilled his cup. He was determined to try harder today, to give her attention. Perhaps things had started well.

'What time are we leaving?' Maura gave him her widest smile.

'After breakfast. We can be on our way and in Foix for a late lunch and find the Irish bar. There can't be too many of them over here.' Brendan was pleased with his last remark and hoped she'd find him witty. He smiled, sure she'd like his plan: lunch together, quality time.

He stood up, but she did not move. Maura was looking at her nails, which she held curled inwards like a cat's claw. She made a low noise in her throat and raised a provocative eyebrow in his direction.

He felt his pulse thump. 'What's the matter, Maura?'

'Ah, I just thought we could . . .' She made a movement with her head, as if she could cajole him from a distance. He frowned. 'We could actually go to Foix tomorrow instead of today, couldn't we?'

'What did you have in mind?'

'Well, I have booked us a secret surprise.' She sat back in her seat and licked crumbs from her lips.

Brendan blinked, feeling suddenly that his plan was veering off course. 'What sort of surprise?'

'Well, I don't want to spoil it—'

'What sort of surprise, Maura?'

'Right, OK, an hour or so away from here is a big lake in a town called Soustons. Well, it's a town but it has lots of facilities. And a beach. I have booked us something special – a surprise, for us to do together.'

Brendan did not move. He eyed her suspiciously. 'What are we doing on this lake?'

'Ah, I have booked us some . . . activities, to share.' She stroked his hand and Brendan's shoulders lifted towards his ears. He saw the jogging pants and the T-shirt and at once he understood.

'I booked it last night after you had gone to bed. It's all arranged. It'll be fun.' Maura clasped her fingers and leaned forward, her eyes bright with hope.

Brendan pressed his lips together. Maura was still smiling. He shrugged. He'd give it his best shot. 'Well, we'd better get ready then. Mammy will wait until tomorrow, I'm sure. I'll ring her tonight and tell her we're coming, will I?'

She scraped back her chair and threw her arms around him. 'Come on then, Brendan. Oh, I am so looking forward to this!'

He followed her, leaving his breakfast untouched, pushing his hands deep in his pockets. He wondered what to do to make the day as successful as the ascent of Great Gable on their holiday years ago. He was at the bottom of a climb, looking up, and he felt his legs grow weak.

Chapter Twenty-Eight

Her smile was wide, a slice of melon. She gaped at the view in Soustons, the thickly wooded shoreline down to the lake, mottled green with water lilies. The smooth surface was flecked with gliding swans, ripples behind them as they slipped through the water. There was a pier made of planks of wood and, to one side, little cabins. Further to the right there were blue and white catamarans, bending and weaving along the lake. Soustons was an ideal place for water sports. Maura clapped her hands together and Brendan thought about the different activities he could try. They drove on to the beach where their bodyboarding instructor had arranged to meet them. Maura carried the holdall, still with its label attached, containing their new sports clothes.

At the *accueil*, the reception area which looked more like a hut, they were met by Mathieu. He wore shorts, a bright T-shirt and orange-framed sunglasses, which lodged on top of his dark curls. He asked them if they spoke French and Brendan explained that he did, so Mathieu told them he would explain everything in English as the instructions were quite complex. Maura had booked two activities: in the early afternoon they would try body-boarding and afterwards they would go for a bike ride. Mathieu would be their instructor for the bodyboarding and he suggested that they change into the wet suits, and he would meet them down by the water.

Maura's smile diminished when she emerged in the wet suit. She moved awkwardly, her body shrugging from side to side on flat feet. She was like a seal, slick and shiny and out of place on land. Brendan had surfed before and he was ready for the lesson. Mathieu would start them both off, and then he would concentrate on helping Maura, the beginner, who smiled and covered her embarrassment by batting mascara-laden lashes at him. The instructor was strongly muscled; he spoke excellent English and Maura giggled and patted his arm. Brendan wondered if he would be able to go off on his own for a few minutes, once Mathieu was satisfied with his competence. He bit his lip. His own voice echoed in his ears. It had been his suggestion to share an activity together, and he ought to stay with her. The instructor gave them a board each, which Maura held out straight in front of her like a tray, and they walked in a line towards the area designated for the activity, Maura at the back, fumbling with her board and trotting and running a bit to keep up.

Mathieu gave them the initial coaching, Maura smiling, then laughing when she slithered off the surface and rolled in the water, her face wet and reddening. Brendan mounted his board; he found it easy and was splashing in the water, watching her.

She looked over at him. 'I'm not sure I'm getting the hang of this. You go off, Brendan. Enjoy yourself. It'll take me a while to get going.'

'Are you sure?' He smiled at her, hopefully.

'I'm a novice. I'll be all right here with Mathieu. You're

much more experienced. Go on with you. I want you to enjoy today.'

Brendan pecked her cheek then swam out into deeper water, enjoying some solitary time bodyboarding; gripping his board as he launched himself through the water, slicing the surf. He felt the power in his legs as he kicked against the roll of the water; he pushed himself forward and felt himself lift and launch on his board. He remembered Yeats and wondered what the poet himself might have written about surfing, had he been given the opportunity. He floated on the surface of the water and turned round and waved to Maura. She waved back. She was still trying to lie on the board which shifted away from her grasp. He would have a few more moments by himself, then go back and help her, and she'd manage fine, just as they had done when they'd climbed Great Gable. He would offer her a hand, encourage her, and she would be pleased with him.

He plunged once more into the rising surf, balancing his board and crashing into the wave, letting it push and support him before he leaned forward and dived down into the water. The swell lifted him and he waited for the next roll, thrilling in the idea that it might be stronger than him; it might throw him up, hurl him down, hold him beneath. Brendan could not remember the last time he had diced so closely with chance, when life was so unpredictable, so excitingly dangerous. He was like a sea creature himself, a velvet dolphin, free and at play in the sea. The water rose and hurled him upwards again and his heart knocked in his chest as he hugged the board and kicked himself forward. The surf was violent and strong, spraying him, and he cried out as he felt the electric pulsing of his skin. The water on his face revived him; he blinked his eyes and looked back towards the shoreline.

Maura was still there, the wet suit bobbing black in the

water, splashing for a moment, and then she disappeared. Her head came up again, her arms waving in the air and threshing hard against the water. He turned to head back as the surf swelled behind him once more. He swam to the shore, his legs strong and his heart pounding, a smile stuck on his face. Maura was spitting and coughing. Mathieu held up her board and she turned to Brendan.

He had seen pictures of the seventies rock singer Alice Cooper, with black make-up streaked down his face. Alice Cooper sang 'School's Out' and the teachers had always played the song at the end of each term in the staff room, singing the lyrics loudly and drinking wine. Maura presented a similar picture to the rock star, wiggly lines of vertical mascara, an insistent symmetry painted from each eye to the corners of her mouth. She saw him staring at her and she was suddenly anxious. Quickly, she dipped her cupped hands in the water twice, three times, splashing her face clean. He put his hand out and wiped a smudge of damp mascara from her cheek. She looked up at him, her face gleaming. A feeling surged through him, not unlike tenderness.

She presented her best smile. 'So, have you had a good time, Brendan?'

'Yes, I've really enjoyed myself, thanks.' He thought for a minute. 'Did you like the bodyboarding?'

She shrugged, her grin wide. 'I'm not much use at these things though. And the wet suit doesn't really do me any favours.'

He nodded. 'Wet suits don't really flatter people's bodies.' He saw her expression change; she was hurt and he immediately regretted the remark. His cheeks burned. His comment was obtuse, crass, and he wondered why he always said the wrong thing to her. She was sweet in her wet suit, smiling and cheerful in the water, and he wanted to say something flattering, something which would make everything all right.

He tried again. 'Can I help you get the hang of it on the board? I mean, I've had a lovely time out there. What if we did a little bodyboarding together? I'm sure I could help you get quite good at it.'

She shook her head. 'I fancy a break, a coffee, maybe a sandwich. I've booked the cycling for later. We'll do that after lunch?'

Brendan turned to Mathieu and thanked him for instructing his wife. He held out his hand and took Maura's and they walked out of the water together. Brendan thought of James Bond and Ursula Andress in her white bikini in *Dr No*. Maura gazed up at him and smiled back.

'This was a great idea, Maura. I'm so glad you decided to organise it. Thank you.' He bent down and kissed her cheek, which was cold and wet. 'Let's get lunch, will we? I need a shower. I'm starving.'

They sat inside a café and ate ham sandwiches, shared a plate of chips and drank coffee. Brendan persuaded Maura that they'd enjoy a doughnut, that it might be good energy food before the cycling, and he bought one for each of them, with jam and cream. She chattered happily, licking sugar from her fingers, and told him that she'd booked a hotel for the evening and they could have a special dinner together. She was fresh and scrubbed clean, her skin flushed from the shower. Her hair was damp and he noticed the little dimples in her cheeks. Brendan took her hand and thought about holding it to his lips. He sat back in his seat, confident in the new Lycra cycle shorts and a bright racing top they'd bought on the way. Maura looked bright and cheerful in a sports shirt and jogging bottoms, and she was clearly excited.

'Well, Brendan, I said you'd never get me on a bike but, I have to say, I'm really looking forward to this part of the day.' He smiled and told himself that things were

197

changing for the better. The shared activities would bring them together. This was a fresh start.

They turned up to collect their bicycles; the *accueil* was a simple reception area, a large shed full of bicycles, surrounded by woodland. Brendan gave his name and the instructor nodded and wheeled out a shiny red tandem. Brendan stared at it; he had imagined himself cycling alone, Maura behind him on her own machine. Their instructor, Louis, explained that the ride should take two hours and they should stick to the designated routes on the signposts. He gave them crash hats to wear. Maura suggested that Brendan take the front of the tandem and she would help at the back. Brendan climbed on and she struggled across the frame, quivering, lifting her leg and nervously putting it down again, until they were in position.

Brendan leaned over his shoulder. 'Just time it with me, Maura. I'll set us off. That is the difficult part.'

The launch was not easy. Maura wailed and wobbled nervously then screamed with excitement, putting her feet down and asking if they could start again. They began, rolled forward, tottered and stopped, Maura laughing and Brendan concentrating hard, a frown on his face. On the sixth attempt, they were off, making precarious pressure on the pedals with Brendan pushing the machine forward and Maura teetering nervously in the saddle behind.

The route took them on a path around the woods. Maura was pedalling furiously, keeping in time with Brendan. He spoke to her over his shoulder, checking she felt secure. She was behind him, balancing awkwardly, as he urged the bike forward, his voice encouraging. He turned them towards an incline and raised himself out of the saddle. Moments later there was a lurch behind him as Maura did the same and, together, their breaths synchronised, they pushed harder on the pedals, propelling the tandem forward. He felt her head rest against his back for a moment, then she wrapped an arm around his waist and held on tightly for a moment before gripping both handlebars again.

The woods smelled of sharp fresh pine and the sun streaked through the gaps in the leaves, creating an enchanted forest of light and dark then light again as the tandem snaked along the paths. Maura was developing confidence behind him, saying little. She was out of breath, occasionally asking if they could stop for a rest soon. Brendan grunted, and heaved the bike around corners, pounding down the pedals and leaning over the handlebars to gain good momentum, deciding that the faster they went the less work Maura would have to do. She stopped pedalling for a moment; there was a groan and she started again, slowly at first, then with more effort.

'You're doing well, Maura.' He heard a moan and she stopped pedalling, and then he felt her kick again.

He decided she needed a break so they turned off the path and stopped beneath a huge tree with drooping leaves and thick gnarled bark. He remembered carving their initials in such a tree, not long after they'd met. MF & BG. Maura Flanagan and Brendan Gallagher. He stood astride the bike, lifted a leg and stood on solid ground, holding the tandem upright.

Maura put both feet on the floor, straddling the bike. 'How do I get off?'

Brendan held the tandem still with one hand and took her arm in the other. He eased her forwards and she stood awkwardly, rubbing her bottom. 'I'll be stiff in the morning. The saddle's really uncomfortable.'

He laid the bike down and offered her his hand, palm outstretched. 'But are you enjoying it?'

'Oh, I'm loving it, spending time with you. It's like a proper holiday.' Her eyes shone.

They sat beneath a tree, Maura bending precariously and easing herself to a comfortable position. Brendan stretched out his legs. They were hairy and pale beneath the shorts. He took her hand. 'I'm so glad you organised this. It's been really good fun.'

She snuggled close to him and put her head on his shoulder. 'Brendan, I'm not very good at the sports. I mean, I was hopeless at school. I was always the one last to be picked in the teams. I wish I was better.'

He wrapped an arm round her. 'We're together and enjoying ourselves. That's the main thing. Sharing something we can both do. Everyone can ride a bike and the open air is so nice.'

She breathed out, chewing her lip. 'That's what has been wrong with us, hasn't it? We need to share things more.'

He nodded. 'Maybe we can start again. I can share what you want to do and you can do the same for me. It'll all be fine.'

She was thoughtful. 'If . . . I mean, if we'd had a family, Brendan—' He lifted a finger and thought about placing it on her lips. Her eyes filled. 'If we'd had babbies, well, we'd have naturally shared all this, wouldn't we?'

He shrugged. 'We're fine, Maura. Don't think about all that. We'll be just fine.'

'I just thought—'

'We'll be all right.'

She snuggled into the crook of his arm, and he leaned over and kissed the top of her head. Her curls tickled his face and he grinned, and kissed her forehead. She smiled. 'Ah, but you're right, Brendan. Everything'll be just fine.'

He stood up and held out his hand. 'Come on, my love. Will we get back in the saddle?'

She allowed him to pull her up and then she straddled

the tandem, frowning at the discomfort. She smiled at Brendan. 'I'm ready for round two.'

Brendan started them off and the bike rode bumpily down the path. Maura giggled and, after a few minutes, he felt her rest her head against his back.

They reached an open road. There was a sharp descent and Brendan saw the opportunity to pick up speed, to free-wheel down the hill, the wind in his face, gravel crunching beneath the bike. Maura squealed behind him, a peal of delight and excitement caused by the thrill of their acceleration. He pressed harder on the pedals to gain as much velocity as he could and then he steered the tandem towards the steep incline. They picked up speed and plummeted down the hill, lurching forward, the wheels spinning and his legs whirling and his hair flattened by the breeze. Brendan lifted his head back and gulped in the passing air. The feeling of freedom filled his lungs as the bike hurtled down the slope and Brendan whooped out loud. Maura's voice lifted on the air and they were both shrieking with joy.

The tandem must have hit a pot hole. Something thudded against him, hitting him in the back, and he felt the bike slip from beneath him. The weight of Maura's unbalanced body slammed against his and he heard her shrieks in his ears as he felt the bike snagging to the left and away from him, causing him to react instinctively. He braked, felt the bike lift behind him and he shot forwards, putting out his hands, crunching down on hard metal and gravel as Maura crashed on top of his shoulders with a howl. He felt the impact and heard a sickening snap and felt himself roll over on the ground, grit embedding in his face. He stayed where he was. Maura clambered to her feet. The groan was his own voice; he tried to sit up and saw Maura looking at her leg. Her jogging bottoms were torn open and blood was trickling from little cuts. Dizziness overtook him and he slumped backwards and heard her repeating his name.

He opened his eyes and tried to sit again. His arm hurt and he couldn't lift it. Maura had her phone out and was speaking into it. He tried to focus his vision. She was kneeling next to him.

'Brendan, how are you feeling? I think you passed out. You're a horrible colour.'

'What happened?'

'We fell. We were going too fast. We hit something – a hole in the road. I've phoned for help. You have a lot of cuts on your legs and I am covered in grazes and – oh, what's the matter with your wrist?'

'Is the tandem all right?'

'Sod the tandem.' Her voice rose in consternation. 'Brendan, your wrist is swelling up and it looks like it could be sprained or even broken.'

He was going to be sick, sitting askew on the gravel with the metal of the bike beneath him. He struggled to his feet but the world around him would not stay steady and he sat down. Maura crouched next to him, her voice soothing as molasses.

'You sit still now. Someone will be here in a minute. Try not to move anything.'

The doctor insisted on speaking in English. Maura was all right except for some cuts and bruises. Brendan had abrasions to his elbow and his legs and he had definitely broken his wrist. The arrangements would be made with the holiday insurance company in Dublin and they would be driven to a hotel. The doctor would ring them in the morning, when Brendan was able to concentrate a little better.

He slept fitfully on his back and couldn't turn over. His

202

wrist was strapped tightly and it throbbed, despite the painkillers. His flesh was scratched, taut and painful on his legs, and his elbow pulsated under the bandage where the skin had been dragged off. He was conscious of Maura in deep sleep next to him. He was worried about what would happen the next day, how they would make the journey to his mother.

The next day, Maura was up early and wearing a flowing skirt which wrapped around her waist and exposed the length of her leg. Little plasters were stuck across her skin. She was wearing the silly sling-backs and a thin, pink T-shirt and complained that her skin would never be the same again on her legs with all the cuts and grazes.

After breakfast, they returned to the hotel room and she phoned the doctor, listening carefully, interrupting only with the words, 'Of course, Doctor, I understand.'

She put the phone down and turned to Brendan. Her mouth was firm: she was back in the reception of the doctor's surgery in Dublin, telling a patient what to do. She was in charge.

'The doctor says you can't drive for up to four weeks.'

'That's got to be wrong.'

'No, Brendan, Dr Poussin was very clear about it. Four weeks is usual, he says.'

He groaned. 'I wish you'd have taken your test back in Dublin.'

'It can't be helped. I can't drive and we're stuck here.'

'Then I'll have to drive.'

'You can't, it's dangerous. Besides, it may jeopardise your recovery. The doctor said so.'

'What'll we do?' He reached for another painkiller. He balanced the sore wrist, in its plaster casing, carefully on his knee.

'We'll go to Saint-Jean-de-Luz and find a hotel. Someone from the centre at Soustons has offered to drive us there in our car, which is lovely of them. They were so nice about it all. Saint-Jean-de Luz looks a nice place, by the sea. We can stay there for a while, make it a proper holiday.'

'But what about my plan to ring Mammy? To take her home?'

'Your mother will have to wait, Brendan. She's not expecting us. No. We'll have four weeks or so there and then when, and only when, your wrist is better we'll pop over and see her.'

'Who knows where she'll be by then, Maura?'

'It's decided, Brendan. The doctor agrees with me and the holiday insurance will help out while your wrist is broken. It's a good job we have it: it means we can claim it all back once we're back, doctor's bills and extras. We just have to think of it as our own holiday. Time for us. It's such a good thing the summer holiday is as long as it is in Ireland. We've been away for over three weeks and another four will still give us time to get back for the new term. Now you lie there. I'll bring you some water and an aspirin and then I'll do the packing. You just rest and leave it all to me.'

He lay back on the bed. His head hurt and his wrist was painful. He closed his eyes, and behind aching lids he heard Maura singing a little tune as she busied herself happily with the packing. The image of the fall was still in his head, the crack of his wrist, and the thud of her body as she smashed against his back, the impact like a sledgehammer. He squeezed his eyelids together. She continued to hum the song as she bustled around the room and it wriggled itself around like a worm in his head as he fell into an exhausted sleep.

Chapter Twenty-Nine

The windscreen magnified the sunlight into pure heat and Evie pulled in to the side of the road to check her map. She was nearly there; she might even have passed it, she wasn't sure. The business card said it was called 'Cave Bonheur' and it was definitely somewhere along this road. She took a swig of water from the bottle and started the engine again, pulling out after the last car and travelling slowly so that she could look for the place. Several cars overtook her, the roaring acceleration in her ears making her jump. Then she saw it. She almost went past it, but for the sign, an incongruous twenty-foot-tall bottle made of wood that signalled her destination.

She parked next to the giant bottle so that she could get out and stare up at it. A two-dimensional bottle of red wine, with the label 'Cave Bonheur', it was made out of plywood. The colours had faded in the sunlight and the grain of the wood was dry and split. Across the bottle label were the words *Dégustation gratuite: vente des vins en vrac*. She had no idea what it meant, but she burst out laughing. It was leaning at an angle, to one side, as if struggling to hold up its own weight, as if it could topple at any moment.

'It must be good, this free wine-tasting. The bottle's pissed already.' She chuckled again.

The building comprised a large house with walls that had once been white, overlooking a paved courtyard. There were shady trees to the side, and the sunlight made dappled patterns on the ground. In the distance she could see rows of vines, neatly ordered, rising like little trees towards the hills. On one side were two converted barns, the doors marked '*Accueil*', '*Dégustation et vente*' and the other '*Privé*'. She pushed open the first door and peered inside. There was a strong, sweet smell in her nose and she saw the glimmer of huge steel tanks.

On the other side was an open barn containing a large tractor. There was a small office inside the barn with the sign '*Accueil*/Reception'. There was no-one there, although the door was open. She peered in, smelling musty dampness. Her eyes were not used to the dark, but she could see the outlines of tables and the shapes of bottles in racks. Something fluttered in the rafters: a bird, or a bat. She went out into the sunlight and strolled towards the main building, under an archway. The brickwork was crumbling; once painted white, a dull grey of bricks mingled with powdery concrete and sand. Cave Bonheur was deserted. A little wind blew dust from the cracks of the paving stones.

Evie walked further towards the little vines, which spread out into the distance as far as she could see, and she noticed the heavy bunches of grapes and picked one to eat. It was sour and she spat it on the ground. The soil was dry, little grains of gritty brown around the green and purple of the vines, which stretched out row upon row in neat ridges.

She walked further along a dusty path, was surprised that no-one was at work. The sun was high in the sky, so perhaps the workers were having lunch. A figure moved in between the vines. It was a boy, haloed in the sunlight, bending and standing again. He was a thin shadow, a moving ear of corn. Evie found sunglasses in her pocket and put them on. Benji waved and started to run towards her. Evie waved back.

He grinned excitedly, rubbing his palm across his neck, delighted to see her. 'I know you will come.' He grasped her hand in both of his and shook it vigorously.

'Hello, Benji. It's nice to see you again.'

Benji beamed. 'Come with me please. I can show you our wine fields.'

He had a natural open face, a good-natured expression, which quickly changed to one of anxiety, a crease between his eyebrows. 'I forget to ask your name.'

She grinned. 'Evie.'

'I take you on a tour of the grapes now.' He took her hand and led her around the vines, talking in his steady English, telling her the names of different wines he made and urging her along, pointing at row upon row of thriving grapes. He was becoming excited and he insisted on telling her facts about each type of grape, the sort of wine it would make and how long it took to ferment. His language was encyclopaedic and studied, learned by rote, and Evie was becoming weary. Besides, she had other things on her mind.

She stopped. 'This is all very well, Benji, but do you think we might cut to the wine-tasting? It's so hot and my legs are tired.'

His face filled with apologies and his forehead creased. He turned back towards the old building. A question was buzzing in Evie's head. 'Could I try a nice glass of red, please? I mean, I've come for the wine-tasting. Only a small one. I have to drive back to Foix.'

Benji was enthusiastic, linking his arm through hers. 'We will start now. And if you like it, you buy the bottle.'

Evie smiled. 'That's grand.' They walked into the stone courtyard. 'I'm quite thirsty after all that.' She stopped for a moment and listened. She could hear music: a guitar and a plaintive voice singing. She listened again. 'Is that a record playing? I recognise that song.' She held her breath and listened. 'It's David Bowie – the song about Major Tom.' She didn't move, taking in the melancholy tones, the lilting voice, the hypnotic strumming guitar. 'That's not him, though, is it, the David Bowie one?'

'That is the *patron*, Monsieur Bonheur. He plays well at guitar.'

Evie agreed. 'I thought this was your own place, Benji.'

He grinned. 'Oh no. I am just the assistant. Monsieur teaches me English and he is kind to give me a job. No-one else will give me such a good job. Here I make the wine and sell it.'

'What does Monsieur do, then?' asked Evie. 'Sit on his lazy backside taking the money and playing on his guitar, I don't doubt.'

Benji looked sad for a moment. 'We don't take much money this year,' he told her. 'We have many people who come in to work and pick the grapes and after Monsieur pays them, there is nothing left.' Suddenly, his face brightened and he ran his hands through the corn-silk hair, which was sticking to his head with the heat. 'Come, Madame. I think, time to taste some good wine now.'

The little office to one side was cluttered with paper and the windows were streaked with grime. In the barn the temperature was much cooler and Benji pressed a switch; fluorescent strips started to hum and flickered with sudden light. There were high rafters and stretching cobwebs and dark brick walls; three tables and benches occupied the space on a cold flagstone floor. The tables were wooden and smeared with filth, mainly soil, red veins of spilled wine and something white and greasy that looked like candle wax, although there was no sign of any candles. The transition from scorching sunlight to the cold barn in which they now sat was a shock. Evie's skin prickled with goose bumps and she wished she had brought her green leather jacket. Benji was in a vest and shorts and she noted the flip-flops on his feet. He didn't seem to care about the temperature. He had a bottle of red wine in his fist and was uncorking it. He had begun to talk like an encyclopaedia again, facts about wine temperature and fermentation, so Evie asked, 'Is this a good wine, Benji?'

'You like wine is strong, full-bodied?' he asked.

Evie replied, 'Like my men,' although straight away she thought that was a silly thing to have said. Benji wiped a glass clean with a cloth and poured wine halfway up the bowl. She sat down at one of the tables and held it up towards the lights and swished it around; it was a deep blood-red and had a thick syrupy swirl.

'This is our Cabernet,' he told her and his face was serious as he watched her sip. She wondered if she should say something about the bouquet of geraniums: she remembered Peggy and Geoff from Marmande and she almost spat her wine out in a sudden laugh.

It tasted warm and tangy on her tongue. She finished it all in a mouthful. 'Bloody grand stuff. I'll have a bottle of this. What's next?'

Benji rubbed his face with his hand. 'Perhaps you can try some of this red wine? It is our best wine, a type of Grenache.'

Evie looked puzzled. 'Is it sweet or one of those sharp tangy ones? I like the sweeter ones myself.'

'Perhaps Madame would prefer to try some of our sparkling wines?'

Evie turned, and saw the *patron* standing tall in his T-shirt emblazoned with a picture of the Rolling Stones, and torn jeans. He was about her age, his skin weathered and dark and his eyes darker, his hair pulled back in a little ponytail. She stared at him. She did not know what to say so she simply said, 'Mr Grumpy!'

He raised himself to his tallest and she could see the effort it took for him to smile at her. 'You are a guest. You are welcome to Cave Bonheur. Can I recommend the *pétillants*? The sparkling wines? They are very refreshing. I have them chilled.'

Evie felt a little irritated with herself for calling him a rude name. She flicked the fringe of blonde hair and considered becoming the pornography character again but, on reflection, Eartha Windass was probably not the best choice of role under the circumstances. However, she would make the effort to be charming and engaging towards this strange man; she'd show her ability to forgive him his rudeness.

She folded her hands together and fluttered her lashes. 'Thank you so much – you are most kind,' and she added, 'Monsieur', and gave him a half-smile by way of reward.

He said nothing. She saw the broadness of his back as he turned towards a fridge, which may once have been white but was now grey with grease and thumb-prints. A cork popped and Benji was ready with a hastily wiped wine glass, which he gave to his boss, who took it without acknowledgement. Evie smiled at Benji and mouthed, 'Thank you.' The *patron* poured a little wine in a glass for her and Benji passed him another, which he half-filled for himself.

'Will you be joining us, Benji?' she asked, showing her best manners.

Benji looked around at Monsieur Bonheur and at the barn. 'No, I have work to do in the fields.' The *patron* grunted assent, a long deep growl in his throat. Benji rubbed at his neck nervously and smiled. 'Until next time, goodbye, Madame.'

Evie waved and called goodbye and Monsieur Bonheur sat down heavily at the bench opposite her, a glass in each hand. 'Will Benji not join us for a drink, Monsieur?'

The tall man shook his head. 'He has work to do. Plenty to keep him busy.'

'He's very good,' Evie prompted. 'He knows everything about the wine. All sorts of interesting facts.'

Monsieur Bonheur nodded curtly. 'Benji is autistic. He's very intelligent.'

'Oh. He's a very nice young man. I met him at the market. Very charming.'

'Excellent worker, reliable, methodical.' Evie stared at him, waited for him to make the first move. He pushed her glass across the table and offered a toast. 'To life.'

She looked straight at him. 'To good health and good times,' she said, suddenly alarmed at being on her own with a changeable man whose eyes scowled at her.

They took a sip and neither of them spoke. Evie contemplated saying, 'Nice place you have here,' but the barn was clearly in disrepair, almost falling down, so instead she said, 'Does this place make you a good living, Monsieur?'

He stared at her and took another swig. 'You're asking me about my profits?' She was conscious again of the way he spoke English, the American lilt. Evie's temper was rising and she tried to hold it back.

'I wouldn't be so presumptuous. I was simply commenting on how you manage to make a living here when the place is such a fecking mess.'

211

His face was serious for a moment, then suddenly a smile filled his face and laughter bubbled from his lips.

'You are too honest, Madame. It is very unusual to find someone who speaks their thoughts as you do. It is not a trait I have seen before in the English, and especially not in a woman.'

'OK,' she huffed and brought her drink down on the table with a bang. 'First of all, I am Irish; I don't give a shite for what you think about the English, but you shouldn't be so sexist about women. Your Simone de Beauvoir would turn in her grave.'

He swallowed his sparkling wine. His eyes developed a steady glow. 'You amaze me, Madame, with your speech, but I find myself agreeing with you.'

'Well, good,' she said and thought for a moment. 'My name is Evie Gallagher.'

He held out his hand. 'Jean-Luc Bonheur.'

She took his hand and wondered if he would kiss it, being French and a gentleman, but he gave it a squeeze in his huge paw and then took it away and filled her glass and his own. She drank another mouthful. 'This sparkling stuff is grand. I will buy a bottle. Maybe two.'

'You are on holiday here.' It was a statement, not a question.

Evie took another gulp. 'I am staying at O'Driscoll's, but then you know that. I have a campervan,' she added proudly. 'I can go where I like and stay as long as I like.'

She scrutinised his face, waiting for him to say something about her being a woman of a certain age, that it was foolish for her to be travelling alone.

He thought for a moment. 'Travelling is good for the soul, good therapy, good to spend one's time meeting new people and visiting new places. A person can only grow spiritually from such an experience. I congratulate you.'

212

Evie closed her mouth and took another swig. 'Have you travelled much, Jean-Luc?'

'I was born with the need to travel. Always.'

She frowned. 'How do you mean?'

'My father was an Algerian sailor. I never met him. But I have inherited his hunger to see the world and enjoy nature and experience life.'

'How can you not have met your own father?'

Jean-Luc was thoughtful. 'My mother knew him only once. I was born in Marseilles. It was 1941. I left home at fourteen to travel and by the age of twenty-three I was living in California.'

Evie leaned forward. 'What made you come back to France?'

He shrugged. 'What makes us do anything at all in our life? Love. Or the lack of love.' He drained his glass and refilled both glasses again.

'You must have had an exciting life,' she said, swallowing the wine, which fizzed on her tongue; it felt refreshingly cool, and new warmth enveloped her. 'Mine has been boring.'

'I doubt that.' He raised his glass. 'You are a woman who is anything but ordinary. Tell me about your life in Ireland.'

'Not much to say.' Evie paused for a moment and then began to tell him about Jim and Brendan and Sheldon Lodge, Anaconda Man and the betting shop, Liverpool and Brittany. She talked about the luck of the Irish, her lucky number four; how she had been so fortunate to get a lift from two lovely girls in Roscoff when the wheel fell off her case, and how she had drunk brandy with a charming German student to escape the chilly atmosphere of Oradour.

He listened, his dark eyes alert to her story, filling her

glass again, sipping the wine to moisten his lips and lifting the bottle to replenish their glasses. She was relaxed, feeling warm and happy in his company. She drank again, the wine fizzing against the back of her throat, and she closed her eyes for a moment. The wine was sweet and Mr Grumpy was talking to her in his soft, gravelly voice, waving his hands and telling her about his passion for music.

Chapter Thirty

She blinked her eyes open. It was a struggle to remember where she was, but the dry taste in her mouth reminded her of all the sparkling wine she had drunk and how desperately she needed to yawn and yawn again. She rested her head on her arms for just a moment and let her heavy lids close as she listened to the murmur of a man's voice.

She was conscious of a thin, blue cover over her body and a hard mattress beneath her. She was in a dark room with pictures on the walls. The heavy wallpaper was covered in lantern shapes in burgundy on a background in shades of yellow. The curtains were closed to keep out the light but birds twittered outside. The red numbers on the little alarm clock showed seven thirty. It was early morning. Dust shifted and held still in the brightness between the curtains and she pulled them open and stared down on the courtyard below.

Evie was in his bedroom and she was sure she had slept alone. She wondered where Jean-Luc had spent the night and where he was now. Her eyes were sluggish and stuck with sleep. The legs of her jeans twisted around her calves and her shirt felt clammy and slept-in. She recalled drinking three bottles of wine with Jean-Luc, and putting her head down on the wooden table to rest. The memory came straggling back to her: she must have fallen into a doze and he had lifted her up and brought her here to sleep.

She slithered from the bed; her shoes were still on her feet and her handbag was placed on the flagstone floor. Besides the dark wooden double bed with its scant covers, there was an old-fashioned wardrobe with a huge mirror and a matching chest of drawers with brass handles. In one corner there was an acoustic guitar placed carefully against a wall, and an amplifier. There were lots of books, some on shelves and some piled on the floor. She picked one up, then another. They were in French; she glanced at the shelves and noticed a few of the books were in English and one was in a language which she recognised from school as Latin.

The surface of the chest of drawers was scratched and there were deep rings made by wine glasses or coffee cups. There was a prescription bottle of tablets, a hip flask of brandy and an empty tumbler, and some framed Polaroid photos of Jean-Luc as a young man with long hair and a serious face and the same brooding eyes. There was a photo of him playing his guitar, wearing a T-shirt that advertised a music festival in California; another photo showed him, again serious, with a laughing blonde woman and a child, a little girl. A later picture, Jean-Luc, hair in a ponytail, with a dark woman who had a short haircut and strong features. There was a silver-framed, older photo of a woman in a brown dress, probably his mother. Evie recognised the sepia style; she had one of herself and her brothers and sisters, her own mammy and da, taken in the late 1940s.

There was a photo of a fourth woman looking directly into the camera, a lively, cheerful woman in her fifties or sixties, a more modern photo taken in the courtyard. There was a signature on the bottom corner which read *'Toujours, Hélène'*. Evie chuckled: Jean-Luc seemed to have had a fair number of women in his life.

She followed the stairs across the landing and opened several doors. There were three other bedrooms, one with a large double bed covered with a mattress and old pillows, the curtains drawn. The other two rooms contained junk: boxes, rolls of wallpaper, magazines in piles and books. There were stacks of vinyl records in a dark case. She pushed open the door to a bathroom equipped with a large white bath and a shower, the neck hanging down to a broken spout. The tiles were cracked and the floor was bare boards. One solitary thin towel hung from a rail. She crossed the landing and went down the stairs into a kitchen, where there was a large range and a wooden table. The wind puffed through an open window, making the thin curtains waft.

There was a vast living room with an open fire, the remains of ash and coal spattered in the hearth. Again, there were more books, one of his jumpers left over the back of a chair, its arms hanging down. The door to the outside creaked when she opened it. The sunlight was still soft outside, but the air had cooled. Cave Bonheur was quiet except for a few fast swallows, which dipped and lifted across the courtyard. Evie went into the little office and through to the barn where she had shared the sparkling wine, but the lights were off. She wondered whether she should take some bottles and leave money; she was uncomfortable about the amount she'd drunk, and resolved she would come back, just to buy some wine.

The little campervan was parked where she had left it. The doors were locked. She fumbled in her bag and found the keys. As she slid into the driver's seat she noticed two

217

bottles of sparkling wine on the passenger seat, bearing the label 'Cave Bonheur'. She scratched her head and started the engine. It was the fourteenth of July, and wasn't four her lucky number? As she pulled out of the driveway, she took care to avoid the huge wooden wine-bottle sign which leaned, Pisa-like, to one side. She wondered whether the last wine-taster had hit it after a good session drinking sparkling wine. She turned onto the road and checked the time. She would be back at O'Driscoll's for the breakfast Paulette would have ready at half eight.

It was two days until she could drink alcohol again, and this time it was only one glass of red, during lunch with Caroline and Nige. The food was delicious and Evie was at ease in their house, which had been cleverly renovated and snuggled in the shoulder of a hill.

'What is this stuff called again?'

'Baba ganoush.' Caroline offered her more of the dip and some crudités. 'It's Nige's signature dish – well, one of them, anyway. He loves to make Lebanese food. He had a Lebanese girlfriend before I knew him. Or was she Turkish?'

Nige started to collect the plates. 'Israeli,' he mumbled and disappeared into the kitchen, returning with strong coffee and some little cakes that looked like sugared shredded wheat. Evie nibbled one.

'This is grand,' she said. 'They are so sweet and full of nuts.'

'Pistachios,' explained Nige, pouring thick coffee into ornate cups. Evie chewed for a minute. Something was on her mind.

'You know the man in the bar who stopped the fight the other night in O'Driscoll's?'

Caroline gave her a look. 'Jean-Luc Bonheur?'

218

'I just wondered why he was so grumpy. Do you know him well?'

Caroline shook her head. 'No-one does. I mean, we've been here what – twenty years. He's always been a bit aloof.'

Nige was refilling the coffee cups. 'He's got worse over the years. I mean, his business wasn't always as bad as it is now. I don't know how he sells any wine.'

'The kid from the village.' Caroline pursed her lips and took a mouthful of coffee. 'He's a bit of a loner too, lives with his widowed mother. He goes up there every day and keeps the place going, I think.'

Evie was about to say his name, Benji, but she thought better of it, and asked a question instead. 'Why is his business so bad?'

'Haven't you noticed his place from the road?' Caroline asked. 'It's practically falling down.'

'No, I haven't seen it.' Evie wondered if her lie was convincing.

Nige poured himself a coffee. 'Since his girlfriend died, he's not really kept it up.'

Evie met his eyes. 'What happened?'

Caroline took over. 'Sad, really. Long illness about five years ago. He nursed her through till the end.'

'No wonder he is so grumpy.' Evie picked up another cake.

Caroline gave her another discerning look. 'Why the questions, Evie?'

The blood warmed her cheeks and she shrugged. 'I just wondered. Is it a good place to buy wine?'

Nige suggested she pop into Cave Bonheur and try it out for herself; the wine was good but the service was terrible. Caroline interrupted. 'You probably won't get a word out of the miserable sod. He doesn't do sociable. I

219

don't know anyone who has a good thing to say about him.'

Evie's mouth was full of words of defence. She had found him funny, generous, good-natured, intelligent. But before that, in the Irish bar, hadn't he been moody, disagreeable? Perhaps that was his natural state. But then she considered – first impressions aren't always right. And he had been charming during their last encounter. Charming and elusive. She decided to say nothing. She ate more cake.

It was six o'clock and Ray was filling up the bar with new bottles from the basement, ready for a busy evening. Paulette was out with the kids so Evie decided to stop for a chat. There was music playing on the jukebox: Ray's favourite, Dropkick Murphys.

'Hi Ray. Good music.'

He smiled. 'Can I get you a drink before we open, Evie?'

'Oh, a sparkling water would be lovely. I'm trying to cut back on the wine.'

'Why's that?'

Evie thought of the free tasting at Cave Bonheur and waking up in a strange bed. She smiled. 'Not sure it's doing me any good. Thought I might go on the wagon for a bit.'

Ray laughed and handed her a glass and an opened bottle. 'I don't believe it,' he told her. She took a mouthful of water, and then another. She was feeling cooler.

Ray suddenly remembered. 'Ah, you had a visitor today. I almost forgot to tell you.'

Evie wrinkled her nose and shook her head in confusion.

Ray was polishing the bar surface. 'Jean-Luc Bonheur came in here, looking for you.'

She tried a casual voice. 'Oh? And what did he want?'

'He said he'd pick you up tonight at seven thirty.'

Her mouth dropped open. 'What for?'

'I thought you'd know. Dinner, apparently.'

She was about to deny it; she was about to suggest the man was losing the plot. Caroline had said no-one had a good word to say about the man. She thought about the two bottles of sparkling wine on the passenger seat of the campervan. She thought again. 'Oh. Grand. I'd better go and get myself ready then.'

Ray grinned. 'Hot date, is it?'

Evie smiled back and brushed a hand through her hair. 'More of a business meeting, I expect.' And she was gone.

Chapter Thirty-One

In her room, Evie tried on the long, African-print dress she had bought in the market, and smiled into the mirror; she would never have worn such a dress in Sheldon Lodge. Mrs Lofthouse and the paradise pink lipstick loomed in her mind, and she grinned as she applied a bit of gloss to her mouth and brushed her hair. She was tanned now and her hair had grown a little, silver through the blonde. At the corners of her eyes were deep lines, skin the sun had not reached, which showed when she squinted or laughed, cream against brown. Evie's reflection beamed back at her; laughter was always a great remedy. She wondered if Mr Grumpy would laugh that evening. It was time for her to leave.

Jean-Luc was waiting outside in a battered red sports car; she'd seen it before when she first arrived at O'Driscoll's. She had parked the campervan next to it. The soft top was folded down and Jean-Luc's hair was now brushed out, a mass of grey curls. The collar to his denim jacket was turned up and he was wearing round sunglasses. Evie slid into the passenger seat and he asked her if she was cold, if she minded the top down. She said she didn't mind at all, it was grand. They drove off, Jean-Luc revving the engine loudly.

She'd expected a simple meal in his house, but they were sitting across a table in a chic restaurant. Evie saw the prices and decided that she would offer to pay. He explained the menu to her and bad-temperedly suggested that she should learn French.

'I think I will,' said Evie. 'I'll ask Ray or Paulette if they will teach me. I'm sure they'll be good at it.'

He looked stung and ordered their food, broodily sipping at the water the waiter brought to the table. The starter arrived and he began to eat, hardly looking at her. Evie asked the waiter for a bottle of red house wine in French and Jean-Luc shot her a sharp look.

'Is that all right?' she asked him.

'I would have chosen a better wine. The one you have chosen is bad – overpriced vinegar.' He exhaled and began to dip bread in the garlic sauce on his plate.

The main course arrived, beef in pastry, and a different sauce, probably mushrooms and cream. The waiter poured the wine into their glasses and she made a point of drinking enthusiastically. 'This is grand,' she said. It was overpriced vinegar.

The silence was accompanied by chewing. Evie decided the atmosphere needed to change; she smiled at Jean-Luc. 'It was kind of you to invite me to dinner.'

He was surprised. 'But it was your idea.'

She put down her knife and fork. 'My idea?'

He munched for a few moments and then spoke. 'After we drank three bottles of sparkling wine, before you passed out, you said to me that I should take you out to dinner.'

Evie blushed. 'And you always do what random women tell you, do you?'

He shrugged carelessly and continued to eat. Then he

223

said, 'You told me that my business was . . . what did you say . . . "a fecking mess". I wondered if you would have some great advice for me, being such an experienced businesswoman.'

She decided he was an irritating rude man. She considered what to say, but Jean-Luc stopped eating and looked at her, his eyes dark embers.

'That was before you told me you were an actor in a pornography film.'

Evie put her face in her hands. 'I said that?'

He nodded.

'And is that why you asked me to dinner? Because I told you to and because I said I was a pornography star?'

He continued to eat, then took a deliberate mouthful of the bitter wine, before wiping his lips with the napkin.

'No, I invited you because I like you. You make me smile. It is a long time since I have smiled like this.'

Evie prodded her food. 'Well, Jean-Luc, if it is advice you want, I have plenty for you. Your wine-tasting place is in need of a good scrub-down. It's filthy. The cobwebs need to go and the walls need painting. The tables need some nice candles and a few little knick-knacks to make it feel like home, and . . . oh, yes – the sign you have outside is shite. No wonder no-one comes in; the place looks like a deserted cowshed *and* it smells like one. Your wine is good but you don't market it properly while you are sitting on your arse playing your guitar and singing David Bowie songs. You need to smarten up your act and get out there and advertise yourself – run a proper shop, rather than leaving it to that poor little kid you boss about and treat like dirt while you mope around and drink away the profits.'

He stared at her and took a mouthful of wine. His lips twitched slightly. She did not understand. He did not look angry or cross or grumpy. He was simply watching her.

224

She put her hands down on the table and stared back. 'So, there it is. There's your advice, Jean-Luc. I've said it.'

He reached out across the table and put his hand on top of hers, his large palm covering her hand. She wondered if he would crush it. His expression was serious.

'Evie,' he began.

She drank more wine. 'I know. Here we go. You're going to get all grumpy and sulky and tell me off.'

'No,' he said and his eyes were serious. 'I am going to offer you a job.'

Chapter Thirty-Two

'Are you going to sit here all day, Brendan, staring at the laptop and humming to yourself?'

Maura was standing in the doorway, her hands in her pockets, her jacket on. She was ready to go.

'What's happening now?' His wrist was sore. For two weeks he had been trying to exercise it each day, raising it heavily and putting it gently on the arm of a chair, but it didn't stop the aching. He was bored. Going out made him tired, but he was stifled within the walls of their small hotel room. Maura had taken on the role of nurse and her voice had become the banging of nails in his head. And their funds were dwindling. He balanced his laptop on his knee and finished an email with his good hand.

His staccato tapping seemed to be giving Maura a headache too. She put a hand to her eyes and said, 'We agreed to go to the little night market. It starts at seven. We said we'd go.' She sounded tired.

He went back to the keyboard, finished an email and pressed *send*. 'You go.'

'By myself, Brendan? Oh, come on. It's not as if you've broken your leg, is it?'

He wanted to snap at her, but he stopped himself and smiled instead. He went back to the laptop. Penny Wray had sent him a lovely photograph of a place she'd visited in Mexico. It was called Xel-Há, and it was a huge Mayan archaeological site where there were water sports such as snorkelling, scuba-diving and swimming with dolphins. He wondered who was pointing the camera at Penny and sharing her holiday with her. Penny, in the crystal-blue waters, wore a snorkelling mask, her hair wet, and her face tanned and smiling. Maura breathed out through an angry mouth with crimson lipstick, a frown line between her eyes.

'Let's go to the market, Brendan. We have hardly been anywhere all day.'

He flicked through the other photos: Penny on a catamaran, her hair blowing back; climbing an ancient pyramid called Chichén Itzá, in bright shorts; a parrot on her shoulder, a splash of feathers in blues and reds and her broad smile filling the frame. Brendan pressed *save* and changed the screen.

'All right, Maura. Let's go to the night market.' He rose wearily and she had his jacket, held out with the arm ready for him to slide in his wrist, which was held stiffly within a plaster cast.

She buttoned it. 'Let's go for a drink later, maybe find a nice little bar and have a wine each and a stroll.'

He raised his shoulders. He thought about saying, 'Whatever you like,' but he had no enthusiasm even to speak a few words. He moved towards the door, thinking of Penny Wray snorkelling in Mexico, his mother basking in the sunshine of the south and he wondered why, even outside the room, he felt like he couldn't breathe. Of course it was the throbbing pain in his wrist and the weeks of being too often inside a stifling hotel room. But it was something else, not just Maura; he couldn't blame her. He wondered sadly if he was just simply incapable of being happy.

The following day at breakfast Maura announced that she wanted to go to Spain. Brendan lifted a cup of coffee with his good hand and sat back in his seat.

'Oh, come on Brendan, we're on holiday. We might not be down this way again.' She stopped talking and thought for a moment. When she spoke again, her voice was soft. 'I saw this article in a local magazine about the Picos Mountains. There's a coach trip where you cross the border to Spain and have an overnight in the Picos. Spain, Brendan – imagine. We could have paella and go up the mountains on one of those chairlifts. There is snow up there, even this time of year, and we could try Spanish wine. We could get a nice meal, see the sights and stay over. It won't be too expensive. We'll manage. We need a trip out anyway. I'm fed up with looking at these walls. What do you think? It'd be great fun.'

Brendan marvelled at her enthusiasm. He was feeling listless. The coffee was cold and filled his mouth with bitterness. He swallowed and put the cup down carefully. 'I suppose you've already booked it on the credit card?' He sounded miserable.

She feigned surprise. 'Not without discussing it with you first.' She leaned over and grabbed his bandaged hand in a moment of excitement. 'What do you say, Brendan? Let's go.' She pulled her hand back.

The waiter took away his half-filled cup. 'All right. You organise it, Maura, and we'll go.'

She was smiling and full of excitement, a child who had got her own way. He pressed his lips together. He remembered how he had felt when they were cycling in

228

Soustons. He had glimpsed a possibility that their intimacy would come back, that the spark would flicker again. It didn't have to be love or passion, but a remembrance of what they once had, the mutual liking for each other. But since his injury, he had felt numb and distant. Her constant enthusiasm annoyed him, made his wrist throb more. She was now fully in charge, as if his broken wrist had taken away his capacity to decide for himself. She had even tried to spoon soup into his mouth one night, feeding him morsels of bread as if he were a child. He felt like something else had snapped with his wrist; any hope of finding what they once had now seemed distant and unlikely. Brendan wondered if there was a way back for him and Maura; if, when they returned to Ireland, they could pick up with their old life together. He felt his wrist throb and doubted it.

Chapter Thirty-Three

It was the third week of Brendan's incapacity; his broken wrist still ached. He was sitting in an air-conditioned coach, reading a book about the Pilgrims' route of Santiago de Compostela and another about the bombing of Guernica in 1937. Maura flicked through a glossy magazine and an expensive book of Picasso's paintings. There was a peace in being absorbed in the books, occasionally looking out the window at the changing scenery, the mountains rising from hills and the snow glinting against blue skies. They arrived in Bilbao in time for a brief stroll and a dinner of *bacalao al pil-pil*, which was a kind of cod stew, best enjoyed with a bottle of local Rioja. Brendan slept soundly despite the aching wrist. He woke the next morning and stood at the hotel window in his boxer shorts, gazing at the mountains. Maura was still asleep so he decided he would take some pictures on his phone and email them to Penny.

After a breakfast of potato omelette and crusty bread in the hotel, they took the coach to Fuente Dé. They queued in silence at the ticket office, their books to their noses, and took the cable car up the Picos Mountains.

Brendan put his books in his backpack as the cable car was hoisted up, parallel to jagged rocks, the ascent efficient and fast. Maura hugged her handbag and gazed out at the scenery. It was warm inside the cable car, nestling close to the craggy rocks, the greens giving way to greys, then broken-tooth rocks holding little snatches of snow before the blanket of whiteness made him blink. He enjoyed the sense of insignificance, overshadowed by crowding mountain crests. It was as if his problems were melting in the sparkling sunshine. The cable car slowed and the passengers put precarious feet onto the firm ground. The perfect peaks were smothered in snow and low-hanging clouds broke around them like mist. He put an arm around Maura's shoulders and wondered why he had done it. He left it there for a moment and then took it away, pulling his phone out deliberately to take selfies with the mountains behind him, and a picture of them both. She tugged away. Her shoulders slumped. He put an arm around her and took another picture of them both, the crags stretching behind them. Her face was serious and she was leaning away from him, her mouth a little grim.

'Isn't this wonderful, up here?' Brendan said when they reached the top. He wondered why she looked so unhappy; it had been her idea. She stood a little way from him, her head down. He suggested a walk and she trudged along behind, looking at her shoes.

They reached a little café and Brendan was about to order two coffees, but Maura shook her head and asked for a sparkling water. They sat together at the table and gazed out across the valley, the cable cars rising through mist. Maura sipped her water in little mouthfuls. Brendan rested his aching wrist on the table.

'This was a great idea to come here.' He indicated the view with his good hand. 'It's spectacular. I wish I had time to come out here for a longer walking holiday, maybe spend a week doing all the walks, or even come out here skiing.' He closed his eyes, saw himself holding two poles, a red bobble hat over his ears and goggles on his face, the mountains huge behind him. In his imagination he was free and happy to enjoy himself.

Maura took another sip and Brendan noticed she was pale.

'Aren't you enjoying the mountains?' he asked her.

'They're wonderful.'

He took money from his wallet to pay the bill. Maura lifted her head. 'Must be the potato omelette,' she mumbled. 'I feel a bit queasy.'

'Maybe it's the height and all the fresh air.' He put the money on the table and rose to go. 'Come on, let's have another stroll. We've an hour before we meet the coach. You never know. It might clear your head and make you feel better.'

He pushed his chair back and was on his way to the door when he heard her chair scrape behind him. She waved an arm, gesticulated to the toilet and then rushed in. He waited for fifteen minutes. When she came out again, Maura's face was tinged green.

The next day they were back in the hotel room in Saint-Jean-de-Luz. Maura was lying on the bed reading Brendan's book on Guernica, even though he had not finished it.

'This is an interesting book, Brendan.' She flicked the pages. 'I never knew much about Picasso. He had an interesting life. He was a bit of a character.'

'Yes, my love.' Brendan was on the floor, his laptop on his knee, his back to the bed, sending an email to Penny Wray, attaching pictures of the Picos Mountains. He looked across at his wife. 'How are you feeling now?'

'A little better, if I lie still. My mouth has a horrible

232

taste in it, like aluminium. I think I'll lay off the wine for a day or two.'

Brendan made a low humming noise. She lifted her head and looked across. 'What are you doing?'

'Sending emails. People at work.'

'You can't possibly be thinking of work, Brendan? It's almost mid-August. You'll be back there in a few weeks. You need to rest.'

He didn't lift his eyes from the screen, but made another low grunting sound between his lips. Penny had been out at sea on a speedboat and seen a tornado. There was a picture of a whirling conical black shape, poised demon-like above stormy waters. Another attachment was one of her holding the fins of two dolphins, leaning forwards, being pulled through streaming water, her mouth open in a scream of delight. Her hair wet and blowing across her face. She was wearing a red bikini top and her body was tanned a deep bronze. The dolphins were rising from the water, their mouths curved in a smile. Brendan smiled too.

'What the hell are you staring at, Brendan?' She had slid off the bed and was behind him close to his back, leaning over his shoulder.

'Maura.' He turned around as best he could, his body twisted. She was looking at the laptop screen.

'Is it pornography you're looking at now, Brendan?' He heard a thump. She dropped *Guernica* on the floor.

'It's a private email.'

'A private email, is it? It looks like a woman in a skimpy bikini to me.'

Brendan's voice took on a whining tone of apology. 'If you must know, she is a colleague from work.'

Maura's hands were on her hips, her face flushed. 'Oh, I'm sure she is.'

'She's on holiday in Mexico. She teaches sport with me. We're good friends.'

'Good friends is it, Brendan?'

'Yes, actually.' He wished he hadn't said 'actually'. He wished he hadn't said anything at all. This was not an argument he intended to have. He turned back to the laptop and saved the photo in a file he had marked 'PW'.

'I'm waiting, Brendan.'

'You'll wait a long time.' He was cross with himself, meeting her clichés with silly retorts. He decided to research the history of Guernica and tapped with one hand on the keyboard. Picasso's painting came up, black and grey, a mass of angular and twisted faces.

'Are you having an affair with her?'

'No.'

'You'd like to though, wouldn't you?'

'No.' His answer was too fast; his voice rose at the end, elongating the 'o', making him sound like he was hiding something.

'Come on then, out with it.'

'I'm not having this conversation.'

'Because you're guilty as hell; you're having an affair – she sends you sexy pictures of herself when you're on holiday, to keep us apart, to wreck our marriage.'

'Don't be silly.'

Maura huffed. 'Oh, I get it all now: why you haven't been interested in me these past weeks; why we have been distant and you've been telling me you don't know how you feel. It's her, isn't it? She's come between us, broken us apart.'

Brendan's mouth was open. 'You have it all wrong, Maura. Penny and I—'

'So it's Penny, is it?'

'She has a name.' He was talking clichés again; he could

234

hear himself; he was in her soap opera. Brendan closed his mouth.

'So how long have you both been at it, you and this Penny?'

'At it?' He shouldn't have repeated her words. She took it as an admission of guilt.

'You and her . . . you and this Penny one . . .' She struggled for a word and one came out, angry, laced with spittle: 'Bonking.'

Brendan laughed at the silly choice, and he knew he had made a mistake.

'You filthy swine, laughing at me, and you and your fancy woman in her red bikini are having sex behind my back.'

He felt his heart quicken. 'Maura, for goodness sake. You're making a fuss over nothing.'

'Over nothing? You and your tart are sending each other private dirty little pictures . . . Oh, you must both have been laughing at me.' Her face was pale now and she was shaking. 'Well you can keep your fancy tart, Brendan.' Maura reached out a hand and found her hairbrush. 'You are a bastard – that's what you are, a conniving cheating lying filthy b—'

The word was lost as she threw the hairbrush. He raised his arm; the brush hit him square on the plaster-wrapped wrist and he yelped. She hurled a small mirror next. He heard it shatter on the floor. She grabbed *Guernica* from the carpet and heaved it at his head. It clattered against the laptop, which skidded across the floor and twisted on its lead. She ran at him, grabbing his hair, digging her fingers into his skin and, just when Brendan thought he might lose his eyes to her claws, she stepped back, her face convulsed, tears boiling. She gasped. Brendan gathered himself in tightly for the blow that would surely come. Seconds passed.

'I hate you, Brendan. You're a cheat and a liar and I'll never forgive you.'

He cringed, his mouth still open, horrified by the mess around him. Someone in the next room banged on the wall, shouting in a gruff voice. Maura pulled on her jacket, grabbed at her handbag.

'Maura—'

'I hate you, Brendan. When we get back to Dublin I want a divorce. And you can just – just – just – fuck off.'

It was a word he had never heard her use. She slammed the door behind her and Brendan felt the finality in his sinews. The room was a mess, the broken glass, *Guernica* with its pages spread like a dead bird, and his laptop upturned with a blank screen.

Chapter Thirty-Four

Evie's first week started tentatively. She was not sure how he'd react when she showed him her ideas for the new fresh look of Cave Bonheur. He had raised his eyebrows at the sparse design of tables and whitewashed walls – a bistro look – and said, 'OK. If you say so.' She bought the paint herself secretly, stowing it in the campervan and smuggling it into the barn, telling him she'd met a man in O'Driscoll's and it was free. They brought in ladders and she and Jean-Luc cleaned the brickwork, revealing a smoother surface below. She noticed how he didn't fuss over her, as Jim would have, when she climbed the small ladder, but how he kept a watchful eye on her, standing close, passing her a brush, holding the paint.

He was able to reach the top of the barn using the high ladder and she marvelled at his strength and determination, whisking cobwebs away with a broom. By the third day, she was exhausted and, at lunchtime, he took her hand, pulled her away from the box of sandwiches she had made hurriedly that morning, and led her into the darkness of the house where he had laid out the long table in the kitchen with food.

'Today, I have made you lunch, Evie.' He smiled and they shared cold meat, crusty bread, olives, fresh tomatoes. He watched her across the table, pulling a chunk of bread for himself and sloshing butter on top.

She frowned. 'You should eat less butter, Jean-Luc. Cholesterol is bad for you.'

He gave a dry laugh. 'And now you are concerned for my health?'

She rocked back in her seat. 'I'd like you alive to finish the job. That's all.' He chuckled and opened a bottle of red wine, suggesting that she should sit in the shade afterwards for a few hours and rest.

By the second week, the walls had been coated with white paint twice and the barn was much brighter. Evie instructed Jean-Luc to clean the fridge, first taking out any bottles of wine and stacking them carefully. His eyes crinkled and he smiled. 'You are my boss now, Evie? OK, so I have to do a good job.'

He had hardly been grumpy at all.

Several days later, she, Jean-Luc and Benji had worked all morning, stacking crates and checking stock. Evie smiled when she saw how fond Jean-Luc was of Benji; how he ruffled his corn hair and asked about his mother, how she was managing by herself since his father died and telling him he could take some chicken home from the fridge for her. Benji gravitated towards Evie, explaining about each grape and how every type of wine was different. His eyes were round with trust and he asked her about Dublin, about her homeland. He had never travelled further than Carcassonne. She asked him to tell her about himself and she found herself stopping work to listen to him talk, waving his hands and talking engagingly about how he'd hated school, how his father had died when he was ten

238

years old and how he'd read the books his mother gave him to teach himself about mechanics, geography and science.

Later in the afternoon, Jean-Luc sent Benji home early with a bottle of wine for his *maman* and some slices of cooked meat. Evie was scrubbing the tables and, when she looked up, Jean-Luc was towering above her. 'Time for a rest, I think.'

He led her into the garden at the back of his house, the neck of his guitar in one hand. There were flowers everywhere growing wild, bees buzzing on the air. They sat on the grass, Jean-Luc strumming quietly. Evie watched him, noticing how he held the guitar lightly, how his long fingers moved over the strings like crawling spiders. He sang a song in French, a plaintive tune, and, although she couldn't understand the words, she knew it was about love. Afterwards she clapped softly. 'That was very good, Jean-Luc. Have you played the guitar long?'

He nodded. 'Since I was six years old. I have taken a guitar with me wherever I have travelled.'

She smiled. 'And you've travelled a lot. I know how important that has been to you.'

The dark eyes met hers. 'And you, Evie. What is important to you now?'

She thought for a moment. 'A month or two ago, I would've said family, but I think that's only because I'd nothing else to say. Family are fine. My son is a sports teacher; he'll be enjoying his summer break in Dublin. He's doing grand. No, now I'd say a good book, travel, independence, friends. To be able to live my life each day exactly how I want.'

He leaned over and squeezed her hand. 'I like what you say. I am very grateful you are helping me with Cave Bonheur.'

By the end of the second week, she'd almost learned the chorus of the French song. It was called '*Ne Me Quitte Pas*' and she had no idea what the words meant but she bumbled along with them and they sang it together as they swept the floor, scrubbed tables and benches and opened the large window. Evie remarked to herself that Jean-Luc had not been grumpy at all. In fact, he'd been very nice company.

At the end of each day, he had offered her money, which she'd refused, as the job wasn't finished. He'd press a bottle of red wine into her hands and then hug her, kiss both cheeks and murmur, '*Merci,* Evie.' She'd take the warmth of his lips on her cheek back with her to O'Driscoll's, meeting Ray's quips about her absence with a grin and at night she'd sleep deeply, her bones aching and a smile on her face.

She was really pleased. The trestle tables were covered with some of the plastic material she had found in rolls at the market. She had chosen a cheerful pattern of purple grapes and wine bottles, and she put little candles in jam jars. Paulette and Ray advised her about the food, a spread of breads and cheeses, salads, fruit and nuts. Benji grinned all day, arranging clean glasses and dust-free wine bottles in an impressive array. She prompted Jean-Luc to show more interest and take more responsibility, lifting the guitar from his hands in the middle of him playing 'You've Got a Friend' and asking him to brush the floor, get rid of all the cobwebs, scrub the fridge, chill the sparkling wine and sort out some music on CD.

Evie had not quite managed to achieve her trump card. She had decided to replace the old sign outside that was leaning over and proclaiming the entrance to Cave Bonheur. With some help from a French phrase book

Jean-Luc had given her and a photo she'd stolen from his bedroom, she had asked a woodturner in the market to make a replacement sign. She was disappointed when he'd said it would not be ready for several weeks, especially since it was such a high price, but the idea was alive in her mind and she had ordered it anyway. The woodturner had said something about it being a special job that would take time but she imagined Jean-Luc's smile when the new sign went up, and she thought it would be worth every penny. The old sign would have to do for now.

The guests came in large numbers: market traders, café owners, friends of Ray and Paulette and Caroline and Nige and others she'd persuaded to come along with the little leaflets and posters. There was an advert outside, by the road, and passing local people and tourists stopped in dozens, leaving their cars on the grass and peeping inquisitively into the barn. Men from the village, who worked in the vineyard from time to time, were on hand to help Benji bring in cases of wine. Over two hundred people attended the day of wine-tasting at the Cave Bonheur, and Evie was shaking hands and promising deliveries while Jean-Luc stood beside her, writing down numbers and orders and translating her words into French. When tourists arrived, Evie spoke to English and Dutch people and met a lovely German couple who bought twenty cases of sparkling wine on her recommendation, for their son's wedding.

Evie leaned on the table as the last people exchanged money for cases of wine. Benji and one of the locals, a man called Gaston, his cap pulled over his ears and his little moustache twitching as he spoke, were lifting boxes and taking them outside to pack in cars and vans. The tables were laden with empty wine glasses, red rim-marks against the plastic cloth. The clearing up would have to be done before she went back to Ray's. She was in paid employment now, having reluctantly accepted a one-off fee for the job – he'd persisted, insisted – so she would take her work seriously and she would supervise the job to the end. She glanced over at Jean-Luc who was wearing his Beatles T-shirt and a clean pair of jeans, spreading cheese on a piece of baguette.

Evie smiled. It hadn't been like this in the shop where she'd sold bread and cakes as a young woman. Old Pat Dixon would never have given her any responsibility. To him she was there to smile at the customers while he rubbed past her too often to get to the doughnuts. She'd never told Jim about Old Pat's suggestive remarks; she had kept a smile on her face and chatted to the customers. She was no youngster now – she would tell Old Dixon where to get off.

She sighed. Given her time again, she could do so much more with her life. She could have been an events organiser, maybe for charity or even for a huge business. She might even have become a manager, got a degree, and owned her own shop. What if, at twenty-one, she could have been here at Cave Bonheur, organising a wine-tasting event and learning French, managing a business? She felt that her life as a young woman, a wife and a mother had passed so quickly and she'd missed out on so many opportunities. An ache settled in her head, between her eyes; she could have made so much more of her time than standing at a kitchen sink making floury potato cakes and ironing shirts. She looked at the dregs in the wine glasses and wondered what she could look forward to now in her life. She picked up an empty bottle, then another, and threw them in the bin for recycling.

'What is on your mind, Evie?' Jean-Luc stopped

munching his bread and cheese. She shrugged and threw another bottle away. 'Today you have done a wonderful job here. You have put Cave Bonheur back on the map. I have made more euros today than in the rest of this year. I will pay you double.'

'You're very generous.' She turned away from him.

'What is it, Evie?'

She wasn't sure. A weighty melancholy was sitting on her shoulders and she shook her head. He looped a bear's arm around her. 'Come. Sit down. Let me pour you a drink. Eat something. You have not stopped all day.'

She accepted the glass of wine he offered, then glanced at the plate he was pushing in front of her, piled up with food. She took a sip and put the glass down. 'Jean-Luc, we must clear up before I go back to O'Driscoll's. It's past ten. Where is Benji?'

'I sent him home. He was falling asleep and his mother is not well.'

'But it's late and there's so much to do.' She was up again, moving around the room, collecting bottles and gathering glasses.

He came over to her. 'Evie?'

'The place is a mess. I'm not coming back tomorrow to sort it all out. There are bottles and glasses everywhere.'

'You are tired.'

'I want to get it all done, Jean-Luc.'

'It is not important. Come and sit down again and rest.'

Evie turned and crashed into him, a bottle in each hand. Her head thudded against his chest and she felt tears on her face. He took the bottles from her and put them back on the table. 'You are exhausted.' She nodded. 'And you were thinking about something. I saw in your eyes.'

Something held tight in her throat; weariness soaked into her bones and she wanted to sit down. Jean-Luc's

243

kindness made a knot in her chest. Suddenly, something inside her broke and her voice came in gulps between sobs. 'I was thinking of – oh, I can't say – just – what a waste it has all been – it has taken me this long – to find out – oh, I don't know, Jean-Luc.'

He put his arms around her and she laid her head against his chest, sniffing, her face wet against his T-shirt. She stayed there a while, listening to his breathing, and she felt his hand against the back of her head, stroking her hair.

'You are a wonderful person, Evie.' His voice rumbled against her cheek. 'What you have done here today, it is a miracle. And what you say, it may be true, it may be not, but today I think to myself, Jean-Luc, this woman has come along to help your terrible life, like some kind of angel.' He laughed. 'All the way from Ireland in a little camping van.'

Evie began to laugh too, her laughter mixed with sobs. 'I'm an Irish angel in a campervan. That's bloody grand. I've heard it all now.'

His face was serious. 'But what you say, it is true, Evie. We must do something with our lives, with all of it. You and I, we should do something with the time we have left. We should make each moment count for us, like each heartbeat.'

Evie wiped her face with her fingers. 'What the hell are you talking about, Jean-Luc?'

'We should find love.' His reply was simple, and he cupped his hands to her face and kissed her mouth. She blinked her eyes and looked at him again, to make sure she was not losing her senses. His eyes were intense. She considered her options, then pulled him against her and kissed him back.

*

'Where the hell have you been, Evie? We thought you'd been abducted by aliens. Paulette was on at me to ring the *gendarmes*.'

Evie put her handbag on the bar. 'I have been busy,' she said coyly. 'I've only been away a few days. Can't a girl spend a few days away enjoying herself? I've had a lovely time. And I've come to a decision. Time waits for no woman. So, anyway, I have come to pay up and get my stuff and go.'

'You're leaving us, Evie?'

'You're only young once,' she told him. 'Besides, I've a car waiting for me outside.'

'You aren't in the campervan?'

'No.' Evie tried to hide her smile. 'The camper is parked up, back at my new home. I'm moving out of here.'

Ray scratched his head. 'New home?'

'It's a long story,' Evie quipped. 'But as I said, you're only young once and I don't want to keep my man waiting, so I better collect my things, pay you what I owe and get properly moved in.'

'New man, is it?'

Evie winked at him. 'Oh yes. I mean, how long does it take to tell you've found Mr Right? In my case, a couple of weeks. Now I've no time to waste, so I'm moving in with him. We're shacking up together. That's it. So, will you sort out my bill, Ray, and I'll pay up and be off. You can give me a hand with my bags. He's in the car outside.'

Ray was still staring as she made her way to the stairs. 'It won't take me a minute to pack. And when I'm all sorted out, you and Paulette must come round for dinner.'

Chapter Thirty-Five

The bed had a new king-sized duvet and they were underneath a dazzling cover, a silky bright purple one Evie had bought in Foix. A tray was precariously balanced on her knee with little coffee cups half-filled and plates covered in crumbs and smears of butter and jam. There was a Sunday newspaper and books, the Zola he had given her in English and the Brontë she had bought for him in French. He was teaching her to speak French; she was copying his voice, imitating his expressions and the movements of his lips.

'Try it again.'

'Why are you laughing at me, Jean-Luc?'

'Say it again. Maybe. *Peut-être.*'

She made her mouth into a little tunnel as she had seen him do. '*Pute être.*'

He laughed again; there were tears in his eyes.

'What've I said?'

He couldn't speak. She sat up straight. '*Pute être. Pute être.* That is what you said.'

He wrapped an arm around her. '*Peut-être* is maybe. You say *pute*. *Pute* is . . . it is . . .'

'What is it I've said?'

'*Pute* . . . It is a – a – a woman who – a woman of the night.' He was still laughing and she grabbed his shoulder.

'Oh hell, I wouldn't want to get that one wrong when I was asked what I want for dinner.' She refilled her coffee and offered to fill his cup. '*Plus de café? Oui, pute être.*'

He was laughing again.

'Jean-Luc, I have never seen you laugh so much.'

He took his coffee. 'It has been a great week together, Evie. I hope for many more. We made a good decision, not to wait, but to be together now. Do you think we are crazy?'

She snuggled down into the crook of his arm. 'Not at all. It's been grand. What's been the best bit of it, for you, this last week?'

He thought for a moment. 'My life has a meaning now.'

'Shite!' she retorted. 'All life has meaning, whether you're on your own or not.'

'You are right,' he said. 'But every day this week, I don't lie in bed or sit playing my guitar or wondering what I should do next; I get up and work on the tractor with the vines, and I know you have good food for dinner and you are here waiting for me . . .'

'So I'm the cook and bottle washer who has got your arse out of the armchair and back to work, is that it?'

He kissed the top of her head. 'Evie, it is good to have you here. You have so much life. This is what you do – you breathe life into an old man in his seventy-seventh year, and his tired empty home.'

'There's been plenty of life in you this week, I'm sure.'

He looked suddenly sad. She picked up a book from the covers. 'So, tell me, what is so good about *Germinal* and this Émile Zola?'

'It is about the working classes of France and how hard

life was for them. It was the late 1800s and they were in the mines and conditions were bad, so they had to make a strike. André Gide said it was one of the best French novels written. I find it very sad.'

The cover showed sepia people bent over, carrying burdens. 'I will enjoy this. It's interesting, how the lives of the poor people were then. It will give me something to think about. Have you started your book yet?'

'I have read much of it already, your Emile Brontë.' He raised a mischievous eyebrow and she caught his expression and smiled at the joke. 'It is good. But what does it mean, the *wuthering*?'

'It's the name of the house.'

'But what does it mean, the English, *wuthering*?'

Evie thought. 'Well the house is up high, isn't it, next to the moors, and so I expect wuthering is to do with the bad weather. Like weathering. You know, windy and all that. Like the characters, totally blown about by passion.'

He smiled. 'She is like you, this Cathy. She has desire and she is *têtue* . . .' He thought for the word. 'Headstrong – wilful, and full of passion.'

She grinned. He was her Heathcliff, brooding, dark, a mysterious man of yearning and sorrow. She could sense it about him, and she wondered if all his past had been miserable.

'You are thinking again, Evie.' He pulled her close and her head rested on his chest. 'Share with me your thoughts.'

She wondered how to phrase it. 'I was thinking about your photos, Jean-Luc. You have had a lot of women. And is that little girl your child? Where is she now?'

He made the expansive shrug she was now used to seeing. It hid deeper feelings.

'The child was born in California. She must be forty-eight years old now, maybe more. Her mother Cindy and

248

I called her Soleil, after the sun. I was twenty-six, maybe twenty-seven, and Soleil was – how can I say – not planned. One day, when Soleil was five years old, I came home from work on construction and Cindy was there with another man. I packed my things and I left. That was it.'

'You've had no contact with her since, your own child?'

'No. I think of her often but – well, I never met my father and I think maybe she will not miss me.'

'You have no other children?'

The shrug again. 'Maybe, maybe not. Who knows?'

'So, what came next then? Who is the dark-haired woman?'

'Sylvie. The Parisienne. She and I spent ten years together. She knew everything of my body but nothing of my mind. After a while there was little left between us and I moved away.'

'So, she was the best one then? The lady in the photo on the end?'

'Hélène. We bought this place together. She was the reason I stayed in one place. She made the money so that I have enough now. She was organised, very practical.'

Evie thought she would have needed to be. 'How long were you together?'

'Thirty years, more. The wine-making was her idea. She was a good woman. I just drove the tractor and filtered the wine and—'

'Played guitar?'

Jean-Luc gave a half-grin. 'I am a man who is all good for nothing. You see what you have found for yourself?'

'I think she was a lucky woman, your Hélène. You must miss her very much.'

'At first, there is pain and the heart dies a little. But you have made it beat again, Evie.' He kissed her forehead.

'You must meet my son, Brendan. He is a lovely young fella.'

'I would like that. You have grandchildren?'

Evie gave a small laugh. 'His wife likes her house spick and span. I'm sure she'd have no place for any little ones.'

'Maybe one day?'

Evie pulled a face. 'You'd get on well with him, Jean-Luc. I must text him; invite him over before the end of the year. What about Christmas? Would that be all right?'

'This is your home, Evie. You invite who you want.'

She beamed at him. 'He's very like his da. Same colouring, same hair. You can't get a word out of him sometimes. Just like his father was. Two peas in a pod.'

Jean-Luc frowned. 'And you miss him, your husband, James?'

'He was Jim, well, his proper name was Seamus. I called him Jim.'

'You had a good marriage together?'

'Oh, I thought so at the time, Jean-Luc. He was a very nice man. Very kind, very steady. But, you know, we never did anything like this. Stay in bed on a Sunday, read books, talk about our feelings and things. And I feel a bit sad saying this but, well, I don't really miss him much any more, not now. At first it was an empty house and it was the little practical things, you know: how do I empty the bins by myself, how do I pay for all the bills? And then I got confused by the loneliness. I ran away for a little time, I sort of gave up on life a bit, went into hiding. But then, I thought to myself, I was just stuck in one place. Stuck in the mud. And I took off. I mean, I didn't know where I was going or what I'd do, but I just took off. I had to. You know, Jean-Luc, you can't love someone else if you don't know who you are and what you want out of life.'

250

'And do you know it now, Evie, the thing you want from life? Now you have travelled across France in your little car?'

'Yes, I think I do.' She looked at the worried eyes, the lines around his mouth. 'This is what I want.'

He kissed her and she was caught in his hug.

'So, what shall we do with today, Jean-Luc?'

'What do you want to do?'

'Well it's Sunday, so maybe a picnic, a little trip out somewhere? You could bring your guitar and we could sit in the countryside and you could serenade me in the sunshine.'

His hand touched her cheek. 'Maybe. Or maybe we could just stay here all day in bed, and talk.'

Evie hugged him, her arms pulling at the back of his neck. '*Pute être.*'

She stood at their wine stall in the market, the buzz of voices in her ears. This was her new venture, running the stall with Benji while Jean-Luc drove the tractor between the vines at Cave Bonheur to check the progress of the grapes and prevent the presence of weeds. Business was increasing, what with Benji's expert knowledge of wine-making to impress the customers, and her patter persuading them to buy more than they needed. Next to her, Benji leapt up and down, talking about the grape harvest and how they would be making the wine in the big vats, how hot the temperature would need to be, and watching the bubbles form and then the deep Claret would pulse in the tubes.

She thought about being in Jean-Luc's arms, that huge hug which enveloped her completely, her face against the rough hairs of his chest, hearing the steady thump-thump of another human heart. She was thinking about the

251

outside warmth of another body, her own feeling of warmth inside, of not being alone. She was strong; she could do whatever she liked now. She could help harvest the grapes, ferment the wine and put it into bottles. She might make cheese; she would have a pantry full of jams and chutneys in the autumn and next spring plant some vegetables, maybe make a coop and keep chickens. The spare rooms needed decorating, their bedroom too. They could even open a bed and breakfast for holidaymakers next summer. She thought about his face, the weathered leather of his skin, the roughness of his hair which crinkled against her fingers, the sinking flesh below his cheekbones. She heard Benji chattering as someone was buying wine and she thought about Jean-Luc back at their place, Cave Bonheur, driving on his tractor around the little vines which were bursting with grapes. Her mouth was smiling.

'Well, you surprised us all, Evie. I think "dark horse" is the phrase that comes to mind.'

Evie looked up to see Caroline, her hands on her hips, a frown on her tanned face, her sudden smile. She was being teased and grinned back. 'Caroline. Good to see you.'

'Who would have thought it, Evie? You and Jean-Luc!'

She was amazed that she had nothing to say. It wasn't long since she had called him Mr Grumpy.

Caroline persisted. 'Well. Spill the beans, Evie. It's been three weeks, hasn't it? Everyone is talking about it. You've saved that man's business; you've probably saved his life.'

She accepted the mug of tea Caroline held out for her, a flask in her other hand. She took a gulp and handed it to Benji, who was eyeing the drink, his mouth open.

'He is a lovely man,' Evie said. 'You will have to get to know him better. Come round and have dinner with us next week?'

Caroline beamed. 'We'd love to. Now, how about you and I take a break? I'm sure Benji can mind the stall while we grab some lunch? I want to hear all about it. Oh, you're such a wicked person, not telling me all the gossip! Jean-Luc—'

Evie breathed out. 'Give me ten minutes, Caroline. I'll just finish up here and leave Benji to it. I need to run a quick errand then I'll join you at your stall; I just have a couple of things I need to do. You'll be all right for half an hour, won't you, Benji?'

'Of course.' Benji grinned broadly, drained the tea and handed the mug back to Caroline, who called, 'I can't wait,' as she walked off, swinging the flask. Evie would follow momentarily; she would call on the woodturner first, who should be at his stall, and ask how the new Cave Bonheur sign was coming along. She thought warmly how Jean-Luc's face would brighten at the new sign.

Evie took out her phone. A customer was at the stall and Benji was offering a bottle of red wine, speaking excitedly in words she couldn't understand, except for '*vin*' and '*plaisir*'. She found a message; it was Jean-Luc's number and he had texted in French. **Tu me manques, mon ange Irlandais**, and she smiled at the words, although she only understood the last part. It was nice being his Irish angel. Then she found Brendan's number and began to slowly write a message. She needed to make sure the words were just right.

brendan, hope all is well & you & maura are enjoying the summer. She paused, remembering Maura, whom she had completely forgotten about, then typed again: **im staying here in foix i am now living**

She stopped to think. She moved her thumb over the letters.

253

Chapter Thirty-Six

Brendan was enjoying the countryside and the cliffs. He felt his lungs expand in the sharp air. His face was tanned and the back of his neck was warmed by the sunshine. Maura had stayed in bed again, claiming he made her feel ill, so he took another bus and found a route on his map. The sensation of being alone was good, his backpack bouncing on his back and the sea breeze in his face as he walked for miles, his head full of thoughts at first and then later calm and quiet.

His wrist was still in the cast after almost four weeks, but the aching had stopped. It gave him a feeling of freedom to be following the coastal path. Brendan walked briskly for three hours; his map suggested that another half-hour's walk would take him to a beach where he could have a late lunch and there would be a bus back to the hotel. He stopped to take photos. The view down from the path was spectacular and he wondered whether he should take up painting or sketching, whether he could render the sweep of the beach and the smooth seas in oils. He thought how he would like to try the twenty-five-kilometre walk from

254

Bidart to Hendaye, waking up early and taking the whole day to complete the journey.

He had rediscovered how much he enjoyed walking, not just the sense of accomplishment but also the way the strong muscles in his legs made him feel powerful and in control as he moved from path to promontory, from beach to clifftop, from sand to grass to rock. The view was broad and open and he couldn't help but make a parallel with his own life, a spectrum of new opportunity to go where he wished and be independent. He thought of Maura momentarily and imagined how it would be if she were walking beside him. She would be wearing the silly heels or the pink trainers, complaining of tiredness, asking how much further they had to go. He imagined her in hiking boots and a waterproof, talking to him about the landscape and asking questions about the geology. He thought of Great Gable and he sighed. It seemed like a long time ago.

He took out his water bottle. He was thirsty; the water was lukewarm but he gulped greedily. Seagulls swooped and soared overhead, the whirling of handkerchiefs. In the distance he could see the ragged brown wingspan of a hovering buzzard. Below, the tide was coming in and the spray rose and slapped against the outcrop of rocks. The beach was a stretch of empty sand except for a lone fisherman and his net.

Brendan's mind strayed back to Maura in the hotel room. She would be asleep or reading a magazine, on her side, her arms around a pillow. Brendan had not hugged her for weeks now, their backs to each other in the bed, their adjacent shoulders cold, turned away at harsh angles. They hardly looked at each other. He did not like being in the hotel room. Now his wrist had stopped aching, he wanted to be out in the fresh air and he thought she'd feel the same. But now the situation had reversed: she was unhappy to stray out of the room most days. She looked pale and was lethargic when she woke, although she would agree to come down for dinner later in the evening, when she usually felt a little better. Meals were now quiet times, where they exchanged a few words, ran out of things to say and listened to the harsh scrape of their forks against the plates.

A darker cloud was coming towards him. There was a new chill in the air, so Brendan reached into his backpack for his cagoule and heaved it over his head, pulling up the hood and snatching at the toggles. Ten minutes later, the rain shower came in and Brendan squeezed his eyes shut against the sudden torrent, feeling his face cooling and then becoming cold. He quickened his pace. Below, he could see a beach with a little wooden shack that he thought might be a café.

It was still raining when he ordered his sandwich and French beer. There was only one other person in the café, an old man who was downing the last dregs of his ale. Brendan gave him a half-smile and looked away again. He heard the chair scrape. The old man moved across to his table, pulling out the chair next to him to accommodate his large belly.

It was dusk when Brendan returned to the hotel in St Jean-de-Luz and he was looking forward to a shower and dinner. In the hotel room, Maura was lying on the bed, asleep. He picked up his laptop and checked emails; nothing from Penny Wray. He was hoping she would send more holiday pictures. He did not think she had returned to Dublin from Mexico; it was three more weeks until the new term started and he wondered if she would have an interview for the new job. He checked his emails again. He'd heard nothing back from St Cillian's: it must mean he had missed another opportunity. Maura was breathing softly. He went into the shower.

She was sitting on the bed when he came out, reading a magazine.

'How are you feeling?' he asked.

She shrugged. He felt sorry for her, seeing the way her shoulders sloped forwards over her reading. 'Maura, the cast comes off next week. We can go to Foix and see Mammy, then we can all three of us make our way back to Dublin in two days, three at the most.'

'And what then?'

He took a deep breath. 'It's all such a mess.'

He saw her swallow hard.

'Do you want any dinner, Maura?'

'I might as well.'

'Have you eaten today?'

She made a face which told him no. He looked at the inky fingerprint smudges beneath her eyes, the grey pallor of her skin. Her hair was not brushed and was flattened on one side. She was wearing pyjamas.

He put his hand out to her and she moved away. 'Come on, let's go downstairs and eat. Maybe you'll feel better. You must be starving if you've eaten nothing all day.'

'I have no appetite.' She took a deep breath. 'How was your hike?'

'Good,' he said, and wondered if he should tell her about Loris the fisherman in the café. She struggled out of bed and looked for something to wear and he decided it was best to say nothing.

She pulled on a dress and tugged a comb through her hair, splashed water on her face and said she was ready. He saw how the dress hung from her shoulders; she was thinner and her suntan was fading. Her eyes were hollow and miserable and she was hunched over, arms folded over her stomach. For a moment, he wanted to hug her. His mobile pinged. It was Evie. Maura's back was turned to him. He quickly read the message to himself: brendan, hope all is well & you & maura are enjoying the summer im staying here in foix i am now living in—

'In a cave?' he gasped.

Maura faced him, her comb in her hand. 'What?'

'Mammy. She says she's living in a cave. With a new man.'

A week later, his hand moved freely. He examined it, as if looking at a long-lost friend. His wrist was pale and somehow thinner after four and a half weeks against the tanned forearm. He flexed it: it still worked. He tried to lift the luggage, but his wrist hurt too much, so he used his good arm to take the bags down one by one, glaring at his wife as he passed her. Maura did not help much; she leaned against the car and squeezed her eyes tight as if in pain. Brendan paid the bill and hoped that he could claim something back from the holiday insurance as he was now almost overdrawn, but decided to say nothing to Maura. As he started up the engine, she closed her eyelids and leaned back in her seat.

His wrist ached but he was enjoying the drive. The scenery changed as they left the coast behind them and moved towards the rising hills and dense forests. Brendan hummed a little tune. They would arrive in Foix in three to four hours and he would find the Irish bar. There could only be one, and someone would know where his mother was staying. The bit about the cave worried him, but he guessed that it was a mistake in her text. Perhaps she meant the name of a hotel. The idea of being in an Irish bar made him think of Dublin and he realised he missed his home. He would buy a pint of Irish stout in the bar, phone his mother, and in a few days he would be back home. He would ignore his domestic problems until then. The little tune bubbled on his lips.

'Please Brendan, don't.' Maura put her hand to her head.

'Is my singing annoying you?'

'It's not that . . .' She looked out of the window. He waited. 'I have to tell you something – I have done something really stupid.' She could not meet his eyes.

His mind raced to the worst thing he could imagine. 'What have you done?'

'I shouldn't have – I have done something terrible. While you were out hiking, I went on your laptop. There were some emails. I opened them up and read them. Then I – deleted them.'

His mouth made a firm line. 'What emails?'

'That girl, Penny. The sporty one at your school. She sent you some more pictures and some emails.'

He looked at the road ahead.

'I owe you an apology. You were right. I know you aren't having an affair with her now.'

He was puzzled and intrigued and angry all at once. 'So how do you know, Maura?'

'Her emails. She said she was returning back to Dublin next week. She said she and Sam were still enjoying themselves in Mexico. They're having the time of their lives scuba-diving. And she says Sam has just proposed, so it's unlikely she's cheating, having an affair with you. I read all the messages. It's obvious from how she writes that Sam is her other half and she's not interested in you in that way. She even said you and I should go to their ceremony at Christmas. I'd got it all wrong. She and you aren't——'

Brendan made a cough to clear his throat. Penny and

Sam? Sam? He thought of Penny massaging his shoulders in the PE office. He thought of her in the red bikini swimming with dolphins. So she was with Sam. She had a boyfriend after all. He exhaled and sadness sank into the deepest place in his chest.

'There's something else.'

He glanced at her and then back to the road.

'You have an interview in two weeks. Early September. At St Cillian's. For a new job.'

He felt anger surge. 'You deleted that?'

'It's in Trash. You have to tell them if you're coming to interview. By the end of this week.'

Brendan rubbed his sore wrist against his forehead. 'Fine. I'll do that. It's just as well I still have time.'

Maura's eyes were on him, glassy with tears of shame. 'I have been really stupid, haven't I?'

'Yes, you have.'

She pursed her lips. 'There's something else . . .'

'What else have you done, Maura?'

'My job at the surgery – well, I've had far too much time off now – five weeks more than I should've . . . I told them two weeks . . .'

'They can't sack you?'

'No, but I had a text yesterday. They've found a replacement to cover for me. And she's doing really well. They like her. So when I'm back they're going to discuss a job share between us, and ask me to think about changing my hours. I will be working less.'

Brendan fixed his eyes on the road ahead.

'I am so sorry, Brendan.'

He couldn't remember the last time she had apologised to him, but he was thinking of an interview at St Cillian's and how it could be a new start. He was thinking of Penny and her Sam scuba-diving together, Sam proposing and

Penny accepting, a Christmas wedding. The hills rose higher on both sides of him and he felt penned in. He gritted his teeth. His eyes hurt.

They drove for an hour in silence, Maura looking at her hands or rummaging in her handbag, Brendan staring at the road, lost in thought. She picked up the road map and flicked through the pages. She paused on one page, took off her sunglasses and stared hard at the map.

'Brendan?' Her voice was suddenly sharp, inquisitive.

He grunted.

'Didn't you say your mother said she was staying in a cave?'

He grunted again.

'It's just, well, here on the map, there are some caves. Maybe she is living near there. What did she say exactly?'

He sighed. 'That she was living in a cave.'

'Look—'

'I'm driving, Maura—'

'Caves, near Foix. Rivière souterraine de . . . La-bou-iche. Underground. River. Caves.'

Brendan glanced at the map. 'Where are these caves?'

'Just outside Foix. We pass right by them. What do you think?'

'Perhaps there's a house nearby. Worth a try,' Brendan admitted. 'If it's on the way, we'll stop in and ask. She might be living near there. We have plenty of time. But she'd be so surprised to see us. I can just imagine the smile on her face as she answers the door.'

Maura dismissed the image of Brendan and his mother rejoicing, found a CD and put it on. She sat back in her seat looking pleased with herself and rummaged in her handbag, finding a packet of mints. She unwrapped two, putting one in her mouth and popping one in Brendan's before offering

261

him a bright smile, pushing on her sunglasses and sliding down in her seat.

The temperature had dropped considerably and his skin prickled with cold. Brendan was encased in darkness and a steady dripping came from a distance. Maura stood at his shoulder. Rocks rose on either side of them, gnarled carbuncles, scored pictures of bison in black and red on the smoother surfaces. Lights illuminated corners and brought the cave drawings into sharp focus, and Brendan imagined how uncomplicated and pleasant life must have been centuries before. His hands were icy, a chill sat in his shoulders. He'd almost expected to see Evie sitting at the kiosk, selling the tickets, but no-one had seen an Irish woman living nearby.

They followed the guide, past white stalactites that hung like daggers overhead, to a bridge. There were waterfalls splashing on either side of them, the flow pooling surf-white and spreading towards darker greys and blues as the water stilled. They crossed the bridge, Maura then Brendan then several other tourists moving single file into the gaping mouth of another cavern. It became dark and there were pendulous nodules, swellings and shiny tissues hanging from a curved ceiling, like being inside an enormous throat. The smell of damp became a wheeze in his chest. The darkness opened; there was the sound of crashing water and they walked into a dreamy blue light. A little boat was waiting for them and they clambered in, packing tightly, while the guide explained that they were in Europe's longest navigable underground river. The water reflected a magical sheen of turquoise and azure and emerald on the rocks. As the boat moved through the still river, the glow caught on Maura's face and illuminated her expression, her eyes shining. The boat took them inside

262

a gorge, golden and scored deeply with time, blue rocks emerging from shadow. Refractive light lapped against the rocks.

'All those years ago, how those people must have lived.' Maura was clutching the guide booklet and bending the page, looking at the English translation. 'We take so much for granted in our lives, don't we? The beauty of those caves . . . how tough their lives would have been just to survive.'

After a moment, Brendan spoke. 'I am glad we stopped here. It would have been awful to have missed out on this place.'

He started the car. Neither of them spoke until they arrived in Foix. They drove around for half an hour but there was no sign of an Irish bar. Brendan asked a passer-by, who just shook his head and walked away. At Maura's suggestion, they stopped at a restaurant to eat and asked the waiter, who did not know. Halfway through their meal, the *patron* came out with a map and showed Brendan the way to an Irish bar, back the way they had come. He said it was called O'Driscoll's and was near Saint-Girons. Brendan's heart lifted and Maura's eyes darted from the map to his face, gauging his thoughts.

Two hours later they were still driving around Saint-Girons. Finally Brendan parked the Panda opposite O'Driscoll's and went over to the dingy-looking building with the dark door. The paint was peeling off in strips. He pushed the door but it wouldn't open. Maura was at his shoulder. He pushed again and then pulled hard, just in case it opened the other way. It would not give. Maura pointed to a sign which said: '*Fermé. Deux jours de congé*'.

O'Driscoll's was closed, and would not open for two days.

Chapter Thirty-Seven

Evie could not sleep. The night was warm and she pushed the duvet away. It was so deeply dark in the countryside; the window was wide open but the room had no light. Jean-Luc was asleep, breathing softly, and she lay against the vast wall of his back. His skin was cold. She moved the duvet to cover him.

Sleep would not come. She was searching for links to her lucky number. Four. He was not born on the fourth day, nor in the fourth month. His birthday was in November, the seventh; 1941 had a four in it, but that didn't count. His name had seven letters. There was no way she could make her lucky number four work with Jean-Luc. But they were lucky nevertheless. Her luck had changed and her lucky number with it. Perhaps seven would be her lucky number now.

It was almost five in the morning, according to the little red numbers on the alarm clock. Dawn creased the skies, the familiar reds and purples blended with the darkness over the hills. She made plans for decorating the other bedrooms, to paint the walls sail-white and raise long curtains which would billow in the breeze.

She thought about Cave Bonheur in winter, the old house with its thick cob walls, a huge log fire in the living room, Jean-Luc singing and playing guitar, a stew simmering on the kitchen range. She put out her hand, feeling the warmth of his cheek and the curve of his mouth. He mumbled and rolled over onto his back, his arm wrapping around her, and she nestled her head in the indentation of his shoulder. There was a fluttering in the window and Evie raised her eyes. She could make out a rounded stare, unblinking and still, looking at her from the window ledge. There was another flurry of feathers. The owl shook out its wings but was still there. She rolled closer to Jean-Luc, closed her eyes and smiled.

When she awoke, there was an empty space beside her. He was gone and it was past ten. She stretched and felt the breeze from the open window against her skin and she wriggled out of the bed and into clothes.

He was not downstairs, but there was coffee simmering steadily on the range and he had left her some bread and fruit for breakfast and her favourite yogurt.

She went outside into the bright sunlight; the tractor was still in the barn but his red sports car had gone. She frowned and went back indoors.

After breakfast, she went into the office, filed a few papers and entered the barn. They would need a new fridge next year, a bigger one for the sparkling wines and perhaps some fine wine glasses. Evie imagined the heavy crystal in her hand, passing the Claret to a customer who would take a mouthful and nod appreciatively. She imagined the pride on Jean-Luc's face as the customer bought cases of wine and, in her daydream, the barn was light and airy and the tables were fashioned from sturdy oak wood, with knots in the curved legs.

She went outside to the open barn and climbed onto

the tractor. Next spring she would learn to drive it. She gripped the wheel and waggled it.

'And I don't see why not.' She could learn to help with the harvests and use the machinery as well as anyone else. She could haul in the crop and crush the grapes in the steel tanks, watching the wine gush. She waved an arm in the air, cutting down an imaginary vine as big as a beanstalk, hacking it with a huge sword, leaning out from the tractor.

'Be careful, Evie. Don't fall.'

Jean-Luc held out a hand and helped her down. She could manage by herself but he was being kind. He kissed her and she tasted brandy on his lips. She feigned annoyance. 'Where have you been all this time, you terrible boozing man? In the pub, drinking?'

He smiled and draped an arm around her.

'I went to town, on business. Afterwards, I saw your friend Ray, in his bar.'

'Oh yes? And what mischief did you both get up to there?'

'I drank one glass with him and then an idea came to me and we shared it. Now we will make the mischief with our own women at home.'

She frowned. 'What on earth are you talking about?'

'After the business, I—'

'What business?'

'Oh, just a few things in town.' He clutched a little bottle in his hand; Evie took it from him and rattled it loudly.

'What's this, Jean-Luc?'

'Well, first I saw the doctor, and he gave me vitamins.'

She gave him the package back. 'You need vitamins?'

'My doctor says they are good for me. Then I went for a meeting with my accountant and the business is doing very well. I think to myself, this is all because of my little Evie, so I have an idea. I go to see Ray for a drink and I tell him that I think you and I will go away for a little time together and he is jealous, he likes the idea too, so today he takes Paulette and the children for a break at the coast for two days. And you and I are going away now, somewhere special.'

She was puzzled. 'Now?'

'We pack the car and go today. It is fine. Benji will look after the grapes for us, and I will call Gaston and some other men from nearby who help sometimes. I will pay them well for extra time. We deserve a celebration.'

Evie grabbed his hand. 'Where are we going?'

'A place where we can drink *txakoli* and *pacherán*; we can eat *brebis* cheese and cross the border and drive through Spain to Figueres and see the works of Dalí and eat paella and stay in a little place I know in the mountains.'

'Jean-Luc, that's grand.'

'Let's do it. Imagine, Evie, we can sit in the sunlight in the Pyrénées Mountains with the sheep and the goats and share a picnic and play guitar, just me and you and nature.'

Evie hugged him. 'You may need those vitamins . . .'

He thought for a minute, unsure of what she had said, and then he laughed.

Two hours later, the yellow Panda stopped outside Cave Bonheur and Brendan stared up at the crooked sign. 'Do you think this is it?'

'The man outside the Irish bar said it was here. This is what he said it was called and it's a *cave*, Brendan.'

Brendan climbed out of the car and went over to peer at the sloping sign. 'This must be it.'

'I thought he was a lovely man. Irish too. Do you think

that he really played his banjo on stage with your mother? He said she had a great singing voice. Can you imagine them singing "Danny Boy" together? I never heard your mother sing.'

'This is it. I think we've found her.'

Maura was still in the car. 'He didn't know the Irish bar was closed either. He seemed very disappointed. He knows your mother, though. And he knows her new fancy man.'

'Don't say that, Maura. They live here. He might hear us.'

'By all accounts he is a strange one. It seems odd that your mother has picked up with a—'

Brendan walked away, towards the buildings where a little campervan with flowery curtains was parked. Maura slid out of the Panda and stood still for a moment, swallowing hard.

Brendan turned to her. 'Are you coming or not?' His voice was a little irritable. He was not sure how his mother might react, and if she was inside the house with her new man, what would they say to him? His heart thumped.

She tottered forwards. 'Hold on a minute . . . I am sure something disagreed with me in that cheap B and B. The coffee was horrible and the milk was off—'

He was already knocking on the door marked '*Accueil*'.

Maura reached him and was clutching her handbag and leaning against the door post, breathing deeply. Brendan looked around him, taking in the trees and the courtyard and the barn with the tractor and the house. He looked out at the little vines like bonsai trees, as far as he could see.

'Perhaps she's in that place over there? It seems to be some sort of manor house.'

'It's all a bit scruffy,' she said.

Brendan ignored her. He saw someone running towards him from the distance, where vines stood in rows. The figure was shouting and waving. It was a skinny boy in jeans with a shock of yellow hair. Benji stopped short and looked at Brendan and Maura as if he thought he had first recognised them but now realised they were someone else; he asked them politely in French if they had come to taste some of the best wine of the region. Brendan explained that he was here to see Evie Gallagher and Benji was a little confused. Maura took over, speaking slowly.

'Evie Gallagher. Where is she? We have come a long way to visit her.'

Benji looked around him anxiously and was not sure how to deal with these people who spoke in loud hesitant French. He wondered if they were the police or people who could not be trusted. He twisted his fingers. 'Evie? She is not here.'

'Where is she?' Brendan and Maura spoke almost together.

'Monsieur and Madame are away. They are back tomorrow. Or the day afterwards. I don't know.'

Maura asked Brendan in English if they should stop and buy some of the wine and Brendan said they should concentrate on trying to find his mother. Benji was confused and waved his hands in front of his face. 'Evie is not here. Maybe she will be here tomorrow. Today she is away with Monsieur.'

Brendan scratched his head. 'Where has she gone?'

'To the mountains.'

Maura looked at Brendan. 'Where's she gone?'

'We must have missed her . . .'

Benji was walking away. Brendan shouted after him: 'We will come back tomorrow and perhaps she'll be here then?'

Benji began to run back towards the vines. He sat down behind a clump of grapes and ran his hands across his face, leaving dirty smears. He would tell Monsieur Bonheur when he came back; he would know how to deal with these visitors. He worried that, although they said they were Evie's family, the man's voice was loud and the woman interrupted him and looked anxious. He was happy to wait, to sit somewhere familiar, and to see what the *patron* would say.

Brendan turned slowly back to the car.

'So, that went well,' Maura shrugged and he ignored her.

An hour later, Brendan shoved his phone back in his pocket and frowned.

'What did she say, Brendan?'

'I can't get a signal.'

'Let's find somewhere for tonight perhaps? I could do with a lie-down now.'

He drove around for half an hour and found them another bed and breakfast place near Foix, which was better than the one they had stayed in the night before. The bedroom was small but clean and it had space for a double bed and their cases. Maura felt tired and disappeared for a long soak in the bath. Brendan sat down on the bed with his laptop and found the email in Trash inviting him for an interview at St Cillian's. He confirmed that he would be available to attend in Dublin in twelve days' time, at the beginning of September. He spent a few moments wondering what a difference the job would make; he could be in charge of pastoral care. He was imagining the interview in his head, and formulating his answers. 'Oh yes – I'm very calm, comfortable at supporting children with emotional or behavioural problems. As a sportsman,

270

I realise the importance of being in a team. I'm not only a football coach but a life coach too. I believe I can make a difference in how young people are integrated into the social network of the school, and made to feel like they belong.' He smiled. Life would be better in a school where he could have responsibility and respect.

He thought about his mother; he had no idea where she was but at least he knew where she was living. He would see her tomorrow, definitely. Brendan wondered about her new man. He doubted that it was anything more than a joke on his mother's part; the man was probably just the owner and she was staying as a paying guest. His mother would not embark on another relationship, not after his father. And besides, she was seventy-five. Brendan wondered why she might need a relationship and he thought sadly that he didn't really need one himself. A pinging sound signalled the arrival of an email in his Inbox and he noticed it was from Penny. He held his breath for a moment, listening to be sure that the splashing of Maura's bathwater had stopped, then he opened the message.

Penny wrote that she and Sam had hired a speedboat and she had spent the day sailing and snorkelling before an evening of cocktails. There was an attachment and Brendan downloaded the photographs and looked at each snap. Penny, her back to him, wearing a green cap and driving a speedboat; Penny again, in a flowery sarong holding up an ice-blue drink filled with fruit. Penny, with her arms around a slender girl in shorts and T-shirt, a girl with a long cascade of dark curls and coffee-brown limbs who was kissing Penny's cheek. Penny was flashing a huge smile and a shining ring at the camera. Brendan hit his thumb pad and saved the pictures in his file marked 'PW'. So that was Sam, the slim happy girl in Penny's embrace. Brendan thought of Penny, her kind words of support in the staff room, the way she would bring him a sandwich at lunchtime. She was a lovely, kind girl and he was just a fool. He closed down his laptop; the disappointment was a thick bitterness in his mouth. In the next room he could hear the gurgling of bathwater as it drained into the plug hole.

Chapter Thirty-Eight

It had been a steaming day in Spain, the soil cracking beneath their feet in the foothills. They bought more bottled water in the little shops as they crossed the border on the way back. It was cooler up in the mountains, surrounded by mist and smudges of cloud which hung and shifted and disappeared. The peaks rose like crowding giants, watching over the sunken lakes and dipping green valleys. The red sports car stopped outside a little white house which nuzzled in the crook of a hill purpled with heather. Jean-Luc turned a key and they went inside, carrying bags of shopping. Evie touched the wooden table and the white-plastered walls, and she peered into the tiny kitchen while Jean-Luc knelt by the fire and coaxed the sticks to catch light, sending sparks flying up the chimney. She put her shopping on the table and he found a bottle of dark liquid in a glass cabinet and uncorked it, pouring them each a small glass. Evie took a sip and held it in her mouth: it was warm and sweet and strong. She closed her eyes for a moment.

'*Pacherán*: it is an honest French liqueur. To good health.' Jean-Luc spoke as he unpacked, putting bread and cheese and fruit in the kitchen. She sat down in the armchair and felt the warmth of the fire flare from the grate, the shadows flickering high on white stone walls.

'I love this cosy little cottage.' She sank back into cushions and closed heavy lids. For a moment, she and Jean-Luc were back in the market in Spain, holding hands, tasting cheese and buying bread. They were inside the cool museum, looking at Dalí's installation of Mae West from the steps, excited by the colours, the painted eyes and the sofa-shaped lips and the coiled curtains of hair. Evie was eating paella in a street café and buying colourful pottery for their home. She must have drifted off to sleep, her head crammed with their day together, when she felt the pressure of his hand on hers. She smiled and snuggled into the armchair, and the air hung with the aroma of brewing coffee.

She drifted in and out of sleep. She could hear him playing the guitar, his soft resonant voice. She breathed out and imagined him in the cottage as a younger man with Hélène: it had been Hélène's cottage and now it was his. Evie hoped they had spent good times together, that his life with Hélène had been as fulfilling as hers was now with him. The logs crackled and spattered in the hearth. She thought of the mountains outside, their protective bulk, and the little cottage in their shelter, and she yawned.

'I don't want to go back tomorrow.'

He was beside her. 'Then we will stay here, Evie. Just us two. For as long as you wish.'

Hours passed and she snoozed again and woke and nibbled at bread and cheese and drank two little cups of coffee and now she was wide awake. Jean-Luc was strumming his guitar and humming a song that she recognised as one by Simon & Garfunkel. She pushed herself out of her seat and grabbed his arm. He put the guitar down.

'Let's go outside, Jean-Luc.'

He asked no questions, but reached for his jacket and one for her and they closed the door behind them.

It was dark outside but for the stars. The hills loomed like distant shadows and the air made them shiver. The moon was a silver coin, which slid behind a cloud and out again. He put his arm around her and they were quiet for a while. In the distance an animal called, a soft yelp to a mate or a pup. Jean-Luc put his face against her hair and his voice was low. '*Mon amour.*'

The moment was heavy with emotion and it was Evie's instinct to lighten it. She put her finger on his lips. 'You French men are the limit, Jean-Luc. A bit of French and a sexy voice and we women are putty in your hands.'

He did not speak for a moment, but wrapped his arms around her and brought her close to his body. She breathed the warmth, leaned her head back against his chest and felt the vibrations as he spoke.

'*Aimons donc, aimons donc! de l'heure fugitive,*
Hâtons-nous, jouissons;
L'homme n'a point de port, le temps n'a point de rive;
Il coule, et nous passons!
Temps jaloux, se peut-il que ces moments d'ivresse,
Où l'amour à longs flots nous verse le bonheur,
S'envolent loin de nous de la même vitesse
Que les jours de malheur?'

She closed her eyes. 'That was lovely, Jean-Luc. Is it a poem? Tell me what it means.'

They turned to look up at the stars. She could not see him as he moved to stand behind her, but she felt his arms tighten. 'Alphonse de Lamartine. He lived in the 1800s. A great French poet. His words are very sad.'

'What is he saying?'

'That we must love while we can today, sometimes our

275

love overflows, but we do not love for long, because time is jealous of our happiness.'

'That is depressing,' she said and for that moment she felt miserable. They were both quiet. Then she said, 'Your Lamartine's full of shite.'

She heard him chuckle. 'Why so?'

She took a deep breath. 'I want to tell you something.'

He was waiting.

'I spent over half my life married to Jim and that was all right. I don't regret it, but it was all about doing the right thing for someone else. I used to make his dinner and iron his shirts but I never did it because of love, I did it for duty or because it was the proper thing to do. I wanted a big family. I had a lot of love going spare, Jean-Luc, and Brendan was the only child I could have and I gave most of my love to him, I probably smothered him with it, hoping he would have a good life. Then, when I was on my own, I realised I didn't even know myself, let alone have any love for myself. Now I have come to France and met you, I am where I should be. Here, with you. And I don't care what your Albert or Alfred de Lamartine says, each moment should be happy and fun and filled with love – we shouldn't hang around worrying about what is going to happen next.' She heard him exhale. 'Especially at our age.'

She knew that he was smiling. She turned and saw the curve of his lips.

'You are right, *chérie*. I think you are right about everything.'

She looked over his head at the canopy of stars. 'We are so small.'

He gazed up and she knew he shared her thoughts. His words were spoken close to her ear. 'But love is big and powerful and perhaps it can be infinite, Evie. Perhaps it can last for ever for us?'

She nodded and he kissed her. He took her hand in his and she noticed how small it was compared to his large palm. He brought her fingers to his lips. 'You have my heart in this little hand.' She put her hand on his chest and he covered it with his own.

Her eyes were steady. 'I will keep it safe.'

He pulled her close and she leaned against him. The moon dipped behind the shreds of a cloud. In the distance, an owl hooted and another replied.

She awoke and the room was yellow with sunlight. She had slept in one of his enormous T-shirts and as she sat up she smiled to see 'Red Hot Chilli Peppers' emblazoned across her chest. She blinked her eyes and saw him, his hair damp from the shower, his back to her as he looked through the window. He did not know she was awake and now she filled the moment looking at him, his wide shoulders and a back still muscled from work. Her eyes took in buttocks, long legs, buttocks again and she slithered out of the bed and tiptoed behind him, the T-shirt baggy below her thighs. She enclosed him in her arms, resting her head between his shoulder blades. Evie heard him make a long, deep sound, a rumble of contentment, and she hugged him closer, breathing his warm skin.

Chapter Thirty-Nine

Brendan wanted to have a shave but she was in the bathroom, taking up all the space in front of the little washbasin. He knew that he was wrong to blame Maura but somehow he wanted it to be her fault; Evie had not been there yesterday and the yellow-haired boy refused to speak to them. He and Maura would have breakfast and then go back to Cave Bonheur and wait outside all morning if necessary. A dark mood squatted on his shoulders. Maura bent over the basin, cleaning her teeth. Spittle and toothpaste were dangling in an elastic line from her mouth and she was staring into the mirror, her face pallid and fretful.

'Come on, hurry up. I need to get to the mirror and have a shave. It's nearly eight thirty.' He could not believe he had spoken to her so brusquely, so he added, 'Please, Maura, come on, love.' He heard her spit hard and turn on the tap and he glanced back into the bathroom. Her eyes moved wildly, like a beaten animal's. He turned away.

They spent the morning sitting in the Panda. He was reading a new book on coastal walks in the south of France and she was looking at the pictures in a French magazine and trying to puzzle out a few words which were the same as English. Brendan glanced at the front cover. A celebrity actress had just broken up with her husband and she was in therapy and a TV presenter was talking about how weight-gain and depression can affect a marriage. It was hot inside the car, even with the windows down. Maura grabbed a bottle of water from her bag and took a few gulps, then replaced the cap and put it back in her bag. She would usually have offered him a drink, carefully wiping the top first. Things were changing.

He stretched his legs out of the car door before standing up and passing the teetering sign near the office, where he walked up and down for several minutes. The camper-van had not been moved. He walked towards the vines, but he could not see the blond boy. The place was deserted. He went back to the car. By two thirty, Maura was asking for something to eat and Brendan started the engine. They would drive to a supermarket and buy a snack, perhaps come back later, when it was cooler.

Evie made a pot of tea; Jean-Luc wasn't a tea drinker but she insisted that it was the only thing to have after their long journey. It would help them cool down and, besides, this was green tea, so it would be good for him. Jean-Luc looked at the pale liquid in the cup and sat back in the armchair, taking a tentative sip. They could unpack their cases later, and put the cheese in the fridge and the bottles of *pacherán* in the cupboard. Evie thought she would make a simple meal of bread and cheese and fruit. Jean-Luc decided to check the grapes later that evening. Evie was puzzled.

'So when do you normally harvest the grapes and make the wine? I'm looking forward to it.'

'You will enjoy the harvest, Evie. It is a special time. There are some people from Saint-Girons who come here each year to help and Benji is expert now about the fermentation and filtration. I love watching grapes become wine in the big vats. And we can work on that too, you and I. It will be magical.'

'When do we start, Jean-Luc?'

'Anytime in the next month or two. When the grapes are ready.'

Evie frowned. 'What makes them ready?'

'The seeds change from green to yellow. They are not so bitter.'

'But is it because of the sunshine?'

'The sunshine, yes, always, and the weather.' He laughed. 'Or the will of God.'

She looked up sharply. 'Do you believe in God, Jean-Luc?'

'I am, I suppose, a pantheist.'

Evie pulled a face. 'You believe in that little fellow with horns and the pipes?'

'No, for me God is in nature, all around in the mountains and the skies and the seas. In nature and the universe. I do not think there is an anthropomorphic God.'

For a few seconds she was stunned. 'I never thought of it that way. I have a lot of things to learn.'

'Who is he, then, your God, Evie?'

She stuck out her bottom lip. 'I went to a Catholic school, St Aloysius. The nuns weren't afraid to give you a good slap. I learned that I wasn't much use for anything and I suppose God wasn't much use to me either, but I believed in him because we were told we had to.'

'And now, what do you believe? You are a Catholic?'

'I don't really think about it much.' She put on her thoughtful face. 'And when I do think about it, I think it might just be a load of bollocks. God only comes out for weddings and funerals or when you want to ask for something. But then there's a lot of goodness in people, isn't there, so maybe that's because of God? I'm not sure. I believe there's something out there which guides us – God, luck, happiness – and it's important to live a good life.'

His expression became brooding. She wondered if she had offended him. 'I might become a Panty-ist, or whatever you just said you were. It sounds like more fun, living in the mountains and going to the coast and just enjoying nature as it comes to us.'

His eyes crinkled. 'I think nature has a lot of answers. We come from the earth and then we go back to it. I no longer believe in the Bible I was raised with, but when it speaks of grapevines and vineyards, that I understand. So I suppose that my religion now is found in grapes, Evie. Every year they grow on the vines and give us good wine and we can rely on them to be there for us again the next year.'

Maura leaned back in her seat and closed her eyes.

'You still feel unwell?' Brendan's eyes were on the road ahead. She nodded. 'Nearly there now. Do you think she'll be in?'

Maura sighed. 'You should have phoned her first.'

Brendan's hand squeezed the steering wheel. His knuckles were white. 'She'll be pleased to see us, Maura.'

She made a soft puffing noise through her lips and Brendan felt his heart thud in his throat. He had come all this way and he had no idea how his mother would react.

He pulled the car in at the opening to the vineyard, where the sign slanted precariously, and he parked the Panda next to an old red sports car.

Evie finished her tea. She thought about giving Jean-Luc a kiss and she rose steadily from the armchair, but the door banged open and Benji ran in. He stopped abruptly, looking at Evie then at Jean-Luc. He moved his hands in front of him, stammering. Jean-Luc spoke to him quietly. Evie understood the words '*calme*' and '*doucement*'. Benji breathed in, and then began to say something between deep breaths – a man, a woman, she heard her own name. Benji ran over to Evie and put his arms around her protectively; her hand was instinctive, she threaded it through his bright hair and over his warm brow. Jean-Luc turned to her.

'Benji said a woman and a man have been here looking for you. He says they are here again, they are outside. Do you want me to go out and speak to them?'

Evie frowned.

'Evie, do you know who they might be?'

'No idea.' She put her arm round Benji. 'I'm intrigued. Come on – let's all go together, shall we?'

There was an abrupt knock at the door. Benji opened wild eyes, but Evie laughed. 'It's fine. The police aren't after me. Unless it was the speed cops who stopped me for going through a red light but that was weeks ago.'

She opened the door and stood still: Brendan was staring at her, Maura just behind his shoulder. Evie grabbed her son and hugged him, her body a flurry of emotion. She seized Maura and pulled her close, Maura's eyes popping with surprise. She clutched Brendan again and squeezed him in her arms, kissing his cheeks.

'Come in. Come in. Oh, what a lovely surprise.' They were in the hallway, not yet into the living room, and she stopped and turned to Jean-Luc. 'Oh, I don't believe it – Jean-Luc, this is my son, Brendan, and this is his wife, Maura. Brendan, this is my – this is Jean-Luc and Benji, who works here with us. Benji, *voici mon fils*.'

Benji's face relaxed and everyone else was smiling. Brendan could not take in what was happening: his mother was blonde now and tanned and speaking French and a tall man was shaking his hand. Maura's eyes protruded as the tall man then kissed her on both cheeks and she beamed at him as he said, '*Bonjour, enchanté*.' Her face happy, like a child's at Christmas.

Evie led the way. 'This is our lounge so you can sit down and put your feet up – oh, and the kitchen is through there. Brendan, why on earth didn't you ring me, tell me you were here? We have a lovely big range; it's grand to cook on. I'll show you round in a bit. And you'll have to come and see outside. Oh, you could do a wine-tasting. Unless you want a cup of tea. No. Stay for dinner. Are you on holiday? You should have told me. Why not stay for a few days, stay here with us? That would be OK, wouldn't it, Jean-Luc?'

He squeezed her shoulder in his hand, and she knew he was happy for her. Brendan was still mystified. Maura tried to help out. 'It was really hard to find you, Mother, but here we are now.'

Evie turned to her and laid a hand on her arm: her eyes shone. 'Let's get this straight, Maura. Call me Evie. Would that be all right?' Maura nodded, glancing at Brendan nervously. Evie thought she looked smaller than she remembered, more anxious, and in their house she seemed unsure of her surroundings; she had the demeanour of a rabbit ready to run.

Brendan opened his mouth to speak but no words came. He thought of his journey and was about to explain how far they had come, but he decided it would be best to talk about it later. He smiled at Evie and she hugged him again and laughed and said, 'Oh, I am so pleased to see you.'

Benji said his goodbyes and left for home on his bike. Jean-Luc was upstairs, bumping about in the spare room, making a bed for Brendan and Maura, and Evie set the table with fruit and nuts: olives, tomatoes, apricots, fresh figs, walnuts, grapes and strawberries. She laid out baguettes and cheeses, plates and knives and she poured red wine into glasses. The four of them ate together, Evie talking about her journey in the campervan. Maura was amazed that she had won so much money on a horse called Lucky Jim and Brendan was quiet, chewing his bread thoughtfully.

Maura smiled. 'We had a real escapade ourselves on the way here. Brendan and I were riding a tand—' He shot her a troubled look and she winced and thought again. She mentioned quickly they had visited some caves nearby, saying how stunning they were.

Jean-Luc spoke for the first time. 'Rivière souterraine de Labouiche. We must go there, Evie. You will love it.'

Evie thought a moment. 'Jean-Luc, why is this place called a cave?'

'*Cave* means wine cellar, *chérie*.' A deep chuckle. 'But there is no wine in the underground caves, just a blue river. We can go there together and drink the beauty of nature.'

Brendan stopped eating and frowned at them both, his knife still in the air.

Evie smiled. 'So this is Wine Cellars Bonheur?'

He murmured agreement. 'And "*bonheur*" means happiness.'

She brought her hands together. 'That is just the best thing.' She thought again. 'Who needs luck when you have happiness? What a grand name for our home.'

Brendan couldn't help himself. 'When are you coming back though, Mammy? To Dublin?'

She turned her head to him. 'Not at all, Brendan. Not ever. This is my home here now. I mean, we might come over for a visit, but I live here.'

Brendan's face tightened. Evie recognised the expression; he was the same as a child, just before a tantrum. His lips compressed, his cheeks reddening – she knew what he was thinking, and that he was frustrated that he couldn't have his own way. She looked at Jean-Luc and saw that he understood too, and she loved him for it; he could see the closeness between mother and son. Indeed, he had loved his own mother with a protectiveness that had been both fierce and possessive. She'd had no-one else and he'd always stood by her. So, he respected Brendan's attachment to Evie, nodded towards her and turned away. She and Brendan would have their discussion uninterrupted. Maura's face was pained and puzzled, as if expecting an argument. Evie decided to take over.

'I live here now, Brendan, and Jean-Luc is my partner. We have been together for nearly six weeks and we are very happy and we intend to stay that way. That is that. Now I am going to clear up the table and I suggest we all go down to O'Driscoll's for a quick drink. I'll make a couple of calls on my smartphone and you can meet some of my friends. Would that be all right? I've so many friends I want you to meet. Ray and Paulette, Caroline, Nige. Oh, it's grand you're here, Brendan. I do hope you'll stay for a day or two.'

Chapter Forty

Brendan turned over, taking the duvet with him and giving Maura the cold side of his back. He had said very little all evening. He was not interested in Maura's chatter. He squeezed his eyes shut.

'I can see why she loves it here. Those people were so nice. Paulette and Ray, what great people, and I did enjoy chatting with Nige. He is such a knowledgeable man. Imagine, all the travelling he has done around the world and still he loves this place the best. Such interesting people.'

Brendan blew a shot of air out of his mouth.

'And Jean-Luc. What a lovely man he is. So gentle and he obviously thinks the world of your mother.'

Brendan thought grimly to himself how different his and Maura's relationship was. Jean-Luc had listened attentively to Evie's conversation all evening, leaning towards her, his arm protectively around the back of her chair, nodding in agreement with her thoughts.

'She's landed on her feet with him and this place, Brendan. And she is happy. You can't deny it.'

He thought about telling her that she should shut up.

Evie and Jean-Luc had kissed and smiled into each other's faces. He had never seen his mammy like that with his father. He was uncomfortable with the whole situation; his mother no longer needed him at all, and he couldn't understand it. He rolled over, pushing his head into the pillow to send the images away.

'So, what about their invitation to stay here for a few days? I mean, we can stay for a while, can't we? It would give you some time with your mother.'

Brendan was counting time in his head. His interview was in ten days. They had not bought return tickets. It was feasible. They could stay for a week. He would not tell Maura, though. He felt peevish and wanted to keep her waiting.

'I'd love to stay here for a while,' she said, hope in her voice. It irritated Brendan that she clearly hoped his mother's new romance would rub off on them. She was chattering, patting his arm, enjoying the experience. He closed his eyes. After a few minutes, she stopped talking and the room was dark and filled with silence. A sigh shuddered through her body as she turned her back to align with his. Minutes passed. He could not sleep. He could feel that she was thinking and he knew she was awake too, but he had nothing to say.

Evie brought a silver coffee pot to the table; Brendan put his head in his hands. She poured coffee into his cup, dropped two sugar lumps in, and paused. His head still rested on his fists, which lifted up the sinking flesh from his cheeks into little rolls. Evie stirred his coffee and poured her own. Moments later, Maura came downstairs, sitting opposite Evie, muttering good morning and running her hand over a tired face.

'Did you both sleep badly?' Evie asked, and Maura

287

groaned softly. She turned to Brendan. 'Why won't you come with me this morning?'

Brendan shrugged and took a mouthful of coffee.

'Will you come with me, Maura?' Evie filled another cup.

'Where to?'

'It's market day in Saint-Girons and I sometimes do the stall there, selling wine. Benji will be there already, setting up, so I am going straight over after breakfast with some food for him and I usually stay for a few hours. Oh, it's a marvellous little market and my friend Caroline will be there with her jams and I have such a good time. My French is getting a bit better and I usually sell lots of bottles to all sorts of people. Lots of them are tourists. You'd enjoy it.' She looked at Brendan. 'Both of you.'

Brendan forced a smile. 'I might go for a walk, Mammy.'

'I'll come with you, if that's all right, Mo— Evie.'

Evie beamed at Maura. 'That would be grand.' She noticed Brendan's eyes move furtively towards Maura's just as his wife's moved quickly away. Evie passed them a plate of croissants. 'Freshly baked this morning. Jean-Luc drove to the *boulangerie* at seven before he went out to do a bit of work. You should go up and see him, Brendan; it is so interesting, all the different things he has to do to make wine.'

Brendan made a little noise in his nose and took a croissant, nibbling it carefully. Maura took one and did the same. Evie exhaled, took a croissant and bit it in half, chewing thoughtfully.

Evie had never seen Maura look so happy. She was watching the people walking past in the market, noticing Benji sell bottles of wine to French customers and to hesitant tourists. She helped Evie to replenish the stall and

288

she stood at her shoulder as Evie sold a case of sparkling wine to an English lady who said she came from Dunstable. When a young couple approached and asked her directly if someone spoke English, Maura gave them a winning smile and said she could certainly help. She told them about the bottles of wine they had drunk at their own table the night before and how good it was and, while Benji poured two small glasses for them to taste, Maura was effervescent, praising the young woman's dress and asking her where she had bought it and complimenting them both on their suntans and wishing them a happy holiday after they bought a case of the red wine.

'You're a natural, Maura.' Evie put her hand on Maura's shoulder and, for a moment, she saw the gentle face of the bubbly girl Brendan had brought home so many years ago.

'She wants to take my job, Evie,' Benji joked, and Maura looked really pleased.

'It's good to have the help here,' Evie told her. 'But you should take an hour off and go round the stalls. You'll love it. You have an hour or so then I'll have twenty minutes. I need to go and see the wood-carver: he is doing a special job for me.'

It was noon and the market was thriving; heat rose from the concrete and people flocked to the shade. Trade was good and Evie hardly noticed the time pass, but it was almost two o'clock when Maura returned, carrying three cartons of couscous and bottles of water. She had other purchases under her arms and her hair was covered in a colourful scarf which she'd bought from the African stall. Her face was flushed and she was smiling. Evie took some money from a French woman and handed her two bottles of red, waving her off with a 'Merci Madame. À bientôt.'

Maura took her place behind the stall. 'I had a lovely chat with your friend, Caroline. She's such a nice person, so genuine. I bought some jam from her and some whisky marmalade. Oh, and the African stall is gorgeous. They were playing music. They had drums – *djembe*, the man told me they were called – and some sort of stringed instrument called *kora*. It was lovely. And I bought a skirt and a scarf. Then there were some lovely ceramic pots and, oh, the chunky jewellery. I wish I'd brought more money. And I got myself a pair of comfortable sandals – look, I bought these so I could stand behind the stall with you. I thought they would be ideal – real leather. And I bought you this – it's called *zaalouk*, with tomatoes and aubergines, and I couldn't walk past the stall, it smelled so good. Is that all right?'

Benji shovelled plastic forkfuls into his mouth and Evie picked up her carton. 'It's a Moroccan dish. I like the aubergines. Lovely.'

Maura was impressed. 'I can't believe how you have changed, Evie. I mean you were in that stuffy old home but look at you now. You speak French, you look completely different and you are so nice—'

'I wasn't nice before?'

Maura put her hand over her mouth and Evie could see the returning memories of their last conversation in Sheldon Lodge in her expression, her face reddening. 'I – I mean, well, back then, it was—'

Evie helped her out. 'It wasn't right for me. Sometimes a change is a good thing and this is a better life here. Me being in that home was no good for any of us.' Her mouth held itself in a grim line for a moment.

Maura was silent, her eyes thoughtful, and Evie thought of the vast gulf that had been between them for years. Perhaps she had disliked Maura simply because she was

Brendan's wife. Perhaps she hadn't fully let Brendan go, allowed him to become the man he needed to be. She wondered whether she hadn't been in the way, as far as her son's relationship was concerned, and perhaps she'd been a little bit jealous of his transferred affection to his wife. She glanced at Maura, who offered a rueful smile. Maura had been good company at the stall, and eager to learn. Evie thought about telling her that she had a lovely smile; she hadn't seen it often.

'Let's have a big supper tonight, all of us.' Evie brought her hands together. 'Sparkling wine, a nice meal; I will make a *clafoutis* for dessert.'

'*Clafoutis!*' Benji jumped up and down, repeating the word. 'It is my favourite. *Clafoutis.*'

'I will do an extra one for you, Benji, *pour ta mère.*'

Maura was puzzled. 'What is it, clafootee?'

'A bit like a cheesecake. I put cherry brandy in mine. Just a little. I must go and buy some fresh cherries – oh, it's a pudding, Maura. Jean-Luc loves it. It has such a light batter.' Evie grinned. 'It might cheer Brendan up a little bit. He's had a face on him like a smacked arse.'

Maura shrugged. Evie was thinking that her son was moody, more reticent than usual, and the relationship between him and his wife had seemed somewhat distant. A good dinner always sorts out marital problems, she thought. Especially if there is plenty of drink on the table.

That evening the wooden table was set with food: bread, glasses and bottles of wine, a casserole steaming in the middle. There were buttered potatoes and colourful plates with peas and beans, yellow and green. Tomatoes and carrots, green leafy salads and dishes Brendan had never seen before, made with peppers and olives and garlic, and bowls of balsamic vinegar with golden oil floating in the centre. Brendan looked at his mother as she busied about, creating dishes with such ease and enjoyment, adding butter and herbs to vegetables she would have previously taken from a tin. She wore a long African skirt that wrapped around and tied at the waist and a T-shirt, dark grey with a splash of batter from the pudding. Her hair, newly washed, was light and soft. Her skin was brown but also firmer, less papery; her movements seemed more fluid and her eyes brighter. He could not get used to the way she would move around the room with her hands full, singing to herself, then find herself in Jean-Luc's arms and smile up at him with such ease and familiarity. He even saw her pinch his bottom and giggle. Brendan was quiet and brooding.

Since she had returned from the market, Maura had not stopped babbling, and his forehead was beginning to tighten. She was following his mother everywhere, watching what she was doing, her hands twitching in the air, ready to help. Jean-Luc washed a few dishes and then picked up his guitar, playing a few chords to himself. After a while, he put it down deliberately and went to the table, pouring four glasses of wine and giving one each to the women. He took the other two and came to sit next to Brendan who was in the armchair next to the grate where the logs were piled high. He handed him a glass and said, '*Santé*.'

Brendan swallowed a mouthful, followed by a second. When he glanced up, Jean-Luc was looking at him, his dark eyes steady. Brendan had the feeling that Jean-Luc understood his thoughts. He was about to attempt conversation when Evie called them all to table.

Chapter Forty-One

Brendan had eaten too much; he had drunk too much wine. Maura's face was flushed in the firelight as she sat opposite him, digesting her second helping of *clafoutis* and sipping brandy. Jean-Luc was strumming his guitar and singing something in French, Evie sitting on the floor at his feet, smiling, waving her hands and talking about her plans to create a bed and breakfast and redecorate the house. Maura was effusive and laughing, an amber glow on her face, her smile lifting her cheeks as she chatted easily with his mother. Brendan looked at his wife and then at his mother. He watched the way Evie was so affectionate towards Jean-Luc and how they smiled into each other's faces and laughed. He caught Maura's eye and plastered a smirk on his face. She grinned at him and then turned back to speak to Jean-Luc. She looked radiant and Brendan wished he could put his arm around her. He wanted to feel like part of a couple, not the moody man on the outside. But mostly, he wanted to be part of a happy couple with Maura again, with the vibrant, chattering woman who spoke so easily to his mother and her new man, and who seemed to be fitting in so well. Maura was relaxed, friendly, and he envied her for it. Something in his heart expanded and became swollen with pride, perhaps even with love, as he watched Maura laugh easily at a joke. He sat firmly in his chair and watched the others enjoy the evening. He swallowed the brandy and it was fierce and hot in his mouth.

Maura was in a party mood. 'Have you played the guitar long, Jean-Luc?' He finished his song and Maura was clapping lightly, her face shining.

'A long time.' His fingers strummed a chord. 'My guitar has been with me since I was a boy; since I first kissed a woman, I learned to play and sing about love and loneliness.' The flames made his eyes thoughtful and a melancholy flickered for a moment. 'Music and poetry, it's the same thing: they break from a broken soul but they heal the heart.'

Evie laughed. 'He does talk shite sometimes, but he's a great fella on the guitar. I never think about putting on the television. We just talk and he plays the music. It's grand.'

Jean-Luc began to play something fast and jazzy, picking out notes easily with thick fingers.

Maura was excitable. 'Can you play any Oasis?'

Jean-Luc began with a few chords she found immediately recognisable. 'Wonderwall'.

'Oh, I love this one!'

He began to sing softly, and Maura joined in, and Jean-Luc looked at Evie. Brendan turned his eyes away as Maura threw her head back and sang from the depths of her lungs. He wanted her to sing it for him, to smile in his direction, but she had her eyes closed, singing for herself now. He wondered if Maura was even aware of him at all. No, her confidence had blossomed tonight. She was in France, in a new place where she seemed really at home; she was talking animatedly to his mother, chattering warmly, even flirtatiously, to Jean-Luc, and Brendan felt left out in the cold. He hoped no-one saw him wipe a tear from his cheek. Maura clapped again as he reached for the bottle of brandy.

'That was lovely, Jean-Luc. I remember that song. It was out when Brendan and I—' She turned to him, and then back to Jean-Luc and her lower lip dropped. 'Years ago.'

'You sing well,' Jean-Luc commented and the skin on Maura's neck became blotchy and pink.

Evie couldn't resist a jibe. 'Not like a frog, Monsieur?'

Jean-Luc bent over and kissed the top of her head. 'Your song moved me that night, Evie. It was a sad song, "Danny Boy". Seeing you there so sure of yourself, so happy, made me realise how lonely I was. I thought you were beautiful that night but the words would not come to tell you.'

She reached up an arm to him. 'So instead you told me I sang like a frog.'

He made a deep sound in his throat, full of emotion. 'You said I was an ugly toad.'

'I thought you were drop-dead gorgeous.'

It took him a moment to understand her words, and then he smiled. Evie laughed, her voice tinkling and full of joy, and Maura joined in. Evie reached for the brandy, filling glasses.

'It's a lovely story, how the two of you met, Jean-Luc.' Maura put a hand to her face: the fire was warm. 'I love a romantic story.' She lifted her eyes to meet Brendan's.

He shifted in his seat. Maura was clearly impressed by Jean-Luc's warmth; she was even developing a friendship with his mother, their heads close together. He clenched his teeth. 'I think I'll go up to bed.'

Evie looked at him. 'But you didn't go out anywhere today at all, Brendan. It's only just after nine o'clock. Stay a little bit longer. We're having such a lovely time.'

'I'm shattered,' he said, as he stood up and stretched.

Maura glanced away. 'Think I'll have an early night

too. Thank you both for such a lovely meal and, well, the music and singing was great. It really cheered me up.'

'It's grand to have you both here, isn't it, Jean-Luc?' Evie's eyes searched his face.

Jean-Luc smiled; he began to pick out the notes for 'Stairway to Heaven' and he sang softly, his voice low and poignant. Evie turned to him, giving him her full attention, as Brendan headed for the stairs followed by a hesitant Maura.

He pulled his pyjamas over his head and Maura sat on the bed, taking off her new sandals. The silence between them hung cold in the air and neither of them knew how to break it.

Then Maura sighed. 'He's nice, Jean-Luc, isn't he?'

Brendan brought his lips together and made a small sound.

'What's that supposed to mean, Brendan? Don't you like him?'

'You obviously do.' Brendan shuddered at the pettiness of his own voice. He saw Maura look at him steadily, unsure how to read his mood. He thought about reaching out, putting an arm round her, but sulkiness squatted on his shoulders and he couldn't move.

'I had such a lovely time today.' Her voice was a whisper.

'You seemed to enjoy being with Mammy at the market and you got on well with Jean-Luc tonight. You looked like you were having fun. You didn't need me at all. I was just a millstone . . .'

Maura couldn't speak for a moment, then she muttered, 'Don't you think we can be good together, Brendan? Like Evie and Jean-Luc? Can't we be more like them, the two of us?'

He shrugged. 'I don't know.'

He turned off the light and climbed into bed. He felt her slide in beside him. It was quiet for a moment, and then he heard her sigh. He breathed out. 'I'm sorry, Maura.'

She sniffed. 'You were very moody tonight, Brendan. I don't understand at all what got into you downstairs.'

He was quiet for a while and, when it came, his voice was hollow. 'I was just tired.'

'You looked unhappy.' Another pause. 'Is it because of me?'

'Perhaps it's because of me.'

'Are you needing a hug? I am.'

He put his arms around her and squeezed her to him, whispered into her hair, 'Oh, Maura, it's all such a mess. I don't know what to do—'

He didn't finish the sentence; she pulled away and rolled over. He heard her snuffling quietly. Brendan put out a hand and touched her shoulder. He wished she would turn back again, tell him he was special, help him to tell her that she had moved his heart this evening, that she had been wonderful and he had truly admired her warmth and friendliness, something he couldn't summon himself. She'd looked beautiful in the firelight and he was jealous of her easy conversation with others and angry with himself for being so foolish. He had wanted her to smile at him, to chatter animatedly to him as she had chatted to Jean-Luc, to look at him as her mother had looked at her new man and he wanted so badly to be able to go back in time, to replay the last few hours again, to be seated at the firelight and to join in the song and put his arms round Maura. But he had failed at the first hurdle and he was failing again. Jealousy stopped his mouth and spread like cement. Maura's sobs became quieter and the opportunity was lost. He waited for sleep.

Chapter Forty-Two

Everyone else was eating breakfast but Maura was still in the bathroom. Evie left her coffee and hurried to the stairs; she could hear Maura retching from the depths of her throat. Evie went upstairs, wondering why Brendan was still downstairs at the table spreading butter and jam on a baguette.

She put a hand on Maura's back, feeling the violence of her gagging, rubbing gently between each heave. Maura was almost vomiting, her face was wet and she was clearly unwell. Evie turned on the tap as the bouts subsided. Maura was trying to apologise between swallowing and sobbing.

'Don't even think about it, Maura. Was it the drink last night? I mean, we drank quite a lot between us . . .'

Maura turned to Evie and her face was washed out. Her eyes glistened and were hollow. She put a hand on Evie's shoulder. 'This is the fourth time this week I have felt so bad. I might be ill. I think it's my nerves. I'm in tatters. Brendan and I – things are not going well between us at the minute.'

Evie stared at Maura's face and was thinking about

something else, a memory, a sensation in her stomach, shreds of her own past. She clutched Maura's arm.

'Come downstairs and we'll get you a cup of tea. You and I need to have a chat, I think.'

There was a long conversation in which Maura and Evie had their heads close together, talking in hushed voices, then Jean-Luc was given his instructions. Brendan stood alone haplessly and followed Evie into the garden, watching Jean-Luc slide into the red sports car. Maura was trembling as she sat in the passenger seat and clicked the seatbelt. Evie gave her a conspiratorial wink and said she would see them in an hour and asked Jean-Luc to pick up some eggs for her so that she could make omelettes for lunch. She waved until they passed the crooked sign, then she turned to Brendan, who was standing next to her quietly. 'You and I need to talk.'

'Is that why you've sent the pair of them off to the shops, Mammy? So we could have a chit-chat?'

She linked her arm through his and turned him away from the house, walking past the barn and the tractor to where the vines grew like little trees. They walked along the path, and she hugged his arm.

'I thought it would be nice for you and me to spend some time, just the two of us, yes?' Brendan smiled weakly and she held his gaze. 'But it's clear you're unhappy and Maura is looking like a wet weekend herself. You hardly said a word last night, and you're just like your father was, with his moods – I can read you like a book. So, how can I help?'

He took a deep breath. 'You can't, Mammy. It's such a mess. When you left the home in Dublin, I was really worried about you. You just took off. Then I found out you were in Liverpool and the next thing I knew you were in France. You never said goodbye or anything. So I came out here to bring you back. I thought you'd need me to look after you. And now things are different. You've changed so much.'

For a second she was angry. 'I was wasting away in Sheldon Lodge, Brendan. Is that what you wanted? I was a little old lady waiting to die in a place that was sucking the soul out of me.'

'No, but—'

'And you say I've changed, but haven't I changed for the better? Haven't I come here and found out who I am and made my own new life? I like it better here, Brendan. I'm stronger and fitter and happier. I'm busy and I have friends and a lovely man who loves me. Don't you think that is a good thing?'

He agreed.

She turned them around and they walked silently back to the house. Inside, Evie went over to the range, heating water, putting tea-bags in the pot, opening a tin of biscuits. Brendan stood behind her, hesitant.

'Mammy, so much has changed in my life too. I came here to find you and then I followed your texts—'

'Why the hell couldn't you just ring up?' Her hands were on her hips.

His face crumpled and she went over to him. 'I wanted to bring you back. I wanted you to need me, to look after you. I wanted to see the look on your face, the joy of it, when I turned up to take you home. And I missed you, Mammy. And I wanted to get away but Maura was always there and it's going badly between us and I wanted to see you. I thought you weren't safe. I mean, you'd gone abroad. I thought . . . I sort of wanted to rescue you, but, but now I'm here and you don't need me and you won't come back home and my own life is such a mess—'

She put a mug of tea in his hands and clasped them

around the soothing heat. He took a mouthful and breathed out.

Her gaze was intense. 'Don't you love Maura?'

'I think I do. But I'm not sure I can make her happy.' Brendan shrugged and he looked like he would cry.

'Does she love you?'

He shrugged again and Evie sighed.

'It's a fecking mess, I'm sure, but these things have a way of sorting themselves out.'

'I don't know how to sort it out any more, Mammy. I don't know what to do next.'

She put her hand on his shoulder and her cheek was next to his. He could smell the warmth of a perfume, a gentle smell of something sweet and woody, and he inhaled. Her hands found his curls and she wound her fingers into them as she had done when he was a child.

'Things will get better with time, Brendan. Stay here. Can you stay for a week?'

He closed his eyes. 'I think so. I need to be at an interview in Dublin in nine days so maybe we can stay for five or six more.'

'Stay, have some time to relax, enjoy yourself, get to know Jean-Luc.' She saw the expression on his face. 'He's not going to replace your dad, Brendan, but he is such a good man. Get to know him a bit. Give him a chance.'

Brendan drank the tea, and stared into the depths of the liquid. Evie went over to the range and started to select vegetables.

Jean-Luc came in followed by Maura, who said she needed to go to the toilet and made a quick exit past the table without looking at Brendan. He sighed. His mother was hugging Jean-Luc, who was mumbling about looking at the equipment and taking the tractor around the vineyard; he had work to do. Evie kissed him, laughing and telling him to be back in three hours as she would have lunch ready.

'Brendan, go with Jean-Luc, will you? I'd love him to show you the wine-making equipment. We have six five-hundred-litre stainless steel tanks in the other barn and all sorts of interesting devices for filtering and bottling and what-not.' She made a small movement with her head, twice. 'Go on with you. You'll enjoy it.' Brendan looked puzzled. Jean-Luc put on his cap and his jacket and Brendan followed him sheepishly, while his mother beamed away at him.

Brendan stared at huge vats and racks upon racks of bottles. The barn was dark and full of cobwebs in the corners but the machinery was pristine. There was even a little ladder that led up to the tap at the top of the vats. Jean-Luc explained the process and Brendan was trying to listen, rubbing his forehead.

Jean-Luc stopped speaking and took off his cap. 'You have no need to worry about your mother, Brendan.'

Brendan did not know what to say. Jean-Luc put a hand on his shoulder.

Brendan began to stammer. 'Please . . . please don't think I was being . . .' He looked at the huge hand, at Jean-Luc, whose gaze was steady.

'Evie is a wonderful woman. She is special.'

Brendan agreed, wondering if he should escape, run away, or stand and listen to a man he hardly knew talking to him about his own mother.

'Evie is my life now, she is everything to me, and I will make sure she is cared for.'

Brendan agreed quickly.

'You can trust me with that, Brendan. With your mother.'

He agreed again and looked anxiously at the door.

Jean-Luc positioned himself in front of Brendan and grasped his hand in his fist. Brendan's colour faded.

'We can be friends, perhaps? I know you must miss your father and, well, I can see you are not happy, but I hope at least you will trust me.'

Jean-Luc was shaking his hand vigorously. Brendan looked at his trapped hand and back to the big man and he swallowed hard.

'Ah, yes, Jean-Luc, all right, so . . . so tell me, tell me all about the fermentation process.'

Chapter Forty-Three

Maura held out the little plastic tube to Evie. The small oval window in the middle contained two vertical red lines. They were clearly red. Maura's hand was shaking.

'Is that positive?' Evie asked and Maura nodded. Evie had been sure of it: hadn't she been there herself, four times? She bit her lip and led her to the armchair. Maura sank into the cushions and leaned back.

'So – how many weeks? Can you work it out?'

'Seven, maybe eight. Now I think about it, it makes sense. We were in Brittany. It was the end of June, beginning of July. Now it's the end of August. I hadn't realised, hadn't given it a thought. Oh, I'm so stupid.'

Evie took her hand. 'How are you feeling about it all?'

Maura stuck out her bottom lip and stared ahead. She was numbed, in shock. In contrast, Evie's thoughts rushed: Brendan, the child, their futures. She shook Maura's arm. 'You're going to tell Brendan?'

Maura did not blink. Her voice was empty and she looked drained. 'I suppose so. I doubt he'll be interested. I haven't the first clue how he'll react.' She thought for a moment and her voice was quiet. 'I'm worried. I don't know if he'll be pleased or angry. I shouldn't imagine he'll be happy. It'll be my fault. To be honest, Evie, I hardly know him these days. I'm keeping the babby though, whatever happens.'

The next day, Evie and Jean-Luc went out in the morning. They spent the afternoon working in the fermentation rooms and in the evening they shared a meal with Brendan and Maura and then proclaimed they were tired and needed an early night. The following day, Maura was retching again in the bathroom and Evie surreptitiously popped her head around the corner and asked, 'Have you told him yet?' only to be greeted by a sad shake of the head.

In the morning, Evie and Jean-Luc went over to help Nige and Caroline with an unexpected problem in the house. Later that day, Evie and Jean-Luc were painting an outside wall together, refusing Brendan's offer of help, and in the evening they went to O'Driscoll's to chat to Ray, Evie telling Brendan he needed to spend some time alone with his wife. Evie was not being very subtle. She could tell from Maura's pained expression, by the anxiety furrowing her brow, that she had not told Brendan about the pregnancy, but Evie did not care about being obvious about her intentions. She was taking desperate measures in a desperate time. When they came home in the evening, Brendan went to bed to read and Maura sat in front of the fire, flicking through a magazine and staring into the sparks. Jean-Luc filled the coffee pot and put it on the range.

Evie went over to Maura. 'Does he know yet? Have you told him?'

'No.'

'Why the hell not?'

Maura's head hung down.

305

Evie was not sure if tears were falling. 'Shall I call him down? Shall I tell him for you?'

Maura sniffed. 'It's so difficult—'

'It was never going to be a bloody picnic in the park.' Evie's teeth were gritted.

'Evie, he'll hardly speak to me. He sulks all the time. When I smile at him, he ignores me. When I say something, he tells me he has a headache.'

Evie put her hands on her hips. 'Get yourself up there and talk to him, Maura. You need his help with this problem and the pair of you need a damn good shaking-up so you can sort it out. There's a babby, for goodness sake.'

Maura looked around nervously. Jean-Luc came to sit by the fire and he breathed out deeply. Evie turned to Maura again and this time her tone was gentler. 'It's difficult, but he has to know what's happening. Maybe then you can both talk about it, work things out.'

Maura smiled weakly and moved towards the stairs. Evie looked at Jean-Luc hopefully. By the time Maura opened the bedroom door, Brendan was on his back, his arms over his head like a child asleep, snoring.

'Mammy, what's going on?' Brendan came downstairs in a T-shirt and shorts, his hair sticking up. Maura was at the table eating toast and Jean-Luc was packing flasks and sandwiches. Evie cut slabs of cake and put fruit in containers.

'I've decided. We're going out for a picnic, the four of us. We're taking the day off and going into the mountains.'

Brendan reached for a coffee. 'Lovely.' His voice conveyed no enthusiasm.

'We'll go in the sports car and you two can follow in the Panda. Is that OK?'

Brendan wasn't convinced. Maura passed the toast and

he accepted it warily. She gave him a careful smile. 'Your mother says they need a break. They have been working hard. Jean-Luc was chopping logs yesterday with Nige and then we did all that painting. I think a little break would probably be good for us all.'

Evie was concentrating hard on looking interested in cutting tomatoes. Jean-Luc did, in fact, look tired, the skin below his cheekbones seemed looser. Brendan shrugged his shoulders and bit into the toast.

They had lunch in the mountains, the picnic cloth spread on the ground between the two cars. Evie was talking about Benji's mum, who had been a widow for ten years and was now unwell, and she said she thought a cake might cheer her up. The sun was overhead and Brendan stretched out on a rug with his book; Maura was trying to rub sun-cream on his face and the back of his neck and he felt irritable. A thin string of clouds hung between the peaks and clung to the sides of the mountains like snow. Some hikers passed, rucksacks bouncing on their backs, boots kicking pebbles into the dust, and Brendan followed them with his eyes. More distant mountains hung beyond them, huge and hazy in the heat, and he could hear the tinkle of goats' bells on the air. Maura bit into her second ham roll and Jean-Luc pulled Evie to her feet.

'Where are you going, Mammy?' Brendan asked.

'Jean-Luc and I are going to take a little walk. We might take a few pictures on my smartphone. We don't have any photos of the two of us.'

'Shall I come?' Brendan instinctively felt Maura turn towards him sharply.

Evie was already on her way, her hand in Jean-Luc's. 'Don't worry, Brendan. We won't be long. I am sure you and Maura have plenty to talk about.'

He watched them go, and then went back to his book. He muttered, 'Like a couple of teenagers,' and straight away regretted it. His voice sounded whining and petty, even to his own ears.

Maura thought for a few moments. 'I think they're sweet.'

'You would.' It was out of his mouth before he'd thought what to say. He stared at the page, his eyes stuck on the same sentence.

Maura rolled over onto her back and began to speak to the clouds. 'We need to talk—'

Brendan had nothing to say. He reread the sentence again twice.

Maura breathed out and started again: 'I need to talk to you about something.'

His mouth twisted in a miserable line. 'Not sure I want to hear it.'

'I'm pregnant, Brendan.'

He read the line again. The words began to move on the page, letters merging and separating, black against white.

'Eight weeks, I think. It was when we first arrived in Brittany. I've done a test.'

Brendan closed his eyes. There was a rushing sound in his ears. He put a hand to his head and felt sweat against his palm. He eased himself to a sitting position and looked around him. The scenery was still the same but something inside him had moved uncomfortably.

'Well, Brendan?'

He was trying to focus his eyes on something – the rolling hills, the grass, the sky; his mouth was full of glue or sand or wood chips and he could not open it. Maura's eyes were glued to his face but she made no sound. She waited, examining his expression, and he felt anger surge in his lungs, making him breathe heavily.

He searched for the hikers: there was a little path, a scar in the mountain face, and they were crawling along it, ant-lines in the distance. He wished he was there with them, away from the picnic rug, away from Maura and away from the news that she was pregnant.

She wiped her forehead with the back of her hand. 'So you have nothing to say to me about our baby?'

Baby. The word rattled in his brain, staccato, machine-gun shots. *Baby.* Rat-a tat-tat. He shook his head. Above the clear blue of the skies, the clouds, swathed mist-like over the mountaintops. He sought out valleys, sweeping green fields, then looked down at the picnic mat: crumbs of bread, a few tomato pips, a liquid ring from a lemonade glass. There was a little blue flower growing by his thigh. His fingers pulled at the leaves, touching the petals. *Baby.*

'So you've nothing to say at all?'

'I've made such a mess of things . . .' He eased himself to his feet, unsteady, shaking, and glanced all around him, looking for an escape. In the distance there was a tall man holding a small blonde woman by the hand. They were walking towards him. He started to move with urgency, collecting plates, wiping away crumbs, folding the picnic rug. Maura watched him. He scanned her face briefly and looked down at his fingers.

'I'm not sure. Not sure what to say. And here's Mammy. Shall we talk about it later, Maura? Later?'

He drove the Panda back to Cave Bonheur in silence, following the red sports car, changing gears deliberately and with studied concentration. Maura looked out of the window. His chest hurt as he thought about his child. He imagined buying cradles and cots and clothes and nappies and then he wondered if he'd become a weekend dad. He imagined Maura meeting someone else, chatting to a new man in the warm, flirtatious, easy way she had talked to

309

Jean-Luc, and the new man being a proper father to his child. He would be out in the cold again, alone. He imagined someone else holding Maura in his arms and Maura looking at the new man as his mother gazed at Jean-Luc. Jealousy and self-loathing became perspiration in his hair, which slid down his forehead, onto his lip. The sun's heat perforated the windscreen and his head ached; each thought that throbbed behind his eyes was rubble and it was piling up and stifling him, stopping his breath.

Chapter Forty-Four

'Mammy, did you know about this?' Brendan stopped outside the front door and turned to Evie.

'Let's go inside the house and talk.'

He turned back to her and his face was aflame. 'No, let's talk here. How long have you known my wife was pregnant?'

Maura put her arm on his. He'd called her 'my wife'.

Brendan pushed her away without realising. 'How long have you all known and not told me?'

Evie spoke softly. 'I guessed. I found her being sick in the toilet. It wasn't hard to work it out.'

'And did you know too, Jean-Luc?'

'I took her to the *pharmacie*.'

Maura tried again to touch his elbow and he ignored her. He breathed deeply, his chest rising and falling, then he remembered her and turned to face her. 'So how long have you known, Maura?'

'It was so hard to tell you—'

'How long have you known?'

She breathed deeply. 'Two days.'

'Two days. And you couldn't tell me?'

'Let's go inside, Brendan.' Evie opened the door. He slumped against the wall and covered his eyes. Evie and Jean-Luc went in, leaving the door ajar behind them.

Maura waited for them to go. 'I am so sorry, Brendan. I tried to tell you but I was worried about what you'd say.'

He gaped at her. 'I – don't know what to say. I mean – is it real? What are we going to do?'

Maura tried again to put a hand on his arm and hold him steady. This time he did not shake her off. She was struggling to make her voice level. 'I am going to have a baby. You are going to be a father, Brendan. I have had a couple of days to think about it all and it is that simple. It's our babby. Yours and mine. If you don't want to be with me, then I'll bring it up by myself.'

He rolled against the door-jamb, raising clenched knuckles to his face. 'If it had been ten years ago, Maura. Even two years ago. But a baby . . . now . . .'

'We didn't plan it, but it's happened. I'm pleased, in my own way. I always wanted a baby – well, to be honest, we both thought it would never happen but I've no choice now. It's here and I'm going to have it and I'm going to love it as much as I can.'

He stared at her.

'And you're its daddy, Brendan. If you don't want to live with us, then that's all right. I mean, I don't want to force you to do something you don't want to do. We've not been getting on too well, and that's not good for a baby. It needs parents who will love it, whether we're together or not.'

He was breathing deeply. 'I don't know what to do.'

She swallowed tears, fighting to be in control. 'I want to be with you and the babby but only – only if you want us. If you don't then we're better . . .' Her voice trailed off. Brendan put out his hand; he thought he might touch her, but he couldn't. He lowered it, pulling it in by his side.

She tried again. 'We're going back in a couple of days, Brendan. You have some time to think. The last thing I want is to force you so . . . shall we see what happens? Will we wait until we're back in Dublin? Will we decide then?'

He nodded and she went into the house. He sank down on the step and bit into his bottom lip. He felt weak, useless, and he brought angry fists to his temples. He hit himself once and the tears started to come. He wiped his eyes angrily, wondering what sort of man he was. He thought again about himself and Maura. A baby.

Tears threatened and again he wiped his face roughly, salt water and snot on his hand. He hung his head and waited for his anger to subside, but it had him by the throat and he could not breathe. He still loved Maura but they had no future if they couldn't talk about their feelings and agree on anything; he hated the situation, he hated himself, but he could not hate the baby. A space opened in his chest, a space for a child, and he gasped with the realisation that his life would change: nothing would ever be the same again.

A hand rested on his shoulder and he thought it was his mother's light touch. He looked up and Jean-Luc came to sit beside him, passing him a glass of brandy. Brendan said nothing and the big man waited quietly. Brendan stared into the glass, swirling the dark oily liquid. He could smell the strong spirits and he inhaled. A sigh shuddered through his body and he took a gulp and said, 'Thanks.' He swallowed a second mouthful and closed his eyes for a moment.

When he opened them, Jean-Luc's soft gaze met his.

Brendan sighed. 'I wish I could go back and change everything. Make everything better.'

Jean-Luc said nothing for a moment, then he patted Brendan's arm with a large bear paw. 'It is fine to have these feelings, Brendan. Anger, jealousy, love – they are all part of passion, and passion is what keeps our hearts beating. She loves you, your Maura.'

Brendan frowned: he was not used to a conversation like this. His father had talked to him about sport and what was in the newspapers, but never love. He said simply, 'The baby?' The big hand came to rest on Brendan's wrist, the one he broke in the fall. Brendan looked at Jean-Luc and raised his eyebrows. 'What should I do?'

Jean-Luc's voice was quiet. 'What we all must do. Give love with all of our heart. Put your wife first. The rest will follow after.'

'Do you think they'll be all right?' Evie was sitting up in bed wearing his Beatles T-shirt. She watched him swallow a couple of vitamins and slide under the duvet. She flicked off the little lamp and snuggled down in the crook of his arm.

'Time will tell.' Jean-Luc's voice sounded sleepy. 'But a baby makes a big difference for them.'

She rolled over to him and put her arms around his neck, and nibbled his earlobe playfully. 'We're going to be grandparents.'

He kissed her cheek and she breathed out. 'Jean-Luc?' She paused for a while to gather her thoughts. 'You know, I think a lot of this is my fault.' He made a low sound, a contented hum, and she closed her eyes. 'I've been too clingy to Brendan. I've made him a bit of a mammy's boy. And he was my only young one, so I wanted to keep him to myself. Does that make sense?' He murmured again, his breath against her cheek. 'And I haven't really given Maura a chance, you know, I never got to know her properly. I just made my mind up about her, and that was that. I used to think she was a bit – you know – false, and conniving, but that was me, seeing her as an enemy, coming between me and my son. I was wrong. I need to embrace them both, don't I? Especially now there's a babby on the way.'

His big arms were around her and for a moment she could hardly breathe. He mumbled, '*Bonne nuit, chérie.*'

She began to chuckle. 'Ah, it will all be grand, Jean-Luc. I know I can sort it all out. I'll make a friend of both of them. It'll be fun, even. I've got to know Maura so much better. She's a nice girl. And Brendan – well, he has a lot more to him than I've let him know. He'll be fine, they both will. Ah, Jean-Luc, isn't it wonderful? We have so much to look forward to.'

She sighed and settled down with her head on his shoulder, staring into the darkness and thinking about a small baby who would come and visit them at Christmas with his parents, who would play outside with toys, who would have a bicycle, who could go with her to the market and meet her friends. Images danced inside her head.

'Jean-Luc,' she whispered into the darkness. She thought about buying the baby a little guitar and she wondered if he would teach the child to play when he or she came to visit, and what was the best age to start. She heard the low rumble of his breathing as it became steady and slow, and she went back to her own thoughts.

Chapter Forty-Five

Jean-Luc was eating sausages when Brendan and Maura came down. Evie threw an arm around his shoulder, almost knocking his fork from his hand. 'I'm giving him a proper Irish breakfast. He has a lot of hard work on today up in the field.' She poured coffee into cups and added, 'I can fry you some sausages too if you want them?'

Maura pulled a face and her pallor explained why she was nibbling at dry toast. Brendan reached for the coffee.

Jean-Luc finished chewing. 'Perhaps this afternoon we can all go somewhere? Or maybe tonight? Evie, you remember the restaurant I took you to the first time?'

'Where the wine was overpriced vinegar?'

He laughed. 'The food there is good. We can all go together?'

Brendan looked grateful. 'I'd really like that.'

'Yes, so would I.' Maura poked at the toast for a moment and left it on her plate.

Brendan gave a little cough. 'Mammy, Jean-Luc. I want to say – I am sorry I have been so difficult these last few days.' Evie held her hands up, but he continued. 'It's been a bit of a shock but Maura and I will work it out in time.

316

We don't want to rush into anything but we'll be going home tomorrow and then we can decide what is best to do for all of us – all three of us.'

Maura pushed her plate away. 'Thanks for your help, Evie, Jean-Luc. I am sorry we have been so much trouble. You've both been very kind.'

Evie beamed at them. 'Not at all. It's been lovely to have you both here. And it's settled. We'll all go out tonight and have a lovely family evening together. I'm sure you'll work it out when you get back to Dublin. You know we're both here for you.'

Jean-Luc scraped his chair back and began to put on his jacket. Evie went over to him, brushed a thread from the material, stood on her toes and kissed him. 'Don't forget you promised me a lesson in French later.' She hugged him, ruffling his hair, and she smiled into his face.

He kissed her again. 'I must go now, *chérie*; Benji will have started work already.'

'Tell him I hope his mammy is better soon. Oh, and I'm making her a cake this morning. See you later for lunch.'

Jean-Luc went out, leaving the door slightly ajar. Sunlight lay across the flagstones, a bright oblong against shadows. Evie began to clear away the plates. 'What'll you two be doing this morning?'

'We'll just read; maybe help you out a bit?' Maura picked up her cup and Brendan's.

'Perhaps we should go out this morning?' Brendan suggested. 'Carcassonne is an hour and a half away. We can be there by half ten. A couple of hours and back here by two. Will you come with us, Mammy?'

'I have plenty to do here; you two should go.' Evie ignored Maura's troubled expression. 'It's your last day and you can't miss the historic city. Off with the pair of you; I will have lunch sorted for two o'clock, then we can

317

spend the afternoon together, all four of us, and go out this evening. I think it's a grand idea.'

Maura hesitated but Brendan took the coffee cups from her. 'We'll go, Maura. It'll give us some time together; help us to start thinking about what to do. I promise not to sulk or be bad-tempered. The break and the fresh air will do you good.'

Evie put the plates and cups in the sink and started to search for flour and sugar and a bowl. Brendan reached for his jumper and Maura's, and she thanked him stiffly as he pushed the door wide open. Evie smiled. They were making progress.

Baking smells filled the kitchen; the air was sweet and heavy. Two fruitcakes were cooling on a rack and fresh pastry had left soft white smudges on Evie's T-shirt and on her cheeks. A quiche, tomatoes, olives and two salads were on the table and she laid out four plates, four tumblers and a carafe of water. She looked at the clock: it was twenty past two. Sun streamed in from the window, a blessing of brightness falling on the table, and little grains of flour were still suspended in the light, motionless. Evie cut slices of bread from a baguette and went to the drawer for knives and forks.

She heard Brendan and Maura before their shadows appeared, surrounded by the light from the open door. Maura was talking softly. Evie raised her eyebrows. At least they were being civil. Brendan came in, full of enthusiasm about the castle and the citadel and the walled town. Maura smiled and handed Evie some flowers, and the scent of lilies filled her nostrils as she found a vase. Maura's voice chimed, 'Carcassonne is a lovely town. It would be great to see it at night, all lit up.'

'Maybe another time?' Evie glanced at the clock without meaning to.

Brendan saw the quiche on the table. 'Sorry we're late, Mammy. It was just such a nice place, Carcassonne. I could have spent all day there. The history is fascinating. We'd have been even later if Maura hadn't reminded me—'

'Can you start to serve up, Brendan, Maura?' Evie wiped her hands. 'I'll just pop up to the fields and give Jean-Luc a shout. He must have lost track of the time.'

She turned under the archway and strained her eyes towards where the path ended and the grapes began. She was not yet accustomed to the bright light and she could not make out any shapes beyond the dark shadows in the distance. She could see the vines, tall and green, stretching out in ranks. She looked again, squeezing her eyes closed against the sunlight. Her chest lurched. Someone was lying down, next to the tractor, on the grass between the vines. She broke into a run; her breath came in hard wheezes and she slowed to a little trot and then began to run again.

Jean-Luc was on his side, slumped on the ground, an arm across his face. Evie fell to her knees, rolled him over and Jean-Luc looked straight at her. His eyes were wide open but they did not move: he did not see her. She pushed an open hand against his chest; she rolled up his T-shirt and put a palm against his skin, against his heart and waited. Nothing. She called his name, called it again, and looked at his face. His tanned skin held a strange pallor. He was completely still, and she thought that it would be possible to touch his open eyes: they were dark, sightless marbles now – he would feel nothing. Her fists clung to his T-shirt; she was flinging herself against him, pulling him towards her, hoping the enormous arms would wrap themselves around her at any moment. He did not move. His body was empty, a shell, there was no life there. He was gone and her voice rose loudly until she was howling into the air.

319

Chapter Forty-Six

Caroline and Nige stayed for the rest of the day. Brendan's French was not good enough to deal with all the people who came into the house and then went again, first the doctor, then the funeral directors. Evie sat at the wooden table and watched people move around her home; she listened to them talking and heard nothing, occasionally inclining her head to answer a question, then returning to her thoughts. Brendan put a cup of tea in her hands and took it away cold. Maura pushed food in front of her but Evie did not notice it was there. She did not move from the table until late at night, when Brendan was so tired he needed to go to bed, and Evie moved to the armchair where she dozed. She was still there the following morning; the embers were ash and she was cold, not noticing as a blanket was wrapped around her shoulders or as the fire was relit and crackled to life.

Outside, the morning was warming, but the house felt gloomy and quiet. Caroline arrived quietly, bringing breakfast. Evie did not move from the armchair and Brendan recalled with sadness the old lady with the translucent eyelids at Sheldon Lodge as she put her hand to her head and gazed around, confused, not remembering. She was staring into the corner and Brendan was momentarily alarmed at her fixed expression until he realised she was looking at Jean-Luc's guitar. A tear trickled down her cheek.

Brendan was upstairs, packing his things, putting clothes into his case then taking them out again. He decided he probably should stay and forget about the interview. Maura's case was empty on the bed and he heard her footfall. She stood in the doorway and watched him pack.

He closed his suitcase and turned to her sadly. When he spoke to her, it was with his head down; he was not sure how he should be with her. 'I'm not sure what to do, Maura. The interview?'

She pursed her lips. 'He looked so healthy, Brendan.'

'I know.'

'Your mammy's devastated.'

'I've never seen her like this.'

'I came up to get extra blankets. She's frozen down there, even with the fire on.'

They crept into Evie's room with a kind of reverence. The curtains were still closed and a Beatles T-shirt was lying across the pillow, the duvet thrown back. Everything was as they had both left it, the morning before.

'Will we find some blankets, Brendan? Best not to take this duvet from their bed. It's the one they slept under—'

They found a duvet in a tall cupboard, folded in plastic, probably new, and Brendan pulled it down. Maura was looking at the photos on the chest of drawers; she picked up the one of Jean-Luc as a young man, with his guitar, and Brendan was about to accuse her of being nosy when he saw tears in her eyes. 'You liked Jean-Luc, didn't you?'

'Didn't we all like him?' She picked up his bottle of

tablets and studied the label. She sighed. 'I've seen prescriptions for these at the clinic. They're beta-blockers.'

Brendan hugged the duvet. 'Come downstairs. Let's get Mammy comfortable then perhaps we should pack. We need to be off soon. That's if we're going. I mean, I've the interview to go to, but I'm not sure it's right to leave, not now . . .'

'Brendan, I think I might just stay here. We both should.' The wrapped duvet was still pulled close to his chest, the plastic making light crackling sounds in his arms. 'I mean, I might stay for the time being. You go back on your own if you need to, have your interview. I will stay on with your mammy for a week or two. She needs someone in the house.'

'You're right, Maura. I'll ask her what she thinks. I mean, it's a bit sudden to go . . .'

'They're not happy with me at the surgery for taking all this time off. It'll be a job share anyway when I'm back. I don't really care any more.'

He did not move.

'You go back to Dublin if you must. Ask your mammy. I can get a flight over later on. And I won't contact you until I come back. I want you to do the same. A week or two apart will give us space to think about what we want . . .'

'From each other?'

'I think you need time to decide about what you want, Brendan. About priorities. And feelings.' She turned abruptly and went down the steps in front of him, leaving him staggering behind her, his arms full.

Maura sat in the huge chair by the fire, her arms folded across her stomach. Brendan was standing and he held Evie close. His shoulder was wet; the material on his shirt was soaked in her tears as Evie clung to him, her head on his shoulder. His arms were round her and her back was shuddering beneath his touch.

'Will I stay here, Mammy? You're upset. You need me here with you.'

'Brendan.'

'I don't have to go. I mean – it's only an interview and you're—'

She sniffled and looked at him. 'You should go.'

'No, Mammy. I'm staying. I mean, I can't leave you all alone, not after—'

'I'm not alone.' She looked around the room. It was full of Jean-Luc's things: his coat, his cap, his guitar.

'I've made my mind up. You need me here. There will be other interviews.'

She stared at him and her eyes were red and fierce. 'No, I don't need you, Brendan. You go back. Have your interview.'

'I'm not going. I'll stay.'

'I said no. I'll manage. I'll be just fine.'

'But, Mammy. I can't go now. Let me stay a few days at least—'

'Go, Brendan. It's an important interview. Let me know how you get on. I have my smartphone. Ring me anytime, or text.' She stopped speaking, taking a breath, wiping her eyes. 'I have Maura here and Caroline, and Benji will be over tomorrow. I'll be . . .' She thought for a moment. 'I'll be grand.'

'Are you sure? I mean, I can stay . . .?'

She smiled, a weak smile, and he hugged her again. She pulled out a huge blue handkerchief and buried her face in it. It was one of Jean-Luc's.

Maura put a hand on Evie's shoulder, her face ashen. 'You should go, Brendan.'

*

323

Hours later, his cases were in the Panda and he opened the door and wriggled down into the seat and sighed deeply. He started the engine and hesitated, peering through the windscreen. They were both looking at him, not moving, not waving. He accelerated and swallowed hard as the car moved forward and out into the road. His mother and Maura were behind him in the distance, becoming smaller. It felt strange to be alone in the car, empowering but somehow hollow.

He pulled out onto the main road and he scratched his head and glanced into the rear-view mirror. Evie and Maura had gone, and he noticed the crooked sign, the big wooden bottle leaning over to one side. He stared at his case on the seat behind him and thought of his mother, of Maura and the baby, and of Jean-Luc. He should have insisted that he stay and be with her, but now he was driving back to the ferry port for an interview at St Cillian's. Brendan felt the sudden sharp pang of loneliness.

Chapter Forty-Seven

The bar was packed out with people. Many of them Evie
had never seen before. Ray had insisted they all meet in
O'Driscoll's after the service for a wake, he would lay on
a spread, and she hesitated in the doorway, gazing around
at the crowds. Maura and Caroline were at her elbows.
Evie breathed in and said, 'Here goes – the gangplank,'
and Caroline whispered, 'Are you sure you'll be OK?'

Evie walked through a line of people who took her
hand, kissed her cheek, hugged her, muttered '*Désolé*',
offered help with the wine harvest and promised a visit.
Everyone gave her their most sympathetic expressions. She
put on her sweetest smile and spoke to each of them –
'Thank you' – '*Merci*' – '*Vous êtes gentils*' – 'I miss him
very much' – 'You're very kind' – until she arrived at the
bar where Ray and Paulette hugged her.

'You'll need a stiff drink, love,' Ray suggested, and a
glass was in her hand. Billy the Banjo was picking out a
soft tune in the corner; voices were hushed and Evie was
aware of a tremor in her lungs, constricting her breathing.
She was determined not to cry. She had sobbed at the
crematorium and the weather made it worse: the sun was

325

slung soft and hazy behind clouds and the distant hills were obscured by a low mist that hung heavy as a sigh. She wondered about Jean-Luc, if he was watching it all, smiling and thinking of nature and pantheism, but she doubted it and she pushed the thoughts from her mind. She'd looked at the coffin, at the dark wood and the gold handles. She knew he was gone from her and her chest was racked with convulsions.

She sipped her brandy and put it down on the bar. She didn't want it. There wasn't much she wanted: the only thing she needed she could never have back again and it was easy to lose herself in thoughts which, when she tried to remember them, amounted to blankness. Maura linked an elbow through Evie's and attempted a question.

'What will you do now? I mean, will you come back to Dublin?'

Evie looked horrified. 'I've no intention of going back to Dublin. I live here. I'll never go in another bloody care home. This is my life.'

Maura looked anxious and Ray leaned across to both of them.

'Just a week or so ago, he came in here for a brandy at lunchtime. He said he was taking you to stay in his little cottage in the mountains. I said I'd take the girls to the coast and we'd all benefit from a day or two off work.'

'I remember it.' Evie forced a smile.

'He knew he was unwell, Evie.'

She blinked hard, as if someone slapped her face. 'He knew? What did he know?'

Ray looked at Maura; they exchanged a glance that Evie did not see, which gave him permission to discuss Jean-Luc.

Ray chose his words carefully. 'He'd been to the doctor's and then to his solicitor. He'd had bad news. He wasn't getting better, despite the tablets, and he said he needed a brandy. We had a long chat. Mostly about you, how you'd changed his life, made him happy. Everything belongs to you, you know, Evie. He had it all arranged.'

Evie took a mouthful of her drink and closed her eyes. 'He's the most perfect man.' She realised that she was speaking of him in the present tense: she could not let him go, not yet, and tears threatened to start again. She looked directly at Ray. 'Do you think it would be all right if I . . .? So many people are here to say goodbye to him and they've all been so kind. Could I – would it be all right to say thank you?'

Ray put his hand over hers, and then he rapped on the bar and said something in French, introducing Evie. The room became hushed. She sipped her brandy again and saw all the faces. She remembered some of them: the two men who had fought in the bar that night; the little man in the beret who had bought her drinks; Paulette; Billy the Banjo and his wife; there were other familiar faces from the market and from the wine-tasting event she had organised weeks ago, when it had all begun. In the corner she could see Benji in a black suit and tie with a tiny lady who was sitting down, her dark hair pulled back. She was wearing a black dress and her eyes were shining towards Evie.

Evie coughed. 'I – I wanted to say thank you all for coming here today to remember. I won't try to say it in French. I am not that good yet, but someday I will be.' She paused, thinking of Jean-Luc, their lessons together. 'I will get much better at French. That is my first promise. My second promise is that I'll always remember the most wonderful man I ever met, Jean-Luc Bonheur.' She stopped again. All eyes were in her direction, all faces sombre. She raised her voice a little. 'We didn't know each other for very long but I knew him long enough for him to become . . . what's the phrase the young ones use today? My soulmate. He is my soulmate, such a lovely kind man.' She stopped. Present tense. She wondered how long it would be before she would stop thinking of him in the present. She carried on quickly. 'A lovely man, intelligent, warm, generous, a little bit sentimental but he had a—'

She clamped her lips together. She couldn't say he had a good heart. She tried again. 'He was full of love and I loved him.' She swallowed once. 'I still love him and – and I want to—'

She paused and fumbled in her pocket and brought out a piece of paper, her hand shaking as she pulled on reading-glasses. She felt Maura and Caroline both put a hand on her shoulder. 'I went on the Google Translate.' There was a small laugh. 'He once said this poem to me – it's French – Alphonse de Lamartine. It sounds beautiful in French and he said it to me when we were together in the mountains and I didn't know what he'd said, what it all meant. After he – after – well, I decided I might – I wanted to know what he'd told me so – so, yesterday, I found it on the Google and I translated it and I want to read it in his memory.'

She took in the people around her, staring at the faces all focusing on hers. She adjusted her glasses and took a shuddering breath, and she read:

'So let us love, let us love; and the transient hour
Let's enjoy in a hurry;
Man has no harbour, time no shores;
It flows, we fade merely!
Jealous time, can it be that these drunken moments
When love fills us with bliss to overflow
Fly from us at the same speed
As do our days of woe?'

She stopped and felt the silence heavy on the air. Then she could hear Maura sniffing behind her. Others were crying, some wiping a single tear, some with wet faces, unashamedly moved. She picked up her small glass and lifted it high, and her voice was slight and weak.

'Jean-Luc Bonheur.'

His surname was lost in the chorus repeating his name over and she slumped back against the bar, the poem clutched tightly in her fist.

When they arrived back it was early evening and a van was parked outside. Three men were packing away their equipment. The huge wooden bottle that sloped at an angle had been removed completely and a new sign was upright in its place. It was beautifully crafted, worked in wood, with the name 'Cave Bonheur' engraved deeply into the grain in black and gold. Next to the lettering was a design of a man in silhouette leaning over, playing a guitar. He had a little ponytail. It was unmistakeably Jean-Luc.

Evie struggled out of Caroline's car and she rushed over. Her face shone. It took her a while to speak, then she said, 'It's perfect.'

Maura and Caroline were behind her, sharing anxious looks.

Evie smiled but there were tears on her face. 'I ordered it for him. It was meant to be a surprise. Oh, he would have loved it.'

Caroline hugged her. 'It's beautiful, Evie.'

She pulled away. 'It's a memorial.' She sighed and went into the house.

Late into the evening, she and Maura were sitting by the fireside. A clock was ticking, but both women were quiet. Wood snapped and crackled and sparks flew up the chimney and they glanced at each other and saw the fire reflected. They were both deep in thought.

Maura spoke first, her hand curved across her belly. 'It's hard to believe there's a little babby in here.'

'Life is funny.' Evie's voice was toneless. 'Someone dies and someone else is born. That is the way of things, isn't it?'

Maura did not know what to say. Evie sniffed. 'Are you looking forward to having this little one, Maura?'

'I will be, when I get used to the idea. I can't imagine it just yet, how it'll feel being big and then giving birth and then bringing up a little human being.'

'You'll be fine.'

'Evie, what if I am all by myself? A single mother? What'll I do?'

'We'll all help out. You'll manage. That's what we do, we women. We manage.'

Maura thought for a moment. 'What if I've lost him, though? Brendan. He was the only man I ever loved. The only one. And I might've lost him for ever.'

Evie raised her head, her stare was firm, and her breath, when it came, was stretched out. 'I know how you feel.' She leaned over and grasped Maura's hand for a moment. They both looked back into the flames and were occupied with their separate thoughts, their separate troubles, their personal pain.

Chapter Forty-Eight

Evie woke up in the early hours, feeling cold, although her arms were wrapped around his pillow. She breathed the fabric in deeply, but could find no smell of him there. There was no reminder of him in the Beatles T-shirt she wore, although it had once been next to his skin. There was no memory of him in their room. She looked for him, but he had left.

She went downstairs. Her feet were ice-cold and pale, and her fingers were becoming numb. She sat in the armchair in the dark and looked at familiar shadows, furniture looming, dark body shapes rising and leaning towards her. For a while she wondered what she would do, what her future would hold. Three months ago she had not met Jean-Luc; now his absence was like a weight that pushed down on her shoulders, constricted her breathing and shivered like winter in her belly. She would move forward but she could not do it yet. It was too early. She still awoke at night and reached out. She still opened her eyes in the morning and looked for him, forgetting that he was gone, and she expected him to walk in at any time in the day whenever a door creaked.

There were things she knew she could not do yet. She could not touch his belongings. She could not look at the tractor, empty and motionless, now back in the barn. She could not bear to flick through the photos on her phone that they had taken together in the mountains, not yet: she had been so happy and light-hearted, those few days before she found him lying still. A knot of anger tightened within her, it glowed like an ember, that he could have known his health was failing and yet he did not tell her. But she knew why and she forgave him.

The room was dark and quiet and his guitar was in its familiar place in the corner. As she blinked at it, she saw a long neck, the shape of shoulders, a waist. She closed heavy lids and she imagined him holding it, the way his arms looped around it and clasped it to his body. It was his first love, and she picked it up and held it tight, her arms around it. He would not come back and she knew that she had no choice but to accept it. But for now she just needed to cry.

A week had passed, one day stretching into another. Maura was asleep. She slept until late in the day, curled in her bed, her face peaceful. Evie locked the door behind her. She was driving the red sports car to the cottage in the mountains. Caroline came along for company, to help with the directions and to support her in a vehicle she was unaccustomed to driving. Evie loved the way the little car handled; she kept miscalculating the gear changes and the accelerator growled and revved beneath her feet, but she was improving her skills. Caroline followed a map she had created from the internet; Evie did not recognise any landmarks and she commented that all bloody hills looked the same. The mountains were steep, whichever path she took, and mist lay thick around each twisting bend.

She slowed down: the roads were narrow and the drop at one side was sheer. They decelerated to a steady pace in second gear when a sheep stepped in front of them and stopped, looking at them blankly before slipping away into a hedge. Evie braked firmly, she and Caroline bumping forward and then back in their seats. She managed a joke. 'We nearly had mutton for dinner.' It was a brave attempt to claw back her happier self, which was hidden somewhere inside, refusing to come out. The mist was damp and heavy, tearing apart into shreds, and Evie thought it was beautiful and it somehow cocooned her, keeping her apart from the world. Caroline was eating salted peanuts and offered her some. Evie turned away and wrinkled her nose.

She recognised the little white cottage when they reached a bend; it was curled up in a little valley and she increased speed a little before pulling up by the door. She held the key in her hand and the door pushed open easily. Caroline was intrigued, her voice trilled with delight as she led the way from room to room, running upstairs and throwing open windows and offering suggestions about colour schemes and grand designs. Evie was thinking about something else and was glad to be downstairs again, sitting at the table while Caroline went into the tiny kitchen to make a cup of tea.

'So what do you think you'll do with this place, Evie?'

Evie gave an exaggerated shrug, the way Jean-Luc used to; she realised Caroline could not see her, so she added, 'I'm not sure.'

'You could let it out, a holiday cottage, maybe? Or you could sell it on? Both ways you could make a tidy amount of money.'

She shrugged again, making a face that showed that she had no interest. Caroline carried on chattering.

'Or you could rent it out. There must be farmers or

people who want to live up here. It's not too far from a major town by car, but I should imagine it gets pretty isolated in the winter.'

Evie stared at her hands. She could hear Caroline pouring water from the kettle.

'I'm so glad he left you something, Evie. I mean, for security. Who knows what the future holds? For any of us.'

She gazed away into the distance. 'Jean-Luc didn't have a family. No-one he knew, anyway.'

Caroline put two cups down and sat at the table. 'Well, at least something good has come from it all.' Evie gave her a sharp look; her friend's expression clouded. 'I mean, at least, you now – you have a home and . . .' Caroline drank her tea and the room became quiet, both women thinking.

Suddenly Evie sat upright. 'I went to see Monsieur Joffert, his solicitor. A lovely man. He explained everything in English. There is a bit of money put aside for Benji too. I told him I want to keep the business going. For Jean-Luc. He said he would give me any help or advice I needed. I planned to spend my last days with Jean-Luc and now I plan to spend all my years in his house.'

Caroline tried again. 'So you're a businesswoman now?'

Evie sipped her tea and then pushed it away. 'It's too soon for all this, Caroline. I'm not rushing myself. I'm sure a time will come soon when I can start decorating rooms and renting out properties and organising a wine harvest and remembering Jean-Luc without feeling so wretched but—'

Caroline interrupted, putting a hand over Evie's. 'Seriously, anything you need, Nige and I are just a phone call away.'

'I'll hold you to that. I know there are so many people

who are out there for me. I'm an independent woman now. I have some decisions to make. But there's no way I'll ever go back to a care home again. It's not for me.'

Evie's eyes darted around the house, thinking about the last time she had been there. If she concentrated hard enough, she would be able to see him lighting the fire, pouring *pacherán* into two small glasses, nuzzling her neck; she could hear his voice, his mouth against her hair. '*Mon amour.*' She swallowed hard. It was no time for sentiment. A moment's weakness brought tears to her eyes and she did not want to provoke Caroline's sympathy. She stood up and her jaw was firm.

'Will we stay over tonight, Caroline? There are two beds made upstairs. Do you think Nige would mind? I fancy a drink.'

Her friend smiled and pulled out her mobile. 'Is reception OK here? I'll tell him I'm staying.'

Evie knew just what to do, as Jean-Luc had. She built a fire and when it was leaping in the hearth, she went to the larder and peered in. There was not much food, but she found potatoes that had started to wrinkle, an onion and a box of eggs. They would eat omelettes. She found a bottle of red wine and the *pacherán*, and the glasses she and Jean-Luc had put to their lips. She laid the table.

Two hours later, the fire roared in the grate and whooshed up the chimney as if the wind was tugging at it. Their plates were empty and they had opened a second bottle of wine. Evie poured the *pacherán* into small glasses. Caroline sipped it slowly. 'I've never had this stuff before. It's so sweet.'

'Jean-Luc loved it. He loved all the lovely things in life, good food, good wine.'

Caroline blinked, pushing her auburn hair away from her face. 'And you, Evie. He loved you.'

For the tenth time, Evie raised her glass. 'Jean-Luc.'

'Jean-Luc.' Caroline drank the small glass in one gulp.

Evie whispered, '*Mon amour*,' and poured them both another.

Caroline sipped at the second glass and said, 'You didn't know he had a heart condition?'

Evie sighed. 'I do now.' She smiled at her friend. 'You know, I'm glad he didn't tell me though. I'd have worried. He looked so well. So big and strong.'

Caroline frowned. 'Didn't he have tablets from the doctor?'

'Loads of them, on the bedside table.' Evie shrugged. 'He told me they were vitamins and I believed him.'

'I wish you'd had longer together, Evie. You made the perfect couple.'

She laughed, a dry little laugh. 'There wasn't enough time for a cross word between us.' There were tears in her eyes and she wiped them away. The alcohol was beginning to take hold. 'Do you know, Caroline, I truly loved that man. I loved him more in a few weeks than I loved Jim in all our married days.' Caroline swayed a little, bit her lip and finished her *pacherán*. Evie poured more. 'He was wonderful, my Jean-Luc. Such a man. He was kind, thoughtful, intelligent, affectionate. He was perfect.'

Caroline nodded and Evie gave a small snort. 'Do you know what I'll remember most about him though?'

Caroline's eyes were round and shining. She held up her glass. 'I don't know, Evie. His sports car? His good taste?'

Evie shook her head. 'Ah, well, no. He had a lovely bum on him.'

Caroline gaped, hesitated, and then both women began to laugh. Evie poured more *pacherán* and they drank and laughed and tears rolled down their cheeks.

'Caroline?' Evie suddenly sat up straight. 'Can we go outside and look at the sky?' Her friend tried to stand, easing herself upright, then she fell backwards into her chair. 'It's just . . . when Jean-Luc and I were here, we did that together. Looked up at the stars and he said a poem for me. Do you think we could go outside?'

They staggered together, arm in arm, one tall, one small, and closed the door on the warm cottage behind them. Outside, they shivered. The sky was studded with diamond stars, as it had been before, and both women gazed upwards. Caroline's voice was a whisper. 'Do you believe he's up there, Evie? Jean-Luc? In heaven?'

Evie turned her head sharply. 'He didn't believe in any of that nonsense, my Jean-Luc. He was a pantheist. As for me, I'm a Catholic, so I always believe there might be a chance. Who knows? He made me feel sure that it's now that matters.' She thought for a moment. 'Ah, Caroline. I had so many good things from him in such a short time.'

They were quiet for a while then Evie said, 'It would be easy to think of him as my last chance of happiness. But that's not true. It's a gift he gave me, happiness. Bonheur. I'll always remember it. It's called the present for that reason. Being happy and living for the now.'

Caroline squeezed her arm and they shambled back into the house together.

The next day, the table was still laden with greasy plates and empty glasses, their bases rimmed with dark red liquid. The two women busied themselves with clearing up. They both felt without speaking it that the house was a kind of shrine, and it should be left tidily for next time.

Evie reached for her coat. 'We'd best be off soon, Caroline. We've all that mist to go through and a few sheep to knock over. Now you've seen the house and you

337

know all about it. I'm glad you came with me . . . Next time we're here, we can bring some paint brushes—'

When she returned to Cave Bonheur, Maura was in front of the fire with her feet on a stool. She was still wearing pyjamas, a dressing gown and thick slippers. It was almost six o'clock. Evie sat opposite, and gave a dry little laugh.

'You're resting well, Maura. That's good.'

Maura stretched out her legs, raised her arms in the air and yawned. 'I'm just enjoying the peace and quiet. It's nice to have time to be by myself and think.'

'When did you get up?'

'A couple of hours ago. I thought I might ring my sister and tell her I'm pregnant. She won't have a clue. I haven't told anyone. No-one back in Dublin knows.'

'You'll have to start telling people soon. Where is it she lives, your sister?'

'She's over in Roscommon. I don't get to see her much: her nursing work takes up most of her time and her three kids and all. She will be so surprised I'm pregnant.'

Evie compressed her lips. 'You have no-one else, no family now?'

'Besides Brendan? No – just Bridget and her husband. No-one else. '

Evie was quiet, imagining her son. He would be back in Dublin, even at work. His last few texts did not mention how the interview at St Cillian's had gone. She knew Brendan well enough to wait for him to bring it up. He would phone her in a day or two to find out how she was, even if he and Maura had agreed not to communicate. She sighed. What they both really needed was to talk to each other, not avoid the subject of the baby and their future together, if they had one. She might tell Maura that, but not yet.

She stood up. 'I'll make us something to eat, shall I?'

Maura wrinkled her nose, uninterested. 'I'm not hungry.'

'Me neither,' Evie admitted. 'But you're bloody pregnant and you should be looking after yourself and I'm a lonely old woman and I need to make a better job of looking after myself too. I've been thinking. We need a healthy eating regime. From now onwards, it's all about getting stronger and fitter. So – off your arse, Maura, get out the rice and I'll dice the vegetables. We're having risotto. And a nice healthy salad.'

Chapter Forty-Nine

Brendan walked into the PE staff room and slumped in his chair, stretching out tracksuited legs.

'You look shattered, Brendan. It feels like we've been back forever, doesn't it? Never mind, it'll be Christmas soon.' Penny Wray picked up a baguette, which was thoroughly wrapped in cling film, and threw it across towards him, a perfect shot. 'I saved you this one: it's brie and cranberry.'

Brendan opened the end of the bread and took a bite, pulling a piece of the plastic film from his mouth and then chewing the sandwich thoughtfully. 'Thanks, Penny – great.'

'Long morning, Brendan?' It was Tony Azikiwe, who dropped into the seat opposite him, his shorts riding up to his thighs. He was the new sports teacher for rugby – fit, huge-chested, shaven-headed except for a few little dreadlocks which dangled across his brow. Kevin Fearon had commented on it this morning, as Brendan collected in the Beckett homework. 'Mr Azikiwe's cool, Sir. He is cooler than you are.' Brendan had grinned. 'He's cooler than all of us,' he'd said, and then he'd told the class to open *Waiting for Godot* at page twenty-two.

Brendan gazed out of the window. They were well into

October already and the weather was becoming chilly. He chewed his baguette and thought how muddy it would be with thirty kids out on the pitch in this rain. Penny sat comfortably beside him and patted him on the shoulder. 'How's it all going, Brendan?'

He nodded and mumbled, 'OK.'

'All' meant that she knew he had not seen Maura for almost six weeks now and he had not heard from her directly, although his mother sent regular updates about the pregnancy. She told him over the phone about the vineyard, how they were beginning to harvest the grapes, and the pauses in her speech showed how badly she was missing Jean-Luc. Brendan sighed. He should be there now, with both of them. He looked at his trainers, spattered with mud, at the jog bottoms he had worn for over a week without washing them. He wasn't taking proper care of himself, and he felt guilt seep into his lungs. He came to school in badly creased shirts, stained sports tops, and his face was often covered with little cuts from careless shaving. There had been no-one home to tell him off when he stuck little pieces of tissue over the nicks. There was just the incessant silence. His reflection in the mirror each morning was tired and a little unkempt. He threw down his half-eaten baguette, still wrapped in cling film, and Tony Azikiwe seized his chance.

'Don't you want this, Brendan?'

In twenty minutes the klaxon would sound for the afternoon's lesson. It was football outside, on the all-weather pitch. Rain hit the window and ran down in wiggly ribbons; outside the sky was battleship-grey.

Penny put her legs up on the table; they were still brown against her white socks and pink trainers. 'They have shortlisted the candidates for my job here,' she announced. 'There are three women: two newly qualified teachers and

341

a woman in her late twenties. They'll be in next week to look around. You must meet them.'

She met Brendan's eyes and he hoped she was not matchmaking. Tony Azikiwe stared at her directly.

'It's a shame you're leaving so soon, Penny. I've only just got here.'

Her laughter was the tinkle of a little bell. 'Sure, we can keep in touch, Tony. My new school is only on the other side of the city. We'll all keep in touch, will we?'

Tony gave a hopeful grin and finished the last piece of brie sandwich. Brendan picked up his briefcase and rooted around inside for his lesson notes. He found his copy of Yeats' poetry and some marking he had to finish this evening. He wondered why he was looking forward to going home. The house would be empty.

It was almost dark when he arrived. It was after six o'clock and his briefcase was heavy. Inside the house it was cold: he had forgotten to reprogramme the heating again and he wondered if it was worth putting it on now. He would have an early night. He felt a dull ache in his stomach and a growling of digestive juices: he hadn't eaten much during the day. He went into the kitchen and opened the cupboards one after the other, finding a tin of baked beans, another of tuna, some salt and a packet of soup. He stood still for a moment and decided he would go to the supermarket, maybe call in for chippers on the way back.

An hour passed during which he traipsed around the supermarket aimlessly, buying biscuits, tins of sardines and cocoa and other things he didn't really like. Shopping for one made Brendan's head hurt. The rain was heavy when he stopped the Panda in the driveway. The lights were on inside the house and he blinked momentarily and rubbed his forehead. He heaved the three bags of shopping into one hand and the chippers and cod in their hot wrapper in the other, and he struggled towards the front door. It was open. He had definitely locked the door before he left. It was all getting to him and he closed his eyes for a moment and felt weary. The handles of the bags were taut and digging into his fingers, leaving deep red marks.

Inside, the room felt a little warmer; he could not remember turning the heating on. He was losing his mind a little; perhaps it was the loneliness, and now he performed one task after another, like an automaton, giving it no thought. He locked the door, hung up his car keys, took off his coat, put the bags in the kitchen, on the worktop, and picked up the battered fish in paper, taking a bite.

He could smell perfume, a soft, woody smell, not unpleasant, and when he turned round, Maura was standing in the doorway. She wore a loose flowery tunic top that hung away from her body, although she did not look any bigger. Her face was calm and there was a soft glow in her eyes. Brendan felt a familiar lurch in his chest. He pulled his hands into his sides and smiled shyly. She looked at him with the same smile he remembered from their first date. He went over to her and wanted to kiss her cheek but instead he stood and stared at her.

'I didn't know you were coming.'

'I got a taxi from the airport.'

'I'd have come and picked you up.'

'I didn't want to bother you.'

They were silent for a moment, and then she said, 'Your chippers are getting cold.'

He fumbled for a plate, two plates. 'Do you want to share them?'

'I'm eating for two, Brendan. I'm trying to eat healthily now. Anyway, I had a meal on the plane.'

They sat on the sofa together, a space between them, and Brendan swallowed cold powdery potato. For a while there was no other sound other than his soft chewing. He put the plate down, the chips half-eaten, and sat back in the seat.

'Well, Maura, how are you?' The question felt silly as soon as he'd said it.

'I'm fine. The babby's fine. I have an appointment with the midwife tomorrow and I'm back at work next week, two afternoons a week.'

'Oh.'

'And I have a scan booked for Friday.'

Brendan wondered if he could ask if he could go along to the scan, after all he was the father. He thought about what to say to her, and he said, 'That's good.'

'So, how about you? Can I ask about the interview?'

'St Cillian's?'

'Yes. How did it go? Did you get the job?'

He examined her face. There was no judgement there in her expression, no hopefulness: she was just interested.

'It was a nice school. Lovely children. The other teachers there were very friendly and the job would have been really interesting, pastoral work and that . . .'

Maura raised her eyebrows. He waited for her to say, 'So you didn't get the job?' He expected her to interrupt, to ask him what went wrong, but she was looking at him. Her eyes were bright and clear, glowing with a steadiness that made Brendan catch his breath.

'I withdrew. I told them the position wasn't for me.'

She was surprised. 'I thought you wanted to work at St Cillian's? I thought you didn't like it much where you are now.'

He ran his hands through his hair. 'To be honest, Maura, St Cillian's is another teaching job. I knew if I went there, I'd have to commit to five years, three at least. I couldn't be sure I could do that with . . . well, I

344

didn't know what to do with us – with everything being as it is.'

Maura was twisting the rings on her finger. 'We have some talking to do.'

'We do, you're right.'

'Have you had time to think about it all?'

'Yes. Have you?'

'Yes. I have thought about it all the time.'

Brendan stood. 'I'll get us a cup of tea.' He went to the kettle and busied himself with mugs, aware that he was putting off the conversation. He changed the subject, calling from the kitchen, 'How was Mammy when you left?'

'She seems OK, Brendan. Some days better than others. She misses Jean-Luc. She keeps herself busy; she's learning French, and she's started to go to yoga in Foix and she's made a new friend or two there. She sees a lot of the O'Driscoll's crowd, and Caroline and Nige. Then there's a lot on with the grape harvesting and the wine-making at the minute.'

'That's good.' Brendan was not sure if it was good or not. 'Does she have plenty of support with the business over there?'

'She has a team of men who helped out with the harvest. They've worked at Cave Bonheur before. They know the ropes. And Benji is always there.'

'I'm sure it's a good life to be had.' He came in with two mugs and put them on the coffee table, flopping down on the sofa beside her. Maura was holding out a list.

'She gave me this. Some books she wants us to send. Jean-Luc had copies in French and she wants us to get her the books in English and post them over.'

Brendan took the list and laughed. 'Dostoyevsky, Camus, Kerouac, Lamartine? George Sand? Marcel Proust!'

Maura was serious; she laid a hand on his arm, touching his wrist with light fingers. 'Does it still hurt?'

He shook his head. It had healed perfectly, aching only when he put too much weight on it. 'Mammy's put some money in our joint account. And some for the babby. I couldn't stop her. She said she and Jean-Luc wanted to make us a little gift. I didn't know what to say.'

Brendan drank his tea. It was hot and burned his mouth. Then he said, 'I'll ring her later. It would be nice to have a chat.'

It was quiet for a while. Brendan stared down at his feet. He was wearing odd socks.

'So?' Maura sat upright. 'What about the elephant in the room?'

Brendan wriggled on the sofa. 'Do you think we should think about putting the house on the market?'

Maura took a deep breath, her face flushed with anxiety. 'So that's it?' She waited. 'Is it over between us? Is it, Brendan? Is that what you've decided? We'll sell the house and split everything up?'

He rubbed a fist in his eye and looked down at his knees. 'That's not what I meant. Is that what you want?'

She turned away. 'You first.'

'Maura,' he began. 'I mean . . . we're having a baby. It's possible the two of us could make it work. I – we – we're going to be parents and maybe you and I could find a way to get on for the sake of—'

She was furious. 'No, Brendan. For the sake of the baby? No. I don't want that.'

'No?' He turned away from her and squeezed his eyes shut.

'No. I'd rather be by myself and bring the child up alone than settle for being second-best, in a second-rate marriage.'

'You think I'm second-rate?'

346

'No.' Her voice was insistent. 'But you said that yourself. You said it just now. You suggested we make the best of it; we stay together for the sake of the child.'

He was silent. He wanted to tell her what was in his mind, in his heart, but the words wouldn't come.

'I care about you, Brendan, but I am no second-choice afterthought of a wife.'

He watched her as she spoke, her voice so determined, and he gave her a little watery smile. 'I'm a fool.'

'No-one's disputing that.' Her words were not without affection.

'Maura, I have missed you.' Her hair had grown and was loose around her shoulders. He thought of how they had first sat on the sofa in his parents' old house, youngsters, green and silly, holding each other's hands and waiting for Jim and Evie to leave the room. 'I mean, I've been useless without you. I don't just mean the practical things. I've missed you. It's not about the baby and I don't care about this house. I've no life without you, no soul. I've realised over these past six weeks or so how stupid I've been. I've let the woman I love slip through my fingers.'

A sigh caught in Maura's throat. 'We've both made mistakes, Brendan.'

'What I said before . . . I didn't mean that I wanted us to stay together just for the baby.'

'What did you mean?'

'I mean, I'm sorry. I've made a mess of things. We needed to talk and I just shut up, closed down. I didn't help at all. I'm indecisive. I'm an awful communicator. I've been jealous, selfish, stubborn, and it's cost me my beautiful wife. I miss you, Maura. I miss you so much it hurts to tell you.' He looked down at his hands.

She swallowed. 'I wasn't any better, Brendan. I could

be bad-tempered and controlling. I think I was frustrated. Things had got into a big rut.'

Brendan recalled her moods, her anger directed full force at him and his mother. It seemed a long time ago. He shook his head. 'That's not what I see when I look at you.'

'What do you see?'

'Someone warm, confident, happy. A woman who sparkles . . . the woman I love.'

A smile twitched on her lips. 'And I see a lovely man, warm-hearted, affectionate, sweet-natured.'

He thought about holding her hand. 'I've thought about you every day though. It's been hard, waking up alone and wondering if I'd see you again. I mean, I thought you might stay in France. You seemed so happy there.'

Maura picked at her fingernails. 'I was. It's a completely different lifestyle and it suits me. I love it there. But you didn't ring me. Or ask to talk to me when you rang your mammy.'

'You told me not to.' He looked at her and a grin broke on his face. 'You said you needed time to think. I picked the phone up every night and thought about it. The same as I thought about ringing Mammy when we were trying to find her in France. It was easier to wait, to put things off.'

'I love it there, though, Brendan. In France. The way of life suits me.'

Brendan squeezed his eyes shut. She was about to tell him she was going back to France. Perhaps she'd met someone. He grabbed her hand. 'I've changed, Maura. I did what you said, thought about things, and now I know what I want.'

'We've both changed a bit, haven't we? We've had time to think about what's important.'

'Am I important?' he asked her and she smiled.

'Most important,' she said. She looked lovely; her mouth curved gently in a smile.

He took her hand and put it in his lap. 'We'll make good parents, Maura.'

'Do you think so?' She sighed. 'But it's not enough, is it? We need to be good for each other.'

'I want to be with you, though. You come first, baby or no baby. I love you, for who you are. You're my wife. I want us to stay together.'

She thought for a moment. 'What's to stop us slipping back into a rut again? What if we stop appreciating each other?'

He looked at her from the corners of his eyes. 'You're happy in France, aren't you?'

'It's a nice way of life. It's beautiful there. Quiet, peaceful. It's a slower pace.'

He glanced at her, watching her expression. 'A good place to start again? A good place to bring up a baby?'

'I'm not sure what you're saying, Brendan. I thought you wanted to be with me.'

He took a deep breath. 'Yes, I do, more than ever, but not here, not in this house. Maybe somewhere else, some-where completely different.'

She looked puzzled. 'What are you thinking of, Brendan?'

'Well, we've been through a lot, you and me. So much happened this summer: Mammy, Jean-Luc, the babby, everything is different now. And I'm not sure I want to teach any more. I'm not sure I ever did. I want a life where we have time for each other, where we can grow together and have the space we need. I think we need to start again, not here, but from somewhere else. From somewhere we can grow together, like the grapes, warm in the sun.'

She breathed, 'In France.'

'Me and you.' He took her hand. 'It's what we need, to be together again.'

Her hand tightened around his. Their eyes connected and held and they both remembered being the same shy teenagers, the future a fast breath in their chests.

Brendan leaned back on the sofa and she hesitated, then she rested her head on his shoulder and his voice was a whisper. 'A fresh start, Maura. That's what we need. A brand new beginning, for the three of us.'

Maura took both his hands. 'That's what I want, Brendan.'

'Somewhere we can be ourselves and have some peace in our lives. Where we're not chasing deadlines. Where we can make every moment count, be the people we really are without so much to keep us apart. Somewhere we can bring our child up and enjoy a different pace of life. I mean, we both know the ideal place, a home we can move straight into, somewhere we can work together and make a living . . .'

Maura's face shone in the light and he saw tears gleaming, and he wiped them away with his fingers. He wrapped his arms round her, pulled her as tightly to him as he could and felt the warmth from her body seep into his and remind him he was alive. She kissed his lips and spoke quietly. 'When will we go? Do you think Evie would mind?'

'I'll make a phone call tomorrow. I'm sure she'll need a hand with the business now. I know she'd let us stay with her. Then when we're up and running, when we're all ready, we can still help her out, and maybe find our own little house nearby. Somewhere we'll settle, happy together, doing what we want, just for us. Somewhere we can make our own future. Somewhere our baby can grow up in the countryside. Speaking French.'

Chapter Fifty

It was silent in the house except for the sound of the men eating; some scraped the remains of the stew from the sides of the casserole, filled their plates again, wiped their bread in the gravy and drank water. They pushed their empty dishes away, one by one, and sat back in their seats.

'*Merci, Evie. Un bon repas!*'

Evie smiled and began to collect plates into tall piles as the men stood up and put on their dusty jackets. Benji was about to lead the way, then he stopped and rushed over to Evie, hugging her, before turning to go. She called after him: 'Benji, I have a cake for your mother. Don't forget to take it with you.' She thought again. '*N'oublie pas. J'ai un gâteau pour ta mère.*' He hurried outside; one or two of the older men followed him, on their way back to work.

'*Gaston. Un moment, s'il te plaît,*' Evie called and the short man with the little moustache in the black cap turned back to her. She thought for a moment, and selected her words. '*Inès arrive plus tard, avec les poules?*'

Gaston grinned. His wife kept lots of chickens which laid lots of eggs, and she had promised to show Evie how to start with her own coop.

351

'*Elle arrivera envers seize heures.*'

Evie counted on her fingers. Sixteen hours on the twenty-four-hour clock. She'd be here at four.

Gaston opened the door wide, zipping his jacket against the breeze and his eyes twinkled. He turned back. '*La langue s'améliore, Evie,*' and he disappeared, back to work.

She was puzzled. 'What does he mean, the tongue is getting better? What's wrong with his tongue?' She went over to the mirror and stuck out a little pink tongue. 'Perhaps he means mine?' She realised he was telling her that her language skills were improving. She closed her eyes. Things still took a while to sink in.

She began to clear the table, wash dishes, and wipe down surfaces. She hummed a little tune, remembering the song she sang with Jean-Luc in the barn when she was helping him. She paused over the words: '*Ne me quitte pas*' and her lips curved in a smile. The words meant 'Don't leave me'. Of course. It wasn't a quick job and, when everything was put away, she sat in her armchair with a cup of tea and picked up one of the books Brendan had sent her: *The Idiot* by Dostoyevsky. She flicked through the pages.

It was her favourite place, sitting in the armchair by the fire. She glanced at the photo in the silver frame over the fireplace. Her new friend Marie-Thérèse – Marie-Thé – from yoga had helped her select the image from her phone and they had taken it to the best place in Foix to have it framed. She saw her face smiling back at her, happy behind the glass. Jean-Luc's arm was around her, the mountains crowding behind them, the sky was the deepest blue. Evie thought about her expression, the innocence and unwavering belief in their future and, as she looked again at Jean-Luc, she thought she could see in his eyes some kind of resignation, a certainty that now was all he had. She was looking too hard.

She put another log on the fire from the stack that rose on either side of the hearth. Her friends had been sympathetic. She rubbed her forehead hard, wondering how she would have managed without them. Caroline and Nige had introduced her to their contact who felled trees and now she had wood enough for the coldest winter. It made a wall on one side of the barn outside, next to the tractor. Caroline and her partner were kind to Evie; Ray and Paulette texted her each day and invited her over to O'Driscoll's at least once a week. There were so many people she had begun to love.

She closed the book and thought of Brendan and Maura. It was only a fortnight since Maura had returned to Dublin, and though she had been idle all the time she had been with Evie, either asleep or with her feet up, Evie had grown to like her. She felt sorry as she'd driven them both to Toulouse Airport; Maura was quiet and fretful, huddled down with her cases in the sports car.

She thought of the phone conversations she'd had with Brendan over the last ten days. She recalled the new enthusiasm in his voice, and how what he had said to her made the tears stream down her face. New beginnings. She glanced around the house, at the tired paintwork, the heavy furniture. An idea came to her. She put the book on the floor and went upstairs. Her tread was light. She passed the main bedroom, her room, and she went back to look in again, her mind full of ideas. The curtains were closed, so she opened them, cracking the top window ajar and a little breeze came in and lifted the seams. There was dust on the dressing table and she smoothed it off with her fingers. There was more dust, lying light as a whisper on his photos, and she picked them up one by one, and examined the faces that had once posed for a camera. There was a new photograph, another of herself and

353

Jean-Luc in the mountains, and she lifted it and touched his face with her fingers. She gave a little laugh: she was becoming as sentimental as him. She wondered if the old bed ought to go. Maybe a four-poster, with purple velvet drapes, or a strong wooden bed with drawers.

'Hmmm.'

On the landing she paused at the room Brendan and Maura had stayed in. That would need repainting, maybe a deep crimson, they might like that. A bit of colour might help them rekindle the passion in their lives. As if they needed much help; Brendan sounded so much happier on the phone since he had given his notice. And he and Maura had a new energy about them, when they'd spoken to her about their plans to move. Evie decided they'd need a new wardrobe. One each. And the spare room would take a lick of paint, ready for any other guests. She arrived at the smallest room, at the end. It was full of boxes of junk: most of it would have to go. The window frame was a dull white and the wood was dry and the edges were jagged. The old checked curtains were dirty at the seams and so thin they quivered in the gusts of wind. The view from the window was framed like a picture, a square of vines in long rows, hills, and in the distance there was the thick mist and then the shadowy bulk of the mountains.

There was a damp patch on the ceiling and the single bulb hanging from a dirty cable; the wallpaper was a dull orange colour with a wavy cream design that might have been fashionable in the 1970s, and it would all need stripping off. A pastel blue or a sumptuous pink paint might be in order or perhaps some sunshine yellow, or wallpaper with rabbits or hedgehogs or adorable bears. She closed her eyes and transformed the room in her imagination. She saw toys and fluffy clothes and a little bed and she imagined voices and laughter. It would be so lovely to have them here, the three of them. Not just for the help with the business, but for the company. For the craic. After all, they were family. More than family – they would all be close. She wondered if they would know the sex of the baby before it was born. It didn't matter: a baby's room could be done out in rainbow colours. She thought, wistfully, that Jean-Luc would now never teach this child to play the guitar, but perhaps one day the child would discover it and the house would once again be filled with its beautiful sound. Jean-Luc would have loved that. And she could watch the baby grow and run about in the vineyard, climb on the tractor, call her *Grand-mère* or just Evie. There were endless possibilities and they were all in her thoughts, in motion, taking shape.

She was downstairs again, washing her cup, looking at the clock. It was gone three and Inès would be here shortly. She pulled on an old cardigan, one of Jean-Luc's, tugged on knitted gloves, and went outside, closing the door tightly to keep the house warm.

The sky was smeared, blotchy and grey, like wet paint; little clouds shifted quickly overhead and the breeze held a chill. She saw the sign for Cave Bonheur and she felt at ease: it was the welcome she had wanted for the place and he would have been pleased. She walked towards the fields where the grapes were being harvested. How difficult it was after she found him lying on the ground, until quite recently, to even say his name. Now it was easier to say it aloud, easier to remember him when talking to others, even though sometimes a pang of regret clutched at her and caught her unawares. This house would always be his place, his home, his business, but now it was hers too and she would be certain to make it work.

The men were busy in the wine-making barn. She'd seen most of them many times before helping Benji, but there were new faces too; so many people willing to help. She could hear their voices as she passed. She would not go in – she wanted this time to herself and, besides, they were so involved in what they were doing, she doubted that they would notice her presence. She walked a little further and arrived at the vines, now stripped, cut down and bleak. They were just sticks, thin withered fingers, twisted stumps. A few dark, gnarled grapes were dried and suspended in clusters here and there, hanging down from shrivelled stalks. The wooden supporting posts remained sturdy, solid and vertical while the vines wasted around them. Snaggles of weeds were pushing through, but the ground was mostly brown soil and little sharp stones. Evie took off a glove and grasped the stem of a vine. It was woody and knotted like rope, surprisingly strong and deeply rooted. Next year the grapes would come again. There would be another abundance of wine.

Vine after vine, in straight rows, sparse little bushes stretched out and upwards to the rising hills. A blast of ice in the wind gripped her bones through the woolly cardigan, and she hugged herself and gazed into the distance. A gust blew her hair back, exposing her forehead, and her eyes watered a little. She breathed in the clean air; perhaps it came down from the mountains; perhaps it would soon bring snow. Winter would be a cold time, but there would be family and friends and the fireside. Then eventually spring would come, and a new baby would arrive; the grapes would begin as buds. That might be the time, this might be the place, to scatter his ashes and to say goodbye. She could not let him go yet, but there would be a new year, and life would begin again.

Evie turned and the wind was at her back as she walked towards the house. A car slowed down and stopped by the new sign and she waved to the woman who was closing the driver's door, watching her opening the boot and pulling out a cage with two chickens in it. The woman called out and Evie called back and smiled. She walked towards her new friend, quickening her pace. There was a lot to do, much to organise and plenty of everything to go round. She began to hum a familiar tune to herself and a smile flickered across her lips. *Ne me quitte pas*. Don't leave me. She'd always have memories; he'd never leave her. She hugged Jean-Luc's big old cardigan close to her, snuggling inside the safe warmth of the wool. The air was bitterly cold and it would not be long before the sky became dark.

As she walked, she counted the months in her head, until Christmas, until the baby was born, looking for the number four. But there were no lucky numbers, only life as it is now, the present, and chances and changes. She would make a new present for herself in her home: a good life for herself and for the others she loved and she would focus on everybody's happiness. She did not need luck now: she had found her own way to be blessed. The present truly was a present, a gift. It was all about finding happiness within herself. No, not happiness. She would call it '*Bonheur*' from now on.